Ties That Bind

Also by Marie Bostwick

Threading the Needle (Cobbled Court Quilts #4)

A Thread So Thin (Cobbled Court Quilts #3)

A Thread of Truth (Cobbled Court Quilts #2)

A Single Thread (Cobbled Court Quilts #1)

On Wings of the Morning

River's Edge

Fields of Gold

"The Presents of Angels" in *Snow Angels*

"A High-Kicking Christmas" in *Comfort and Joy*

Published by Kensington Publishing Corporation

Ties That Bind

MARIE BOSTWICK

KENSINGTON BOOKS
www.kensingtonbooks.com

KENSINGTON BOOKS are published by

Kensington Publishing Corp.
119 West 40th Street
New York, NY 10018

All Kensington titles, imprints, and distributed lines are available at special quantity discounts for bulk purchases for sales promotion, premi-
ums, fund-raising, educational, or institutional use.

Special book excerpts or customized printings can also be created to fit
specific needs. For details, write or phone the office of the Kensington
Special Sales Manager: Attn. Special Sales Department. Kensington
Publishing Corp., 119 West 40th Street, New York, NY 10018. Phone:
1-800-221-2647.

Kensington and the K logo Reg. U.S. Pat. & TM Off.

ISBN-13: 978-0-7582-6928-7
ISBN-10: 0-7582-6928-5

First Kensington Trade Paperback Printing: May 2012
10 9 8 7 6 5 4 3 2 1

Printed in the United States of America

With thanks . . .

To my editor, Audrey LaFehr, and my agent, Liza Dawson, who never allow me to settle for less than my best; to my husband and family, for putting up with my crazy schedule and many moods; to my sister, Betty, who offers encouragement with liberality and criticism with grace; to my Very Sparkly Assistant, Molly, who keeps my books, calendar, and life pretty balanced, considering; and to Anne Dranginis, whose friendship I value and whose insights regarding courtroom drama and family law made this book more interesting; and to the readers whose appreciation and encouragement are the greatest rewards of writing.

Prologue

Margot Matthews

"People are like stained-glass windows. They sparkle and shine when the sun is out, but when the darkness sets in, their true beauty is revealed only if there is a light from within."

Elisabeth Kübler-Ross said that, and I've been thinking about it a lot lately. Maybe that surprises you. Most of the people I know, apart from my close friends, would be surprised to know I can quote from Kübler-Ross, and for one simple reason: I am nice.

I am. That's how people describe me, as a nice person, a nice girl. That wasn't so bad when I *was* a girl, but when you move beyond girlhood into womanhood, people tend to confuse niceness with lack of intellectual depth. And if that nice person is also a person of faith, they think you're as shallow as a shower, incapable of introspection or academic curiosity. But mine is an examined faith, composed of inquisitiveness, discovery, and introspection. However, it didn't begin with me.

I have known and loved God for as long as I can remember. It was as natural to me as breathing. As I've grown older and met so many people who struggle with the meaning and means of finding God, I have sometimes wondered about the validity of my faith. Could something so precious truly come as a gift?

I can't answer for anyone else and don't presume to, but, for myself, over and over again, the answer has been yes. I don't understand why the searching and finding should be so simple for some and so arduous for others. I only know that I have been blessed beyond measure or reason. But while peace with God came easily to me, peace with myself has been elusive.

From adolescence onward and with increasing anxiety as the minutes and years of my biological clock ticked on, I waited for the missing piece of myself to arrive, the better half who would make me whole: a husband. And with him, children, a family. That's what I'd always wanted, and that, I was sure, was what would make me happy. But after reading and meditating on Kübler-Ross, Brother Lawrence, the apostle Paul ("I have learned the secret of being content in any and every situation"), I finally realized that I was not happy with myself because I had never learned to be happy *by* myself.

And so, more than a year ago, I broke it off with my boyfriend, Arnie Kinsella. It was hard, but it was for the best. I like Arnie, but I wasn't in love with him any more than he was in love with me. Even so, if he'd asked me to marry him, I'd have said yes in a heartbeat. I know how terrible that sounds, but it's the truth.

My friends—Evelyn, Abigail, Ivy, Virginia, everybody from my Friday night quilt circle—applauded my decision. They said I deserved the real thing—head-over-heels, candy-and-flowers, heart-throbbing, heart-stopping L-O-V-E.

A nice thought, but it's never going to happen, not to me. And if finally acknowledging that didn't quite make my windows blaze with light, at least it saved me from further humiliation and the weight of impossible dreams. I was over all that and I was over Arnie Kinsella.

Or so I thought. Until today.

✒ 1 ✒

Margot

December

Today, I turned forty.

I wanted to let this birthday pass unnoticed, but when my lunch break came I decided I deserved a treat and walked around the corner to the Blue Bean Coffee Shop and Bakery, known to locals in New Bern, Connecticut, as the Bean.

My table was near a window frosted with little icy snowflake patterns where I could watch people bundled in scarves, hats, and thick wool coats scurrying from shop to shop in search of the perfect Christmas gift. When the waitress came by I ordered a plate of nachos, loaded with extra everything including so much sour cream they ought to serve it with a side of Lipitor.

Six bites in, a glob of guacamole and chili slipped off my chip and onto my chest. Dipping a napkin in water to clean up the mess only made it worse. My white sweater looked like a toddler's finger-painting project. I was on my way to the restroom to clean up when I spotted Arnie sitting in the back booth with Kiera Granger. That's where people sit when they don't want other people to know what they're up to. It doesn't do any good. Everybody in New Bern is well informed about the business of everybody else in New Bern.

On another day maybe I'd have been able to forget the sight of Arnie and Kiera sitting in the dimly lit booth, heads together, hands nearly but not quite touching as they talked intently, so intently that Arnie didn't even see me, but not today. I left my food and twenty dollars on the table and ran out the door and into the street, wishing the blustery December snowfall would turn into a blizzard and hide me from the world.

With only five shopping days until Christmas, Evelyn would need all hands on deck, but I couldn't face going back to work. I fumbled around in my bag until I found my cell phone. Evelyn answered on the fifth ring.

"Cobbled Court Quilts. May I help you?"

I heard a car round the corner; the engine was so loud that I'm sure everyone within three blocks could hear it. I stopped in my tracks, hoping the heap would pass so I could continue my conversation. Instead, it slowed to a crawl and the noise from the engine grew even louder. I pressed the phone closer to my left ear, covered the right with my free hand, and shouted into the receiver.

"Evelyn? It's Margot."

"Margot? What's all that noise? I can barely hear you. Where are you?"

"I'm going home."

"What?"

I held the phone directly in front of my mouth, practically screaming into it. *"I'm going home. I'm not feeling very well. I'm sorry, but . . . aack!"*

A blast from the car horn nearly made me jump out of my skin. It was more of a bleep than a blast, the kind of short, sharp tap on the horn that drivers use to alert other drivers that the signal has gone green, but what did that matter? At close range the effect was the same. I yelped and dropped the phone, dropping my call in the process.

When I regained my balance, my phone, and some of my composure, I turned toward the street and saw a low-slung, bright blue "muscle car," rusty in spots and with multiple dents, a tailpipe choking clouds of smoke, topped by a roof rack carrier piled high with possessions and covered with a plastic tarp that was held in place by black bungee cords—sort of. The tarp was loose on one side, exposing some boxes, a big black musical instrument case, and a hockey stick. Quite a collection.

The driver was a man about my age with black hair receding at the temples and brown eyes that peered out from rimless glasses. A boy of twelve or thirteen sat slumped in the passenger seat, looking embarrassed and irritated. The driver said something and the boy cranked down the window. The driver shouted to me, but I couldn't make out his words over the roar of the engine.

What kind of person shouts at strangers from their car? Or honks? In New England, honking in a situation that is short of life threatening is up there with painting your house orange or coming to a dinner party empty-handed. You just don't do it.

Climbing over a snowbank and into the street, I noticed that the car had Illinois plates and a Cubs bumper sticker. Were they visiting relatives for Christmas? If they were, I probably knew the family. So no matter how rude he was, *I* had to be nice.

Shaking my head, I mimed a key in my hand and twisted my wrist, signaling him to shut off the ignition. Instead, he shifted into neutral. That reduced the engine noise to a loud hum rather than an earsplitting roar. Better, but not much.

"Sorry!" he yelled. "If I turn it off, I'm not sure I'll be able to start it again. Can you tell me where Oak Leaf Lane is? We're lost." The boy, who I supposed must be his son, slumped down even farther in his seat, clearly humiliated by his dad's admission. I smiled to myself. Teenagers are so painfully self-conscious.

"Turn around, take a right at the corner. Oak Leaf Lane is the third right after the traffic light. Beecher Cottage Inn is down about a quarter mile on the left, if that's what you're looking for. Or are you staying with family over Christmas?"

Still grinning, he shook his head. "Neither. We're moving here." The man leaned across his son's lap and extended his hand out the window so I could shake it. "I'm Paul Collier. This is my son, James. James is starting as a seventh grader at the middle school after the holidays and I'll be starting a new job at the same time."

"Dad!" James hissed. "You don't have to tell her our life story."

Paul Collier rolled his eyes. "I wasn't. I was just making introductions. This is the country, James. People in the country are friendly. Isn't that right, miss?"

He looked to me for support, but I decided to stay out of it. Paul Collier seemed nice, but I had to wonder how he was going to fit into New Bern. The residents of New Bern *are* friendly but, like most New Englanders, they are also proud and a bit reticent. They like for strangers to act . . . well, a little strange, at least initially. And they don't like it when strangers refer to their town as "the country." Makes us sound so quaint.

I bent down to shake his hand and changed the subject. "Well, it's nice to have you here. On Christmas Eve, we have a carol sing with hot chocolate and cookies on the Green. That's the park in the center of downtown," I added, realizing they might not be familiar with the term. "And if you're looking for a place to attend Christmas services, New Bern Community Church is right on the Green too."

"Great! I was just telling James that we needed to find a church first thing."

His enthusiasm piqued my interest. Most men don't put finding a church high on their list of priorities when they move to a new town. My gaze shifted automatically, searching out his left hand, but I couldn't tell if he was wearing a ring.

What was I doing? When was I going to get over the habit of looking at every man I met as a potential mate? Even if this man was single, his hair was too dark and his forehead too high. Not my type. And he was probably too short. And anyway, I was through with all that. And even if I hadn't been—which I was, I absolutely and forever was—Paul Collier's response to my next question would have settled the matter.

"So, you've moved here for a new job?"

"I'm a lawyer. I'm starting at Baxter, Ferris, and Long after Christmas."

A lawyer. Of course, he was. It was a sign, a clear sign that I was supposed to learn to be content as a single woman and stay away from men. Especially lawyers.

I let go of his hand and took a step back from the blue heap; he couldn't be a very successful lawyer if he was driving such a pile of junk. "Well . . . good luck. Have a good Christmas."

"Thanks. Same to you, miss. Or is it missus?"

He was awfully direct, another quality that doesn't go over well in New England.

"Margot," I replied, leaving his question unanswered. "Margot Matthews."

"Nice to meet you, Margot. Merry Christmas."

He put the car back into gear, revved the engine, made a three-point turn in a nearby driveway, and drove off, leaving my ears ringing. Or so I thought, until I realized that the buzzing was coming from my phone.

"Sorry, Evelyn. I accidentally dropped the phone."

"What happened? It sounded like an airplane was about to land on top of you."

"Just a car driving by. Listen, I don't think I can finish the rest of my shift. . . ."

"Something you ate at lunch?"

"Sort of," I replied. "Will you be all right without me?"

"Sure. I mean . . . if you're sick, you're sick. Do you think you'll feel better if you just lie down for an hour? Maybe you could come in later."

Evelyn is not just my boss; she's also my friend. She doesn't have a deceitful bone in her body, but something about the tone of her voice made me suspicious.

"Evelyn, you're not planning a surprise party at the quilt shop, are you?"

I told her, I told all my friends, that I don't want to celebrate this birthday. Why should I? There is nothing about being forty and still single that's worth celebrating.

"No. We're not planning a party at the shop. Take the afternoon. But you've got that meeting at church tonight, don't forget. Abigail called to see if you'd pick her up."

The meeting. I was so upset that it had completely slipped my mind.

I sighed. "Tell her I'll pick her up around six fifteen."

In the background, I could hear the jingle of the door bells as more customers entered the shop. I felt a twinge of guilt. I almost told her that I'd changed my mind and was coming in after all, but before I could, Evelyn said, "I've got to run. But feel better, okay? I know you're not happy about this birthday, but whether you know it or not, you've got a lot to celebrate. So, happy birthday, Margot. And many more to come."

"Thanks, Evelyn."

∞ 2 ∞

Margot

I built a fire in the fireplace and stood watching the flames dance before settling myself on the sofa to work on my sister's Christmas quilt. Quilting, I have found, is great when you want to think something through—or not think at all. Today, I was looking to do the latter. For a while, it worked.

I sat there for a good half an hour, hand-stitching the quilt binding, watching television and telling myself that it could be worse, that my life could be as messed up as the people on the reality show reruns—trapped in a house, or on an island, or in a French château with a bunch of people who you didn't know that well but who, somehow, knew way too much about your personal weaknesses and weren't afraid to talk about them.

When I picked up the phone and my parents started to sing "Happy Birthday" into the line, I remembered that being part of a family is pretty much the same thing.

"I'm fine. Really. Everything is fine."

"Margot," Dad said in his rumbling bass, "don't use that tone with your mother."

I forced myself to smile, hoping this would make me sound more cheerful than I felt. "I wasn't using a tone, Daddy. I was answering Mom's question. I'm fine."

My mother sighed. "You've been so secretive lately, Margot."

Dad let out an impatient snort. "It's almost as bad as trying to talk to Mari."

At the mention of my sister's name, Mom, in a voice that was half-hopeful and half-afraid to hope, asked, "Is she still planning on coming for Christmas?"

"She's looking forward to it."

Looking forward to it was probably stretching the truth, but last time I talked to my sister she had asked for suggestions on what to get the folks for Christmas. That indicated a kind of anticipation on her part, didn't it?

"She'll probably come up with some last-minute excuse," Dad grumbled.

In the background, I could hear a jingle of metal. When Dad is agitated, he fiddles with the change in his pockets. I had a mental image of him pacing from one side of the kitchen to the other, the phone cord tethering him to the wall like a dog on a leash. Dad is a man of action; long phone conversations make him antsy.

"Wonder what it'll be this time? Her car broke down? Her boss won't let her off work? Her therapist says the tension might upset Olivia? As if spending a day with us would scar our granddaughter for life. Remember when she pulled that one, honey?"

A sniffle and a ragged intake of breath came from the Buffalo end of the line.

"Oh, come on now, Lil. Don't cry. Did you hear that? Margot, why do you bring these things up? You're upsetting your mother."

"I'm sorry." I was too. I hadn't brought it up, but I hate it when my mother cries.

"I just don't know why you're keeping things from us," Mom said.

"I'm not keeping anything from you. But at my age, I don't think I should be bothering you with all my little problems, that's all."

I heard a snuffly bleating noise, like a sheep with the croup, and pictured my mother on her big canopy bed with her shoes off, leaning back on two ruffled red paisley pillow shams, the way she does during long phone conversations, pulling a tissue out of the box with the white crocheted cover that sat on her nightstand, and dabbing her eyes.

"Since when have we ever considered you a bother? You're our little girl."

"And you always will be," Dad said. "Don't you ever forget that, Bunny."

Bunny is my father's pet name for me—short for Chubby Bunny. My pre-teen pudge disappeared twenty-five years ago when my body stretched like a piece of gum until I reached the man-repelling height of nearly six feet. I haven't been a Chubby Bunny for a quarter century, but Dad never seemed to notice.

"It's Arnie, isn't it? Is he seeing someone else?"

Mom didn't wait for me to answer her question, but she didn't have to. Somehow she already knew. How is that possible? Is that just part of being a mother?

"Don't you worry, Margot. Arnie Kinsella isn't the only fish in the sea."

"Maybe not. But all the ones I haul into my boat seem to be bottom feeders."

"Stop that. You can't give up," Dad said with his usual bull moose optimism and then paused, as if reconsidering. "You still look pretty good . . . for your age."

Ouch.

"You know what I think?" he asked in a brighter tone before answering his own question. "I think maybe your husband's first wife hasn't died yet."

"Werner!" My mother gasped, but why? Was she really surprised?

"What?" Dad sounded genuinely perplexed. "At her age, a nice widower is probably her best shot at getting a husband. I'm just saying . . ."

"Hey, guys, it's sweet of you to call, but I need to get ready to go."

"Are you going out with friends? Are they throwing you a party?" Mom asked hopefully and I knew she was wondering if my friends had thought to invite any bachelors to the celebration.

"I've got a meeting." Not for two hours, but they didn't need to know that.

"On your birthday?" Dad scoffed. "Margot, they don't pay you enough at that quilt shop to make you go to meetings after hours. I keep telling you to get a *real* job."

Yes, he does. Every chance he gets.

I used to have a "real job" according to Dad's definition. I worked in the marketing department of a big company in Manhattan, made a lot of money, had profit sharing, a 401(k), and health insurance, which I needed because I was forever going to the doctor with anemia, insomnia, heart palpitations—the full menu of stress-related ailments. After I moved to New Bern and started working in the quilt shop, all that went away. Insurance and a big paycheck aren't the only benefits that matter—I've tried to explain that to Dad. But there's no point in going over it again.

"It's a church meeting. I'm on the board now. Remember?"

"Oh. Well, that's different, then."

My parents are very active in their church. Mom has taught fourth grade Sunday school since 1979. When there's a snowstorm, Dad plows the church parking lot with the blade he keeps attached to the front of his truck and shovels the walkways. No one asks him to do it; he just does. That's the way my folks are. They're good people.

"What a shame they scheduled the board meeting on your birthday," Mom said.

"This is kind of an emergency thing. We've got to pick a new minister to fill in while Reverend Tucker is recovering."

"Oh, yes," she said, remembering our last conversation. "How is he?"

"Better, I think. I'll find out more tonight. Anyway, I've got to run. Love you." I puckered my lips and made two kiss noises into the phone.

"Love you too, sweetheart. Happy birthday! If that sweater doesn't fit, just take it back. But promise me you'll at least try it on before you return it."

"I'm not going to return it."

"Well, there's a gift receipt with the card if you do."

Dad cleared his throat. "And there's a hundred-dollar bill in there too. That's from me. Buy yourself something nice."

"Thanks, Dad. But you didn't have to do that."

"Why not? Can't a father spoil his daughter on her birthday? After all," he chuckled, "you only turn forty once."

Thank heaven for that.

"I don't care how old you are, Bunny. Don't forget, you're still our little girl."

As if I could. As if they'd ever let me.

After I hung up, I went back to work on the quilt. This time I left the television off and just focused on the stitches, trying to make them small and even. It's a very soothing thing to stitch a binding by hand, almost meditative. With my tears over Arnie spent, I turned my thoughts, both hopeful and anxious, to Christmas, and my sister.

Mari's full name is Mariposa. That means "butterfly" in Spanish, so when a bolt of fabric with butterflies in colors of sapphire, teal, purple, and gold on a jet-black background came into the shop, I made two important decisions—I would use it to make a quilt for Mari *and* I would invite her and my parents to come for Christmas.

It's been five years since the last time we tried it. Olivia, my niece, was only a few months old. I'd seen the baby a couple of times, but my parents had never met their granddaughter. There is a lot of bad blood between my sister and parents. I talked Mari into coming to Buffalo for the holidays, but at the last minute she called and canceled. Mom was crushed and cried. Dad and Mari got into a shouting match. It was awful. Mari blamed me. It was almost a year before she'd answer my phone calls again.

That's why making a second attempt at bringing the family together for Christmas really was a big decision, but I had to do it. When I saw those sapphire blue butterflies, the exact blue of Mari's eyes, I knew I had to take the chance and at least try. Honestly, I didn't really expect Mari to say yes. At first, she didn't.

"No, Margot," she snapped, almost before the words were out

of my mouth. "I am *never* going back to Buffalo. Too many bad memories."

"No, no. Not Buffalo. I didn't say that. Come here, to New Bern."

In truth, I *had* been thinking we'd get together at Mom and Dad's, but perhaps things would go more smoothly if we met on neutral ground.

"New Bern is beautiful at Christmas. There's a huge decorated tree on the Green and they outline all the buildings with white lights. You and Olivia can stay here and I'll reserve a room for Mom and Dad at the inn."

Would the inn already be booked for Christmas? It didn't matter. I talked as fast as I could, spinning out a vision of the perfect Christmas, making it all up as I went.

"My friends, Lee and Tessa, have a farm outside of town where we can cut our own tree. Lee just refurbished an old horse-drawn sleigh. I bet Olivia has never been in a sleigh! And the quilt shop has an open house on Christmas Eve with cookies and punch and presents. Everyone will make the biggest fuss over Olivia, you'll see. I'll ask Charlie, Evelyn's husband, to dress up as Santa Claus and deliver her presents!"

Would Charlie agree to that? I'd get Evelyn to ask him. He'd do it for her.

"And after the open house we can decorate the tree together and go to the midnight service at church, all of us together, the whole family, and . . ."

"No, Margot . . . just. Wait. Give me a second to think."

I clamped my lips shut, closed my eyes, said a prayer.

After a long minute, Mari said, "I don't know, Margot. It's just . . . we have plans for Christmas Eve. Olivia is going to be a lamb in the church nativity play."

"Oh, Mari! Oh, I bet she's adorable!"

"She is pretty sweet," she said in a voice that sounded like a smile. "I had to rip out the stupid ears on the costume three times, but it turned out so cute."

"I'd love to see her in it. I bet Mom and Dad would too. Would you rather we all came to Albany for Christmas?"

"Nooo," Mari said, stretching out the word for emphasis. "Very bad idea. Too much, too soon. But . . . what if we just came for Christmas dinner, just for the afternoon? I think that's about all I can handle this time."

This time? Did that mean she thought there might be other times too? I was dying to ask, but didn't. She was probably right. After so many years apart and so many resentments, an afternoon together was probably as much as anyone could handle.

It was a start. Sometimes, that's all you need—a decision, a second chance.

Sitting quietly and sewing that bright blue binding inch by inch to that border of brilliant, fluttering butterflies, covering all the uneven edges and raveled threads with a smooth band of blue, seeing all those different bits and scraps of fabric come together, stitch by stitch, into a neatly finished whole helped me look at things differently.

Coming upon Arnie and Kiera in the restaurant was a blessing in disguise, I decided, an opportunity to change my outlook, a chance to quit feeling sorry for myself and find peace and purpose in my life as it was, not as I wished it to be. I came to this conclusion just as I placed the final firm stitch in the edge of the binding. When I was done, I spread the quilt out on the floor.

It would have been easy enough to create a pretty pieced quilt using the butterfly focal fabric. Every quilt I've made has been a variation on that theme, but this time I wanted to try my hand at appliqué. Having taken that leap of faith, I decided to go one step further and create my own design. And rather than planning out every little detail of the quilt, I decided to gather up my fabrics and just "go with the flow," letting inspiration come to me as it would, leaving myself open to the possibility of new ideas and insights.

The center medallion, which I'd come to think of as "the cameo," was an ink-black oval appliquéd with flowers and leaves and fat curlicues, like dewdrops splashing on petals, all drawn by me, in teal, cobalt, azure, butterscotch, honey, and goldenrod, colors I'd picked up from the butterfly wings. The cameo was framed by curving swaths of sunshine yellow, making the oval into a rectangle. Next, I built border upon border upon border around the edges of the rectangle to create a full-sized quilt; three plain butterfly borders, of varying widths, and the same number and sizes of sawtooth and diamond borders, one with the diamonds all in yellow, another all in blue, a third with colors picked at random, and a thin band of black to make those brilliant colors even more vibrant. Finally, I dotted the top with individual appliquéd butterflies "fussy-cut" from the focus fabric and placed here and there on and near the cameo and borders.

That idea had come to me at the last moment, but it made a world of difference. It was almost as if a migration of butterflies had seen the quilt from the air and come to light gently upon the smooth expanse of cloth, taking a moment of respite in that rich and lovely garden of color before going on their way. That's how I felt looking at it, rested and renewed, hopeful, ready to rise again and resume the journey.

It was the most beautiful quilt I'd ever made, and it had come about all because I'd been willing to lay aside my old habits and leave myself open to new possibilities. There was a lesson in that.

God had something new in mind for me, something better, I was sure of that. And, though I can't tell you how, I was sure it had something to do with my family, my sister, my niece. If I was never to have children of my own, perhaps I was to play a role in Olivia's life? I barely knew her, but I longed to shower my little niece with love, to regain my sister's friendship and heal the wounds that had torn us apart.

Maybe this would be the year that we could all finally put the past behind us. Maybe this Christmas would be the moment and means to let bygones be bygones, the year we would finally cover all the raveled edges and loose threads of the past and be a family again, bound by blood, tied with love, warts and all.

Maybe.

❧ 3 ❧

Margot

The church vestibule was cold and a little gloomy. The big over-head chandeliers were dark so the only light came from a few low-watt faux-candle wall sconces topped with tiny gold lamp-shades. Though the sanctuary had been decked for Christmas more than two weeks before, the clean, sharp scent of cedar and pine boughs hung in the air. That's the upside of an unreliable furnace; chilly air keeps the greens fresh longer.

Abigail stood on the mat and stamped the snow off her boots. "We're late," she said in a slightly accusing tone, nodding toward a trail of melting slush left by those who had arrived first.

It wasn't my fault. Abigail left me cooling my heels in her foyer for ten minutes while she was in the kitchen giving Hilda, her housekeeper, last-minute instructions about Franklin's dinner. I almost reminded her of that, but then thought better of it. I've known Abigail long enough to know she doesn't mean to sound snappish. She just hates being late. When you think about it, it's kind of sweet that she fusses over Franklin's dinner like that, as though they'd been married three months instead of three years.

If I ever get married, that's just how I'd want to treat my husband, as though we were newlyweds forever. I wish . . .

I stopped myself. I wasn't going to go there. I was going to stick to my resolution, be content in every situation. And what was so bad about my situation anyway? Things could certainly be much worse. Think of poor Reverend Tucker, lying in a hospital bed.

"Have you heard any more about Reverend Tucker?" I asked as I followed Abigail down the stairs. "Mr. Carney made it sound pretty bad."

"Ted likes to make things sound bad," Abigail puffed. "Makes him feel important to get everyone else in a flutter. There's no such thing as a *good* heart attack, but Bob will be fine. I called the hospital and pried some information out of the administrator."

I'll bet you did. I smiled to myself. Abigail is one of the biggest donors to the hospital and about fifty other charities. She has clout in New Bern and no qualms about exercising it on behalf of people she cares about.

"I insisted that they put the same doctor who treated Franklin on the case. He's the best cardiac man in the state. Don't worry, Margot. After a few months of rest and rehabilitation, the good reverend will be back to his old self."

"That's a relief. I can't imagine anyone else being able to fill his shoes."

"Nor can I. But we will have to find someone to replace him, at least for the next few months. On such short notice, especially right before Christmas, I don't suppose we'll have much to choose from in the way of candidates. But," she said with grim determination, "beggars can't be choosers. We'll just have to find ourselves a warm body and hope for the best. I just hope Ted doesn't let the meeting drag on and on. I don't want to be here all night."

"Well, there's only one item on the agenda. All we have to do is discuss the candidates and vote for an interim minister. How long could that take?"

Abigail arched one eyebrow. "Obviously," she said, "you don't know Ted Carney as well as I do."

I was sketching lines of intersecting squares along the margin of my legal pad, thinking about side dishes to serve with the Christmas turkey. Somebody coughed and I jumped, startled by the noise, worried that I'd missed something.

I hadn't. Ted Carney was talking. Still.

When Abigail and I arrived, Ted, president of the board, was reminding everyone that the pastor was already scheduled to take a sabbatical in the spring. Ted proposed we extend the sabbatical to six months, giving Reverend Tucker plenty of time to recover, and that the Tuckers stay at Ted's cabin on Lake Winnipesaukee, leaving the parsonage vacant to house the interim pastor. Everyone liked the plan and voted in favor of it. So far so good. Now all we needed to do was choose our interim pastor. Easy.

But instead of getting directly to a presentation of the candidates, Ted began going through a list of every minister who had served in the pulpit of New Bern Community Church for the last two hundred years and spelling out the relative strengths and weaknesses of each one—in excruciating, mind-numbing detail.

No one was listening.

Deirdre Camp was making a grocery list. Pat Boyd was holding her BlackBerry, surreptitiously checking her e-mail. Waldo Smitherton, who is ninety-six, was dozing, but there was nothing new about that. He sleeps through most board meetings. The only person who appeared to be listening was Miranda Wyatt; her eyes were glued to Ted.

Abigail, obviously irritated, was drumming the table with her fingers. I wondered how much longer she'd be able to control her temper. I looked at my watch.

"Oh for heaven's sake, Ted! Get on with it!"

Seventy-eight seconds. Pretty impressive. For Abigail.

Ted sputtered like a jowly bulldog and glared at Abigail. "Excuse me," he said. "Were you wishing to address the chair or the board? I believe there needs to be a motion before you can do either."

Ted likes to invoke *Robert's Rules of Order*—usually incorrectly. It makes Abigail crazy.

"No! There doesn't! This isn't a formal meeting and we're not ready to take a vote, so we don't need to make a motion! What we need to do is find a pastor before Christmas. So, do you have any résumés for us to consider or not?"

Abigail's outburst elicited stirring among the benumbed board.

People sat up and stopped their doodling. Pat powered down her BlackBerry. Adam Kingsbury elbowed Waldo, who woke with a start and shouted, "Aye!" thinking it was time to vote.

Scowling, Ted pulled a small stack of papers out of a weathered brown briefcase.

"Is this all we've got to choose from?" Pat asked. "Two résumés?"

"I'm afraid so," Ted replied apologetically. "And they aren't résumés so much as information sheets. I typed them up myself. The pool of candidates available in time for Christmas is very small and I wasn't able to reach either of them on the phone. One is flying to Europe and the other is on a backcountry ski trip. However, I did put in a call to Reverend Oswald, head of the Eastern Conference, who is on a mission trip to Malawi. Before we were cut off, he told me a little bit about the candidates. They're fresh from seminary, but Reverend Oswald said either would be an excellent choice."

Abigail leaned close to my ear and hissed, "If we've only got a choice between one embryo parson and another, then why did he subject us to that endless lecture?"

Miranda raised her hand before speaking, as usual. Miranda is a third-grade teacher. Ted smiled and yielded the floor. Abigail rolled her eyes.

"Pardon me, but might it be a good idea to find a guest preacher for Christmas and fill the position later when there are more available candidates? Ted's inspired comments on the qualities of a true minister made me think we shouldn't rush this." Miranda smiled sweetly. Ted ducked his head in a sort of "oh, it was nothing" way.

Abigail's eyes darted from Miranda's face, to Ted's, and back to Miranda's. "Is she flirting with him?" she whispered.

I shrugged. It was possible. Ted was a widower and Miranda was divorced. It was hard for me to imagine anyone being attracted to Ted romantically, but they say everybody is right for somebody—a rule that seems to apply to everyone but me.

"Miranda makes a good point," Ted said, flashing a wide smile in her direction. "We could bring in a guest pastor over the holidays. Reverend Flatwell is avail—"

Ted was interrupted by a collective groan.

Floyd Flatwell is a retired minister who is always willing to fill in for a pastor who is sick or away on vacation. Before he'd retired from ministry, Floyd had retired from a career as a golfer. He never won a major tournament, but he had played on the professional circuit. If you're looking for someone to preach for one Sunday, possibly two, Reverend Flatwell is a fine choice. But more than that? Uh-uh.

Four years previously the church gave Reverend Tucker a two-week trip to Israel as a gift to celebrate his fortieth year in ministry. He caught pneumonia on the flight home, so the congregation got to listen to Floyd Flatwell preach sermons about spiritual insights he'd gained on the links—lots of references to following through, keeping your eye on the ball, and heaven as the ultimate nineteenth hole—for four weeks in a row.

Abigail said what everyone else was thinking. "Absolutely not. We have more visitors on Christmas than on any other day of the year. Do you think a sermon comparing the journey of the three wise men to the rigors of tackling the back nine at Augusta—with descriptions of every hole—is going to convince them to come back?"

Glancing at Miranda, who was looking at her lap, Ted shifted his shoulders. "If that's how everyone feels, we'd better look at the candidates on hand." Ted picked up the first résumé and started telling us what we could have read for ourselves.

"Anthony Ferrari graduated from seminary last spring. He's done volunteer work with at-risk youth and served as a chaplain for a police department in Worcester—"

Waldo Smitherton interrupted with a raspy bark. "Ferrari! Sounds like a pricey sports car. We don't want a minister who drives a fancy car. Wouldn't look right."

"He doesn't *drive* a Ferrari," Ted said. "It's his name. He's of Italian descent."

"What?" Waldo cupped his hand to his ear. "He climbed the Martian Crescent?"

Ted raised his voice a couple of notches. "He's Italian!"

Waldo frowned. "I don't know about that. My brother's wife

was Eye-talian. Nice girl, but too fertile. They had nine kids. Drove my brother to the poorhouse."

Squinting his birdlike eyes, Waldo addressed the group. "We just spent good money repainting the parsonage. If some family with a buncha kids moves in there, we'll have to redo the whole job. Is this fella married? How many children they got?"

"Four," Ted admitted. "With another due to arrive in April."

There was a murmuring among the group.

"Moving on," Ted said wearily. "Philip A. Clarkson also graduated from seminary in the spring. He is forty and *un*married."

Abigail kicked me under the table. "Unmarried," she mouthed.

"Stop it," I mouthed back, just as clearly.

"In addition to a Divinity degree," Ted continued, "Reverend Clarkson has a Master of Social Work. He spent sixteen years working in the field, first in a home for senior citizens, then a rural hospital, and finally in a large metropolitan high school."

"Philip A. Clarkson," Deirdre mused. "He wouldn't happen to be related to Philip R. Clarkson, would he? My sister is a member of his congregation in Boston, one of the largest churches in the denomination. He's a wonderful speaker!"

Ted beamed. "Yes, I believe this is his son. My phone connection to Reverend Oswald was poor, but before we were cut off he said this is Reverend Clarkson's only child. If he's half the orator his father is, we'd be very fortunate to hire him."

There were murmurs of approval as the board took in this information.

"It's too bad we don't have time to bring him in for an interview," Miranda said. "But imagine! Having the son of such a famous pastor here in New Bern! I think Ted did an amazing job, finding such a well-qualified candidate in less than a day."

Adam Kingsbury, who is in his fourth year of what was to be a two-year term as church treasurer, no one else being willing to take on the job, was chewing nervously on his thumbnail.

"Ted, we haven't discussed finances. How are we going to get money to pay an additional salary? What about insurance?"

Ted held up his hands. "It's all going to work out. We'll be able to put our new pastor on the Conference's insurance plan. As far as his salary," Ted drew his bushy gray eyebrows together, "I think we're going to have to put off plans for a new furnace."

"Oh, no!"

"Not again! We barely got through last winter."

"I know, but I don't see another alternative. Do you?" Ted let his gaze rest on Abigail, who ignored him.

"That's it, then. We'll just have to make do with the old furnace and pray that God makes it last another year. Now," he said, clasping his hands together, "it sounds like we've settled on our candidate. We just need someone to make a motion. Margot?"

I looked around at the others, surprised that Ted would call on me to make the motion and more than a little annoyed to see the wide smile on Abigail's face. I knew what she was thinking, and I was having none of it. Single I am and single I will remain. I have accepted this, so why can't everybody else?

I felt a kick under the table and jumped. Abigail, still smiling that irritating smile, tipped her head to one side, urging me to get on with it.

"I move that we call the Reverend Philip A. Clarkson as interim pastor of the New Bern Community Church."

"Second!" Abigail chirped so loudly that she startled the again- dozing Waldo, who jerked his head up and shouted, "Aye!"

4

Margot

Abigail flipped down the visor and peered intently into the narrow mirror while she applied her lipstick. "Watch out for potholes, Margot. You're making me smear it."

I kept driving, keeping the wheel exactly where it was, saying nothing.

"I don't see what you're so upset about," she said, running her fingernail around the edge of her lips. "All I did was suggest that you'd be the perfect person to welcome Reverend Clarkson. You're so hospitable. Everyone knows that. Besides, you were the natural choice. Everyone else has families. They're all busy getting ready for the holidays."

"And I suppose I'm not!"

Abigail jerked in her seat, surprised by my outburst.

"Just because I'm single doesn't mean I have nothing to do! And I do have a family! They're all coming for Christmas! So I've got plenty of things on my plate already—*especially* since I'm single! I don't have a husband to help me with the preparations. And I don't have time to be a one-woman welcome wagon! And even if I did, you only volunteered me because you're trying to set me up with the new minister."

Abigail was quiet for a moment. "I'm sorry, Margot. That was insensitive of me. You're just as busy as the rest of us; I know that. Being single has nothing to do with it. It just seemed to me that . . . well, your faith is so important to you. I thought a nice, unmarried man of the cloth might be the perfect match for you. I was only trying to help."

"I don't want that kind of help. I'm perfectly happy being single."

Abigail put the cap back on her tube of lipstick and closed the visor. "Of course," she said flatly. "Anyone can see that. You positively radiate joy and contentment."

"I'm fine. I have a nice home, a good job, and *most* of my friends are lovely people. Let's just leave well enough alone, all right?"

Abigail looked shocked. "Why? I've *never* left well enough alone. Not when I saw the possibility of getting something better. And I want something better for *you,* not me. What's so terrible about that?"

"Nothing," I said, feeling guilty for snapping at her. Abigail really does mean well, but she's so . . . insistent. "But I believe I'll be a lot happier if I just embrace myself and my life as it is and get over the idea that I need a man to be complete as a woman."

"Well, of course you don't! What a silly idea. Is that how you've felt? Truly?"

I nodded sheepishly as I turned my car onto Commerce Street.

"Really," Abigail said, in a slightly disbelieving tone. "Well, then I applaud your enlightenment—however recent it may be. That whole 'you complete me' bunk is just that, a lot of sentimental hoohah invented in Hollywood. Or some such place.

"If a man alone can make you happy, then my first marriage should have made me the happiest woman on earth. Woolley Wynne was handsome, very rich, and very generous, a rare combination, and he adored me. At first. But I wasn't happy with myself. I was forever regretting my lost love, the man who'd made me truly miserable, which, for a lot of young women, seems to be an incredibly magnetic quality in a man.

"Why is that, do you suppose? Why should a young, attractive, intelligent, and interesting woman, as indeed I was at the time, scan a horizon thick with potential suitors only to say, 'Aha! Another opportunity to suffer!' and then run headlong toward the man best equipped to ruin her life?"

"I don't know."

"Nor do I," Abigail said. "But that's exactly what I did. Thank heaven I'm past that stage. You couldn't *pay* me to be twenty-five again, Margot. You really couldn't."

Abigail is so rich she doesn't need anybody to pay her to be anything, but I do understand her point. There are plenty of things bothering me about this birthday, but I truly would not wish to be younger. I like knowing what I know now, the assurance and resolve that a full log of life experience brings. I only wish I'd had this ... wisdom, I suppose you might call it ... back before I had closed quite so many doors and wasted so much time. Maybe everyone feels this way at forty. Maybe that's how it's supposed to be. If time and breath were infinite, we wouldn't value them like we do. Looking at Abigail, beautiful and energetic and full of life in her middle sixties, a troublemaker in the best sense of the word, makes me think that there is still time for me to get it right.

"I think the reason Franklin and I are happily married," Abigail continued after pressing her lips onto a piece of folded tissue, leaving two mauve half-moons on the white paper, "is because we were happy before we married. We were two satisfied, fully formed individuals before we fell in love. Being married has just enhanced that. Maybe that's what you need, Margot, to find a man who can be a friend first and a lover later."

"I've had men friends, Abbie. Lots of them. Every time I develop a romantic interest in a man, he backs off and tells me that he just wants to be friends."

"And then you never see them again?"

"Usually," I said, thinking of Arnie. New Bern is a small town so, of course, we run into each other. But it's always awkward.

"Well, then those men weren't really your friends, were they? 'Let's be friends' is one of those things people say to get themselves out of a relationship without looking bad. What they really meant is that they'd assessed the possibility of a romantic relationship with you, thought better of it, and decided to move on, getting as far away from you as fast as possible without breaking your heart," Abigail said matter-of-factly.

"Which they managed to do anyway."

Abigail patted my shoulder sympathetically. "I know. They were stupid. Complete idiots. I've so often heard you jest that you're not looking for Mr. Right anymore, that you'd be willing to settle for Mr. Good Enough. But Mr. Good Enough *isn't* good enough. Not for someone as special as you."

"Oh, Abbie. You're sweet."

"Ha! Well, we both know *that's* not true. But I do admire you, Margot, and I'd like to see you happy. I did have matchmaking on my mind when I volunteered you to welcome the new minister, but now I think romance may not be the best thing for you, not just now. At the moment, I think you'd be better off to find a friend. A real friend, someone whose interests and passions match your own, who understands how you think, who can offer you sound advice and take it too, is one of the greatest gifts on earth. That's what Franklin and I have. And that, more than anything, is what holds us together."

I pulled the car into Abigail's driveway. All the lights were off.

"So," she inquired, "do you have time to go over to the parsonage and greet Reverend Clarkson? If you're too busy with your family, I can . . ."

"No. That's all right. I'll do it. I don't mind."

"Thank you."

"You and Franklin are lucky."

"We are. And," she said, reaching into the depths of her purse and pulling out a blue box tied with white satin ribbon, "my birthday wish for you is that, someday, you will be just as fortunate."

"You didn't buy me a present from Tiffany's, did you? Oh, Abbie. You shouldn't have." I turned the key in the ignition and the engine stopped.

"Open it! You didn't suppose I'd forgotten, did you?"

Inside the box, on a bed of pale blue satin, was a necklace, a sterling silver key pendant decorated with a pink enamel heart, hung on a long silver chain. "Oh, Abigail! Oh, it's beautiful! I just love it. Thank you."

"Take good care of that. It's the key to your heart and very precious. Mustn't be given to anybody who is anything less than your soul mate. Oh, I almost forgot. There's a card that goes with your present." She rustled through her handbag. "Hmm. I must have left it in the house. Come inside and I'll give it to you." She opened the car door.

"That's all right, Abbie. Give it to me at the quilt circle."

"It's a very funny card," she said, climbing out of the car. "I spent a lot of time picking it out. Come along, Margot. I insist."

She started walking toward the house, not looking back because it would never occur to Abigail that anyone, particularly me, would fail to follow her instructions once she insists upon something.

I got out of the car. Abigail knows me too well.

5

Margot

We went in the side door. Abigail snapped on a light and we walked through an orderly anteroom with winter coats and hats hung on pegs and boots—garden boots, hiking boots, riding boots, snow boots—standing at the ready in tidy pairs on grooved trays designed to catch mud or melting snow. Three open cupboards on the opposite wall held an assortment of sports equipment—tennis rackets, golf clubs, and cross-country skis. Abigail is very athletic.

The kitchen was just as well organized, with gleaming copper pots hung on a rack over the stove, a long wall of cream-colored cabinets with dishes lined up like museum collectibles behind doors of beveled glass. Of course, Abigail has much more storage space than I do, and a full-time housekeeper, but I couldn't help but feel a little twinge of self-reproach when I compared Abigail's tidy kitchen to mine.

I've got to reorganize my kitchen. Soon. Maybe tonight. The last thing I need this Christmas is for my mother to come into my house and start throwing out little hints about me being messy or, worse yet, putting on an apron and starting to clean. The minute she walks into my house and starts picking up things, or pulls my vacuum out of the closet, I feel like I'm nine years old again.

I leaned against the counter, tapping my foot while Abigail opened a kitchen drawer and looked through a blue-flowered file folder for my card.

"It's not here," she said, frowning. "Hilda must have moved it. I've told her a million times ... Never mind. I'm sure it's on my desk." She walked to the hallway.

"Abigail, it's all right. Really. Why not wait and give it to me later?"

"No. It's a birthday card and I want to give it to you on your birthday. Come on."

I followed her down the hallway and into the dark living room, completely unsuspecting until Abigail turned on a table lamp and everyone I know and care about in New Bern—Evelyn, Charlie, Garrett, Franklin, Ivy, Virginia, Tessa and Lee, Madelyn and Jake, Dana, Wendy Perkins—jumped out and shouted, "Surprise!"

I stood frozen, utterly shocked. Evelyn came over to give me a hug. "Don't be mad. I told you that we weren't planning on giving you a surprise party at the shop. You didn't say anything about a party off-site." She laughed and everyone joined in.

My plan for celebrating this birthday was not to. But when I saw my friends popping up from behind the furniture like jacks-in-the-box, complete with silly grins and funny paper hats, I reconsidered.

After the shouts and the hugs, the kisses and congratulations, Evelyn and Madelyn brought out a beautiful cake, shaped like a bed and draped with a fondant icing quilt in pink, green, and white patchwork squares with four tall pink and white twisted candles, like four carved bedposts on each corner of the cake.

"Oh my!" I exclaimed, leaning over and gently poking the fondant with my finger to confirm that it truly was a cake. It looked so real, like a quilt on a doll's bed. "Who thought this up?"

Virginia, who, in her eighties, is more on the ball than most women half her age, waved her hand over her head. "Guilty!" she called out. "Though it wasn't exactly my idea. I saw something similar on the Internet." That's what I mean about Virginia; though her specialty is meticulously and exquisitely handmade quilts using heritage techniques, she is always willing to try new things. Virginia has more Facebook friends than I do.

"And Madelyn baked it," Tessa added, beaming as proudly over her best friend's accomplishment as if it had been her own. "Isn't it amazing? You know, if Madelyn hadn't decided to become an innkeeper, she could have made her living as a baker."

I looked up at Madelyn, who was shooting a look at Tessa. When Madelyn, widow of an infamous Wall Street financier, was living a glamorous life in New York, the paparazzi followed her everywhere. But now I've noticed that she doesn't really like being the center of attention.

"It's beautiful, Madelyn. Too beautiful to eat."

"It better not be!" she said, putting her hands on her hips. "I spent all morning baking it. Go on, Margot. Blow out the candles before the bedposts burn down."

"Yeah," Garrett, Evelyn's son and the Cobbled Court Quilt Shop's official "web dude," agreed. "Get on with it, Margot. I'm starving!"

I leaned over and pursed my lips, ready to blow, but was stopped by Ivy, who cried, "Wait a minute! Don't forget to make a wish."

I paused for a moment, wondering what to wish for. It seemed I already had so much. But then I remembered what Abigail had said about Reverend Clarkson in the car and what I'd said back: "You can never have too many friends."

Closing my eyes, I made a silent wish about myself and friendship and Reverend Clarkson. When I was done, I leaned down again and blew out all four candles in one breath, never supposing anything would come of it.

༄ 6 ༄

Philippa Clarkson

I have to go to the bathroom. I really, really do.

If Tim were here, he'd give me a hard time for not remembering to go before I left. But why would I? It was always his job to remind me. Well, not his job exactly, but he always did remind me and I came to depend on him for that. And so many other things. Funny the things I miss about him, even now. Funny to think I'd ever miss being teased for having a bladder the size of a thimble.

I could have gone when I stopped for gas near Sturbridge, but the line to get into the ladies' room ran out the door. Why can't people who design buildings figure out that women need twice as many toilets as men? It's all a matter of clothing complications and personal plumbing. Don't architects take anatomy in college? Anyway, I didn't stand in line and wait because I was afraid I'd be late to meet this person . . . what was her name?

I'd written it down on a scrap of paper and stuck it in my coat pocket before I left, but repeated groping through my pockets unearthed only an ATM receipt, a business card for my gynecologist, a used tissue, and three cherry-menthol cough drops. I have a cold.

I have to go to the bathroom and I have a cold and, for the life of me, I can't recall the name of the very first person I'll meet from my very first congregation. This does not bode well. Why can't I remember? I'm usually so good with names.

I'm nervous, that's why. Who wouldn't be? Getting your first pulpit is as good a reason as any for a case of nerves, especially under these circumstances.

What *is* that woman's name? I know it starts with an "M." Mary? Marion? Margaret? That's it. Margaret. I think it was Margaret . . . or something like that. No, it was Margaret. Definitely. This is no time to start second-guessing myself.

But it's hard not to. I've been waiting for a church of my own for so long. And I don't just mean the months since I finished seminary, months spent living at my parents' house while meeting with and being rejected by various pastoral search committees. I've been waiting for this moment, or rather been drawn to it, for most of my adult life.

The calling to ministry is exactly that, a calling, a thing you respond to not because you want to but because you have to. That's how it was for me. When I was little, people always used to pat me on the head and say, "So, are you going to be a minister like your dad when you grow up? Are you going into the family business?"

I never came right out and said, "No way!"—pastors' kids tend to learn the art of diplomacy at an early age—but that's what I was thinking. I knew exactly what responding to the call to ministry entailed. As a child, I wanted nothing to do with it.

What I did want was money in the bank, a nice car, bright red with a convertible top with an enormous dog who would sit in the backseat, marriage and a family, at least two kids and preferably three, a big home with one bathroom for every bedroom plus one more for show, and my name on the deed. No more parsonages for me.

Everything started off according to plan. I received a scholarship to James Madison University, beginning in the business school because I figured that was the surest path to getting a balanced checkbook and the deed to a house, hating it, transferring to marketing, then communications before making peace with my inclination to the helping professions and landing in the department of social work.

So I wouldn't have a big bankbook or a big house, but at least I'd have a paycheck, chart my own course, and be doing something meaningful. At least I'd avoided the religion department. That had to count for something, right?

Wrong.

I liked social work, but something was missing. I tried changing jobs. If working with seniors wasn't filling my cup, then maybe helping hospital patients would, or working with kids. Each job was satisfying in its own way, but it wasn't enough. The thing that kept me up at nights was the fact that, according to various rules and policies, I was not supposed to talk to my clients about the one thing many of them needed most—God. Sometimes I did it anyway and it got me in trouble. Once it got me fired.

In my heart, I knew it was coming but, even so, when the principal, Janice DeCarlo, called me into her office and told me she had to let me go, it was a shock.

"You know I hate doing it, Phil." Janice always called me Phil. "You're the best social worker we've ever had, but I can't keep pretending to look the other way. . . ."

"I know. You're right. I'll be more careful."

Janice smiled and shook her head. "No, you won't. You were praying with Brent Ragozine right outside the library. Don't say anything. Or make promises we both know you can't keep. Your instincts are good," she said, handing me a letter of dismissal, "but you're in the wrong place. Go do what you're *meant* to do. Be a minister."

I took the letter, folded it in half, and laid it on my lap. "I suppose you're right."

"I am," she said, rising from her chair and coming around to my side of the desk. "You may not realize it, Phil, but you're actually having the best day of your life."

Janice was right. The calling to ministry had always been in me. Finally admitting it came as a relief.

But why did the call to my first church have to come right before Christmas? And why to Bob Tucker's church? I've heard him speak. He and Dad go way back. The man can preach the paint off the wall. He'll be a hard act to follow. As the only child of Reverend Philip Clarkson, I already know all about bringing up the rear.

I wondered if the search committee knew about my dad. Probably. I've met with seven pastoral search committees since May. In each case, the first thing they said to me after "Please, sit down" was "Your father is a wonderful speaker!"

Translation? "Your father is a wonderful speaker, so we figured you must be too. The apple doesn't fall far from the tree, right?"

Yes and no. There is so much I share with Dad—a love of the outdoors and good music, a tendency to tear up during sad movies, and a deep, abiding love of and desire to serve God. But I am not an apple from the Clarkson tree. I'm adopted. My parents, Philip and Joyce, look like an ad for Scandinavian Airlines—tall, blond, and Nordic—whereas I am short, dark, and Hispanic. My birth mother was Puerto Rican. Judging from the tight curls in my hair, my father may have been African American, but no one knows. Every adoptive child grows up wondering why their birth parents gave them up, but I was able to work through most of that. My career in social work helped me understand that, sometimes, the most loving and sacrificial choice a woman in dire circumstances can make is to release her child to the care of someone else. And, growing up in a caring, stable, faith-filled home helped too. My parents and I do not share even one drop of the same blood, but they love me like their own, and that has made all the difference for me.

Another thing my parents, specifically my father, do not share with me is exactly what all those search committees were looking for—an inspired gift of oratory. He has it. I don't. That's why I've been passed over for so many pulpits.

But finally, I've got a church and six months to prove myself. Dad assures me my preaching will improve with time and practice, but Dad is a very reassuring sort of guy. Very supportive. Almost too supportive, if such a thing is possible. Dad and Mom always told me that I could do anything I set my mind to. It's a totally appropriate parental response when talking to a five-year-old, but after her teens, a person is looking for a more realistic assessment of her abilities and talents. It's simply not possible for everybody to be good at everything, is it?

They're good parents. The best. I'm lucky to have them. And

I'm lucky that this position opened up without time for the folks in New Bern to take me for a test run before deciding to sign on the dotted line. If I'd had to guest preach before getting the offer, would I have found myself driving south just two days before Christmas, my car-top luggage rack loaded down like Santa's sleigh, carrying everything I would need for a six-month sojourn in New Bern, Connecticut? I doubt it. God moves in mysterious ways.

But as I popped another cough drop into my mouth, I couldn't help but wonder what God had in mind, giving me a cold just before my preaching debut? Then I remembered Second Chronicles 12:9, "My grace is sufficient for thee: for my strength is made perfect in weakness."

I looked in the rearview mirror, caught sight of Clementine, who was half-asleep, head lolling against the backseat, and smiled, the way I always do when I look at her, the last gift Tim gave me before he died. I wonder if he knew how much she would come to mean to me? That the necessity of caring for Clementine would be the thing that would roust me out of my mourning and force me to rejoin the human race. I bet he did.

"I know what he'd say if he were here. He'd say, 'Gee, Pippa, if God is looking for a way to display heavenly strength through human weakness, who better than you to demonstrate the principle?' " I laughed, hearing his voice in my head, and looked in the rearview mirror again. "What do you say, Clemmie? Think he's right?"

She opened her big brown eyes, yawned, and sneezed, which, in Clem-speak, means she agrees 100 percent.

I made good time. In fact, I arrived fifteen minutes ahead of schedule.

It was tempting to park my car downtown and stroll across the snow-covered Green and the sidewalks, peer into the shop windows of my new community and the faces of the people I had come to serve, but I decided to save that for another time. The bathroom situation was getting urgent. It was a charming little village, though— picturesque, homespun, and frosted white, a picture postcard for Christmas in New England. I was sure I was going to like it here.

I pulled up to the church, tempted to park in the spot that said "Reserved for Pastor," but that seemed a little presumptuous, so I found a spot on the street. I pulled on the parking brake and turned off the ignition before climbing out of my red 2001 Jetta convertible, one of the few components of my original life plan that survived more or less intact. Of course, my fantasy car had sleeker lines, fewer miles on the odometer, and a more reliable heater, but I like my car.

And I like my new church!

It's a beauty, a tall and typically New England structure, simple and symmetrical and covered in white clapboard. It stands at the western end of the Green, a solid and constant presence, built to withstand age and the winter blast, inviting without being intimidating, roomy enough to admit all who care to enter, just as it should be.

I stood on the sidewalk and craned my neck so I could see all the way to the top of the steeple, then closed my eyes to offer a prayer of thanks for my journey, a plea for blessings upon my new congregation, and for strength made perfect in weakness. It was, of necessity, a short prayer. I left Clementine asleep in the backseat while I searched for a bathroom. The church doors were locked, but the parsonage was open.

No one responded when I carefully opened the door and called hello, thinking Margaret Whatever-Her-Name-Was might have arrived first. It felt strange to enter without being invited, but I was desperate.

The foyer had wide pine planks on the floor that led to a narrow hallway. The first door I opened was a coat closet, the second a guest bathroom, recently remodeled with white subway tile. After washing and drying my hands, I decided to take a quick tour of my new home.

It was as pretty inside as it was out. The kitchen was compact but serviceable, with white cabinets, black and white linoleum, and a tiled backsplash that looked original but had new white grout that made it look fresh. The paint throughout the house was pristine and the carpeting smelled new. I would have to keep a close eye on Clementine.

There was a lovely formal dining room I doubted I'd ever use. The living room was nice too, but the furniture was more casual with big overstuffed chairs and sofas upholstered in cabbage rose chintz. A little fussy for my taste, but pleasant enough. The study was lined with painted wooden shelves filled with Bibles, concordances, commentaries, lexicons, study guides, and various theological works as well as a good selection of novels, biographies, and mysteries. A desk stood near the window, dark wood with claw and ball feet and a faux-leather desk chair, the kind you get at those big office supply stores. It looked comfortable, but at odds with the antiques. Besides that, the only furniture in the study was a floor lamp, a side table, and two brown and burgundy striped club chairs placed at a conversational angle in front of a fireplace. It was a small room but cozy. This would be my refuge of choice on chilly winter evenings.

I wanted to go upstairs and see the bedrooms, but the woman from the church was due to arrive any minute. Peering out the front window, I saw Clementine's head visible in the backseat. I ran outside and unlocked the car. "Come on, Clemmie! Hop on out and have a look around. What do you think?"

She climbed out of the car, looked left and right, and then sneezed vigorously.

"I know. Pretty nice, huh? Look at this yard. Plenty of room to play out here."

She sneezed again and started pacing back and forth across the snowy lawn, tramping down a path. I laughed. She does this every time. Just as Clementine found her spot, I heard the sound of footsteps followed by a yelp of surprise and a crash.

Turning, I spotted a tall, blond woman sprawled on the sidewalk. A splash of red against the white snow startled me, making me think she'd been seriously injured. But when I ran to her side, I saw a broken casserole dish lying on the sidewalk. The red gore was only spilled tomato sauce.

I squatted down next to the woman. "Bet that hurt. Anything broken?"

"No," she replied and then looked down. "Nothing besides my dish. My pride is a little bruised, though."

While the woman climbed off the ground, Clementine arrived on the scene, sniffed the ground, and began wolfing down the spilled casserole.

"Clementine!" I scolded. "Stop that!"

"It's okay. It was supposed to be dinner for our new minister." The woman shrugged. "Somebody might as well enjoy it."

"Oh! Then you must be Margaret," I said with a smile, extending my hand.

She frowned and pressed her lips together. "Margot," she corrected me and shook my hand. "Margot Matthews."

I smacked myself on the forehead. "That's right! Margot. We've been expecting you."

Margot's eyes went wide. She blinked twice, looked at me, then Clementine, then back to me. "You were? I mean . . . Yes. You were."

"Are you all right?" I asked, wondering if she'd hit her head when she fell.

"Oh, yes. I'm fine." She pressed her lips together again, looking down as she patted Clementine on the head. "I just didn't realize that Reverend Clarkson had a dog." She paused, then looked at me with a deliberate smile. "Or a wife."

I grinned, finally understanding her reaction. "I don't," I said with a laugh. "I mean, *I'm* Reverend Clarkson. Reverend Philippa Clarkson. And this is Clementine," I said, looking down at Clemmie, who had finished her snack and was sitting on her haunches, licking the last traces of tomato sauce from her muzzle. "She's big enough to be a horse, but she's actually an English mastiff. Both of us are unmarried. Well . . . I'm a widow."

Margot's eyes grew even wider. "Philippa Clarkson? Not Philip? You're our new interim minister?"

"That's what the contract said. I hope that's still okay with everyone."

Margot frowned again, but only for a moment. "Of course," she said firmly. "Why shouldn't it be?"

She put out her hand for me to shake again. "It's nice to meet you, Reverend. Welcome to New Bern. I'm sure you'll be meeting everyone soon, but with Christmas so close, I'm all that was available in the way of a welcoming committee. But I'm afraid I'm not doing a very good job," she said, looking down at the broken dish.

"That's all right. I had a cheeseburger on the road. But I wouldn't mind a cup of tea about now, and a briefing about the church and town. Do you have time?"

"Of course, Reverend. Happy to."

"Please, call me Philippa. I know I have to get used to the title eventually, but every time someone says 'Reverend Clarkson,' I start looking for my dad."

"All right, Philippa," she said with a smile. "I can do that."

7

Margot

Clementine padded into the kitchen, flopped down next to the stove, and went immediately to sleep, snoring and twitching her feet as she dreamed. Philippa opened cupboards, scavenging for a teapot, tea, and sugar while telling me how excited she was to be in New Bern and how nervous she was about preaching the Christmas services. I thought she was just being modest.

"I'm not," she assured me, opening a corner cabinet that held canned vegetables and peering into it. "Trust me. My sermons are nothing to write home about."

"But," I protested, "your father is—"

With her back still to me, she held up her hand. "Reverend Philip Clarkson, the preacher's preacher. I know. But there's no such thing as a preaching gene, and if there was, I wouldn't have inherited it. My parents adopted me at birth. Spending your whole childhood listening to brilliant sermons is no guarantee either. In seminary, I got a C in preaching—the only C of my entire academic career.

"Here we are!" she exclaimed and pulled two white ceramic mugs out of a lower cabinet. "Who keeps their mugs on the bottom? Do you think it would be all right for me to switch the flour and baking stuff to the lower cupboard?" Without waiting for an answer, she began removing all the mugs from the cabinet.

She was petite, not more than five foot three, with a slim waist and thin wrists. She had a lithe build and moved gracefully even while wearing black, fur-lined ankle boots. Her skin was dark, the color of coffee with a touch of cream. Her hair was blackish brown, a halo of tight corkscrews that stopped halfway between her jaw and shoulders. She wore bright pink nail polish that matched her pink cable knit sweater and charcoal denim leggings that stretched tight over muscular calves.

Before tea, I had helped unpack the car. While carrying in a pair of skis, she told me that she loved sports and the outdoors. She'd met her husband, Tim, through a bike club. Until his illness, they had enjoyed hiking, biking, kayaking, and cross-country skiing. At that moment, wearing those clothes, she looked like anyone you might meet in New Bern, a customer who might come into the shop looking for a few yards of fabric, or maybe a teacher at the elementary school. What would she look like standing in the pulpit with a white neckband visible above a black robe and an embroidered gold clerical stole hanging from her shoulders?

Obviously, Philippa Clarkson wasn't what I'd expected. But had I known beforehand that he was really a she, I still don't think I'd have pictured someone who looked, acted, or sounded like this. She was feminine but athletic, humble but decisive, intelligent without being intimidating. Something in her straightforward manner, how she was aware of her strengths even while she acknowledged her weaknesses, told me that this was a woman at peace with herself and with God. Inner light positively streamed from Philippa Clarkson.

I liked her a lot. I hoped everyone else would feel the same. And I hoped that she really was better at preaching than she thought.

"C isn't so bad. It's average, right?"

"Yes," she said, pouring steaming water into mugs and setting one in front of me before sitting down on a kitchen stool, "but when Philip Clarkson is your dad, people expect you to be quite a bit better than average. Did you know that two of my dad's sermons were on the syllabus of my second-year preaching course at seminary?" She raised her eyebrows to emphasize her point.

"I can see where that could be a little daunting. But I don't think anyone in New Bern is expecting you to be like your—" I stopped myself, thinking about our meeting and how thrilled the board had been at the prospect of having an offspring of Philip Clarkson in our pulpit. "You'll be fine. Of course you're nervous. Your first sermon in your new church is bound to induce a few butterflies."

"A few," Philippa said with a wry smile. "And the timing only adds to the pressure. At Christmas, people expect to hear a sermon that will elicit tears of joy, peals of laughter, banish all doubts, and jolt them into a deep and spiritual renewal that will last . . . oh, at least until Easter." She laughed.

"I'm not saying that there's absolutely *no* possibility that my sermon will elicit that sort of response but, if it does . . . it won't be because of me. Know what I mean?"

She scooped two spoonfuls of sugar into her teacup and stirred. "A Christmas miracle. That's what I need."

Margot

I love working on Christmas Eve. I love waiting on harried husbands who seem to have only recently gotten the memo that the countdown to Christmas can now be measured in hours. I like seeing the relief in their eyes when I assure them that yes, she is going to absolutely love it, and I like knowing that it's true. I like picturing the delight on the faces of the quilters who will open those packages the next day. But what I really like about working on Christmas Eve is Cobbled Court Quilts' annual open house.

Evelyn puts out platters of cookies and carafes of hot cider for anyone who comes into the shop. People come to eat, to chat, or to pick up a few last-minute treats for friends or themselves. Some bring along quilting projects they need to finish up before Christmas and sit down to chat while they stitch up a binding or sew on a few embellishments. Everyone makes comments about not needing to add even one more cookie to their waistlines, but by the end of the day, the platters are always empty. After we ring up the last sale and lock the doors, Evelyn brings out some appetizers and one last plate of cookies and we have our staff party.

Everyone gets a gift from Evelyn, some fabric or a pattern book she's chosen especially for that person, and we all exchange the Secret Santa gifts. This year, I drew Virginia's name. At first I was stumped. What can you give an eighty-year-old woman that she doesn't already have? But while I was poking around an antique store, I came across a beautiful thimble in Virginia's size, sterling silver with a band of wild roses around the base, dating from the 1890s. The asking price was quite a bit more than we're supposed to spend on our Secret Santa gifts, but I couldn't resist.

I smiled as I walked to work, thinking about the party and how pleased Virginia would be with her gift, and how great it was that my family would be together for Christmas.

I wouldn't have said it to him but, like Dad, I'd been afraid that my sister might back out at the last minute. However, I talked to her yesterday and everything is still on track. I can't wait to see Olivia! When I saw her last, her two front teeth had been loose. Had they fallen out since then? Grown back?

Evelyn, Virginia, and Charlie are coming to dinner too, which is good. I might need a little help in the kitchen and Charlie will be only too happy to help. It's going to be a lovely Christmas.

As I rounded the corner, passing a red-cheeked Santa who was ringing a bell and soliciting donations for charity, I ran into Ted Carney and Miranda Wyatt. Miranda was hanging on Ted's arm, laughing at something he'd said. They were so intent on each other that they nearly knocked me over. Abigail was right. There was definitely an attraction there.

"Sorry, Margot!" Miranda laughed and turned to Ted with sparkling eyes. "Guess we should look where we're going." Ted smiled and laid his hand over hers.

"That's all right," I said. "Say, Ted. I thought you were heading out to your daughter's this morning?"

"Oh. Uhhh. I decided to put it off until this afternoon. Miranda and I had some church business to talk over. We need to come up with a plan . . . for replacing the boiler."

Though her expression didn't change and she continued to cling to his arm, Miranda gave Ted a sideways look that made me wonder if she was annoyed at his very transparent attempt to conceal their relationship. I wondered too. But, as I learned a long time ago, you can lose a lot of sleep trying to figure out why men do the things they do.

"So," Ted said brightly, changing his tone and the subject,

"how's our new minister? Settled in? I'm sorry I'll miss his Christmas sermon. If he's half the preacher his father is, it should be something special."

"Flashy preaching isn't everything, you know. And anyway, he's a she. The Reverend Philipp*a* Clarkson," I said, putting special emphasis on that last syllable. "And she seems very nice. I think we made a good choice."

Ted's head hinged back in surprise. "Philip—pa? But . . . the paperwork said . . . I thought we were hiring a man. . . ."

"Must have been a typo."

Miranda drew her hand out of the circle of Ted's arm. "What difference does it make? We hired Reverend Clarkson based on experience, not her gender. Didn't we?"

"Certainly," Ted replied, reaching up with his now-unoccupied arm and pulling his hat down more securely on his head. "I'm just surprised, that's all."

"So was I," I agreed, smiling at Miranda, who was now frowning at her escort.

I was trying my best to help Ted out, but he wasn't doing a very good job of helping himself. Ted had been widowed for quite a while. Possibly he was a little rusty at interpreting feminine signals.

"I'm just not sure how the men in the congregation will respond to this," Ted mused, looking down at the ground. "If I had a problem, I don't think I'd feel comfortable unburdening myself to a woman."

"Why not?" Miranda bristled. "The women of this church, myself included, have been going to Bob Tucker for counsel for years."

Ted's head jerked up and he looked at Miranda, realizing his error. "Oh, yes. Of course. I didn't mean to imply there was anything wrong with the Reverend Clarkson's being a woman. It's just a surprise. Like Margot said."

He turned toward me with a slightly panicked expression, silently begging me to come to his rescue. I made another stab at it.

"When I met her, I dropped my casserole dish," I said, carefully wording my response. Dropping that casserole had everything to do with the icy sidewalk and nothing to do with my surprise at our new minister's gender, but if Miranda thought it did, what was the harm? Ted really seemed to like her. It'd be a shame if they fell out over something so minor.

"Right!" Ted said gratefully. "It just comes as a bit of a shock. We've never had a female minister in New Bern before."

"It was bound to happen sooner or later. Our denomination has been ordaining women for more than half a century," Miranda said curtly. She looked at her watch. "I have to run."

"Let me walk you to your car." Ted smiled and held out his arm gallantly. "The sidewalk is icy."

"I'll be fine. Thank you for lunch, Ted. Merry Christmas, Margot." She marched away.

Ted stood on the sidewalk, watching her go. "Merry Christmas," he called after her. "I'll call you when I get back. We can finish talking over options for the boiler."

Miranda didn't say anything, just raised her hand over her head without turning around; a wave, but not a friendly one.

Ted looked at me. His shoulders drooped in disappointment.

"Did you buy her a Christmas gift?" I asked.

He shook his head. "I thought it was too soon. This is the first time we've gone out."

I turned around and looked down the street toward the florist shop. "Kinsey's is open. Go ask Marcia if there's still time to deliver a Christmas arrangement to Miranda's house today. Not a poinsettia. Too impersonal. Cut flowers, red carnations would be perfect."

"Do you really think that will help?" he asked hopefully.

"Well, it sure won't hurt. Merry Christmas, Ted."

❦ 9 ❦

Margot

On Christmas morning, I got to church an hour early to save spots for my friends. It was an easier job than in years past because I only had to save places for Evelyn and Charlie. Virginia was supposed to join us, but Evelyn called early to tell me Virginia had woken up with a cold and decided to stay in bed.

"Will she be well enough to make it for dinner?"

"She said she'd try, but not to count on her. We brought her breakfast and opened presents with her this morning. Her nose is red and she's sniffling, but she's fine." Evelyn chuckled. "Charlie and I gave her a new serger for Christmas. I think this cold is a convenient excuse to stay home and play with her new toy. If she doesn't make it for dinner, we'll drop off some leftovers on the way home. Don't worry."

It was just as well that I only needed to save two extra places. The church was packed—and beautiful. The candles of the Advent wreath and the long tapers fixed to evergreen swags at the end of every pew filled the air with a warm glow and scent of vanilla and melting wax; a sea of scarlet poinsettias carpeted the steps and the raised altar where Philippa sat in her black robe topped with a shimmering white and gold embroidered clergy stole, looking composed but serious and very ministerial while the organist played a prelude of carols.

It was a beautiful and reverent setting, but I had trouble keeping my mind focused on the sacred. Fifteen minutes before the service, every pew was filled—except mine. I'd lost count of how many times I had to explain to people that yes, the seats next to me *were* taken. The closer we got to the top of the hour, the more awkward I felt saying this.

Thankfully, just as the organ moved into the full-throated, pull-out-the-stops crescendo that signaled the end of the piece, Evelyn and Charlie came scurrying up the aisle. They squished past the knees of six other people to reach the center of the pew, murmuring apologies as they did. Evelyn sat down with a relieved whoosh of breath.

"Sorry."

"Where were you?" I whispered.

"Fruitcake emergency. Don't ask." She cast a pointed look in Charlie's direction.

"Is it my fault that you left the platter on the stove top, right next to an open flame?" he hissed. "It could have been worse. Before we got married you didn't even *own* a fire extinguisher. . . ."

I closed my own eyes, but not in prayer. I was trying to keep from laughing. The prelude finished just in time and we rose to sing "Hark! The Herald Angels Sing."

It was a lovely service. No orchestras, or trumpet fanfares, or processions of live camels and donkeys to the nativity, but lovely. The music was sweetly familiar, carols I've sung since childhood, and the story of the first Christmas stirred me to wonder and gratitude, as it always does. And the sermon was . . . Well, it wasn't bad.

The message was spot-on, very clearly laid out. In fact, I think if I'd *read* the text it would have stood up very well against just about any Christmas sermon I'd ever heard.

But I didn't read it. Philippa did. Word for word, and rather slowly, in a voice that was still raspy from her cold. She looked into the faces of the congregation only rarely and when she did, it was with a startled jolt, as if she remembered one of her seminary professors or, perhaps, her father admonishing her to make eye contact with her audience. After she did, she'd look down at her notes, clear her throat and pause for a long, uncomfortable moment before beginning again, as if she'd lost her train of thought.

Evelyn leaned toward me and whispered, "This is our new minister?"

I nodded. "For the next six months. She's very nice. I like her. You will too. But . . . first sermon and all. She's a little nervous."

"Does she quilt?" Evelyn asked, not unkindly. "She needs something that will help her relax. Otherwise, six months could feel like a long time."

Philippa stood near the doors of the sanctuary, wishing the congregants a merry Christmas as they filed past. We were nearly at the end of the exit line, which gave me ample opportunity to hear what people were saying to each other about our new minister. The reviews weren't great.

As we neared the door, I could hear what people said to Philippa as they passed. Reverend Tucker nearly always had compliments and congratulations heaped upon him after he preached. The response to Philippa was much more reserved. People welcomed her to town, thanked her for coming on such short notice, shared memories of sermons her father had given (I saw what Philippa meant about her father. He cast quite a shadow) and wished her merry Christmas. Hardly anyone complimented her sermon.

Waldo Smitherton was the only exception, but he'd slept through the whole thing. He always does and then he always stops to wring the minister's hand and bellow, "Wonderful sermon, Reverend! *Wonderful!* Enjoyed it *very* much!"

Once I asked Reverend Tucker if that bothered him. "No," he said. "I think he really does enjoy it. At Waldo's age, a nap is as good for the soul as a stern rebuke."

After saying the same to Philippa, Waldo started to totter away, then spun around to face her again. "Wait a minute. *You're* Reverend Clarkson?"

Philippa nodded. "Yes, sir. I am."

He hobbled back and shook her hand a second time. "Waldo Smitherton—oldest member of the congregation. Stick around and you may get to preach at my funeral."

Philippa smiled. "I hope not. Not for many years to come anyway."

Waldo looked Philippa up and down, narrowing his eyes. "Huh. You don't look like your dad. Anyway, I thought they were sending your brother."

"No, Mr. Smitherton. I don't have a brother."

"But Philip Clarkson is your father?"

"He is, sir. My adoptive father."

Waldo considered this.

"Well. If you were raised by the Reverend Clarkson, we can't have gone far wrong calling you." He bobbed his head approvingly. "He's a good man. Though, I hope you won't mind me saying, you're a darned sight prettier than he is. A *darned* sight prettier!"

Philippa laughed. "I don't mind at all, Mr. Smitherton. Merry Christmas, sir."

"Merry Christmas to you, Reverend," Waldo said and toddled off, cane in hand.

I was next in line.

"Well, at least I've won over one member of the congregation," Philippa said, still smiling as Waldo retreated. "One down, four hundred and ninety-nine to go."

"Only four hundred and ninety-eight," I said. "I'm already a member of your fan club."

"And you can add our names to the rolls as well," said Charlie as he put out his hand. "I'm Charlie Donnelly and this is my wife, Evelyn Dixon Donnelly."

Charlie put his arm around Evelyn's shoulders and beamed. Charlie and Evelyn have been married for more than a year now, but it's clear to anyone with eyes in their head that the honeymoon is far from over. They're so sweet together.

"Very nice to meet you," Philippa replied, gripping Charlie's hand, then Evelyn's. "You're Margot's boss, aren't you? She's told me so much about you, all of it good. I feel like I know you already."

"I feel the same way about you," Evelyn replied. "And for the same reason. Welcome to New Bern, Reverend. I hope you'll drop by the quilt shop sometime."

"I intend to. I'm hoping to make the rounds of all the businesses and meet the merchants after I'm settled in a bit."

"Fine idea. Be sure and drop by the Grill. Some of my staff could do with a dose of religion." Charlie winked. "Seriously, come by the restaurant for lunch. My treat."

"I might just take you up on it. Margot says the Grill is the best restaurant in town."

"It is," Charlie said stoutly. "I'll not deny it."

Evelyn gave Charlie an affectionate glance before returning her attention to Philippa. "We're having an open house at the shop in January to kick off our winter classes. I'd love for you to drop by. It'd give you a chance to meet the teachers and a lot of very nice quilters. Who knows? You might even decide to enroll in a class yourself."

Before Philippa could respond, Charlie jumped in. "Come for the food, if nothing else. I'm making basil chicken skewers with peanut dipping sauce, mini-quiche with Gruyère and dill, pea pods stuffed with shrimp, and some of those horrible little cocktail wieners wrapped in bread dough that Evelyn likes so much. What do you call those things?" he asked, turning to her.

"Pigs in a blanket," Evelyn replied, ignoring Charlie's eye rolling.

"Pigs in a blanket." He made a face. "Terrible. How did I fall in love with a woman who has such plebeian taste in appetizers? Anyway, you should come, Reverend. The chicken skewers alone are worth the price of admission."

"Thank you," Philippa said. "I'd like to. It sounds like fun."

"Good!" I said. "It's the third Tuesday in January. Is that night good for you?"

Philippa grinned. "At the moment, my dance card is wide open."

"That'll change," Charlie assured her. "And quickly. New ministers are always in demand. You'll see."

"I hope you're right," Philippa said. "It feels strange being new in town."

By this time, the church was nearly empty; everyone had rushed off to celebrate Christmas with family and friends. It occurred to me that, perhaps, her arrival being so unexpected, no one had thought to invite Philippa over for Christmas.

"Philippa, I know it's short notice, but do you have plans for the rest of the day? Why don't you come over and have dinner at my house?"

"Oh," she said hesitantly, "you're sweet, but . . . I should really go home and catch up on some things, finish unpacking. I couldn't impose on you."

"Don't be silly, woman!" Charlie barked, using his traditional rebuke, and then turned red as he remembered whom he was speaking to. "I mean . . . Reverend . . . Pardon me. It wouldn't be an imposition. We'd be honored to have you join us."

"He's right," I agreed. "We've got plenty of food. Virginia, Evelyn's mother, was supposed to join us, but she came down with a cold. It's thrown off my whole seating arrangement. You can't spend Christmas alone."

"She's right," Charlie agreed. "That won't do at all. So get your coat and come along. I won't take no for an answer."

Evelyn laughed. "That settles it, Reverend. When Charlie makes up his mind about something, there's no point in resisting. Charlie is quite irresistible," she said in a slightly flirtatious tone, taking his arm. Charlie grinned and stood up a bit taller.

"Well, since you put it like that. . . . Just let me run home to change out of my party frock," she said, glancing down at her clerical vestments, "and take Clementine for a walk. Can I bring something?" she asked and then laughed. "Not that I have anything. I haven't had a chance to do much grocery shopping yet, but if you need some low-fat blueberry yogurt, I can help you out. Or dog kibble. I've got a fifty-pound bag of that."

"Just bring yourself," I said.

"And an apron," Charlie added.

Evelyn rolled her eyes. "Charlie! Reverend Clarkson is a guest!"

"What? She can chop vegetables, can't she? Anyone can do that. Besides, giving guests something to do helps them feel at ease."

❧ 10 ❧

Philippa

I stood at the cutting board in Margot's cheery kitchen, wearing a borrowed apron and chopping onions.

"Good knife work," Charlie said as he looked over my shoulder. "You can always judge a cook by the way she handles an onion."

Margot, who stood at the stove, stirring an enormous pot of mashed potatoes, turned to look at me. "Wow. You should feel very proud, Philippa. I've known Charlie for years and he's yet to say anything nice about my cooking skills."

Charlie walked over to the stove, picked up a spoon, dipped a tiny taste of potatoes from the pot, and frowned. "And today will do nothing to change that, Margot. You need more salt in these potatoes and more butter. A lot more butter. Christmas is a full-fat holiday. There'll be no watching of waistlines today. Not in my kitchen."

"Technically," Margot said as she tossed a palmful of salt into the pot, "it's *my* kitchen, Charlie. But I'm not trying to keep down the calorie count. I ran out of butter."

"You ran out of butter?" he gasped. "On Christmas? How is that possible?"

"I had it on my list," Margot said defensively, backing away as Charlie elbowed past her to turn off the burner under the potatoes, "but there was so much to buy...."

"Never mind," Charlie said, holding up his hand. "I'll run to our house and get some more. Leave the potatoes until I get back. Take the rolls out of the oven when the timer goes off." He slipped his arms inside the sleeves of his coat.

"Hey, Charlie? As long as you're going out, check the temperature in there, will you?" Margot jerked her head toward the living room. "I don't know where my sister could be. Dad hates it when people are late."

"Don't worry," Charlie replied. "Evelyn's on top of it. She's used to dealing with grouchy old men. Anyway, your sister's not late. Not yet. The way things are going it could be hours before we're ready to serve." He gave the swinging door that separated the kitchen from the living room a push and disappeared.

"Very funny!" Margot called before turning to me. "I know he sounds awful, but that's just Charlie's way. He's really just a big teddy bear."

As if to confirm this observation, the kitchen door swung in the opposite direction and Charlie stuck his head through it. "By the way, Margot, what you lack in culinary skills, you more than make up for in presentation. The table looks beautiful," he said and, without waiting for her response, popped out just as quickly as he'd popped in.

"See? Charlie's a bit rough around the edges, but he has a good heart."

I nodded. "He's fine. I've always enjoyed a good curmudgeon."

Margot giggled. "You came to the right town for that. Wait until you meet Abigail. She makes Charlie look like a poseur but, if she likes you, you won't find a better ally in this town than Abigail Spaulding."

"Then I guess it's a good thing she wasn't at services. Don't think I made many allies today."

Margot carried the wastebasket over to my side of the kitchen. "Don't talk like that," she said as she scooped up the detritus of my handiwork, a pile of papery onion skins, and dumped them into the trash. "It was fine. I thought you made some very good points. It was fine," she repeated, as if saying it twice would make it true and as if fine was the same as good.

"Waldo Smitherton was very taken with you, and Charlie spoke well of your knife skills. Coming from him, that's a real compliment. I'm not kidding."

She stood next to me, staring at the cutting board as I took the last onion, made six quick, deep cuts into the flesh, another six crossways, then chopped through the onion with a speed which was, I'll admit, a little show-offy. But I think I can be forgiven for that. I've spent hours watching celebrity chefs perform this dazzling bit of showmanship and even more hours mastering it. Until now, I'd had no opportunity to display my skills to anyone besides Clementine. She hadn't seemed that impressed.

"Wow!" Margot said. "Where'd you learn that?"

I shrugged, unwilling to admit how many late nights I spend watching Emeril and Rachael and Jamie. After Tim died, cooking shows became my sleeping aid of choice.

"I've always liked to cook. Tim used to say it was my beef bourguignon and chocolate lava cake that convinced him to marry me."

Margot made a sympathetic little noise. I'd told her about Tim when we met at the parsonage, right after she'd told me about her breakup with her old boyfriend. Every psych textbook I've ever read says that the best way to draw someone out is just to listen, but I don't think that's always true. Sometimes, when a woman shares a secret, especially one you can tell she didn't plan on sharing, it makes her feel better if you tell her one of your secrets in exchange, as a sort of pledge of good faith. There's probably an official phrase for this in textbooks about interpersonal communications, but I've always called it "trading hostages." That's what I did with Margot.

I wasn't surprised that she'd shared personal information with me and so quickly. People have always told me their stuff, even before I was ordained. Maybe I'm easy to talk to. I hope so. Sometimes people just need a safe place to unload their troubles.

Don't get me wrong, telling Margot about my broken heart, how Tim's death left me in mourning not just for my best friend and lover but the death of all the plans we'd made for children, a home, life as we had thought it would and should be, wasn't just for her benefit. Sometimes I need to share my stuff too. A minister has to choose her confidantes with care. However, Margot seemed trust-worthy and entirely honest, guileless even. More importantly, I liked her.

It was sweet of her to invite me to Christmas dinner, especially at the last minute. But as I stood in Margot's kitchen chopping vegeta-bles, I felt emotional, almost teary, and not because of the onion.

Christmas is a day for celebration and hope and gratitude. I know because I just preached a whole sermon on the subject. I have every reason to feel hopeful and grateful. God gave me a church for Christmas—a lovely church in a charming Norman Rockwell village filled with kind-hearted people who take in stray pastors and invite them to Christmas dinner at the last minute. I should be happy. In-stead, I am suddenly swamped by loneliness and longing. I miss my family and I miss Tim. I miss all those connections and complica-tions that make life such a struggle and give it such meaning.

This is a nice town, but I don't know this place, these people. I am a stranger here and it feels strange. Things will look brighter after the holidays, I suppose, when my work will begin in earnest. On the other hand, maybe they won't. The reaction to my sermon was, unfortunately, about what I'd expected it to be. That doesn't bode well for my future in New Bern. But one way or another, I'll soon be too busy for introspection. What a relief. It is more blessed to give than to receive and, for me, usually much easier.

Contrary to Charlie's prediction, Margot's sister was late for din-ner. Very late. Repeated calls to her cell phone went unanswered. Margot's dad grew increasingly irritated as the minutes ticked past. He paced in front of the fireplace, clanking his ice in his glass, occa-sionally fishing out a piece and chewing on it, and grumbling.

"Margot, did you tell her that dinner would be served at two?"

"Yes, Dad."

"Well, why isn't she here? It's quarter to three. And here we all sit, waiting, while the turkey dries out."

"Not at all," Charlie assured him, though we both knew it wasn't true. "The turkey is on schedule. Can I refill your glass, Werner? There's plenty of eggnog."

"I'll do it," Margot said, taking her father's glass and scurrying into the kitchen.

"I'm sure she'll be here soon," Evelyn said. "She probably ran into traffic."

"The roads were so icy coming down here," Margot's mother said, turning to Evelyn. "There were spots where we couldn't go more than fifteen miles an hour."

"*We* got here," Werner harrumphed. "Right when we said we would."

Margot returned from the kitchen with her father's glass. Werner stood directly in front of the fire with one arm crossed over his chest, tossed back half his eggnog in one gulp, and started chewing on another ice cube. I've never known anyone who drank eggnog on the rocks, but I suspected, for Werner, the ice was more about giving him something to do than keeping his beverage cold.

"I tried Mari's cell again," Margot said. "No answer. Maybe we should go ahead and eat."

The table was pretty, with a long, low line of white poinsettias wrapped in gold paper and ringed by white votive candles for the centerpiece and set with gold-rimmed china and tall crystal goblets that sparkled in the candlelight. Charlie and Evelyn had brought a bunch of white and gold Christmas crackers to the party, a gift sent by Charlie's sisters in Ireland, and put one next to each place setting.

Charlie demonstrated how to pull on the strings to open the cracker. The resulting pop made everyone jump, and the sight of Charlie wearing a pink paper crown on his head made everyone laugh, easing the tension. For a few minutes the room was filled with sounds of popping paper and the sight of adults looking silly and pleased in their own paper crowns, showing off the cheap plastic trinkets they found inside the paper tubes.

Margot filled goblets with champagne. Charlie carried the turkey in from the kitchen and placed it on the sideboard, carving knife at the ready. Though it was his daughter's table, Werner instinctively placed himself at the head of it. When everyone was seated, he bowed his head to bless the food, but his wife laid a hand on his arm.

"Werner, perhaps *Reverend* Clarkson should say the prayer?"

He looked at me, frowning. We were all members of the same denomination, but Werner Matthews seemed uncomfortable with the idea of a female minister. He'd barely talked to me all day. It didn't bother me; I'd run into that sort of thing before and would again.

"Please, Mr. Matthews," I said, bowing my head slightly, "you go ahead."

After Mr. Matthews prayed, Charlie carved and served the bird while the rest of us passed bowls and platters from hand to hand, filling our plates until there wasn't room for so much as an additional cranberry. The turkey was a little bit dry, but that didn't seem to make any difference to anyone but Charlie, who grimaced slightly when he took his first bite. Everything else was delicious. Now that the food was on the table, Margot's father was more relaxed, which seemed to come as a relief to Margot.

He was an interesting man, bristly, but clearly dedicated to his family and just as clearly used to being in charge of everything—his business, his wife, and his daughter. Margot was forty, a woman with a home of her own and a successful career, yet her father spoke to her and of her as though she were still a girl, a good girl and the apple of his eye, but a girl just the same. And Margot responded in kind, deferring to his opinions.

I wondered if she was aware of how her personality altered in the presence of her father. Was that the price of being her father's favorite, a price she had decided was worth paying? Or had she and her sister, as so many siblings do, simply fallen into the roles assigned to them when they were born—good child, bad child, rebel, saint?

Being an only child does have some advantages. For me, there was no jockeying for position or need to curry favor, no fear of losing parental approval. I was always my father's favorite, the tablet upon which he inscribed all his hopes and unfulfilled expectations. It's something of a mixed blessing. Those tablets are heavy.

Still wearing his purple paper crown, Werner sawed a chunk of turkey breast into bite-sized pieces while talking to his daughter. "I gave your car a once-over before I came inside, honey. You need new tires. The tread is low on the back right side. It's dangerous to drive on a tire like that, especially in this weather."

"I know, Daddy. But I'm thinking of getting a new car, so I didn't think it made sense to replace the tires now."

"A new car?" Werner frowned, reached for the cranberry sauce, and heaped the last of it on his plate. Without being asked, Lillian got up from the table and carried the bowl into the kitchen, presumably to refill it. "What's wrong with the car you've got?"

"Nothing, but it has a hundred and fifty thousand miles on it. And it's not great in snow. I was thinking about looking for something with four-wheel drive."

Werner speared a piece of turkey with his fork before carrying it to his mouth and nodded, all for keeping his daughter safe. "Well, you make sure you call me before you go buying anything. Remember what happened when you bought that Pinto wagon."

Her cheeks flushed pink. "Dad," she said quietly, "that was twenty years ago."

"Biggest lemon on the lot," he said, going on as if he hadn't heard her, grinning and turning to address himself to Charlie. "Needed a new transmission. And that dealer knew it too. That's why he gave her such a 'deal' on it. He sure saw her coming." Werner chuckled and chewed. "Didn't he, Bunny?"

Margot looked down at her plate and nodded.

"So you just make sure you call me before you sign *anything* this time," he said, pointing his fork at Margot.

"Yes, Dad."

"I can drive down, give it a test drive for you, and help negotiate the deal—make sure they don't stick you for any of those crazy 'extras' and dealer fees."

"I'd hate to make you drive all the way from Buffalo just to—"

Werner beamed and patted his daughter's hand. "I'd go to the ends of the earth to help my little girl. You know that."

A ringing sound, like an old-fashioned alarm clock, came from the kitchen. Margot jumped to her feet just as her mother came through the kitchen door holding a full bowl of cranberry sauce in one hand and Margot's cell phone in the other.

"That's probably Mari," Margot said, smiling with relief.

"Hope she's just late and not lost," Werner said, addressing his comments to the table. "Or broken down somewhere. Wouldn't surprise me. *She* drives an Audi."

He rolled his eyes meaningfully and then, seeing that Margot had covered her ear with her hand so she could hear what the caller was saying, lowered his voice.

"Or she did the last I heard. She only lives a few hours south, but she can't be bothered to come see us. And she never invites us down there, not even for Olivia's kindergarten graduation. Never calls unless she wants something. I told her about buying an Audi, didn't I, Lil? Those things are always breaking down and they cost a fortune to fix. I told her over and over, but would she listen?"

Lillian, who was only half listening to him, her attention (and mine) being divided between her husband's monologue and Margot's phone conversation, which was filled with too many long pauses and short responses to be a chat between sisters, frowned.

"Sweetheart," she said, clamping her hand over her husband's without looking at his face.

Werner put down his fork, looked at his wife with surprise and then at Margot. By that time, we were all looking at Margot.

"Yes. All right. We'll be right there." Margot ended the call and turned to face her parents. Her eyes were wide and her face drained of color.

Lillian rose from her chair. "What is it?"

"There was an accident. Black ice, the policeman said. Mari skidded off the road and went over an embankment. He didn't know how long she'd been there before they found her. He found Mari's phone on the floor and saw I was the last person to call. . . ."

Werner got up and stood next to his wife. "Where are they now?"

"In an ambulance. Two ambulances. One for Mari and one for Olivia."

Lillian's hand covered her mouth. For a moment, she dipped lower, as if her knees might give way, but Werner grasped her around the shoulders and pulled her body in close to his.

"How bad is it?"

Margot shook her head. "I don't know. The officer just said we should get to the hospital as soon as possible. But," she said, choking on her own words, "I think it's bad, Daddy. I think it's very bad."

∞ 11 ∞

Margot

Everything was upside down.

My dad has always been the impatient one, the person who honks at people who drive even one mile per hour under the speed limit and barks at checkout clerks whose registers run out of tape. But when we got to the hospital and had to wait while an officious woman scanned our identification and attempted, unsuccessfully, to print out our visitor badges, it was my mother who bristled at the delay.

"Our daughter is here, Mariposa Matthews, and our grand-daughter, Olivia Matthews," Mom snapped. "They've just brought them in. There was an accident. A serious accident! Why are you keeping us waiting?"

"It's for your own protection," the woman replied dully, frowning as she tapped on the computer. "And the protection of the patients."

"I don't *need* to be protected!" My mother's voice rose to a nearly hysterical pitch. "I need to see my daughter and my grandchild, do you hear me? Right now!"

Dad put his arm around Mom and patted her on the shoulder. "Calm down, Lil. Miss, can't we leave our identification here with you and get the badges later?"

The woman glanced up at him. For a moment, I thought she was going to waver, but then she pressed her lips together. "I'm sorry, sir. Hospital policy. Every visitor must be cleared through security and wear a badge."

Philippa, who'd volunteered to come with us while Evelyn and Charlie stayed at my house to clean up, stepped up to the desk and took off her coat, revealing her collar.

"I'm Philippa Clarkson, the new pastor at New Bern Community Church."

The woman looked up from her keyboard in surprise. "That's my church. You're taking over for Reverend Tucker?"

"Just for a few months, until he's feeling better."

"I'm sorry, Reverend. I didn't recognize you. Normally, I never miss services, but I wasn't able to go today. I'm new here and you know how it is," she said with a trace of bitterness. "The low man on the totem pole gets stuck working the holiday."

"That's all right, Cheryl," Philippa replied, glancing at her name tag. "It's good of you to sacrifice your own Christmas celebrations to help people who are going through such a hard time. Do you think it might be possible to let me escort the Matthews family back to the ER? Since I'm a member of the clergy . . ."

Cheryl bit her lower lip. "I don't know, Reverend. It's kind of irregular and, like I said, I'm new here. I went six months without a job before I found this one. I don't want to risk losing it, but . . ."

She looked at Philippa and then at my parents, her eyes resting a moment on my mother, who was weeping on Dad's shoulder.

"Let me check with my supervisor."

Five minutes later, a tired-looking nurse wearing a cranberry red cardigan and necklace of red, green, and blue Christmas lights ushered us to a waiting room. "Dr. Bledsoe will be right in to talk to you."

My mother clutched at the nurse's arm. "Where are they? When can I see them?"

The nurse smiled sympathetically and rubbed her palm over the back of my mother's hand. "Soon."

Mom sat down on a beige sofa with her pocketbook in her lap, clutching at the handle, her back stiff and eyes alert, as though she were waiting for a bus and was afraid she might miss it. Dad sat down next to her, but she seemed not to notice.

"Perhaps I should go find somewhere else to wait," Philippa said, looking at me uncertainly.

"No," my father said hoarsely. He glanced at my mother, who was staring straight ahead. "If you don't mind, Reverend," Dad said, looking up at Philippa, "I'd appreciate it if you could stay with us for a while. At least until the doctor comes."

Philippa nodded and sat down in a chair across from my parents.

I hesitated before following the others through the door. Sensing a presence, I looked down the hall to see a man with gray hair and black-rimmed glasses who was taking off a blood-spattered lab coat while the nurse in the cranberry sweater stood behind, holding out a clean one, guiding his arms into the left sleeve, then the right, before nodding her head toward me, toward me and the door of the room I dreaded to enter.

❧ 12 ❧

Philippa

I stood with my back against a pistachio-colored wall, taking a moment to catch my breath while Margot and her parents were in one of the administrative offices, filling out paperwork. My cell phone went off, vibrating in my pocket and making me jump. Looking down at the screen, I was happy to see the words "Mom and Dad."

Mom was on the kitchen phone and Dad on the bedroom extension. They'd called to wish me merry Christmas and get the reviews on my sermon, but I didn't want to talk about that. The only thing on my mind was the Matthews family.

"It was so awful. She was alive when the ambulance arrived, but there was nothing they could do. Apparently, the car skidded off the road and over an embankment. It was a back road, not very well traveled. They think she was trying to take a shortcut so she'd get there faster. There's no way of knowing for sure how long the car was down there before someone noticed the broken guardrail and stopped to investigate. Could have been hours. Anyway, by the time they found her . . ."

"Oh, that poor family," my mother murmured. "To lose a child and a grandchild . . ."

"No," I corrected her. "Only Mari was killed. The granddaughter is alive. At least for now. The doctor didn't offer much hope of her surviving the night."

"Have they seen her yet?"

"She's in intensive care. They have strict rules about visitors. I don't suppose it makes any difference. She's unconscious."

"Even unconscious people are sometimes aware of the presence of others," my father said. "If the worst happens, it would be a great comfort to the family to see her now. At least they'd have the memory of seeing their granddaughter alive, and knowing she died surrounded by people who love her.

"Encourage the doctors to let them see her, Pippa," he continued, using his pet name for me. "A minister can have a lot of influence inside the walls of a hospital."

"True," I said, remembering how a quick flash of my white collar got Margot and her folks past the security desk. "I'll do that. But I feel at such a loss. Acing three sections of systematic theology does not prepare you for something like this. I feel like I'm flying by the seat of my pants here. . . ."

"Get used to it. The feeling never really goes away. Just don't try to come up with any words of wisdom," my father cautioned. "That's the last thing they need or are prepared to hear right now. Just be there for this family. That's all for now. Later, things will get more complicated. Death, especially of an adult child, always comes with baggage. But you can do this, Pippa. If not, God wouldn't have put you there."

"Thanks, Dad."

"Call and give us an update when you can. In the meantime, we'll be praying."

I heard the sound of urgent footsteps coming down the corridor and looked up to see the nurse in the cranberry sweater, Polly, coming toward me. "Hey, I have to go, but I'll call you later. Merry Christmas."

"Merry Christmas," they chorused. I ended the call just as Polly reached me, a little out of breath.

"Father Clarkson . . ." She stopped herself and shook her head.

"Sorry, I'm Catholic. Your collar keeps throwing me. Reverend Clarkson, I think you'd better come down to the office."

"Why? What's happened?"

"I don't know. A policeman came looking for the Matthews family. He's talking to them right now. I just thought you might want to be there."

❧ 13 ❧

Margot

How long did my sister lie dying at the bottom of that snowy ravine, shivering as the snowflakes, softly treacherous, fell on the car, covering the evidence of her peril in a shroud of white while, only miles away, everyone walked on eggshells as Dad chewed his ice and called her inconsiderate and irresponsible and I hid out in the kitchen, thinking the same thing? How long? Minutes? Hours?

Olivia knows, but she can't tell me. Her tiny body is small and still under the white hospital sheet. Her thin chest rises and falls with the mechanical regularity of a metronome, the pace of her breathing dictated by the ventilator.

She barely knows me. I'm not even sure she knows my voice, and I don't want to distress her, cause her to wonder, even in a twilight moment of semiconsciousness, why a stranger is in her room, so I say nothing. Careful not to disturb the needles, I hold her hand, hoping she'll think I am Mari and rest easier, believing her mother is at her bedside. If she wakes, though the doctors continue to tell me there is little chance that she will, someone will have to tell her what happened. Me, I suppose. I can count on my fingers the number of times I've been in the same room with my niece. Even so, I'm responsible for her now.

I don't know how much time elapsed between the moment

Mari's car skidded off the road and help arrived, but it was time enough for my sister to realize the seriousness of the situation, to confront the reality of death, and in a lurching and painful scrawl, to scratch out a note leaving her child to me, a note that went unnoticed until the battered body of Mari's car was dragged up the embankment and the tow truck driver notified the police of his discovery.

When they told me about the note and what it said, I didn't know what to think, or say, or do. I heard the words, but couldn't respond to them, as if I, too, were trapped in some twilight sleep, unable to move, or believe, or understand why this was happening.

Is this my fault?

I wanted a child desperately. But not like this. Not in exchange for my sister's life. Not a child I am afraid to love, a child who will be mine only for an hour, a day, or two, who will slip away without recognizing my voice or seeing my face, and whose death will burn a brand of guilt into my heart forever.

I didn't mean it to turn out like this.

I want to wake up. I want to wind back the clock to yesterday and beyond, to find the moment where everything went so wrong, before the arguments and accusations, the jealousy and judgments, the thoughtless words, the icy patches, the skidding tires, the fall, the silence, the sirens, and the silence again, the terrible, terrible silence that will never be broken now.

I want to wake up. I want everyone to wake up.

❧ 14 ❧

Philippa

I've only been in New Bern for a week, but I'm on a first-name basis with much of the hospital staff. Cheryl was working the security desk when I arrived. When I reached into my purse in search of my driver's license, she waved me off.

"Don't need it, Reverend," she said and pulled a laminated tag out of her desk drawer. "My supervisor said to make you a permanent I.D. badge. Now you won't have to waste time talking to me anymore."

"Thanks," I said, slipping the chain with the badge hanging from it around my neck. "But I don't consider talking with you a waste of time. How's your family?"

Her face lit up. "Great! Rich got called back for a second interview. Thanks for praying, Reverend. We sure could use the income."

"When's the interview?"

"Thursday at two."

I pulled a notebook out of my purse, the one I use to keep track of people's prayer requests, and jotted down the information. "Thursday. Two o'clock. I'll be praying."

When I got to the nurse's station, I asked Trina to tell Margot I was there.

"You can tell her yourself, Reverend. She's passed out on a sofa in the waiting room." Trina, whose brisk, efficient manner masks a very tender heart, sighed. "I tried to convince her to go home and get a little sleep, but it was no good. Can you talk to her? She looks just awful."

"I'll do what I can. How is Olivia? Any change?"

"You know I can't discuss a patient's condition," she scolded, "not even with you."

A buzzer rang. Trina looked up and down the hall, searching for a white-uniformed subordinate. "What's the point in being the charge nurse if there's nobody to be in charge of?" she grumbled, getting to her feet.

"I can tell you one thing," she said, looking over her shoulder before walking quickly down the corridor. "Three days ago, nobody would have given you odds on Olivia lasting out the night. But she's still here. She's a little fighter, that one. She just might end up surprising everybody."

Margot was asleep on a vinyl sofa. She lay on her back with one arm crossed over her face to block out the fluorescent glare of the overhead light and the other drooped limply off the sofa cushion, dangling near the floor next to an empty bag of cheese puffs and a paper cup half-filled with cold coffee.

"Margot?" I whispered.

She jumped at the sound, her arms jerking as if she'd received an electric shock.

"I'm awake!" She sat up, blinking her eyes several times. "What is it? Is something wrong? How long have I been asleep? Why didn't somebody wake me up?"

"It's okay. Olivia's fine. I brought you clean clothes and something to eat. Charlie baked you some cookies and made me promise to make you promise to eat them." I lifted the paper grocery bag I was carrying.

"Thanks," she said, blinking again. "I'm not hungry right now. What time is it?"

"Four-thirty."

She really did look awful. Her hair was flat on one side and poufed out on the other. There were mascara smears under her eyes and a coffee stain on her sweater.

"Margot, go home for a few hours. You need to get some sleep."

"I did get some sleep," she said defensively, glancing down at her watch. "I just slept for three hours. I feel fine."

I doubted she'd been asleep anywhere near that long, but I wasn't there to start an argument. I tried another tack. "Your parents called me from the road. They'll be back in a couple of hours."

I had offered to arrange a service for Mari at the church, but the family didn't want that. Instead, Werner and Lillian accompanied Mari's remains on the seven-hour drive to Buffalo, where they had made arrangements for interment in a local cemetery and a brief private graveside service conducted by their hometown minister. Margot stayed in New Bern to watch over Olivia. Given the circumstances and the seriousness of Olivia's condition, I suppose it made sense. However, I was concerned that Margot didn't have a means of saying her farewells to her sister. Funerals aren't for the dead, but for those who are left behind.

"When your parents get here, why don't you go home for a little while? They could call if there is any change. You could be back here in ten minutes. I'm teaching a new members class tonight, but if it'd make you feel better, I could come to the hospital after."

Margot shook her head and rubbed her eyes. "Thanks, but no. I'd never forgive myself if Olivia suddenly woke up and I wasn't here. Or if she . . ." Margot stopped, refusing to give voice to her worst fears. "I'm not leaving."

"Margot, you're stubborn."

"I never used to be, but when it comes to Olivia . . ." She shrugged, unable to explain this sudden personality shift.

"Maybe your maternal instincts are kicking in."

"Maybe."

❦ 15 ❦

Philippa

By the time I finished my talk on the history of New Bern Community Church, a history I'd only acquainted myself with the night before, the twelve people in the newcomers class were looking a little glazed.

"Let's take a few minutes to stretch our legs and get something to eat. Coffee and cookies are on the table in the corner."

I filled a paper cup and held it out to Paul Collier, who was standing next to me at the refreshment table.

"Decaf?" he asked.

"I'm not sure. The hospitality committee set everything up."

"Better not," he said, taking a chocolate cookie instead. "Can't risk losing my beauty sleep. I need all the help I can get."

He was joking, of course. Paul Collier wasn't a handsome man, but he wasn't unattractive either. He was about forty-five and had a nice smile but, other than his height, which I guessed to be six-three or maybe six-four, his physical appearance was in the solidly average range. But he seemed easy to talk to and had a good, somewhat self-deprecating sense of humor. Earlier in the evening, during the introductions, I'd learned he was a lawyer, specializing in family law, and was a single parent to a twelve-year-old son, James. They had just moved to New Bern from Chicago.

"So," Paul said as we moved to the center of the room, "what's it like to teach a new member class when you're a new member yourself?"

I grinned. "You may have noticed there were a few holes in my recitation of the church's history."

"Seemed fine to me. Very interesting." He yawned.

"Yes, I can tell."

"Sorry," he said. "I was up late last night reading case files."

"So? Chicago to New Bern. You in culture shock?"

"It's going to take a little adjusting, but it seems like a nice enough town. Not that I've had much chance to investigate. I'm still trying to get the boxes unpacked. You haven't heard of any jazz clubs in the area, have you?"

"Jazz clubs?"

"I play baritone sax. Back in Chicago I was in a combo with some of my old high school buddies. We played in a neighborhood club a couple times a month—just for fun. Mostly we got paid in cheeseburgers and pitchers of beer. I was hoping to find someplace nearby where I could find some people to jam with once in a while."

"Sorry. I don't know of any place in New Bern with live music. But we could consider starting a jazz service on Sunday mornings."

Paul grinned; he knew I was teasing him. "Yeah? Think the town is ready for that?"

"Uh. Probably not."

Paul popped the last piece of cookie into his mouth and smiled. "So, speaking of culture shock—how are you? New Bern is a little different from Boston. How is your daughter adjusting to the move?"

"My daughter?"

He raised his eyebrows. "Clementine?"

I laughed. Paul had arrived late, in the middle of my introduction. "Clementine is my dog, a one-hundred-and-twenty-pound English mastiff. I don't have any children."

"Ah. That's a relief. When you told the story about ripping the heads off the stuffed animals she got for Christmas and pulling out the fluff, I was concerned. Thought she might have some sort of deep-seated emotional problems."

"Not Clementine. Aside from her tendency to decapitate her toys, she's the sweetest dog in the world. What about your boy? How does he like New Bern?"

"It's early days yet." Paul looked down into his cup of water. "I think things will be easier when he makes new friends. James is a good kid, but when you're twelve . . ."

"The world revolves around you and your friends," I said with a nod. "I was a school social worker before I was a minister. Twelve is a tough age to make a move, but whether he realizes it or not, James would have missed his mother more than his friends."

"What else could I do?" Paul said.

Earlier Paul had explained that his ex-wife, James's mother, had been admitted to Yale Law School. That was what had precipitated the move.

"Melanie was a court reporter when we met, hadn't even been to college, but she was already talking about law school. What with the baby and then our marriage and divorce and . . . well, a lot of stuff . . . it wasn't easy, but she did it. And, hey! She got into Yale. That's a big deal. I got my degree from Chuck's Good Enough Law School."

"Sure you did."

"Michigan State. It's a good school, but it ain't Yale. Yale doesn't admit just anybody. Certainly not guys like me."

"If you go around saying 'ain't' all the time, I'm not surprised."

"You think? Maybe that's what went wrong with my application." He smiled. I liked Paul Collier. I liked his modesty and his sense of humor.

"According to our custody agreement, I could have stopped her from moving out of state, but," he shrugged, indicating that the idea had never really been worth considering, "after she worked so hard, that wouldn't have been fair. And it wouldn't have been right to have James so far away from his mom either. So, here we are." He tossed back the rest of his water.

I'd only just met Paul, but his decision to move for the sake of his son and ex-wife said a lot about his character.

"Say, I'm hosting a little New Year's Eve party for the junior high youth group. Seven o'clock. We'll have pizza, games, even set off a few fireworks. Do you think James would like to come? Tell him it'll be my first time meeting the kids too."

"That's nice of you, but . . . I don't know if I'll be able to talk him into it. He's been kind of a pain since the move."

"Tell him about Clementine. No twelve-year-old boy is going to pass up the chance to meet a dog the size of a horse."

"You know, that might just do the trick. I'll give it a try."

He grinned, which made him almost handsome, but maybe that was just his personality. He seemed like a sweet guy. He said he'd been divorced for six years. I wondered why he was still single. Clearly I wasn't the only one who was wondering about him. Jeannine Baskins and Andrea Rizolli were standing together in the corner, whispering and casting furtive glances in our direction.

"Well," I said, looking at my watch. "We'd better get back to it. Nice chatting with you, Paul."

"Thanks. Me too," he said as the group started moving back toward the circle of chairs. "I'll see you Friday."

"Friday?"

"When I drop James off for the party?"

"Oh, right. Drop him off at eight." I nodded quickly, feeling stupid. "And you can pick him up just after midnight."

By the time I stowed the folding chairs, wrapped up the leftover cookies, washed out the coffeepot, turned off the lights, locked up, and drove to the hospital, it was almost nine o'clock. At that hour, the hospital corridors were nearly empty, but as I hustled down the hallway, I heard the sound of familiar voices and tears, tears that turned to sobs. Fighting back a sensation of sickness tinged with panic, I quickened my pace. It couldn't be Olivia, could it? Only four hours had passed since I'd left, and everything had seemed fine then. Olivia was a fighter, just like Trina said.

The sound of my steps rang off the linoleum floors and in my ears, mixing with the sound of sobbing that grew louder as I approached the end of the hall, rounded the corner, and entered the waiting room.

My heart sank, seeing exactly what I had most feared—Dr. Bledsoe, looking exhausted and at a loss as he watched the Matthews family crying and clinging to one another like shipwrecked mariners hanging on to rocky cliffs in a stormy sea, hanging on for the hope of life and the fear of death.

"What happened?" I asked quietly, addressing the doctor.

Margot answered for him, lifting her head from her father's shoulder, her nose red and running, her eyes shimmering with tears. "She's awake! She's going to live!"

↶ 16 ↷

Margot

The doctor cleared his throat and said, "I'm not trying to rush things, but I've got an aneurysm that I need to check on."

Dr. Bledsoe could learn a few things about bedside manner, beginning with his tendency to refer to patients as ailments, but he saved Olivia's life, so I was willing to overlook that.

"Yes, of course. We're just so happy," I said, wiping tears from my eyes. "Thank you so much. I just . . . I wish I had words—"

He held up one hand, cutting me off. His face was grim. "Don't thank me yet. This is a very encouraging development, but we're still not out of the woods."

My mother clutched my hand so hard I could feel her nails digging into my palm. "But . . . you said Olivia is going to live."

The doctor shook his head. "Forgive me. I didn't mean to imply anything else. Barring any unforeseen circumstances, Olivia will live. When I first examined her, I didn't think she had a prayer of regaining consciousness."

"She did have prayers," Dad said firmly. "Hundreds of them. And they've been answered."

"Well, I certainly respect your beliefs, Mr. Matthews," the weary physician said dispassionately. "I've been a physician long enough to know there is always hope, even in seemingly hopeless cases. But at the moment, our concerns must turn to the quality of life Olivia may have. Her injuries were severe. It's too soon to know, but there may have been damage to the brain. In any case, we're looking at a long period of recovery and no guarantees as to the outcome."

"What does that mean?" I asked.

The doctor cleared his throat and motioned for everyone to take a seat. Philippa glanced at me with raised eyebrows, not sure if she should stay. I pointed to a nearby chair. Anything that the doctor was going to say, Philippa could hear too. My parents took a spot on the sofa, Dad's arm draped protectively over Mom's shoulder.

"It means," the doctor said soberly, "that we are going to do everything possible to help Olivia breathe, eat, talk, walk, think, and do all the things that a normal six-year-old should be able to do but, at the moment, there is no certainty that we'll succeed."

"Speak plainly. What are her chances of living a normal life?" Mom asked in a sharp voice that was so unlike the patient, soft-spoken woman who raised me.

The doctor didn't seem at all offended by my mother's tone. He was undoubtedly used to dealing with families under stress. "We're looking at weeks, and probably months, of treatment and therapy, but it is impossible to predict how effective those treatments will be. It's possible Olivia will make a full recovery, but," he said, turning toward me, "it is more likely that she won't. I'm not trying to be negative, Miss Matthews. I just want you to have a realistic picture of what you're facing."

I took a moment to collect myself, taking in a deep breath and letting it out slowly, suddenly aware of the complicated and miraculous nature of that seemingly simple act, an act my niece, whose life my sister had entrusted to me, could not perform on her own. This was not the time to give in to my emotions. For Olivia's sake, I needed to be strong and think clearly.

"I understand. Thank you for being so up front, Doctor. What happens now?"

"We'll need a thorough neurological evaluation. That will give us a better idea of her cognitive function. And we need to wean her off the ventilator, see if she can breathe on her own and for how long. That's the benchmark that will determine whether we continue rehabilitation or begin searching for a long-term care facility."

Dad frowned and sat up taller in his seat. "If you can get her off the ventilator, how long would it be before she could be transferred to a hospital in Buffalo?"

The doctor looked at me cautiously before answering. "I assumed, since the mother named Miss Matthews as guardian, that any program of rehabilitation would take place in New Bern. Is that not the case?"

He addressed the question to me, but Dad didn't give me a chance to answer, interrupting with questions of his own.

"Named her guardian? A note scribbled on a bit of paper when my daughter was dying? Out of her senses with pain and fear? Under the influence of drugs?"

My cheeks went hot. I hadn't told Philippa about the results of Mari's toxicology report. There hadn't been any reason to.

Mari had made a lot of mistakes in her life and, yes, abusing drugs and alcohol had been among them. But all that changed after Olivia was born. Mari wasn't high when her car slid off that icy road, and though I'd been raised never to contradict my elders, especially my father, I couldn't sit by and let him imply otherwise. Somebody had to stand up for my sister.

"Not drugs, Daddy. Anxiety medication. They found the prescription in her purse. And the toxicology report showed that she hadn't taken more than the recommended dose."

The prescription had been filled only recently. My sister was anxious about seeing my parents, but the medication wouldn't have impaired her driving or her ability to think clearly. Why was Dad implying otherwise?

"Prescription or not, it was still a drug." Dad crossed his arms over his chest. "A note scribbled out on a slip of paper while she was dying," he repeated flatly. "In pain, in fear, under the influence, and not witnessed by anyone. That hardly qualifies as a legal last will and testament. It'd never hold up in court."

Words like "legal" and "court" clearly made the doctor nervous. He cleared his throat and gave Philippa a sideways glance, as if hoping she would interject something.

"Mr. Matthews," Philippa said, picking up on the doctor's signal, "you didn't raise objections to Margot's guardianship before. When the hospital said that Margot, as guardian, was the only one who could visit Olivia in the ICU, you went along with it."

"Well, yes," Mom said, giving Philippa a curious look, as if she didn't understand what she was getting at. "At the time, we were just happy to have someone by her side. We didn't want to raise a fuss about who was in the room, as long as Olivia wasn't alone. That was the important thing. We assumed that once Olivia was better, if she got better, Werner and I would take over as guardians. Buffalo is a wonderful place to raise children."

"So is New Bern!" I said defensively and then stopped myself, surprised by my tone. "What I mean is . . . New Bern is a very nice community. The schools are good. It's quiet here, very safe. And . . ." I looked at my parents, who were looking at me, blankly, as if they couldn't quite grasp what I was driving at.

"Mom, Dad . . . Olivia is six years old. By the time she graduates from college, you'll be eighty."

Now it was my father's turn to be defensive. "So what? I'm in great shape for my age. So is your mother. We'll be around for Olivia's graduation. My father lived to ninety-eight. Never retired. Never gave up driving. Helped me pour the foundation for our new garage the month before he died. Remember?"

I did. Grandpa Matthews was a bear of a man, strong of opinion and body, and active right up to his death. Dad was very much his father's son. But that wasn't the point.

"I remember. But Mari named me as guardian. She wanted *me* to raise Olivia."

Dad walked across the room and perched on the arm of my chair.

"Bunny," he said gently, laying his heavy arm across my shoulders and squeezing my forearm, "I know how much you love children. And I know how much you've wanted a family of your own, but you're not in a position to take care of Olivia."

I pushed myself sideways in my chair, moving from under his grasp, so I could look my father in the eye.

Until that moment, I don't recall ever having disagreed with him—not out loud—that was my sister's job. Mari was the pot-stirrer. I was the peacemaker. But there is a price to keeping the peace and, sometimes, it's too high.

"Why would you say that? I own my own home. I have a job, a savings account. And I'm forty years old. I'm an adult, Dad. I have been for a long time. I haven't borrowed a dime from you since the day I graduated, not even when I was laid off. I've always taken care of myself and I can take care of Olivia too."

My mother leaned forward in her chair. "Margot, Dad isn't saying that you can't take care of yourself. We're very proud of you. It's just that—"

"Just that what?"

"Don't interrupt your mother. And don't speak to her in that tone!"

"I'm sorry," I said, purposely modulating my voice and opening my hands, trying to adopt a less defensive posture. "I'm not trying to be disrespectful, but . . . you can't have it both ways. You can't say you're proud of me in one breath and say I'm unfit for mother-hood in the next. It's not fair," I said, swallowing hard as I felt my eyes begin to tear. "And it's not true."

His expression of anger replaced by sympathy, my father reached out and touched my shoulder again.

"That's not what I meant. You'd be a wonderful mother, but a child needs two parents. That's what Olivia should have had all along, a real family, with a mother *and* a father. Now she can." He squeezed my shoulder. "You see that. Don't you, Bunny?"

❧ 17 ❧

Margot

Philippa was insistent. "Now that Olivia is stable you need to go out. Do something normal, see your friends."

"She's right," Nurse Trina said. "The sofa in the waiting area is starting to form a dent where you've been sleeping on it. If anything happens, I'll call you. You should get out for a little while at least. You haven't set foot outside the hospital since Christmas."

Was it only Christmas since all this had begun? It seemed so much longer.

Since the accident the hospital had become my whole world. It was hard to remember that, outside those walls, not so far from the smell of disinfectant and the yellow-white glow of fluorescent lights, the soft squashy sound of nurses' rubber-soled shoes on linoleum floors, the beep and buzz and whoosh of medical machinery, the clatter of soda cans falling from vending machines in the waiting rooms, and the drone of televisions left on through the night by patients who couldn't sleep and loved ones who wouldn't, life went on just as it always had.

Philippa and Trina had a point. Now that the immediate danger had passed, I had to reconnect with the outside world and my community. If I was going to raise a child on my own, I would need help. I would need my friends.

* * *

It was New Year's Eve, but the Cobbled Court Quilt Circle was gathered up in the workroom above the quilt shop, just like every Friday.

Only two weeks had passed since I'd been in this same room, at my usual spot in front of the same sewing machine. Tonight, however, I hadn't sewn a stitch. My glass of wine stood on the table untouched, next to a brownie with one bite out of it and my cell phone, out where I could see it and answer immediately if Trina called. So strange that things were so normal.

"I'm sorry," I said, pausing to take a breath. "I don't mean to keep going on. You probably have plans for the evening—parties and dates and things."

"Not me," Virginia said. "I haven't gone out for New Year's Eve in forty years. It's dangerous; too many drunks on the roads. I'll be in bed and asleep by ten o'clock."

"Which is the same time I'm due to meet Charlie at the restaurant," Evelyn added. "Until then, I'm all yours."

Ivy, who was stitching the binding, used her teeth to bite off the end of a thread. "I've never had a date for New Year's. I never have any dates. Isn't that sad?"

"We're your dates," Virginia said. "Just like every Friday."

"I'm not sure that counts."

"Why not?" Abigail asked, pausing to pick some stray threads off her black velvet skirt. I've never seen anyone quilt in an evening gown, but Abigail acts as if it were the most natural thing in the world. "I have more fun sewing with all of you on Friday nights than I ever had when I was dating."

"Including your dates with Franklin?" Ivy asked.

"Franklin was different. A prince of a man," Abigail said, looking rather regal herself. "If not, I'd never have married him. Ivy, most men are either perfect boors or perfectly boring. You, of all people, should know that."

"I suppose." Ivy sighed as she pulled a new length of thread from the spool.

Abigail frowned. "Oh, for heaven's sake. First Margot, now you. You're not moaning because there's no man in your life, are you?"

Ivy's face broke into a grin and her mask of misery disappeared. "No. I'm just hungry. I figured I'd stand a better chance of snagging the last brownie if you felt sorry for me."

"You're terrible," Abigail scolded, then handed her the plate. "Here."

"Sure you don't mind?" Ivy's hand hovered over the brownie as she scanned the faces of the group. "Anybody? Last chance."

Abigail held up her hand. "I'm having trouble squeezing into a bathing suit as it is. I don't know why we're going out," she grumbled. "Our flight to Bermuda leaves at ten-thirty. We'll be lucky to get five hours sleep. And I don't see why we always—"

"Yes," Evelyn interrupted, giving Abigail a pointed look over the top of her reading glasses and tilting her head in my direction. "Your life is a perfect nightmare, Abbie. Too many parties. Too many trips to exotic locations. Absolutely fraught with worries and problems."

Abigail took the hint. "Oh. Yes."

She turned to look at me. "Margot, that was an extremely insensitive thing for your father to say, but I'm sure he didn't mean it."

"Oh yes, he did. I've said the same thing myself. And in this very room."

"Well, in a perfect world," Ivy mumbled through a mouth full of brownie, "I agree with you; a family with two happy, loving parents is the ideal. But the world isn't perfect, and my kids are much better off living with just a mother than they would be living with a mother and an abusive father. Don't worry so much. You'll be a great mother, Margot."

"I hope so. My mother was a great mother, and my father . . ." It felt a bit disloyal, speaking about my dad to my friends, but I really needed to talk this out with people who I trusted, who would tell me the truth.

"He has his faults, but he really cared about us. He just didn't always know the right way to show it. In a lot of ways, he and Mari were just too much alike." I sighed. "Do you think I'm being self-ish? Maybe Olivia would be better off with my folks."

Evelyn put down the quilt block she'd been trimming and looked at me. "Do you really believe that?"

It was a good question, but hard to answer.

In many ways, my childhood was idyllic. My mom stayed home to take care of my sister and me, fixing us a hot breakfast and walking us to the bus each morning, welcoming us back from school with a glass of milk and homemade cookies every afternoon, helping us with our homework, tucking us into bed every night. Dad worked hard, but he always made time for us, especially when we were little. In the summertime, we loved to help him work in the garden, growing beans and tomatoes and fat orange pumpkins to carve into jack-o'-lanterns in the fall. In the wintertime, he'd take us sledding and skating and help organize snowball wars for all the kids on our block. And he built us a tree house that was the envy of the neighborhood.

My father was and is a very loving man. But Dad was also a hard man, a man of high standards, standards he applied to himself and to his children. That's not all bad. I owe much of my success to Dad. I wanted so much to make my father proud, and I worked hard to do so.

But it was different with Mari.

School was a struggle for my sister, even when she worked hard. By the time she got to junior high, she stopped working hard. I think she got tired of putting in so much effort and seeing so little result. That's when her relationship with my father started to un-ravel. The blunt-spoken criticisms Dad intended as encouragement and advice, my sister took in the worst possible light. Mari started to talk back and act out. She flaunted the rules, skipped class, ignored curfews, started hanging out with a rough crowd, and did everything possible to push my father's buttons.

It worked. Our formerly calm and happy home became a battleground with daily arguments erupting between my father and sister while Mom and I played duck and cover, she in the kitchen and me in my bedroom, waiting for it all to be over.

One day, it was.

Three days after her sixteenth birthday, Mari ran away. My parents were frantic. They called the police, even hired a private investigator. No one could find her. We didn't hear from her for almost four years.

She called me from a rehab center. I was twenty-three, recently graduated from college, working at an entry-level marketing job in Manhattan, living in an apartment with two other girls. I talked my roommates into letting Mari move in after she finished rehab, and they agreed. Mari came to live with me, but she didn't stay for long.

For years, that was the pattern. Mari would disappear for months or years at a time, then she'd reappear, call me or Mom, usually me, from some rehab program, ask to move in with one of us while she got her life on track, only to jump the track after a few weeks or months and disappear again.

Seven years ago, Mari called from Pittsburgh to say she was back in rehab and needed my help. She needed money. Enough so she could rent a place of her own until she could find a job. Moving back in with the family, she told me, put too much pressure on her, summoned up too many bad memories and old patterns.

"I know you've been burned before, Margot, but it's going to be different this time. I promise. I'm going to get clean and I'm going to stay clean. I swear I am."

I'd heard it all before, of course, word for word, but there was something in my sister's voice, desperation, but also a kind of hope, that made me want to believe her. If she'd just been asking for a place to stay, I'd have said yes without any hesitation. But she wanted money. The office rumor mill said that a round of layoffs was due any day and that the marketing department would be first on the chopping block. I'd bought a weekend cottage in New Bern only a year before. After the down payment and closing costs, I only had six thousand left in savings. My rent in Manhattan ran twenty-five hundred a month, so that wasn't much of a safety net. And as much as I wanted to believe what my sister said, that this trip to rehab would be her last, I knew that handing money to an addict and expecting them not to spend it on drugs was like putting a sirloin steak in front of a dog and asking him not to eat it.

"Mari, I want to help, but . . . things are hard for me right now. There's a rumor that my company—"

"Margot, I'm pregnant."

"You're what?"

I'd heard her perfectly well; I just couldn't believe what I'd heard.

"Pregnant!" she shouted and then squealed with excitement. I couldn't see her face, but I could hear her smile through the phone line. "I didn't plan it. But now that she's coming, I'm just so happy."

"She? It's a girl?"

"Well, it's too early to know for sure but, yeah, it's a little girl. I'm sure of it. And, Margot, I'm going to be a good mother, I am! I'm going to turn my life around for good, for both of us. I *have* to. But I need your help. Just for a little while. If it were just for me, I wouldn't ask, but . . . Please, Margot . . . We've got no one else to turn to."

"What about the father?"

"I don't know who it is," she said softly. "I know how bad that sounds, Margot. I know I've screwed everything up, but . . . but that's all over now. Please don't judge me."

"Oh, Mari."

The plaintive tone of her voice pulled me up short, filled me with shame. What had I done or said to make my sister think that I stood in judgment over her? No one in this world can afford to throw stones, me least of all.

"I'm not judging you. I just want to help you. Did you talk to Mom and Dad?"

Mari was quiet for a moment. "I called them first."

I didn't ask what their reaction had been. I didn't have to. If it had been good, she wouldn't be calling me.

"No," I said firmly, answering Evelyn and settling the matter in my mind. "My parents are too old to parent a six-year-old."

I didn't tell them about my other reasons for reaching this conclusion. Even among your closest and best-intentioned friends, some things should remain private. Just as I was bound by blood to help my sister when she asked, so I am bound by my faith to honor my father and mother. But honoring my parents didn't necessarily mean doing everything they wanted me to do—not when conscience and common sense told me to do otherwise. Not when the interests of a child were at stake.

And didn't the admonition to respect parents extend to my sister too? Whatever mistakes Mari made in her life, when it came to mothering, she was dedicated and selfless, doing for her child what she could not or would not do for herself. She would have walked through the fires of hell for Olivia. In some ways, she did. Everything she did, no matter how hard, she did with Olivia's welfare in mind.

Now I had to do the same.

"So, what do you do now?" Ivy asked. "Will you sue for custody?"

"I don't want to," I said. "I don't think families should have to go to court to settle their differences."

"But if it comes to that, will you?"

"My parents have hired an attorney."

Evelyn offered to give me a lift home, but I want to walk. I'm hoping the cold air will clear my head.

Since the accident, I feel like I've been living underwater. People say things to me, but the words are muffled in my mind. They do things to me, but I am numb to their impact, unable to understand their actions or sort out what provoked them. I'm going through the motions, doing what I must, but stupidly and slowly, as if trying to wake from a deep sleep, to shake off a bad dream that refuses to end.

No one is on the street this time of night. The shop windows are dark and the doors all locked. It is snowing, but lightly. Banks of clouds cover the moon, and the only light comes from the soft glow of the antique style street lamps. I walk west down Commerce

Street, moving from one lamp to the next like a sailor following a line of buoys that lead to a safe harbor. I try to think, to feel, to figure out what I should do, but the thoughts, feelings, plans come to me in a chaotic jumble and leave no marks, bouncing in and out and off so quickly that I can't sort through them.

Glancing across the street to the Green, I see a figure in white standing in the shadows, just at the spot where a circle of lamplight gives way to the darkness. For a moment, before I remember that I don't believe in such things, I wonder if I am seeing a ghost, if perhaps my sister's soul is searching me out. The prospect isn't as frightening as I'd have thought.

My heart pounds and I feel a sudden lurch of joyful expectation, the first full-blown emotion I've felt in days, like pushing up from the bottom of a deep pool and discovering I can breathe again. But as I step off the curb, I see that the apparition in white isn't a ghost, only a snowman made by children who were playing on the Green. The pounding in my chest stops, or at least ceases to make itself felt, and suddenly, I am underwater again.

Walking across the snowy street, I feel wet on my cheeks and know that I am crying, that my body is responding to the grief that I won't let myself feel.

I want to see my sister. I want to bring her back, to see her one more time, to ask her what to think, how to feel, how to do the one thing I have never been able to do—fight—to ask her if she is sure, really sure, that this fight is worth it.

If Mari is not here to raise Olivia herself, is it really so important which damaged and dysfunctional member of the family fails to fill her shoes? Now that she is far from this world, removed from the wounds and recriminations of the past, able to see life, not just as it is now but as it will be in time to come, past walls that separate what seems to be and into the substance of what is, perhaps she has changed her mind.

I want to ask her so many things, and so on the dark and deserted Green, with icy flakes of snow hitting my face, mixing and melting as they meet the warmth of my tears, I do what Mari and I used to do when we were little and built snowpeople in the park, in those days when my left hand was always cold because Mari was forever losing her mittens and I always gave her one of mine, back when we were young enough to believe that snowmen could come to life and too young to imagine unhappy endings: I pretend.

"Are you sure?" I ask the snowman, my absent sister's stand-in. "I know you're angry with them and I don't blame you, but if this is just about getting back at Mom and Dad . . ."

The black pebble eyes stare at me accusingly.

Do you really think I'd let my personal grievances get in the way of what's best for Olivia? This isn't about me and you know it. It's about him. About them.

"I know. . . ."

And I do know, in a way I never did before. My father has done and said some awful things, but I've always excused him because I believed that the good in him outweighed the bad and because, if I am honest, the worst of it was never directed at me. Mari bore the brunt of his anger, and I let her. I never said anything because I was afraid of rocking the boat and violating the complicated set of rules that are the cost of keeping the peace and my father's favor.

Just like Mom.

Is that where I learned it? I suppose so. Mom never sat me down and explained the rules, but her example spoke louder than words. Beyond a shocked exclamation of his name when he said something careless and hurtful, she never confronted Dad, never called him out, never stopped him or stood up for us. Was it because she, too, was afraid of losing his love? Or because she had some misplaced idea that love and loyalty to a husband meant supporting even his most incendiary impulses? Or just because she didn't know how?

My father had hired a lawyer. He was taking me to court to nullify my sister's dying wish. And Mom was letting him, or at least not stopping him. How could they?

For a moment, the moon peeped out from behind a cloud, illuminating the frozen-featured snowman and the crescent of orange rind that looked like a wry smile.

Are you really surprised?

I was. Maybe I shouldn't have been, but I was. Was the prospect of me parenting Olivia so unthinkable that they were willing to tear apart what was left of our family to prevent it? Was it worth it? Was it?

The clouds moved in again and it was harder to see. I moved closer to the white figure and whispered urgently, "Are you sure this is a good idea? At least they've had some experience raising children. What makes you think I'll be a good mother?"

My nose was running. I swiped at it with the back of my gloved hand and accidentally knocked the snowman's carrot nose to the ground, where it rolled off into the shadows.

I bent down, searching for a knob of orange on the field of white, but I couldn't see it. Instead, about two feet away and just behind the snowman, I discovered a child's lost mitten, knitted, red with a little band of white snowflakes around the cuff.

Clutching the mitten to my chest, I sank down to the ground, leaned back against the cold pillar of the snowman's body, and sobbed, crying and keening for all we'd lost, pent-up grief pouring from me like floodwaters breaching a dam, leaving me drained, exposed, and able to feel again.

☙ 18 ☙

Philippa

This is probably a minority opinion, but I like junior high kids. Sure, they're loud, awkward, overly dramatic, and they think they're far wiser than the evidence would suggest, but aren't we all? The thing I like about kids this age is that they are less jaded than older teens, more vulnerable, more willing to believe. For good or for bad, junior high kids take things to heart.

That's why I willingly opened my house to eighteen loud, goofy young teens on New Year's Eve, because it's important to support them during these impressionable years—to accept them for who they are, to make them feel part of the church, to listen without lecturing, all while pointing them toward God's highest and best. And if you can do all that while playing really silly games and eating endless numbers of cheese and pepperoni pizzas . . . well, you've got yourself a youth group.

It was nearly midnight. So far the kids had consumed nine large bottles of soda and seven extra-large pizzas, though one pizza was consumed by Clementine, who snatched it off a table and snarfed it down while we were playing the snow boot relay.

Now, their boots were back on their feet and the whole gang was outside, greeting the New Year amid a silvery gold shower of sparklers and a barrage of snowballs. When they came inside, they'd be hungry again. Bottomless pits, these kids. Especially the boys. And so cute.

But I couldn't say that I would be sorry when their parents came to collect them at twelve-thirty. I'd never been so exhausted.

I stood at the living room window, yawning, watching the kids leap and slide and dance around in the snow with their sparklers like a bunch of arctic fireflies. They were all having a wonderful time. Almost all of them.

Cheeks still red with the cold, James Collier came in and sat down in a chair near the fireplace. Clementine, who had been sleeping off the pizza, lumbered slowly to her feet and laid her head in his lap.

"She likes you."

He smiled. He's a nice-looking boy with brown eyes and dark hair. I noticed a couple of the girls whispering and giggling about him earlier. It was pretty much the same reaction his father elicited among the women at the new members class. Girls are always interested in the new guy. I wonder if any of us ever progress much beyond junior high?

"She's nice," James said. "Biggest dog I ever saw."

I walked to the fireplace and put another log on the fire, then sat down in the chair opposite James. "You should see her father. Male mastiffs can weigh over two hundred pounds. Clemmie's petite. Only one hundred and twenty."

James looked impressed. "How much dog food do you go through?"

"About a bag a week, plus snacks. And as much pizza as she can steal."

"Wow!" James put a hand on each side of Clementine's head, scratching both her ears at once. Clemmie sighed and made a groaning noise to signal her pleasure. "She must poop a Volkswagen! Sorry," he said, turning a little red.

I smiled. "Actually, that's a pretty accurate description. I am the proud owner of a special-order, extra-large pooper-scooper."

"Gross!" James looked down at Clemmie's huge head, his expression a blend of disgust and delight.

"So, James, why aren't you outside with the others? Don't you like sparklers?"

He shrugged. "I don't really know anybody."

"You must miss your friends in Chicago," I said. He nodded.

"I'm new in town too. But I'm getting to know people. It takes a while."

James kept his head down, staring at Clemmie. "I don't know why we had to move," he mumbled. "This town is so boring. There's not even a movie theater."

"Well, there's the Red Rooster."

James glanced up and rolled his eyes. "*Two* screens. And the movies are all in French."

I pressed my lips together to keep from smiling. "I don't think they're *all* in French. But, yes, I heard it was an art movie house. They probably have some foreign films. There's a multiplex in Torrington, though. I hear there's a laser tag place there too. We might go there on a field trip sometime. What do you think?"

He shrugged again. "Yeah."

"I know New Bern isn't Chicago," I said. "It isn't Boston either. But if you give it a little time, I bet you'll get to see and do things in New Bern that you never would have in Chicago."

He looked up with a doubtful expression. "Like what?"

"Well . . . like making friends with a dog that's nearly the size of a horse. You never did that before, did you?"

"No," he admitted, his smile returning.

"And," I said, shifting to the edge of my chair, "I bet you never played Cream Puff Toss before either." Clementine's ears perked up, as if she somehow understood what I was saying.

"Cream Puff Toss?"

Trying to stifle a yawn, I heaved myself from my seat, glad that this would be our last activity of the night. Clementine rose too, ready to follow me. "It's like an egg toss, but with cream puffs. It's a game and dessert all at the same time. And it makes a great big mess. I've put down a bunch of plastic sheets in the sunroom.

"Can you run and tell everybody to come inside? I've got to get the cream puffs and find my camera."

And a roll of paper towels, I reminded myself. No matter how much the kids enjoyed the game, I doubted their parents would be excited having a bunch of hyped-up, sticky kids jumping all over their clean car upholstery. Definitely not a formula for endearing myself to New Bern's adult population.

"Why the camera?" James asked, getting up from his chair.

"So we can take pictures, of course." I've played this game with kids before. It inevitably ends in a food fight, cream puffs being lobbed like fat, frosted grenades, and kids getting hit in the face. It's a great photo op. "Hey, you want me to get a picture of you and one of the girls?" I asked, teasing. "I saw a bunch of them looking you over."

James didn't answer, just grinned and headed toward the back door.

❦ 19 ❦

Margot

As we passed through the arched doorway of the courthouse, Arnie stopped to smooth his tie and revisit the conversation we'd had when I asked him to represent me.

"Margot," he said, and then paused to clear his throat. "I don't want to belabor the point, but I want to be clear. Our relationship in this matter is strictly professional. You're the client and I'm the attorney and . . ."

"For heaven's sake, Arnie! Are you seriously suggesting that I'd hire you in some pathetic attempt to rekindle our relationship? What do you take me for?"

"Sorry," he mumbled, his eyes darting around the courthouse to see if anyone was listening to our exchange. "But, given our history, I thought it was important to say it. I believe in being up front about these things."

"Good!" I snapped. "Then let me be as up front as possible. I'm not interested in love, romance, or marriage—particularly to you. The only thing I care about right now is Olivia's welfare. And to guard it, I wanted the best attorney in town. Unfortunately for me, Franklin Spaulding is in Bermuda with Abigail, so I had to settle for *you*, the *second*-best attorney in New Bern. Is that up front enough for you?"

I'm not often given to angry outbursts, but honestly! Arnie is cute and yes, there was a time when I would have cut off my right hand to wear his ring on my left, but he isn't exactly Johnny Depp, is he?

Arnie, looking as if he didn't quite know me, fumbled with the top button of his blue pinstripe suit jacket, unbuttoning and rebuttoning it, and clearing his throat again. "Right. Sorry. I just . . . well, I didn't want things to be awkward between us."

"No," I said. "We wouldn't want *that,* would we?" Sarcasm is not my style either, but I'd had just enough of Arnie and his ego for one day.

Arnie stared at me. "Margot, are you all right?"

I threw up my hands. "Of course I'm not all right! My sister is dead, my niece is in the hospital, and I'm going up against my parents in court! I suppose things could be worse, but I don't even want to imagine how."

Arnie pulled the white handkerchief from the breast pocket of his jacket and held it out to me. I waved it away.

"I don't need it," I said and swiped my eyes with the back of my hand. "All I need from you right now is to go in that courtroom and fix this mess. Got it?"

Arnie nodded. "Got it."

I've fallen down the rabbit hole, into a strange, upside-down place where people you've known all your life suddenly go missing and those who are left start saying things and doing things you could never have imagined in your wildest dreams or your worst nightmares. But it wasn't a dream. It was much too real.

My parents were already in the courtroom when we entered, sitting at a table next to their lawyer. Mom glanced at me briefly with an awkward smile, but my father wouldn't acknowledge me. He looked right through me, the way he used to look through Mari when he was angry with her. Why? I wasn't the one who'd called in the lawyers.

The bailiff announced the entrance of the judge, the Honorable Homer W. Treadlaw. No kidding, that was his actual name. With a moniker like that, I suppose he just had to grow up to be a judge.

But from the scowl on his face and the growl in his voice, my first impression was that Homer W. Treadlaw didn't like his chosen profession. He seemed irritable and impatient and anxious to be anywhere but where he was.

When the judge entered, we got to our feet, just like people do on television. He squinted at us through the lenses of his thick glasses, as if wondering which of us had called this meeting and why in the world he had to attend.

"What's all this about?" Judge Treadlaw rumbled, glancing down at a file on his desk. "Custody battle? Isn't this something you could work out among yourselves? You're all family, aren't you? Can't see why you people need to come in here and waste my time."

My parents' attorney, Cynthia Hoffman, a pretty red-haired woman about my age, rose to her feet. "That's the last thing my clients wish to do, Your Honor. This won't take long, I assure you. This isn't a complicated case." She smiled.

"It better not be," the judge said, his expression unchanged.

"It isn't," she repeated. "The question of custody has already been established."

It had?

I looked a question at Arnie, who shifted his weight forward, preparing to spring from his seat and object as soon as he knew what there was to object to.

"My clients," Ms. Hoffman continued, gesturing toward my parents, "are the grandparents of Olivia Matthews, age six, whose mother was tragically killed in a single-vehicle accident on Christmas Day."

The judge nodded along with Ms. Hoffman, indicating his familiarity with the situation. "Yes, read about it in the paper. Very sorry for your loss," he said.

"The child's father is unknown," Ms. Hoffman continued. "Since Mr. and Mrs. Matthews are her closest living relatives, and since both the Matthews and the minor child are residents of the state of New York, and since the minor child is still in a precarious position medically, someone responsible must make decisions regarding her treatment and rehabilitation.

"Mr. and Mrs. Matthews recently made an appearance before the family court in Buffalo, requesting custody of Olivia Matthews, which was granted. All the Matthews are asking is that you register the New York judgment, giving the order full faith and credit in Connecticut. The question of custody has already been settled. Mr. and Mrs. Matthews are the rightful and legal guardians of their granddaughter, Olivia Matthews."

Arnie was quick to rise, but I was quicker, leaping to my feet and spinning sideways to face my parents.

"You went to court without telling me? Are you serious? While I was at the hospital, missing my sister's funeral because the last words she wrote asked me to take care of Olivia, you two were sneaking behind my back and telling a judge that—"

Judge Treadlaw smacked his desk with his gavel, just once, and frowned more deeply than ever. "Mr. Kinsella? Control your client."

I felt the weight of Arnie's hand on my shoulder as he pressed me down to my chair. "Let me handle this."

"I'm very sorry, Your Honor," Arnie said in a serious tone. "It won't happen again. But, as you can see, my client was shocked by the news that her parents had gone behind her back and yours, by applying for custody in a New York court without her knowledge and without informing the court in either state of the full facts of the case."

"And those are?" the judge asked.

"That Mr. and Mrs. Matthews are not Olivia Matthews's closest living relatives. My client, Margot Matthews, sister to the deceased and aunt to the minor child, has as much claim on that title as her parents, particularly since the deceased, Mariposa Matthews, wrote a note, presumably after the accident but before help arrived, stating her wish that, in the event of her death, Olivia Matthews should be raised by my client."

Arnie glanced in my direction. The judge leaned down and squinted at me, as if sizing me up. "Do you have the note? Let me see it."

Arnie stepped out from behind the table and carried the crumpled scrap of paper, dotted with four brown bloodstains, to the bench, placing it in the judge's outstretched hand. The judge read it.

"Ms. Hoffman," he said, lifting his head and glowering at the other attorney. "You promised me this would not be a complicated matter. That means you're either ignorant of the law or a liar. I am not impressed, young woman. And I am not pleased."

Ms. Hoffman got to her feet, a bit red in the face. "I am sorry to have displeased Your Honor. However, I respectfully suggest that the judgment of the New York court should stand. It's a question of jurisdiction. Both Mr. and Mrs. Matthews and their granddaughter are residents of New York—"

"But the accident took place in the state of Connecticut," Judge Treadlaw rejoined, cutting her off. "And the child is hospitalized here in Connecticut. And the child's aunt, whom, it would appear, the mother expressed a dying wish to see as guardian, is likewise a resident of the state of Connecticut—where I happen to be a judge!

"Do not presume to instruct me in questions of jurisdiction, Counselor. I've been sitting on this bench since you were in grade school. I know the law, far better than you do, it would seem. Tell me," he said, holding up the letter, "were you aware of the existence of this note?"

Ms. Hoffman straightened her shoulders. "I was only recently engaged to represent the Matthews. I was out of town for the holidays. . . ."

"So was I," Treadlaw grumbled. "In Miami. Wish I'd stayed there."

"I was unable to meet with my clients until this morning. And . . . I'm afraid I may not have had time to make myself fully aware of the facts of the case." Ms. Hoffman coughed and turned a bit redder.

"So you're pleading ignorance? Well, I'm still not impressed, Ms. Hoffman, but it's better to be ignorant than to be a liar."

The judge turned his head sharply toward my parents. "And you," he said, addressing my father, "did you tell the New York judge about this letter?"

Dad shook his head. "No, Your Honor. That letter was written when Mari was in terrible pain and under the influence of drugs. She didn't know what she was doing. Our other daughter, Margot," he said, turning his head toward me but still not making eye contact, "has no experience as a parent. She's unmarried and works in retail. How can she hope to support a child on her salary? And who would take care of Olivia while Margot was working? My wife and I already raised two children. We can provide our granddaughter with the love and material support she needs. I think that we would be much more suitable—"

Judge Treadlaw held up his hand, indicating he'd heard enough. "What *you* think carries no weight here, sir. The only thing that matters in my courtroom is the law. Mr. Matthews, you came very close to running afoul of it by concealing everything you know from the court in New York. Very close indeed. However, because I assume that your recent loss has muddled your thinking, I am going to overlook it . . . this time. But from here on out you had better be completely truthful with your attorney and this court.

"And you," he said, glaring at Ms. Hoffman, "had better do a more thorough job of interviewing and prepping your clients. Do I make myself clear?"

"Yes, Your Honor."

The judge got to his feet. Without being told, the rest of us did the same.

"I am going into my chambers to call Judge Morrisaney in New York. When he hears the whole truth of this case, he will certainly rescind his ruling. This matter will be decided in *my* courtroom, under *my* jurisdiction."

Treadwell leaned forward, placing both of his big hands on his desk and glowering. "I am not pleased. Not with any of you. If, however, when I return from my chambers, I learn that everyone has come to their senses and reached some reasonable compromise regarding the custody of this child, my opinion may change.

"Family members, especially those who have already undergone such a terrible loss, should not be quarreling among themselves. While I'm gone, I hope you come to your senses. Work this out, people."

❧ 20 ❧

Margot

We didn't work it out. We tried. At least, I did.

When I was little and we questioned his judgment or rules, Dad would say, "Because I'm your father and I said so. It's my way or the highway."

He meant it too; we knew that. I chose Dad's way. Mari chose the highway.

Given that, you might think I was happy to see my father taken down a peg in that courtroom, but you'd be wrong. My dad is strong, stubborn, and sometimes careless with his words, but I never doubted his love for me, even when I doubted his wisdom. And more often than not, time and a bit of reflection would help me see that Dad was right. And on the few occasions when he wasn't? I let it pass. That's just my nature. I've never liked confrontation. Most things aren't really worth arguing about.

But some things are. Olivia's future is one of them. While I would have been open to finding some sort of middle ground with my parents, I was not going to let Dad steamroll me. Not this time.

When Judge Treadlaw returned from his chambers and learned we had been unable to come to an agreement and were resolved to continue the custody battle, he was still displeased. He granted temporary custody of Olivia to a guardian ad litem, who we were scheduled to meet with the next day.

The snow was still mounded on the New Bern Green and icicles hung like crystal garlands from the eaves of every building in town, but the day was sunny and bright so Arnie and I walked from his offices to our meeting the next day. As we walked, Arnie explained that a guardian ad litem is someone appointed by the court to represent the interests of someone who cannot represent themselves in a legal matter. My parents and I would have input regarding Olivia's care, but her guardian ad litem would be the one making the decisions. Olivia's guardian was an attorney named Geoffrey Bench.

"I don't know him well," Arnie said. "But we've met at a couple of Bar Association receptions. He seems like a decent guy—about fifty, a sportsman, likes to ski. As I recall, he has a little cabin in the Berkshires, on the river. He's into fly fishing."

"Considering you only met him a couple of times, you seem to know a lot about him."

Arnie shrugged. "Bench is chatty. He's actually pretty interesting. Most of the lawyers I know can't talk about anything besides work. The main thing is to get along with him, cooperate with his decisions. It's important that he like you. He is Olivia's temporary guardian, but he'll be making a recommendation to the judge about who should be named as permanent guardian—you, your parents, or someone else."

I stopped in the middle of the sidewalk and grabbed Arnie's sleeve. "Someone else?"

"It's not going to happen. I shouldn't have said anything."

"But you did! And now it's out there! Are you saying the judge could give someone else custody of Olivia? Someone besides me or my parents?"

Arnie sighed impatiently. "Look, it's an incredibly unlikely outcome. I mean, Olivia has two sets of caring, responsible family members vying for custody, so that is the natural choice. But if for some reason the judge decided that you and your parents weren't fit guardians, it's possible that he could grant custody to someone else or make Olivia a ward of the state."

"A ward of the state? You mean he could put Olivia into foster care? Or up for adoption?"

The thought that Olivia, after all she'd been through and all she'd lost, could actually be forced to go and live with someone who didn't know the least thing about our family history and all that my sister had done and sacrificed for Olivia was terrible to me.

"Technically, yes. But that's not going to happen, Margot. I promise. Either you or your parents will get custody of Olivia. Hopefully you. Treadlaw might not be my favorite judge, but he's not crazy. Now, come on. I don't want to be late."

Feeling a little better, I fell into step beside Arnie. "Why don't you like Judge Treadlaw?" I asked. "Because he's so cranky?"

Arnie shook his head and shoved his hands in the pockets of his overcoat. "Cranky judges are a dime a dozen. Treadlaw is lazy. He's got another two years before he retires, but if you ask me, he checked out a long time ago. He relies on other people to get into the meat of the case, instead of getting his hands dirty by sifting through the details personally. I'd say there's about a ninety percent chance that Judge Treadlaw will go with Geoff Bench's recommendation. That's why it is very important for Geoffrey Bench to like you. You've got to win him over, Margot."

"How am I supposed to do that?" I asked nervously. I didn't like the idea that Olivia's welfare rested with this man whom none of us had met.

"Well, I don't know," he said as I followed him up the gray granite steps to the courthouse. "Make him some cookies. Or a quilt. Develop a sudden interest in fly fishing. Do whatever it takes, just make him like you."

He stopped on the top step and turned to face me. "It shouldn't be that hard, Margot. Everyone likes you."

The meeting room was sparsely furnished with a long oak conference table and a dozen very uncomfortable wooden chairs. Arnie and I were on time. So were my parents, who arrived alone. I wasn't sure if they had fired Ms. Hoffman or if she'd fired them. When Arnie asked about her, Dad told Arnie he was perfectly capable of representing himself and that he had better things to spend his money on than lawyers.

"We've always been careful with our money. That's why Margot was able to go to college without taking out a single loan. And if Mari had wanted to continue her education, we'd have paid for that too," he declared. "Children are expensive. You can't send a kid to college on what you make selling fabric and thread."

My mother reached out and touched Dad's arm. "Werner," she said quietly and tipped her head toward me, as if reminding him of my presence.

"I'm just saying," he said. "A woman alone, working for minimum wage..."

"I don't work for minimum wage, Dad. And, financially, I'm very responsible. I learned that from you. I own my car and I don't carry a balance on my credit cards. The only debt I have is my mortgage. When I bought my house, I put fifty percent down."

"Sure," he said, actually looking at me for the first time in days, "back when you were working in New York and made a good salary, you could afford to do that. You had money in the bank. What about now?"

"Pardon me, Mr. Matthews," Arnie said in a firm but cordial tone, "but I think we'd better talk about something else. Or, perhaps, we should all just sit here quietly and wait for Mr. Bench to arrive."

Arnie's advice was sound, but I couldn't bear the idea of sitting in a room with my parents and saying nothing, as if we were combatants in some cold war, only able to communicate through negotiators. After an uncomfortable moment I said, "Have you been to the hospital recently?"

"Of course," Dad responded irritably, taking my question as an accusation.

"We were there last night," Mom said. "Trina said we'd just missed you."

"I had to go to work. Evelyn, Virginia, and Ivy are at a quilt show in Vermont for the rest of the week. Evelyn offered to cancel, but she'd have forfeited the money she paid for the booth space if she did. I stayed late last night. I'm just so far behind. . . ."

"Think how much more behind you'd be if you had a child to add to the mix," Dad said. "What are you going to do then? Leave Olivia in the care of some teenaged babysitter? Or fall behind on work? Which will you neglect, Olivia or your job?"

Arnie put his hands on the table as if to come to my defense, but my mother beat him to it, interrupting his protests.

"Werner!" she exclaimed.

"What?" Dad spread his hands innocently. "I'm just trying to tell her how things are. Olivia is a sick little girl. How is Margot going to have time to work and take her to doctor and therapy appointments? And how are you going to pay for it? Do you even have health insurance?"

I do, but I pay for it myself. It's costing me a fortune. Evelyn would like to offer health benefits to her employees and she's even had me get some quotes, but it's just not something the shop can afford right now.

"Maybe next year," she'd said, after I handed her the most recent quote, which was 14 percent higher than it was the year before. Yes, maybe next year. But somehow I doubt it.

"I'm not trying to be mean," Dad said, in a somewhat more modulated tone, "but these are things you have to think about. I care about you, honey. And I care about Olivia. I want the best for her. She deserves to be raised in a stable home with two parents who have the time and money to take care of her, just like you were."

Arnie, whose eyes had been shifting between my father and me during this exchange, as if he were watching a tennis match, interrupted. "All due respect, Mr. Matthews, being raised in a two-parent home is no guarantee of a happy childhood. If she were here, I think Mari would agree."

"Arnie!" I exclaimed in a voice that was curiously like my mother's and just as shocked as hers had been when Dad insulted me. I appreciated his willingness to stand up for me, but there's no point in challenging my father—I know. When Dad is challenged, he just digs in his heels.

Dad glared at Arnie, ready with an angry retort just as the door opened and Mr. Geoffrey Bench arrived on the scene. Excellent timing.

He was, as Arnie had said, about fifty, maybe a little older, and tall. His hair was graying, salt-and-pepper, but his eyes were blue and he had a fairly healthy tan, which was surprising considering it was January. I was also surprised by the width of his shoulders. There's no reason lawyers can't be muscular, I guess. But the only attorneys I've ever really known well are Arnie and Franklin. It's been a while since either of them lifted anything heavier than a book on case law.

Mr. Bench grinned as he came through the door and quickly shook everyone's hands, congratulating Arnie on a win in a malpractice case he'd tried recently. He was—I don't know how to put it—vigorous, I suppose, and charming. Purposely charming—like he was campaigning for office. His teeth were very big and very white. I wondered if he bleached them.

"Sorry to be late," he said. "I was tied up on a call." He pulled out the wooden chair at the head of the table. The legs made a scraping sound on the floor.

"Hope you'll excuse the accommodations," he said, looking around the room, "but my office is being repainted. Usually, this room is used for jury deliberations. I think they made it as cold and uncomfortable as possible to encourage quick and unanimous verdicts." He smiled at his joke—so did my father—and placed a battered brown briefcase on the table.

"Which, Judge Treadlaw informs me, is something the three of you have been unable to reach." He looked up with a questioning expression. No one said anything. Dad crossed his arms over his chest.

"Right." Mr. Bench took a seat and pulled some papers out of his briefcase, handing one set to me and the other to my parents.

"What's this?" Dad asked.

"Questionnaires. Just something I like to do so I can get to know you. I'd appreciate it if you could fill them out and give them back to me next time I see you."

I glanced over the first page. The questions were pretty standard: name, birthday, place of birth, education, work history.

"I'll be conducting interviews and home visits with each of you before I make my report to the judge," Mr. Bench continued. "But right now, I want to talk about Olivia. I dropped by the hospital first thing this morning and looked in on her."

He had? I was impressed. He'd only been on the case a little more than twenty-four hours.

"I also talked to her doctor. She's got a long way to go, but certainly seems to be making a remarkable recovery. She must have a guardian angel by her side."

"Oh, yes," my mother said emphatically. "And a lot of prayer."

Mr. Bench nodded deeply. "Best medicine there is. But now that Olivia is conscious, I understand from the nurses that she is starting to ask questions. She wants to see her mother. No one has told Olivia about her mother's death?"

I shook my head and looked at my folks. This was one of the things we had disagreed about.

"It's too soon," Dad replied. "And Olivia is still weak. A shock like that could set her back. She's not ready to hear it. She's just a little girl. I'm not convinced she understands what is going on."

"We've got to tell her something, Dad."

"Later. When she's stronger. Right now, I think it would be best to tell Olivia that Mari was hurt in the accident and is too sick to see her."

"But that's a lie!" I exclaimed and then, seeing the set of my father's jaw, backed off a little. "I know you're trying to protect her, but she has to hear the truth eventually. If she finds out later that you were . . . that we didn't tell her everything that happened, she might resent it. She might never trust us again. I know she's just a child, but she's a person. She has a right to know the truth."

I turned to Geoff Bench. "Doesn't she?"

* * *

Mr. Bench walked us to the bottom of the stairwell and excused himself, saying he needed to stop by Judge Treadlaw's office.

"Very nice to meet you, Miss Matthews. I'm only sorry it had to be under such tragic circumstances." He smiled a sad little smile, bobbing his head before turning and climbing the stairs.

As soon as we were outside, Dad turned sharply to the left and walked away without saying anything. Mom gave me a quick squeeze and went after him. Arnie and I turned to the right and hurried away. We both needed to get back to work.

"It doesn't seem like your mother is quite as adamant as your father," Arnie said. "Do you think there's any chance that she'll be able to talk him down off the ledge? Get him to settle this reasonably?"

"I doubt it," I said. "I don't think she's happy that this is ending up in a courtroom but, like Dad, I think she believes that raising Olivia in a two-parent home is more important than respecting Mari's dying wish. And I've never heard her voice an opinion that's contradictory to my father's."

"Well, that's too bad. Still, you did a good job today." Arnie clapped me on the back as though I were a runner who had just come first across the finish line. "You made a good impression on Bench. He likes you. I knew he would."

"I wasn't trying to impress him. I just don't think we should lie to Olivia."

"I agree. So did Bench, and that's what matters. Round one goes to you."

"Stop that." I frowned and pulled my coat closer around me. The temperature had dropped while we were in the courthouse. "This isn't a contest. These are my parents we're talking about. There are no winners and losers here."

Arnie stopped in the middle of the sidewalk. "This is a court case. Your parents are suing to *win* custody of Olivia. If they succeed, that means you lose—and so does your niece. So get your head in the game, Margot."

He shoved his hands into his coat pockets and started to walk again. "And don't feel bad about scoring points with Geoff Bench. We need him on our side. Cheer up. You did good. You won."

"It's hard to feel like a winner when the prize is getting to tell a six-year-old child that her mother is dead. How am I going to do it, Arnie? What am I supposed to say?"

‹♦ 21 ♦›

Margot

Arnie was no help. I don't know why I even bothered to ask him. If you're looking for first-rate legal advice, Arnie Kinsella is your man. For personal advice, I knew it was smarter to rely on my friends. However, they weren't available. Evelyn, Virginia, and Ivy were all in Vermont. Abigail was in Bermuda and would be for weeks to come.

Dana was on the phone when I entered the quilt shop. When the bells jingled to announce my arrival, her head bobbed up like it was on a spring. "Oh, good! You're here. This is the day care. Jordan is throwing up. I've got to leave a little early. Do you mind?"

"Not a problem. Things seem pretty quiet."

"Thanks," she said with a relieved sigh.

Business was more than quiet that afternoon; it was absolutely dead. Between three o'clock and quarter to six, I sold a half yard of fabric—four dollars and fifty cents plus tax—and a package of plastic replacement bobbins—seven dollars. I hoped things were going better for Evelyn and the others up in Vermont. Eleven dollars and fifty cents in the till would barely pay our heat and light bill for the afternoon, let alone my salary.

I tried to work on the books, but it was no use. After the third time I made a mistake in my addition, I gave up and decided to fold fat quarters instead. It's a pretty mindless task, but it didn't stop me from worrying about what I was going to say to Olivia. Someone had to tell her the truth; I just wished it could be someone else.

Just as I was getting ready to close out the register, the doorbell jingled again and a voice called out, "Is it okay to bring a dog into the shop?"

"Sure," I said. "We're cat-free today." Petunia, our regal and spoiled shop cat, can usually be found soaking up the sun in the display window, but since Virginia was in Vermont, Petunia was taking the day off.

Philippa came in with Clementine trailing behind, padding along on her saucer-sized paws. "Hi, Margot. Is Evelyn around?"

"She's out of town until Monday. But if you're ready to try quilting, I can help you. We've got a bunch of new classes starting soon." I gave her a yellow brochure with our class listings. She glanced at it and slipped it into her purse.

"I wish I could, but I'm swamped. I've got committee meetings every night this week, hospital and nursing home visitations, a sermon to write, and a sudden onset of premarital counseling sessions. It seems like half of New Bern's single population decided to get engaged over Christmas and married before June."

She smiled and patted Clementine's big head. The dog stretched out her neck, yawned, and flopped onto the floor like a sack of meal. Philippa dug a tissue out of her pocket and blew her nose. Her eyes looked tired and her face was puffy.

"Are you coming down with something?"

She shook her head as she pinched her nose with the crumpled tissue. "I'm fine. It's just another cold. The boiler keeps breaking down.

"I was taking Clem out for a quick walk before my meeting and thought I'd bounce an idea off Evelyn, but maybe you can help me. Did you know that six premature babies are born at the hospital every month? Maybe we should start a quilt ministry for preemies. It would be such a good way to reach out to the community. If enough people got involved, we might expand the ministry to pediatric patients too. Not all the kids, just the really sick ones who are there for a long time."

"Kids like Olivia?"

"Like Olivia," she confirmed with a nod. "Do you think Evelyn would be interested in heading up something like that?"

"Definitely. And if she can't, I will."

"Thanks." She gave me an appraising look. "How are you? I take it the custody battle is still on?"

"Oh, yes. My parents got a New York court to grant them guardianship. They didn't even tell the judge anything about me— or Mari's note!" I blinked hard, trying to keep hold of my emotions. "The Connecticut judge rescinded the ruling. He named a lawyer, whose name is Geoff Bench, to serve as a kind of temporary guardian. . . ."

"A guardian ad litem?"

I nodded, remembering that Philippa had once been a social worker and knew all about these things. "Anyway, it's all a big mess. I can't believe that my own parents would do something like that— sneak around behind my back."

"I'm sorry," she said. "You've been through an awful lot lately."

"Well, it's not all bad news. Olivia is a little better every day. She's fully conscious now. And asking questions . . ."

Philippa took her purse off her shoulder and put it on the counter, then pulled out a stool and sat down. "About your sister?"

"I have to go over there tomorrow and tell her, but I don't know what to say."

Philippa sighed sympathetically. "It'll be hard, no use pretending it won't. Just tell the truth. Keep it simple. If she has questions, answer them, but don't give her more information than she asks for. She's only six. You can talk about heaven, but it's important that you help her understand that her mother is not coming back. Children that age have a hard time accepting that earthly death is forever."

"Me too," I said as tears fell from my eyes. There was no point in trying to keep them back. "I don't know why Mari's life had to be so hard. And so short. I don't understand why this had to happen to her, or to Olivia, to any of us. And, if it had to happen, why couldn't it have been after Christmas? We hadn't been together as a family in years. If we'd had a chance, maybe we could have patched some things up, you know? I would have liked to see her one more time. I never got to say good-bye."

Philippa's own eyes teared, but she didn't speak. I was grateful for that. She didn't question my faith because she knew that faith and questions are not mutually exclusive. She didn't offer any explanations or theological theories. She listened to me. That was what I needed.

"My father said some things today. . . . They really got under my skin."

I laughed and wiped away a tear, thinking what an understatement that was. My father was always saying stuff that got under my skin. If parental commentary were classified into food groups, Dad would have been those popcorn hulls that get stuck between your teeth and turn your gums red and puffy—irritating, but nothing to get worked up over. Normally, I didn't. But today my father's comments contained more than a kernel of truth.

I wiped away the last tears and looked Philippa in the eye. "Am I ready to be a mother? I mean . . . am I qualified?"

She took in a breath and blew it out slowly, considering my question. "I've never been a mother, so maybe I'm the wrong person to ask. But don't you think that every mother worries if she's up to the task? It seems to me the first qualification for parenthood is love. You've got that part down pat."

"But," I countered, "my father is right; love doesn't pay the rent. It's one thing for me to live on cheese sandwiches and optimism with no benefits, but Olivia will need more than that. Even after she recovers from the accident, she's going to need clothes and shoes and maybe braces for her teeth, a chance to go to college . . ."

"True," Philippa replied. "But you're perfectly capable of doing that. With all your experience in marketing?" she asked, as if questioning why I would doubt my own abilities. "You might have to find another job or work someplace where they could afford to pay you more, but if it came to it, you'd do that for Olivia, wouldn't you?"

It was true. I love working at Cobbled Court Quilts, but if Olivia were given into my care, I would do whatever I had to do to support her, even take another job. If I could find one.

"I only ended up in New Bern because I was downsized and couldn't find work in the city. After I moved I couldn't find work here either. What makes you think the same thing wouldn't happen again?"

Philippa's smile returned. "Because people around here know you now; they know what you're capable of. I can't tell you how many times your name has come up in conversation since I came to New Bern. People like you, and they respect you. If you put out the word that you were looking for work today, you'd have three offers by tomorrow. I'm sure of it."

I wished I felt as sure as Philippa did, but there was some truth in what she said. When I came to New Bern, I was a stranger. Now I had all kinds of contacts. I never told Evelyn about it because I wasn't interested, but the director of the Chamber of Commerce had called once and asked if I'd consider heading up their marketing department. It didn't pay nearly as well as my New York job had, but it was more than I made at the quilt shop—and it had benefits. But money wasn't my only concern.

"My mom stayed home to raise her children," I said. "I know that isn't something all children can have, but I'm worried about balancing work and motherhood. What if I have a big project that requires a lot of overtime? And what if Olivia gets sick? Or doesn't recover fully? Dr. Bledsoe said she could be facing months, maybe even years of therapy. Or what if she—"

Philippa held up both hands as if shielding herself from the onslaught. "Let's just take a deep breath, okay? I know you're single, but you're not exactly all alone in the world. If you needed help, don't you think that your friends from the quilt circle, or church, or one of the scores of other friends you have in this town, would come to your aid? Just like you do when they need your help?"

She had a point. In the days and weeks since the accident, Evelyn, Ivy, Virginia, and the others had rearranged their schedules and taken on extra hours so I could be at the hospital with Olivia. People from church had sent prayers, and cards, and so many casseroles that I didn't have room for them all in my freezer. And, of course, if our situations had been reversed, I'd have done the same for them.

When Dana asked, I'd been only too happy to finish out her shift so she could pick Jordan up from day care.

"Margot," Philippa said evenly, "at the risk of sounding clichéd, it takes a village . . ."

"I know."

"Your sister was a single mom. She had to deal with the same kinds of pulls and pressures you will, but with fewer resources and less support. If you stop to think about—"

Philippa stopped in mid-sentence, examining my face.

"This isn't just about being a single parent, is it? What's the matter, Margot? You can tell me."

If I hadn't already been crying, the concern in her voice would have brought me to tears. I looked away, searching my heart for the answer to her question.

"I always wanted to be a mother. It's something I've dreamed about, prayed for, my entire life. But . . . if I had known that the price of answered prayer was my sister's life . . ."

My hands shook. The light was too bright. I closed my eyes, trying to banish the images that were burned in my brain, the face that haunted my dreams and left me awake and gasping in the night, the daytime visions that always loitered in the back of my mind, truant thoughts that refused to go where I sent them, pictures of pale, pulse-slowed hands that scrounged through the glovebox searching for a scrap of paper, the sound of the pen scratching across it, the painful scrawl that I barely recognized, those few words that were all she had strength and time enough to write . . .

Margot,
I've tried to hang on, but I don't think anyone is coming.
I want you to take Olivia. You've always wanted children. I know you'll love her and take good care of her.
Tell Mom and Dad that I'm sorry. Tell everyone I'm sorry.
Tell Olivia I love her. Tell her over and over.
Mari

I lowered my eyes, looking down at petite Philippa. "My parents were always telling Mari she should try to be more like me. It created a wedge between us. I tried to make it up to her, to help her as much as I could, but I think that just made it worse. She resented having to take my help.

"And I resented her. I was angry that she made everything so hard for everyone, that she'd torn our family apart. I resented the fact that she resented me even while she was accepting my help. And when I found out she was pregnant, I was so jealous. It didn't seem fair! I had done everything I was supposed to do, played by all the rules. But my sister, who returned home only long enough to empty my refrigerator and my bank account before disappearing and breaking my heart, again, was given the child I wanted so much and had been denied.

"I was so sure that I would have been a better mother than Mari. How could I even have thought such a thing?"

I covered my mouth with my clenched fist. Philippa rose from the counter stool and stood in front of me, lifted her hands to rest on my shoulders.

"I didn't mean it, Philippa. If I could, I'd take them all back, every jealous thought, every resentful word and action. I loved my sister. I wish I had shown her how much. I'm sorry. I'm so sorry."

She nodded. "I know," she said quietly, her eyes so filled with understanding and compassion I didn't deserve that it made me weep.

"God forgive me," I whispered.

"He does, Margot. He does."

22

Margot

Philippa, who was making her own rounds at the hospital, walked me to Olivia's room before going to look in on Waldo Smitherton. "You can do this. Just remember what I said about keeping it simple, okay?"

"Okay."

Philippa smiled and patted me on the shoulder before heading down the hall. I paused and took in a deep breath before gingerly pushing the door of Olivia's room, half-hoping to find her asleep. But when I stepped inside, Olivia turned to look at me. Her eyes were so big in her little face, so much like Mari's.

Nurse Trina looked up and smiled as I entered. "Looks like you've got a visitor," she said cheerfully as she adjusted the drip on Olivia's intravenous tube. "And she's brought you another present."

Trina put her hands on her hips and shook her head, pretending to scold. "Olivia Matthews, you are entirely too popular. If your grandparents and auntie keep bringing you presents every day, we're going to have to get an extra room just to store them."

Olivia looked at the nurse, but remained silent. She still wasn't talking much. Dr. Bledsoe said that wasn't surprising. She tired easily and was still in pain. However, the doctor assured me that, cognitively, Olivia was doing well. In a few days, assuming she continued to progress, Olivia would be moved to the pediatric ward. It would be good for her to be around other children.

Trina smiled and patted Olivia's arm above the tape that secured the IV needle. "I'll be back later, sweetie. Hey, guess what? You're going to get some ice cream for dessert tonight."

"She's swallowing just fine now," Trina said, addressing me before turning back to Olivia. "What kind do you want, sweetie? Vanilla or chocolate?"

"Chocolate," Olivia said.

"Then chocolate it shall be," Trina replied brightly. She walked toward the door, giving me an encouraging pat as she passed. She knew why I'd come that day.

"I like chocolate ice cream too," I said. "But chocolate mint is my favorite." I pulled up a chair next to the bed and put my present, a stuffed orange and white striped cat with a big white bow around its neck, on Olivia's stomach.

She reached out her needle-free arm and stroked the chenille fur. "He has a squashy tummy."

"That's what I like about him. He'll be nice to sleep with."

Olivia nodded. "Do you have a cat?"

"I used to when I lived in New York. Her name was Gracious, but I called her Gracie. She was black with four white socks and a little patch of white right here," I said, pointing to my forehead. "She liked knocking things down. I used to come home from work and Gracie would have pushed all the pencils off my desk. Once, she even pushed a vase full of flowers off the table."

"Did it break?"

"No, but there was water everywhere. Gracie jumped down and started lapping it up."

"Maybe she was thirsty," Olivia said practically. "What happened to her?"

"She died and went to heaven. She was pretty old."

Olivia nodded acceptingly. "I always wanted a cat, a real one," she said, tipping her head toward the toy while she continued stroking it. "Mommy is allergic."

"I remember," I said. "We couldn't have cats when your mommy and I were little. That's why I got Gracie when I grew up and got my own place, because I couldn't have a cat when I was a girl."

"You should get another," Olivia said.

"Think so? Maybe I will."

She smiled. It was the first real smile I'd seen from her since the accident, and it melted my heart. She was too little to have lost so much. I couldn't tell her. I just couldn't. But I had to.

"Olivia . . . we need to talk about Mommy."

She stopped petting the stuffed cat and looked up, her saucer-wide eyes riveted to mine. "When is she coming to see me?"

Don't cry, I told myself. *Whatever you do, don't cry.*

I took a deep breath. "Olivia, do you remember the accident?"

Olivia turned her head away and put her hand up to her mouth, sucking on her little finger a moment before answering. "I remember the car sliding and that my head hurt. There was blood and I was cold. Mommy was in the front seat and I was in the back. I wanted her to come to me, but she couldn't. She told me not to cry. She promised everything would be all right."

"Do you remember coming to the hospital?"

She shook her head. "I remember the ambulance. The men put Mommy in another ambulance. I wanted to talk to her, but I couldn't because they had that thing . . ." She cupped her hand over her mouth, pantomiming what she didn't have words for.

"The oxygen mask," I said.

"They had it over my face. But I saw Mommy. She was asleep. The man said they were going to bring us both to the hospital."

She rolled on her side to face me, clutching the cat to her chest with one hand and grabbing the bedrail with the other.

"When can I see her?"

"Olivia, I have to tell you something. Something sad. Mommy was hurt very badly in the accident, even worse than you were."

She let go of the bedrail and put her little finger back in her mouth. She stared at me with cautious eyes, as though a part of her sensed what I was leading up to but was warning me not to say it.

"Do you remember what I said about my Gracie? How she died and went to heaven?"

"She was old," Olivia replied in a slightly impatient voice, leaving the extension of that thought, that her mother was *not* old, unsaid.

"Usually, people and animals don't die and go to heaven until they get old. But sometimes, if a person is very sick or is very hurt, they can die before they are old." I paused for a moment, looking at Olivia, hoping to see a flicker of understanding in her eyes, hoping I would not have to say the words out loud. There was none there, just that same cautious gaze.

"And that's what happened to your mommy. She was hurt very badly, Olivia, so badly that the doctors couldn't make her better and so she died and went to heaven."

Olivia's brown eyes filled with tears and she frowned. Her pale complexion flushed red. I couldn't tell if she was sad or angry or both.

"Well, when is she coming back?" Olivia asked in that same impatient tone.

"Heaven is forever," I said, feeling my own eyes begin to tear. "People don't come back from heaven, sweetheart. But someday you'll go to heaven. So will I. Grandma and Grandpa too. And we'll all be there with Mommy and we'll be so happy. And we'll be together always."

"Let's go now. I want to see Mommy *now*," Olivia demanded, her face flushing brighter as the volume of her voice increased. "Now!"

Philippa had warned me not to say too much, to keep it simple and wait for Olivia to ask me questions rather than supplying her with answers she was not ready to hear or capable of understanding. I tried, but I don't know how well I succeeded. Whether you're six or one hundred and six, it is hard to make sense of the senseless, the unfair, the early death of a woman who, after so many years of drifting, was finally getting her life under control, leaving behind an orphaned daughter who hadn't done anything wrong.

"Livie," I said gently, using Mari's pet name for her, "you can't go to heaven yet. Not now, sweetheart. You won't die for a long time." I reached out, trying to take her hand, but she slapped it away.

"I want to see Mommy now. Make her come back!" She glared at me as if I was the enemy, as if I had kidnapped Mari and was holding her hostage.

"I know, honey. I know. I wish I could. I miss her too. But when people die they don't come back. Not ever," I said firmly.

Philippa had been very clear on this, telling me that I must use the word "die," not euphemisms like "passed away" or "lost," and that I must make it clear that the dead never return. I understood why I had to say it, but I felt so cruel.

"You're lying," she insisted, glaring at me.

I shook my head, ever so slightly. Olivia grabbed the toy cat around the throat and flung it across the room.

"You're lying!" she shouted. "She *is* coming back! She is! She wouldn't leave without saying good-bye! She would never, ever leave me! You're lying!"

Olivia's shouts became hysterical screams. She grabbed the bed-rail and shook it hard, as though trying to break it down, but she was so small and weak that the best she could manage was a metallic rattle. Furious and frustrated, she began clawing at her arm, trying to rip off the white tape and pull out the needles while she screamed, not words, just screams, high-pitched and hysterical, a howl of animal rage.

"Livie!" I jumped up and pushed the red call button that hung on the bedrail, then leaned across the bed, covering her body with mine to try and stop her from ripping out the IVs. Barely a moment later, the door pushed open and a nurse rushed in. She must have heard Olivia's screams even before I pushed the button.

Quickly and expertly, murmuring soothing sounds even as she pinned Olivia's little arms to the bed, the nurse immobilized my sobbing niece. "It's all right, honey. Everything is all right."

A moment later, Trina strode into the room carrying a syringe, as though she'd been prepared for this, far more prepared than I. Tears I had expected, and questions, and even denial, but not this rage.

I barely knew my niece. Before the accident, our cumulative contact could be measured in days. But this was Mari's child, an image of my sister, the sister that I had always loved but never really understood.

All my doubts and insecurities came rushing back. What had Mari been thinking when she wrote my name on that scrap of paper? What made her think I would know how to raise her daughter? This was the first conversation I'd had with Olivia since the accident. Look how I had bungled it.

"Olivia," Trina said calmly as she injected the contents of the syringe into Olivia's intravenous tube, "it's going to be all right, sweetheart. You need to calm down, okay? We're giving you something to help you sleep a little while."

Soon, Olivia's little limbs relaxed. Her sobs subsided, becoming a series of choked hiccups. Her eyes closed, but tears still tracked down her cheeks.

I stood at the side of her bed, my fingers curled around the railing as I gazed down at her little face, matching her tear for tear. "I'm sorry."

Trina stood next to me and moved her hand in comforting circles between my shoulder blades.

"I should have found a better way to tell her."

"There wasn't a better way. It's tragic and it's not fair, but someone had to tell her. The job fell to you. There was no way to sugarcoat it. Don't blame yourself."

"She blames me," I whispered, glancing down at Olivia, who was twitching in her sleep.

Trina nodded. "It won't be the last time. I've got three daughters. Getting blamed for things that aren't your fault sort of comes with the territory."

❧ 23 ❧

Philippa

I knocked on the door softly, thinking he might be sleeping.
"Come in!" Waldo bellowed.

He was sitting up in his hospital bed, looking thinner but alert. He squinted when I approached, as if trying to bring me into focus.

"It's you!" he exclaimed in cheerful surprise, then coughed a few times before grabbing a pink kidney-shaped basin from the bedside table and spitting into it. My stomach lurched and I looked away.

"Sorry, Reverend."

I lifted my hand, waving off his apology. "You're looking much better, Mr. Smitherton. How do you feel today?"

"In pretty good shape for the shape I'm in. Kind of surprised to find myself still here. Think the docs are too."

True enough. This bout with pneumonia would surely have felled most men his age, but Waldo Smitherton wasn't most men. Standing on heaven's doorstep, he had rallied, made a sharp about-face and returned to the land of the living.

"If it's a surprise, then it's a good one."

"Hmm," he murmured and reached up to adjust his hearing aid. "You know what they say: Only the good die young. Heaven knows I'm ready anytime. I've done everything I ever wanted to and then some. At this point I'm just taking up space. Hey, did Sylvia give you that file yet?"

Sylvia was the youngest of Mr. Smitherton's four daughters, a spry sixty-nine-year-old with her father's blue eyes and fatalistic sense of humor. Following his instructions, she had delivered a blue accordion file folder marked "Obituary" to my office earlier in the week. It was filled with newspaper clippings, three medals for cross-country skiing (Waldo had been quite an athlete before a crash and a torn ligament ended his skiing career), a copy of his honorable discharge from the Army Air Corps, a letter of commendation for his role in helping capture a German artillery battery, two yellowed résumés, professional and volunteer, the latter longer than the former, a self-published family history of the Smithertons penned by Waldo several years before, and pictures of Waldo and his late wife, Rachel, on trips to many foreign countries, including Russia, Sweden, Italy, China, Thailand, the Galapagos, and even Bhutan. The date on that photo, the last trip he'd taken before Rachel died, was ten years ago.

Think of it. I doubt most people could locate Bhutan on a map, but Waldo Smitherton had traveled there at the age of eighty-six. What an amazing man.

"Sylvia brought it by on Tuesday."

"Good. If it comes to it, I want you to give me a good send-off."

I nodded. There was no point in arguing with him. Waldo had accepted the fact of his mortality and wanted everyone else to do the same. He wanted his eulogy to remind his daughters, particularly the older three, Gloria, Cynthia, and Rose, who did not share their father and younger sister's Yankee practicality, that he'd lived well and had no regrets. He didn't want them wallowing in grief when he died.

"You'd think the girls would have made their peace with it by now," Waldo had confided to me on my previous visit. "But they're sentimental, all three of them. Can't think where they got it. Their mother wasn't like that. Thank heaven for Sylvia. You can talk sense to her."

In spite of the fact that his three eldest were septuagenarians, Waldo still referred to his daughters as "girls" and displayed a touching, fatherly concern for them. He was one of the kindest men

I'd ever met. If Tim had lived to old age, I bet he would have been a lot like Waldo.

Waldo squinted again, looking me up and down. "Reverend," he said flatly, "you look awful. Are you coming down with something?"

"I'm fine. Just a little tired. I was up late working last night."

Waldo shook his head. "And then you had to get up early today and visit some old codger in the hospital."

"I like visiting you," I said. "You're one of the most interesting people I know."

"Then you should get to know some more people," he said. "Besides being older than dirt, there's nothing all that special about me. Now you listen to me, Reverend. You're trying to do too much. Bob Tucker's just the same, and look what happened to him. Pull up that chair and rest yourself," he commanded, nodding toward a straight-backed metal chair near the door. "Take a load off."

I did as I was told, and gratefully. I really was tired.

"Say, how are things with Margot's niece?" he asked. Waldo kept himself well appraised about the lives of his fellow church congregants. "Terrible thing for a child that age to lose a parent. I lost my father when I was twelve. Did you know that?"

"I did," I said. I'd read about that in Waldo's family history. His father had died of an infection, before the invention of antibiotics. Waldo stepped into his father's shoes, dropping out of school at fifteen to take a job as an errand boy at a newspaper so his siblings could continue their education. Later, Waldo learned to set type. He worked as a printer at the same paper for fifty-five years, retiring at seventy.

"Olivia is getting stronger every day," I continued. "You might pray for Margot, though. She's going to have to tell Olivia what happened to her mother today."

"That's a tough one." He shook his head sorrowfully.

"Mr. Smitherton, I've been meaning to ask you something. Looking through that file, I was simply amazed to see how well-traveled you are. . . ."

"Oh yeah, Rachel and I were real globe-trotters. Visited thirty-three different countries on six of the seven continents. We skipped Antarctica. Rachel said that New Bern in January had enough ice and snow. She didn't need to travel thousands of miles to see more."

"I hope you don't think I'm prying, but how were you able to afford it? I mean, I didn't think that printers made all that much money. You helped your mother financially while she was alive and you had four daughters to raise."

"And they all went to college," Waldo said proudly. "Every one of them. As soon as the girls were old enough to work, they did. All that money went into their educational fund and we supplied the rest, though some of the girls had scholarships too. But we were always savers; that helps. And we lived within our means. Drove used cars, had a nice house but not a big one, didn't buy things we didn't need, fixed old things rather than bought new. Rachel always kept a garden." He smiled, as he always did when speaking of his late wife.

"She knew how to stretch a dollar. The woman could get three good meals out of one chicken. And we were all blessed with good health. That helps. Costs more to spend three days in the hospital than a month in South America. Nothing against these doctors," he said, "but given the choice, I choose South America."

I laughed. "Me too."

"Now let me ask you something," Waldo said. "Next time you come to see me, could you bring me communion? I missed it this month."

I opened my big black handbag. "Way ahead of you," I said and pulled out my portable communion kit. "And I brought you some DVDs of the Sunday services you've missed. Also a couple of John Wayne movies, *Fort Apache* and *She Wore a Yellow Ribbon*. I'm sure they've got a video player around here somewhere."

"Well! Isn't that something? Now this is what I call service." Waldo shifted himself a little higher on his pillow and winked at me. "Keep this up, Reverend, and I'll remember you in my will."

After my visit with Waldo, what I really wanted to do was go home and sneak in a nap before my next appointment. Instead, I rode the elevator down two floors to check on Margot, but when I got there, Trina told me Margot had already left.

"Oh? How did it go with Olivia?"

"Not well. Olivia got hysterical and Margot left in tears." Trina frowned and shook her head.

"I just can't see why such bad things have to happen to such nice people. If I get to heaven, I'd like to sit down and have a long talk with the good Lord, because as far as I'm concerned, he's got some explaining to do." She paused, letting a small smile come to her lips. "On the other hand, I'm sure he thinks the same thing about me."

"And all the rest of us," I said.

"I suppose. But don't you sometimes wonder why the world is so messed up? I mean, one minute everything is fine and the next minute . . ."

Trina snapped her fingers and the sound echoed in my head. Without warning, the room started to spin. I closed my eyes. A groan, and the remains of my breakfast, rose to my lips. I tried to swallow them both back.

"Reverend Clarkson? Philippa? Are you all right?"

Eyes still closed, I shook my head. "Sick," I mumbled, reaching my hand out to the wall in an attempt to steady myself.

In an instant, Trina transformed from amateur theologian to practical nurse. She grabbed a nearby plastic wastepaper basket and held it under my chin, patting my back as I vomited into it.

"Do you feel faint?" she asked when I was done emptying my stomach. I nodded and she guided me to a chair, instructing me to put my head between my knees. It didn't help. Even with my eyes closed, it felt like the room was spinning.

"Wait right there," she commanded. "I'm going to get the doctor."

❧ 24 ❧

Philippa

I sat with my bare feet dangling over the edge of the examining table, wearing one of those stiff, crinkly paper jobs that have replaced traditional cotton hospital gowns, and tried to absorb the diagnosis.

Dr. Mandel, who said I could call her Rhea if she could call me Philippa, stood about five foot one, had reddish hair that was giving way to gray, a well-padded frame, and a grandmotherly manner. At the moment, she was just what I needed.

"Don't look so shocked," she said and scribbled on her prescription pad. "Unless your fertility doctor in Boston performed the procedure while you were under anesthesia and without your consent, you had to know this could happen. Artificial insemination does have a tendency to result in pregnancy. Didn't they explain that part to you?"

She ripped the top sheet of paper off the pad and handed it to me. "Here's a prescription for prenatal vitamins. Congratulations, Philippa. You're going to be a mom."

"A mom..." I held the prescription in my hands, each corner pinched between my fingers, and stared at it. "A mom."

"Are you all right?" the doctor asked, her smile fading. "You're not having second thoughts, are you?"

I blinked quickly and shook my head. "No. Absolutely not. It's just . . . We'd done the procedure so many times. I'd kind of stopped believing it would ever work."

"Fortunately," the doctor said as she opened a drawer and pulled out a pair of latex gloves, "it only takes once. We'll do an ultrasound in a few weeks, but for now, I'd like to give you an internal exam. Don't worry, it'll be quick and it won't hurt the baby. Just lie back and put your feet up. Scoot a down a little, please. That's right. Good girl."

She snapped on a gooseneck exam lamp and adjusted it so she could see better.

"Sorry my hands are so cold. Just try to relax," she said. "Think lovely thoughts, dear. Think about holding your baby."

I tried to follow her instructions, but the idea of a baby, my baby, our baby, mine and Tim's, was still a thing beyond imagining. It seemed like a dream. For so many years, it had been.

Tim and I always planned on having children, but we decided to wait a few years before starting a family. I was a social worker, later a seminary student, and Tim was a special education teacher, so we weren't exactly rolling in dough. We decided to build up our bank account before having a baby. We had plenty of time, or so we thought.

Every month, we gave 10 percent of our income to the church, used 80 percent for our living expenses, and put the remaining 10 percent into a special bank account for our someday baby—the "junior fund," we called it.

We were just seventeen hundred dollars away from our twenty-five-thousand-dollar goal when Tim was diagnosed with stage three colon cancer.

With aggressive treatment, including chemotherapy, we were told that Tim's chance of survival would be close to 60 percent. Tim was always an optimist, always figured that everything would turn out and so, initially, he wasn't nearly as worried about the success of his treatment as he was about what it would do to our plans for having a baby.

Before the chemotherapy, we visited a fertility clinic and had Tim's sperm frozen. Tim painted an amusing portrait of a grim-faced nurse with no eyebrows and man hands who pointed to a stack of magazines, gave him a plastic cup, and told him to "ring if he needed anything"—but as far as Tim was concerned, this was just a blip on the radar screen of life. Once he was done with the surgery and chemo, he assured me that everything would return to normal and we would spend the rest of our lives together, growing old and wrinkly in tandem. "After all, I've got a better than fifty-fifty chance."

In time we came to realize that those odds weren't good enough. The cancer spread and the chemo treatments weren't working. In the last weeks of his life, one of the things that brought Tim comfort, aside from his faith, was the thought of our someday baby. He talked about that a lot. He made me promise that, boy or girl, I'd raise our child to be a Red Sox fan.

Tim needed to talk about the future he wouldn't live to see, and I let him, but it was hard. Having a baby was the last thing on my mind. All I cared about then was Tim. I didn't want to imagine a world that didn't include him. And I couldn't imagine raising a child without him by my side.

One day, I told him so.

Tim reached out his hand, asked me to help him roll over so he could see me better. I stood up, grasped his bony arm, careful of the IVs, and wedged my other hand gently under his back to give him a boost. He was starting to have problems breathing by then. I remember how raspy his voice sounded.

"Do you know what's going to happen in the second after I die?" he asked.

I shook my head. I could not imagine that. I didn't want to.

"The world is going to keep on spinning—just like it has since the beginning of creation. Clocks are going to tick, tides are going to come in and go out, couples are going to fall in and out of love, and you're going to feel very sad."

"Don't." I put a finger against his lips. "Please. I don't want to talk about it."

His eyebrows, or rather the place his eyebrows used to be before the chemo robbed him of his hair, drew together. He frowned and pushed my hand away. Weak as he was, he was still strong. Stronger than me.

"Not talking about it won't make it go away, Pippa. I'm going to die. After I do, I know you're going to be sad. But not for always. Life will go on."

"No. Not for me."

"It *will*," he insisted. "One day you'll wake up and hear the birds outside the window and you'll stop to listen and then you'll stop again, realize that, for a while, you forgot to remember to be sad. And when that happens, I don't want you to feel guilty about it, okay?" He reached across the white sheet and interlaced his fingers in mine. "Okay?" he repeated, in a gentler voice.

I bobbed my head because I couldn't speak.

"Good," he said, accepting my nod as confirmation. "And someday, I don't know when, but someday, you're going to wake up and decide that you're tired of being alone. You're going to want a family, a baby. Two babies. Who knows? You might even meet somebody and fall in love and want to have a baby with him—and that's okay with me. . . ." He paused for a moment, thinking. "As long as it's not Scott McNally. Remember him from college? What a jerk. Always hated that guy."

I laughed and wiped my eyes with the back of my hand. "Fair enough. I won't fall in love and make babies with Scott McNally."

"Good. But if you fall in love with somebody else, a non-jerk, then fine. You don't need to feel guilty or disloyal. You have my blessing. I want you to be happy, Pippa. And if you don't meet someone and fall in love, I want you to have a family anyway, just like we always dreamed we would.

"After I'm gone, take the insurance money and the junior fund, anything that's left after you pay for the funeral and the medical bills the insurance won't cover, and use it for the fertility treatments. I was talking to one of the doctors and he told me . . ."

I turned my head away. "Honey, I'm tired. Can't we talk about this later?"

His eyes flashed with a hard, dark expression I had seen only rarely in our eight years of marriage but recognized. When Tim looked like that, he had made up his mind and nothing on earth was going to get him to change it.

"No. We're almost out of later. We've got to talk about it now. There aren't a lot of advantages to being on your deathbed, but one of them is that you get to set the agenda."

"Kind of like how you get to control the remote during football season?"

"Exactly like that. Pippa, listen to me. We can have a baby, our baby. . . ." He paused and his eyes glowed with sweet anticipation, as if there really was a *baby,* not a test tube of frozen sperm and a 5 to 20 percent chance of fertilization, as if he could see beyond the shadow of death into a future that held new life. "This is the chance of a lifetime! Don't you see?"

I couldn't. Not then. It would be a long time before that would happen.

Tim grabbed my hand, pressed it hard to his lips, trying to kiss me into understanding.

"It's hard, I know, and sad, but . . . oh, baby, it wasn't all sad! I've loved you so much. How many people get to have what we've had? For a day or even a year? How many? I don't want our story to have a tragic ending. And I don't think it has to, not if we've got someone to pass it all on to, the good times, all the memories. Promise me you'll tell the baby about all of it—how we went camping on our honeymoon and the tent started to leak, about the time I caught the ball in Fenway Park, and how we took that bike trip across the whole state, all the way from Boston to Pittsfield. . . ."

"And the red-tail hawk flew right over us for the last five miles. . . ."

His smile beamed. "Yes! Wasn't that something? Tell him that, Pippa. Tell our baby everything we ever did together! Promise me you will."

"I will. I promise."

After Tim died, I forgot about that conversation. Well, not forgot about it so much as I chose not to remember it. The grief over my beloved's death was so immense that for a long time I felt dead too. I could not imagine ever feeling any other way.

But just as Tim had predicted, life went on.

For the first two months after Tim died, I found it a struggle even to get out of bed, let alone leave the house or go to class. I suppose it might have gone on longer if not for a knock on my door one afternoon in early October. There was a man standing on the stoop wearing blue jeans, a red flannel shirt, and holding a puppy—if a thirty-five-pound dog, no matter how young, can ever really qualify as a puppy.

The man, a breeder of English mastiffs, was Ben Abbott. The puppy's name, he informed me, was Clementine. "That's what I've been calling her anyway. You can always change it if you want to."

"You must have the wrong address. I didn't buy a dog."

"Maybe not, but your husband did, about six months ago. Well, not a dog exactly, but he paid in advance for a puppy from Esmerelda's next litter. She's a champion, my Esmerelda. I don't normally sell her pups to people who aren't planning on showing them, but your husband insisted you needed a mastiff and, like I said, he paid in advance."

"Oh, Mr. Abbott. I think there's been a misunderstanding. I don't know anything about puppies and, anyway, this just isn't a good time for me."

Ben Abbott sucked on his teeth for a moment. "Here," he said and thrust the dog into my arms.

Even at eight weeks of age, Clementine was more than an armful, so heavy I nearly dropped her. Unfamiliar with dogs, I held her stomach up, like you would a baby, with her ear flopping backward over my arm. She yawned, stretching her neck, then opened her enormous brown eyes and stared into mine.

Needless to say, I kept her.

There were days, particularly the day when I came into the living room and saw that Clementine had chewed up one entire arm of the sofa, ripping the upholstery and pulling out the stuffing with her teeth, that I wondered what in the world had possessed my husband to buy me a dog. But he knew what he was doing. Clementine was a great companion, and a much-needed distraction from my grief. Most importantly, she got me out of the house. First, just out into the yard, then to the end of the block and back, then on longer walks where neighbors came out of their homes to pat Clementine, say it was good to see me again, and sometimes invite me in for coffee. In the spring, when Clemmie's legs grew longer, I even put her on one of those extendable leashes so she could lope along next to me during bike rides. If not for that, I'm not sure I'd ever have ridden again. Oh, yes. Tim knew exactly what he was doing.

After a year, I returned to seminary, enrolling in two courses that first semester, three the next, eventually working up to a full load, slowly returning to the land of the living, the place where people exist in anticipation of what is to come.

And one day, about two years ago, just as Tim predicted, I went through most of an entire day before I remembered to be sad. It wasn't that I had forgotten about Tim, just the opposite. While cleaning out some closets, I found a bunch of old photograph albums and spent an entire morning going through them, remembering all our good times together and feeling so grateful for what we had shared. But I wanted to share it with someone else, to pass on the stories, the lessons, the love that I had known with my precious husband. I wanted a baby, Tim's and mine.

I called up the fertility clinic and got more information on artificial insemination. The costs weren't as high as I had feared, nor was the procedure particularly complicated. The medical bills, the funeral, what I had spent on living expenses during those months of depression and grief had used up a lot of the junior fund and the life insurance, but there was enough left to pay for several attempts at artificial insemination.

I prayed about it, talked to my parents and the seminary chaplain about it, and decided to go ahead with the procedure. At thirty-eight, I was a little older than most first-time mothers, but I was healthy. But after four attempts, I still wasn't pregnant. My doctor suggested adding fertility drugs to the regime. They didn't help.

Much as I wanted a child, I began to wonder if this was what God wanted for me. Perhaps my calling was to ministry and ministry alone. I spent a great deal of time meditating on the passage in Luke in which the rich young ruler walks sadly away after the Savior tells him to give all he has to the poor and follow him. "There is no one who has left a house or parents or brothers or wife or children for the sake of the kingdom of God who shall not receive many times more in this present time, and in the age to come, eternal life."

After more prayer and more conversations with people I trusted, I reached a decision: I would undergo ten procedures, and if they didn't work, I would accept that God's plan for my life didn't include parenthood and move on. Why ten? Because that was all the remainder of my savings would pay for and because the last treatment would occur shortly before my fortieth birthday, which seemed a good time to stop. Unexpectedly, that final treatment coincided with a phone call telling me that I was to fill the position of interim pastor at New Bern Community Church and that I was needed in New Bern almost immediately.

That's why this pregnancy had caught me by surprise. After nine unsuccessful attempts at artificial insemination, I didn't really expect the tenth to work. Emotionally, I had already moved on. On top of that, I was so overwhelmed with packing, moving, and trying to get a handle on my new responsibilities that I barely had time to eat or sleep. I simply forgot all about the fertility treatment. I chalked my fatigue up to overwork and long hours, not the possibility of pregnancy.

But it was true. Dr. Rhea Mandel, the head of obstetrics at the hospital and, therefore, someone who ought to know what she was talking about, had told me I was going to have a baby. Lying on the exam table, covered by a paper gown and a sheet, I felt two tears slip silently down my cheeks.

Once again, Tim was right. This was the chance of a lifetime.

After the exam, Dr. Mandel, Rhea, helped me sit up again. She took a seat on a rolling stool.

"Everything looks good. But it's early days yet. And at your age..."

I finished the thought for her. "It's possible that I'll lose the baby. I know."

The doctor nodded. "It's sad when that happens, but when it does, there is usually a good reason. If you get through the first trimester, you should have no problem carrying to term. But until then, you might want to keep this quiet."

I nodded. "My parents will be over the moon when I tell them, but I don't want to before I'm pretty sure everything will be all right. And I don't want anyone in town to know, not yet. A few people in the church are still adjusting to the idea of a female minister," I said, thinking of Ted Carney. "The thought of a pregnant female minister might not go over too well. I don't want anyone to think I'll fall down on the job just because I'm having a baby. I'm going to go on just like I was before."

Rhea laid both hands flat on her thighs and raised her eyebrows. "Oh, no, you're not. You have got to slow down, Philippa. Get eight hours of sleep a night. A nap in the afternoon. Eat regular meals. Your schedule makes a medical resident look like a slacker. No wonder Bob Tucker had a heart attack."

"But . . . this is my first church. I can't slack off. There's just too much to do."

"Well, then you'd better find some people to help you do it," she said in a stern voice before getting to her feet. "I'm not kidding. You cannot continue working fourteen-hour days, not if you want to carry this baby to term. Get some people to help you. Isn't that what people in churches are supposed to do? I thought that was what the whole 'love your neighbor' thing was about."

She walked to the door. "At your age, and as hard as it was for you to get pregnant, you won't get another chance." She pointed a scolding finger at me. "Do not blow this, Philippa. I mean it."

I nodded. "I won't."

"Good." She opened the door and winked. "Congratulations. I'm very happy for you."

❦ 25 ❧

Margot

Evelyn hefted an enormous pile of fabric bolts off the cutting counter and carried them toward the shelves. Working in a quilt shop is a lot more physical than most people realize. That's why Evelyn is in such good shape.

It's been a long winter marked by snowstorm after snowstorm. Three- and four-foot icicles hang from the eaves of every building in town, and stories of soggy ceilings and hundred-year-old barns collapsing under the weight of the snow are common. That probably explained why we'd had a full roster for our "Easy Breezy Beach Tote" workshop and why so many students stayed after class and bought more fabric to make more totes; everyone is hoping for an early spring and dreaming of sunny summer days.

The bolts—a rainbow of hot pinks, brilliant blues, turquoise, buttercup, and lime green—towered almost to the top of Evelyn's head, covering her face and mouth, making her response to my question sound like, "Drubgum. Fwoost? Ahbetweepburgenzwip."

"What?" I laughed and grabbed five bolts from the top of the stack. "Try again."

"I was just asking if there's something going on between you and

Geoff Bench. This is the third time you've had lunch with him this month."

"Fourth," I corrected and then blushed, thinking how that sounded. I carried a bolt over to the pink section and reshelved it. "We're just getting together to talk about Olivia and fill in some paperwork. He has to do that. It's his job."

Evelyn dropped her pile of fabric on the floor, picked up two green bolts, and carried them over to the green section. "Has he had lunch with your parents four times this month?"

"He's met with them," I said defensively.

Evelyn shot me a meaningful glance.

"Oh, stop it. They're not here as often as I am. Buffalo is a seven-hour drive. And Dad has had a lot of work. Plumbers always do in winter; people's pipes freeze. I'm the one who sees Olivia every day, so it's only natural that Mr. Bench needs to talk to me more than to my parents."

My daily visits to the pediatric ward of the hospital haven't done much to improve my relationship with my niece. The other children on the ward, the ones who were well enough to respond, like me and call me Auntie Margot. Olivia barely looks at me or speaks to me, or to anyone, including my parents. Which, I'm ashamed to admit, makes me feel a little better.

Everyone says Olivia is grieving and I just need to give it time, but I wonder. Could she be trying not to grieve? Not to feel? It's hard to know what is going on in someone's mind if they won't talk to you. Either way, I'm worried about her. And Olivia is only one of my worries. Geoff Bench is also on the list.

What goes on between Geoff and me is more a monologue than exchange. At our last meeting, we spent perhaps five minutes talking about Olivia and the rest of the hour discussing fly fishing and scuba diving in the Caymans—two subjects on which I had almost nothing to add beyond nods, smiles, and an occasional, "Really? How interesting." I was trying to do what Arnie had told me to do—make Geoff like me. So far, it seems to be working. Maybe too well?

"It's only natural that Geoff talks to me more frequently than my parents," I told Evelyn. "We've got a lot of things to discuss."

"I'm sure you do," Evelyn said evenly.

"Stop!" I laughed and wedged a bolt of bright green polka-dot fabric onto a shelf. "I am *not* interested in Geoff Bench."

"Ah, but is he interested in you?"

"No," I insisted. "I'm a good listener and Geoff is a good talker. That's it. Now, is it all right if I go to lunch or not?"

Evelyn returned the last bolt to the proper shelf. "Sure. The rush is over. I'll probably spend the rest of the afternoon sewing samples."

I nodded and grabbed my coat off the rack near the door. "I'll be back by two."

"Take all the time you need."

"Thanks," I said, "but an hour will be enough." More than enough.

According to news reports, the groundhog did not see his shadow on February second, which means that spring is supposed to come early this year, but I see no sign of it. The snow is piled so high that there's no place left to put it. The sidewalks are less sidewalks than narrow paths between waist-high snow canyons. Who ever came up with the idea of basing weather prognostications on the whims of a rodent, anyway?

Though it's only a short walk from the quilt shop to the café, the cold air felt good. I was glad for the chance to get outside and clear my head before my lunch appointment.

It's not that Geoff is a bad guy, but . . . he makes me uncomfortable. He hardly ever blinks. And he has a habit of talking about his wife, not in a good way. How she doesn't understand him and how she's always away in Florida, working on her tan and spending his money, or in New York, visiting her sister and spending more of his money.

I'm used to men talking to me about their woes with women. Sometimes I think I must have some sort of sign reading THE DOCTOR IS IN printed on my forehead in magical ink that only men with girl-friend troubles can see. I listen, offer advice and, more often than not, it works. I've gotten invited to a lot of weddings that way. I don't mind really. If you can't straighten out your own love life, the next best thing is helping other people straighten out theirs, right?

But this is different. Geoff is married. I don't think he should be talking to me about his wife, especially not in such a negative way. I mentioned it to Arnie, but he didn't seem concerned.

"He's a talker, likes to hear the sound of his own voice. So what?"

Well, Arnie is probably right. I'm sure that there's nothing more to it than that. But...

One time when Geoff was walking me to my car after a meeting with Dr. Bledsoe, he insisted my coat was too thin, took his off, and put it, and his arm, over my shoulders and left it there. It was windy. Probably he was just trying to keep the coat from blowing away. And another time when he was pointing to a line on some papers I had to sign, his elbow brushed against my breast, but I'm sure that was an accident. He apologized after, though he continued to look straight at me, with that gaze that makes the hairs stand up on the back of my neck.

I didn't mention any of this to Arnie, of course, because I thought it would sound silly. Arnie is all about evidence and facts. Hair standing up on the back of my neck doesn't qualify as either.

"But I wish he wouldn't talk to me about his wife," I said. "It doesn't seem very professional."

"It isn't," Arnie said. "But maybe she really is as bad as he says. Maybe he just needs to vent."

"I wish he'd vent to somebody else. I don't like it, Arnie. And I don't like him."

I felt a little bad, almost guilty, admitting this. I've always liked everybody—almost everybody. My mother always said that if you search for the best in people you're bound to find it. Maybe that's what I needed to do. Just try a little harder to like Geoff Bench, focus on his good qualities instead of letting myself be bothered by little things. I'm sure it was all perfectly innocent. After all, who'd make a pass at me?

Almost as if reading my thoughts, Arnie said, "I know. But try a little harder, okay? It's only for a few more weeks. And it's a good sign that he likes to talk to you. Once this is over and the judge gives you custody of Olivia, it'll all have been worth it. You'll see."

To have Olivia safe and secure in my home, to see her heal and grow in a loving, caring environment, to fulfill my sister's dying request, I would put up with anything. It would be worth it fifty times over.

By the time I reached the restaurant, I felt better. When I saw Geoff through one of the restaurant windows, already seated, smiling and waving at me, I smiled and waved back.

"No dessert?" Geoff asked when I pushed the menu back to his side of the table. "That apple pie sounds pretty good."

"I'm trying to lose a few pounds."

"Why?" Geoff made a face that was meant to convey his surprise. "You look great. Wish Laura kept herself up like you have. She spent two weeks at a spa last summer and it didn't do a bit of good. Cost me five thousand dollars. We have a whole gym set up in the basement. Weights, treadmill, elliptical trainer, the works. She never uses it. She's going off to the spa again next week and taking my credit card with her."

He sighed and then looked up at me, eyes trained on mine. "Come on," he urged. "Have a piece of pie. If it'll make you feel better, we can split it."

I looked at my watch, grateful for an excuse to break his gaze. "I can't. Evelyn's alone in the shop. I need to get back."

"All right," he said. "Next week."

He smiled and I forced myself to smile back, wondering how many next weeks I would have to endure before I could bring Olivia home for good.

~ 26 ~

Philippa

As I walked him out of my office, Ted Carney stopped and turned to shake my hand. "I hope you weren't offended, Philippa, but I'm a man who believes in speaking his mind."

"Of course not, Ted. Honesty is the best policy."

Ted buttoned his overcoat. "Always a pleasure to see you, Reverend."

I forced a smile and opened the door. Honesty *is* the best policy; I believe that. And when you can't afford to be honest, silence is golden.

"See you on Sunday."

Ted left. I turned around, leaned back against the door, and closed my eyes.

Sherry, the church secretary, closed a drawer on the filing cabinet. She's in her mid-fifties, stands a hair over five feet two inches in heels, is as efficient as a high-speed calculator and as loyal as a spaniel. I don't know what I'd do without her.

"How'd it go?"

I shot her a look.

"Well, *I* think you're getting much better," Sherry said, reaching for a tissue and blowing into it. Sherry and I have been trading the same cold for three weeks. The fact that the furnace keeps breaking down doesn't help. At the moment, the thermometer in the office reads fifty-six. "Anyway, there's more to being a good pastor than sermonizing."

Sherry means well, but I really don't feel like talking about it right now. I don't feel like talking about anything right now. Meetings with Ted have that effect on me.

"What do I have for the rest of the afternoon?"

Sherry glanced at her desk calendar, but before she could answer my question, her eyes screwed shut and her mouth gaped open as she took in three big gulps of air and then expelled them all in a tremendous sneeze. "Ah-ah-ah-*choo!*" She grabbed another tissue and wiped the wet away from her nose. "Sorry."

"Bless you. Did the furnace company say when they were coming?"

"They were supposed to be here at eleven. I'll call and see what's keeping them," she said, jotting a note before reading off the day's agenda.

"You're meeting Paul Collier for lunch at the Blue Bean at one-thirty. Jennifer, Brenda, and Paula are coming in at three to talk about Vacation Bible School—apparently they're in some disagreement about which curriculum to choose. You've got a premarital counseling session at four. . . ."

"Alex Dane and Tracey Sampras, right?"

"Right," Sherry said and then frowned. "I don't know about those two."

Neither did I. During our first meeting, they got into a huge argument about how much Tracey was spending on her wedding dress and then launched into another about whether or not they should have a flower girl and ring bearer. My standard agenda for a second session of premarital counseling would be to go over the results of a compatibility assessment they'd taken during the first session, but Alex and Tracey had been too busy arguing to take the test. It didn't matter. I already knew what I needed to know about this couple. My job today would be to get them to reconsider their engagement. Hopefully, they would be more willing to listen to me than they were to each other.

"And after that?"

"Stewardship committee meeting at five-thirty and choir at seven. Oh! And John Wozniak called. He'd like to come in and talk to you, as soon as possible, he said. He wouldn't tell me what it was about." Sherry flipped a page on the desk calendar. "You could squeeze him in tomorrow at two forty-five."

I shook my head. John Wozniak is a steady sort of guy, reserved and quiet, doesn't like to talk about himself. If he called saying he needed to see me as soon as possible, there was a good reason. "Let's see if he can come in at five."

Sherry clucked her tongue. "And when are you supposed to have dinner?"

"After choir. I'm having a late lunch."

"And who is going to feed Clementine?" She crossed her arms over her chest and I fought to suppress a smile. Sometimes Sherry is more mother hen than secretary. She has a good heart, though.

"Well . . . I was sort of hoping you might drop by the parsonage on your way home. Would you mind?"

The telephone rang. Sherry swiveled in her chair and reached for the receiver. "You know I don't, but you can't keep saying yes to everyone. You'll wear yourself out!" Her scolding expression melted as she picked up the phone and said sweetly, "New Bern Community Church. May I help you?"

"Thank you," I mouthed and started to head back toward my study.

I had a little under an hour before I was supposed to meet Paul for lunch. I should spend that time in my office, pounding out yet another sermon that would fail to meet with Ted Carney's approval. Instead, I made a sharp about-face, walked to the coat rack, and took my blue snow parka from one of the hooks.

"Excuse me just a moment, Jennifer." Sherry pressed the telephone receiver flat against her chest. "Shouldn't you be writing your sermon? This is the only block of time you'll get today."

"I'm going for a walk." I slipped my arms into my parka.

Sherry's eyebrows arched. "It's twenty-five degrees outside."

"I know," I said as I zipped up my coat. "But the sun is out. I want to soak it in before the next storm. I'll be back at two forty-five."

It felt good to be outside. I've always been active, even in the winter. When Tim and I got engaged, instead of a diamond, he gave me a kayak and a set of his-and-hers cross-country skis. I couldn't have been happier; diamonds were never my style. But I haven't been skiing once this year, partly because I've been so busy, but mostly because I didn't want to risk anything happening to the baby. Dr. Mandel said that I should be fine through the fourth month, but why take chances? It's still hard to believe that I'm really pregnant.

At night, I lie very still, trying to feel something, a movement or ripple or bubble, a sensation of blood flowing swifter and stronger through my veins (my new hobby is voraciously reading everything I can about pregnancy and childbirth. That's how I learned that my blood volume will increase by 25 percent before the baby is delivered. Miraculous!) or any sort of concrete physical evidence that would confirm Dr. Mandel's diagnosis.

My nausea is all but gone, though fatigue is still a problem. The other day, I sat down to work on my sermon and ended up falling asleep with my head on my desk, drooling on the pages I was supposed to be editing. Good thing the office door was closed. What if someone had come in? But I bet Bob Tucker had fallen asleep on his desk plenty of times. Being pastor of New Bern Community Church is a job that comes with too many hats and not enough help. However, if my meeting with Paul Collier went like I hoped, I'd have one less job to do.

Given the hours I was working, my exhaustion wasn't necessarily because of the pregnancy. Of course, my breasts are sore, but it's the same sort of soreness I feel just before my period. And that brings up another kind of worry.

Every morning I wake up and walk slowly to the bathroom, scared that a show of blood will dash the hopes I still barely dare to have. Faith is the hope in things not seen and I've based my life on that hope but just now, I wish I had some hard evidence. I wish I was fat and bloated. I wish my pants wouldn't button and my shoes were too tight.

And I wish I could share the secret. I wish I could infiltrate the circle of strollers and mothers who congregate over tall skim lattes in one corner of the Blue Bean Bakery and quiz them about what they felt in their first, second, third month of pregnancy, and confirm that it is normal for your body to feel so normal when it is doing something so monumental, to ask if they felt so excited, and so afraid, and afraid to be so excited, when they were in my shoes.

There are no children's boutiques in New Bern, but Kaplan's carries a selection of expensive infant wear, all-cotton jumpsuits and sleepers in bright bold stripes and polka dots, imported from Sweden, designed to catch the eye and open the wallets of indulgent grandmothers. I'm dying to go in and buy the striped royal blue and bottle green sleeper worn by a headless white mannequin in the display window. It's the exact same color as Tim's favorite rugby shirt, the one he wore almost every Saturday of our married lives. But I resisted the urge. It's too soon to buy a layette, and I don't want to face Mrs. Kaplan's questions about who is having a baby. I bought my mother a Kaplan's cashmere scarf for her birthday, and by the time I walked out the door, Mrs. Kaplan had extracted the full history of the Clarkson family and my adoption into it.

I took a right turn into the alley, thinking I'd cut through Cobbled Court. Evelyn was standing in the bowfront window of the quilt shop, hanging strings of shiny red hearts from the ceiling to complement a display of red, white, and pink fabrics, an homage to Valentine's Day. She smiled and motioned for me to come in.

It was warm inside. Virginia, Evelyn's mother, was sitting in a straight-backed chair at a large quilting hoop near the window, stitching a red and white star-patterned quilt. Evelyn turned as I came through the door and hopped lightly down from the display, clutching two extra strings of hearts in her hand.

"Don't let me interrupt you."

"I was just finishing up," Evelyn replied and turned around to face the window. "What do you think?"

"Looks good."

Virginia glanced up. "Hearts for Valentine's Day? Not exactly a surprise. Liza would have come up with something more original—folded fat quarters into rosebuds, or hung the whole thing with papier-mâché Cupids."

Liza, I had been told previously, was Abigail Spaulding's niece. Before leaving New Bern to take a job at an assistant curator at an art museum in Chicago, she worked at the quilt shop and created window displays and fabric arrangements.

"Well, I'm not Liza. My creative juices flow in different patterns. Speaking of patterns," Evelyn said, looking at the quilt her mother was working on, "that is coming along nicely."

I moved next to Evelyn and looked over Virginia's shoulder. Using incredibly small and even stitches, the older woman was creating an intricate pattern around each block that looked like a series of fat, intersecting plumes.

"How do you do that?" I didn't see any outline or tracing on the quilt. "Do you just make it up as you go?"

Virginia answered, but didn't look up, still focused on her work. "No, but this is one of my favorite patterns. I've done it so many times that my fingers have pretty much memorized it."

I leaned down closer to the quilt, fascinated, trying to see if there were any differences between the stitching on the various blocks—not that I could see. I looked up at Evelyn. "Is that usual?"

Evelyn shook her head silently, her expression indicating that I ought to be impressed by what I was seeing. I was.

"It's really not that big a deal," Virginia protested. "It's just a matter of practice. Old as I am, I've had plenty of time for it."

"Well, I'm just amazed, Virginia. I could never do anything like that."

"Sure you could. I could teach you. Come to think of it," she said, finally turning her sharp gaze toward me and frowning a bit, "why haven't you signed up for quilting class? Evelyn said you were thinking about it."

"Oh," I replied feebly, "I've been so busy. . . ."

Evelyn began to murmur something understanding, but was interrupted by her mother. "Nonsense. Everyone needs to take a break now and then."

Before I could say anything in response, Virginia deftly tucked her needle into the quilt, hopped out of her chair, walked to the counter, and pulled a yellow brochure from a clear plastic holder that sat next to the cash register.

"Here," she said, thrusting a brochure into my hand, "take a look at these."

Margot had given me this same brochure before, but I'd stuffed it in my purse without ever reading it. There were at least a dozen classes listed, some of which had already started, but one in particular caught my eye—the Ladies in Waiting baby quilt class, taught by Virginia, on Thursday mornings.

"This seems interesting," I said, pointing to the listing.

Virginia leaned closer to the yellow paper and squinted through her glasses, then looked up at me. "You don't want that one. It's for expectant mothers. Margot offers babysitting for the big brothers and sisters up in the workroom—very noisy. Never fails, but one of the toddlers has a meltdown and the whole class gets interrupted while the mother calms the child. That's why the class runs eight weeks instead of the usual six; we go at a snail's pace."

Eight weeks. According to Dr. Mandel, that was about the same time I should be able to feel the baby begin to kick. For reasons that I couldn't quite explain, this seemed like some sort of omen to me.

"Eight weeks is perfect. I'm a slow learner."

"The class meets during the workday," Virginia said doubtfully.

"Weekday mornings are a better fit for my schedule. I'm booked with meetings and church activities nearly every night, and weekends are even worse. Besides, I'd love a chance to connect with some young mothers. The church is trying to reach out to more young families; this might be a perfect opportunity." This was all true.

"But," Virginia protested, "what would you do with a baby quilt?"

I pressed my lips together to keep myself from blurting out the secret I so wanted to share and racked my brain for an answer that wouldn't be a lie.

"Would a baby quilt class use the same principles as a regular quilt class?" For all I knew, baby quilt construction and standard quilt construction might be a case of apples and oranges.

Virginia nodded in response. "The technique is the same no matter the size of the quilt."

"Well, if the point is for me to learn quilting, it really doesn't matter what class I take, does it? When I'm done, I can always donate it to the hospital."

It was true, I could. That wasn't my intention, but honesty didn't require me to share that with Virginia.

As God was knitting my child together in secret, cell by cell, organ by organ, feature by feature, I, also in secret, would make my baby's quilt, choosing each fabric, stitching each seam myself, threading them with hopes and prayers and dreams for the tiny stranger I already loved with my whole heart.

Feigning interest in a fabric display, I turned my back toward Virginia and Evelyn, not wanting them to see how excited I was.

This was it! The answer to my longing for a community of mothers I could learn from, the fulfillment of my desire for some tangible evidence that my baby was real, the hope of things I could not see and could not talk about, not yet. My prayer had been answered, and so perfectly, before I had even known what I was praying for.

A bolt of fabric covered with bright hearts in primary colors caught my eye. I'd read somewhere that bright colors are good for babies' developing eyesight. I composed myself and pulled the fabric from the shelf.

"Can I use this?"

"Of course," Virginia said. "But . . . you're sure you want to make a baby quilt?"

Evelyn, who had been watching our exchange with an amused expression, rolled her eyes and took the bolt from my arms.

"Mom! How many times does she have to say yes?" She laid the fabric on the cutting board and started rolling it out. "Some salesman you are. How are we supposed to make a living if you keep try-ing to talk people out of taking our classes?" Evelyn winked at me.

"I wasn't trying to talk her out of it," Virginia groused. "I just wanted to make sure she'd be happy with the class."

"Oh, I will be," I assured her and dug my wallet out of my purse. "Definitely."

❧ 27 ❧

Philippa

After settling on the colorful heart fabric for my border, I chose my pattern—a quilt that featured what Virginia called "square in a square" blocks. Next, I picked out a score of additional fabrics in primary colors with prints and pictures that would be exciting for little eyes to search out. The process took quite a while and I was very nearly late for my lunch meeting with Paul Collier.

Scurrying through Cobbled Court, I met Margot, who was just coming back from lunch with Geoff Bench. When I told her that I was going to take Virginia's quilting class, she squeezed me and let out an excited little whoop.

"You'll love quilting, you really will. And Virginia is the best teacher there is. I'm so excited for you! Let me see your fabric!"

"I can't right now. I'm late for an appointment," I said, glancing at my watch. "But we'll get together soon. There's something I want to talk to you about anyway."

"What?"

"I'll tell you later. Unless Paul Collier is up for my idea, it won't matter anyway."

"Paul Collier? The man who moved to town right before Christmas? The one with that ugly car? What does he . . . ?"

"No time to explain right now," I said and started backing down the alley. "Call Sherry at the office and see if she can find a time for us to get together. Bye!"

I stood at the door of the restaurant and scanned the tables for a moment before I noticed Paul waving from a booth in the far back corner of the café.

"Sorry," I said, dumping my shopping bags and purse on the seat before sitting down. "I got waylaid in the quilt shop."

"It's all right. I just got here myself."

The waitress, Laura Ayers, whom I'd met and talked to several times before, approached with menus and asked if she could get our drink order.

"I'd like a Coke," Paul said. "With lots and lots of ice."

"Can I have a cup of tea?" I asked. "And a glass of milk?"

"Regular or herbal?"

"Chamomile if you have it." Laura nodded and scribbled on her order pad. "How's your dad, Laura?"

Last time I was in, Laura told me that her father, a widower who lived in North Carolina, was going in for a quadruple bypass. She was very worried about him and wanted to go down for the operation, but couldn't afford to take the time off.

"Better," she said with a smile. "My sister was able to go and help out."

"That's great. Hey, I saw you on Sunday but didn't get to talk to you after the service."

"I slipped out during the last hymn," she said apologetically. "I had to work the breakfast shift."

"That's all right. I hope we'll see you again."

"Oh, yeah," she replied in a tone that made me know she meant it. "It'd been so long I kind of expected the ceiling to cave in on me, but it didn't, so I'll be back. Maybe next time I'll bring my girls with me—if I can roust them out of bed. Teenagers." She rolled her eyes and shoved her notepad into the pocket of her black apron.

"I'll go get your drinks and come back for your order. Oh, and the soup of the day is Brunswick stew." She shifted her gaze left and right, to see if anyone was listening. "Avoid it," she whispered before walking away.

Paul chuckled. "I like her."

"Me too. Her husband walked out five years ago and left her with three daughters to raise, but she never complains, always has a smile on her face." I glanced at the menu and decided on a mushroom and Swiss burger with sweet potato fries.

"You learned all that, and about her dad's illness, and got her to come to church for the first time in years just in the time it takes to order lunch?" Paul let out a low whistle. "I am impressed. You're very good with people."

"Apparently much better than I am in a pulpit," I mumbled as I reached for my water glass, thinking back to my meeting with Ted.

Paul cupped his hand to his ear. "I'm sorry?"

I waved off his question. "Nothing. Let's talk about you. Then I will tell you more about what I'm going to try and talk you into."

"Sounds safer to talk about you," he said with a look of mock concern. "What's up? Something's bothering you. I can tell. I'm good with people too, you know."

"It's nothing," I said, unfolding my napkin. "It's silly."

"You can talk to me. Or are you worried about sharing confidences with a member of your congregation?" he asked and then answered his own question. "Well, that's probably smart. Wait. I've got an idea."

He stretched his hand across the table. "Give me a dollar."

"What?"

"Give me a dollar."

Shaking my head while trying to suppress a smile, I reached into the side pocket of my purse and pulled out a dollar. "Here."

He stuffed the bill into his breast pocket. "You have now hired me as your attorney. That was my retainer."

"A dollar?" I laughed. "That's not much of a fee."

"Well, I'm new in town and times are hard. Now, as I'm sure you're aware, there is a little thing called attorney-client privilege. That means you can tell me anything, and I can't talk about it. So, come on, shoot. I'm all ears."

"It's nothing. Really. I'm just irked about a meeting I had with Ted Carney."

Paul nodded as I spoke. "He's in charge of the church, right?"

"President of the board."

"Which kind of makes him your boss?"

"Exactly. And he's not very happy with me. Part of this, I suspect, is that he thought he was hiring a man and ended up with a woman—a case of mistaken identity, you could say. We didn't get off to a good start. Ted thinks I'm putting too much focus on counseling. But what am I supposed to do about that? When people need to talk, I can't turn them away. Ted was miffed because an unexpected counseling session made me late for the stewardship committee meeting recently and because I skipped a meeting of the music and worship committee in favor of counseling a couple who were contemplating divorce." I started fiddling with my purse, zipping and rezipping the pockets so Paul wouldn't see the anger on my face.

"It's not that choosing what cantata the choir sings at Easter isn't important. It is. It's just that I don't think a committee filled with gifted musicians necessarily needs me to sit there while they do it. Especially when the marriage of a couple with two little kids is hanging in the balance!"

"Is that what you told Ted?"

"Word for word!" I said defensively and then, realizing how I sounded, lowered my voice. "Probably I could have found a more diplomatic way to express my opinion. But if I had the choice, I'd do things exactly the same way. That couple has decided to give things another go. They're seeing a really good marriage counselor. I think they're going to make it."

"Good. I think you made the right choice. Was that Ted's only criticism?"

I shrugged. "Well, he'd never come out and say so, but on top of my not being my father's son, I think he's irked that, biologically, I'm not my father's daughter either. He thought he was hiring a Philip Clarkson clone, and instead he got me."

Paul looked confused.

"He's upset that I'm not my dad, thinks my sermons could stand a lot of improvement. He also thinks I'm in over my head administratively. I don't necessarily disagree with that. But I do disagree with his method of addressing the problem. He wants a more experienced minister to be my mentor."

Paul scratched his ear, thinking. "Well . . . would that be so bad? This is your first job in ministry. When I was a new lawyer, freshly hired by the firm, one of the partners mentored me, quizzed me for my bar exam, had me sit in on meetings. . . ."

I shook my head. "You don't understand. He doesn't want just anybody to mentor me. He wants my father. Specifically, he'd like Dad to come to New Bern and guest preach once a month. You know, show me how it's done. Since he can't get a Philip Clarkson clone, he's trying for the genuine article."

Paul made a sucking sound with his teeth. "Yeah, I can see where that would be a problem for you. What did you tell Ted?"

"What could I tell him? He's my boss. I told him I'd talk to Dad."

Laura came back with our drinks and set them down on the table, along with a basket of bread and butter, then took our orders. Paul asked for a plate of loaded nachos. That sounded so good that I almost asked Laura to bring another order to go with my burger, but I restrained myself. When Laura left, I practically fell on the breadbasket, grabbing the biggest roll, smearing it with a thick layer of butter, and taking a bite.

I looked up at Paul, who was looking at me. "Sorry," I said with my mouth full and pushed the basket toward him. "I had a small breakfast."

It was true. These days, two slices of toast, two fried eggs, a glass of milk, a glass of orange juice, and a piece of leftover apple pie *is* a small breakfast for me. I'd woken up too late to fry any bacon and I was all out of blueberry yogurt and granola.

"Anyway," I said between bites, "I'll work it out one way or another. Anytime you start a new job, there's bound to be a few bumps in the road. It takes time to get used to working with new people."

"Yeah," Paul said as he broke a roll in half and buttered it. "My new boss and I aren't quite on the same page yet either. Truth is, I just don't like the guy. He never shuts up. But he's the boss. . . ." Paul shrugged and popped a piece of bread into his mouth.

"Who's your boss?"

"Geoff Bench. He's head of the family law department."

"Geoff Bench?" I took a sip of my tea and washed it down with a gulp of milk.

"Do you know him?"

"No, but I know someone who does—Margot Matthews."

"Margot Matthews," he mused, then took a swig of soda from his glass and thoughtfully crunched a piece of ice between his teeth. "Is that the Margot who sings in the choir? Tall, blond, pretty eyes?"

"You've met her?"

Paul looked down, suddenly intent on tearing the rest of his roll into smaller bites. "Sort of. She gave me directions one day. So she's one of the Matthews in that custody case Geoff is working on?"

I nodded.

"Huh. Guess I should have put two and two together, but it's a common name." Paul took another drink, chewed another mouthful of ice. "She's, uh . . . well, she's cute, isn't she? Pretty eyes."

"Beautiful eyes," I said and smiled to myself, thinking that getting Paul to agree with my plan might be easier than I'd originally thought. "And very nice. I think you'd like her. In fact, Margot is part of the reason I wanted to talk to you today—"

Paul held up his hands, cutting me off. "Oh no. I'm sure she's nice, but I'm not interested in being set up with anybody right now. And, anyway," he said with a frown, "I don't think she likes me."

"Don't be silly, Margot likes everyone."

"Everyone but me. Anyway, it doesn't matter. I've got my hands full just dealing with a new job, a new house, and an unhappy teenager. A new girlfriend is the last thing I need."

"Things not going any better with James?"

"The principal called me. James is failing two classes, hasn't been turning in his homework. He had an A- average back in Chicago. Sometimes I used to worry that he was a little too obedient, you know? Too compliant." He snorted, as if amused by his former naïveté. "Not anymore. I grounded him. I had to do something, right?"

"How did James respond to that?"

Paul shrugged. "He said it didn't matter because he didn't have any friends anyway. And then he said that he wanted to go and live with his mother. The way he's been acting, I'd almost be willing to let him."

"Is that an option?"

"No. Melanie's so busy she barely has time to think, let alone take care of James. She was supposed to have him last weekend, but she canceled because she had to write a paper for her contracts class. James was pretty upset. I don't really blame him. I made him leave his home and friends so he would be able to see his mom, and now his mom doesn't have time to see him." Paul sighed again and rubbed his hand back and forth across his forehead as if his head hurt. "So, thanks for trying to set me up, but . . . no thanks. My life is complicated enough right now."

"I'm not trying to set you up," I protested. "At least not romantically."

It was true. Of course, had I realized that Paul had noticed Margot and found her attractive, I probably would have. Margot was so sweet and Paul was such a great guy. Now that I thought about it, they were well matched in many ways. They were intelligent, hardworking, and funny. They shared a love of children, a sincere faith and, whether they would admit it or not, they were both lonely. If I'd been looking to play matchmaker, I'd have been hard-pressed to find a better couple to practice on than Paul and Margot. However, my interest in getting those two together was purely practical.

"I'd like for you to meet Margot," I said, ignoring the suspicious expression on Paul's face. "I think there could be something in it for all three of us."

Paul pushed himself back from the table a bit, unconvinced. I closed my eyes and tried to collect my thoughts. It wasn't easy. I was so hungry that I was having a hard time concentrating. The breadbasket was empty. I'd eaten three rolls to Paul's one. Where was my cheeseburger?

"I was hoping you and Margot might consider taking over the junior high youth group. We've got eighteen kids coming regularly now. Even if I weren't already so busy with my other duties, that's too many for one leader to handle. And the kids really could benefit from having a male and a female leader. Kids this age are more likely to open up and talk to someone of their own sex.

"I picked you and Margot because you're both energetic, and fun, and you like kids. You'd be a good influence. And I think it could be as beneficial to you and Margot as it would be to the kids. With this custody battle going on, it might help Margot's cause if she could show the judge that she has experience with children. And I thought this might be a good chance for you and James to spend time together doing something fun. If you were leading the group, he'd have to show up every week. The sooner he gets to know the other kids in town, the sooner he'll start making friends."

Paul moved closer to the table, took another large drink of his beverage and a correspondingly large mouthful of ice. He chewed on it for a long time, his thick, dark brows drawn together in a slight frown.

"You don't think James would feel weird about having his dad be his youth leader? You don't think that would make him seem like even more of an outsider?"

I shook my head. "My mom was the youth leader at my church and, if anything, it only made me more popular. Mom was teaching the kids about God, but she was also the one who took everyone out for hot fudge sundaes, and hay rides, and ice skating parties. The kids were crazy about her. Seeing how everyone related to her helped me see her not just as a mother but as a person, an interesting, likeable human being and someone I could relate to as well, someone who really cared about other people. Her example had a tremendous impact on my life. She was the one who really inspired me to go into ministry."

"Not your dad?"

"Dad too, but in a different way. Dad is a preacher, but my mom is a pastor. The original word, you know, from the Latin, means 'shepherd.' That was my mom, a shepherd, caring for each individual little lamb. I'm very like her."

I stopped, realizing how long I'd been going on. Laura came to the rescue, carrying a tray loaded with food. Everything smelled so delicious. It was all I could do to keep from grabbing the burger with one hand, the sweet potato fries with the other, and stuffing both into my mouth, but I restrained myself long enough to bow my head to say a silent (and very sincere) prayer of thanks before diving in.

"The thing is," I said through a mouth half-full of cheeseburger, "this would be a great help to me and to the church, but I think it could be a help to you and James too."

Without saying anything, Paul took his now-empty bread plate and, using his fork, pushed a pile of his nachos onto it, then shoved the plate in my direction.

"Here."

I swallowed and looked at him doubtfully. "You sure?"

"Of what?" he asked with a grin. "That you need the nachos more than I do or that I'd be a good youth leader? Answer 'A' is absolutely. I've never seen a woman with an appetite like yours. I'm a little less sure about 'B,' but . . . I'm willing to give it a try."

"Thanks, Paul. I really appreciate it. You're going to love these kids, you'll see. So will James."

He picked up a tortilla chip, scooped up a pile of chili and cheese, and lifted it to his lips, but stopped just short of taking a bite. "And you think Margot Matthews will be interested in helping too?"

"Absolutely. I'm sure of it."

❦ 28 ❦

Philippa

"What do you mean you're not interested?" Virginia squawked, dogging Margot's heels as the younger woman carried a bolt of blue gingham cloth to the display shelves. "I met him and his boy on Sunday. Seems like a very nice man, perfect for you. He goes to church, has a good job. What's wrong? I thought you like lawyers."

My lunch with Paul ended a little earlier than I'd figured, probably because I wolfed down my food, and a good part of Paul's, in record time. With a few minutes before my next appointment, I decided to pop over to Cobbled Court Quilts to talk to Margot about the youth group. Her reaction wasn't exactly what I'd expected.

Margot squatted down to reach the lower shelf. "In case you hadn't noticed," she said, forcing the fabric into a narrow opening in the middle, "I'm kind of up to my ears in lawyers just now."

Virginia's eyes went wide behind her thick glasses, giving her an expression like a bug that has just heard something shocking. "This is not just any lawyer we're talking about, Margot! This is no namby-pamby, stamp-collecting Arnie Kinsella, no bleached-tooth, smarmy Geoff Bench. . . ."

Evelyn, who was standing at the notions display, emptying out a mailing carton filled with various pins and needles and sliding them onto racks, interrupted her mother with a laugh. "Mom, you've never even met Geoff Bench. How do you know he's smarmy?"

"Because Margot told me about him."

"I never said Mr. Bench was smarmy," Margot protested as she got to her feet and returned to the checkout counter.

"You didn't have to," Virginia retorted. "He *sounds* smarmy."

"Seriously, Margot," the older woman said as she returned to her quilting hoop near the window, stopping to scoop Petunia, the rotund shop cat, into her arms before sitting down, "just because Arnie Kinsella broke your heart doesn't mean you need to write off every lawyer on the face of the planet."

Margot pressed her lips into a thin line as she opened the drawer of the cash register and started counting bills and change. "Thank you, but I am not interested."

"Why not? Weren't you listening to what Philippa told you? The man thinks you have beautiful eyes!"

"Pretty," I corrected.

"Pretty," Virginia conceded. "Fine. Pretty is a start. Isn't it?"

Margot ignored the question and kept to her task, her lips moving silently as she added up a pile of quarters and scribbled the total onto a slip of paper.

Virginia sighed heavily and stroked Petunia, who glanced up at her and yawned. "I don't understand," Virginia said, addressing the cat. "As long as I've known Margot, she's been desperate for a man. Now a nice, churchgoing lawyer says she has pretty eyes and Margot won't give him a second glance."

Margot slammed the register shut. "I am *not* desperate! Not anymore. Not about men. The only thing that I'm desperate about these days is helping Olivia heal and winning this custody battle."

"Good for you!" Madelyn Beecher exclaimed.

Madelyn, whose bed-and-breakfast caters to quilting groups, had stopped in to pick up a few supplies.

"Desperation isn't attractive. It's also a slippery slope. I'm proof of that. I was so sure I needed a man to make me feel worth something that I ended up compromising every part of me that was worthwhile. Now I prefer to think of men as accessories." Madelyn sniffed. "Attractive to have, possibly useful, but not a necessity. Life enhancing, not life saving."

"Is that what you tell Jake?" Evelyn teased. "That he's an accessory?"

Madelyn smiled and dropped her detached demeanor. "Not exactly. But Jake understands my need for independence. That's one of the things I love about him."

"I don't understand you people," Virginia said. "Can't Margot be an independent person and still give this man a chance? Independence isn't all it's cracked up to be, you know. I've been independent ever since my husband died and I can tell you right now, it's not as much fun as it looks. Especially when you're my age. There's a lot to be said for growing old with someone," she said quietly, looking down as she stroked the cat.

Evelyn put down a package of pins and went to her mother's side, leaning down to kiss her on top of the head.

"You know, I think we might be getting a little bit ahead of ourselves," I said. "I don't think the fact that Paul noticed Margot and thinks she has pretty eyes means he is quite ready to propose, or that Margot was his primary motivation in saying he'd help with the youth group, though it may have been . . . an enhancement," I said, shifting my gaze to Madelyn, who smiled at me.

"I'm sorry, Margot," I said and put on my jacket. "I wouldn't have bothered you with this right now except I thought you'd love the kids. I know they'd love you. I figured it might impress the judge too, but you've got too much going on."

"Philippa," Margot said in a pained voice. "I hate letting you down, but . . . "

"It's okay. Don't worry. I mean it." And I did too. The last thing I wanted to do was add stress to Margot's life. "I'll find someone else to help."

"Who?" Margot asked.

Well, that was a good question. Like many churches, ours suffered from an unfortunate adherence to the 10–90 rule, meaning that 10 percent of the people were doing 90 percent of the work. The largest percentage of the congregation seemed content to let the smaller percentage, or the minister, do the heavy lifting. After all, isn't that what ministers are paid to do? Dr. Mandel was insistent that I had to slow down a bit. But at that moment, I couldn't think of anyone who would be willing and capable to step in and help with the youth, at least no one who wasn't, like Margot, a member of the 10 percent and therefore already too busy.

Of course, if I let the word out that Paul Collier was willing to serve as co-leader, there were probably any number of single women who'd be willing to help. New Bern is a little short on eligible bachelors. But somehow, I didn't think this would bring out the kind of leader I was looking for.

"Don't worry about it," I said. "I'll find somebody."

Margot came out from behind the counter and followed me to the door. "Are you sure?"

"I'm sure. See you all later," I said, giving a wave to the group and a smile to Virginia. "And I'll see *you* at quilt class."

"Looking forward to it," Virginia replied. "Wash that fabric and iron it before you come to class. With a baby quilt, I think it's best."

"Will do."

I opened the door and felt Margot's hand on my arm.

"Philippa? Wait a minute."

It wasn't until I'd said my prayers and gotten into bed that I remembered to call my father. It was a call I dreaded making, but there was no reason to. I should have known my dad better than that.

"Dad, are you sure?"

"I'm not interested, Pippa. Absolutely not. I'm surprised you'd even ask."

"I had to. I told the board president I would."

"Well, he should have known better. Having a mentor might be a good idea, but having a father mentor his daughter? No way. That's a recipe for disaster. And having someone else step into your pulpit and 'guest preach' for you once a month is a terrible idea too—no matter who the mentor is. The way you get to be a better preacher is by doing it, not by having someone else do it for you. What was your board thinking?"

"I doubt it was the board's idea, Dad. Ted Carney thought this up all on his own. He's a big fan of yours, talks about you all the time."

Dad made a grumbling noise in his throat. "Ministers don't have fans, Pippa. Or if they do, they shouldn't. Anyway, please tell Mr. Carney that I said no. He's just going to have find someone else to be your mentor."

"You know," said my mother, who had been listening in on the extension, "that's not a bad idea. Phil, you must know people who might be willing to serve as a mentor to Pippa. You could make a few calls. Would you mind if he did that, honey?"

"No," I said, "it would be great to have someone who'd talk me through a few of the pitfalls and politics of all this. Some days I feel like I'm in way over my head."

"If it's any consolation," my father said with a smile in his voice, "I still feel like that."

"But it's hard sometimes, not having anyone to talk to. Today I had lunch with a member of the congregation and ended up unburdening myself about my frustration with Ted."

"Oh, honey," Mom said in a scolding tone. "You know better than to do that, especially if the object of your frustration is the president of your church board."

"I know. I know. But it's okay. Paul won't say anything to anyone. He's a lawyer. Actually," I said, smiling to myself, "he's *my* lawyer. I paid him a dollar so he can't talk to anyone about what I said at lunch. Attorney-client privilege."

"You paid him a dollar and now he's your lawyer? What do you need a lawyer for?"

"I don't, Dad. It was kind of a joke. Anyway, don't worry. Paul knows how to keep a secret. He's a really nice man."

"Oh? Is he single?"

I sighed and shook my head, knowing exactly where this conversation was going. "Yes, Mom. He is single. But there is nothing going on between us; we're just friends."

"You and Tim were just friends when you met."

"This isn't like that. I'm not interested in Paul romantically. I'm not interested in anyone in that way."

"Tim has been gone for such a long time, sweetheart. Don't you ever get lonely? I just want to see you happy."

"I am happy. In fact, I'm happier than I've been in a long, long time," I said, looking down at my still-flat stomach and imagining my baby, curled up like a question mark inside me with arms and legs sprouting from the tadpole body that, according to one of the pregnancy websites I'd bookmarked, was now about the size of a kidney bean. Bean. I had been thinking that I needed some sort of nickname for this baby, something sweet but gender-neutral. Maybe this was it.

"But, Pippa, don't you ever—"

"Joyce," Dad said in a warning tone. "Leave it. Pippa knows her own mind. And she knows if she's happy or not. She certainly sounds happy."

"I am."

In a few more weeks I'd be able to tell them why, but not yet. Not until I was sure that everything was fine and that the little bean inside me was safe and growing and healthy.

"Well, if you're happy, I'm happy. Good night, sweetheart."

"Good night. I'll call again soon."

I hung up the phone and set the alarm clock to go off six and a half hours later. Another short night. But it had been a good day, certainly a productive one.

Sunday's sermon was still pretty rough, but with a little encouragement from me, the Vacation Bible School committee had reached consensus on a curriculum. On top of that, Alex Dane and Tracey Sampras had decided to call off their engagement, choir had gone well, the stewardship committee had reluctantly but unanimously voted funds to replace the broken banquet tables in the fellowship hall, the boiler was working again, Paul Collier and Margot Matthews had agreed to serve as youth group leaders, John Wozniak, who had just been diagnosed with lung cancer and didn't know how to tell his wife, whose own health was frail, had agreed that he couldn't keep it from her and had decided to ask his son and daughter to come to town and help him break the news, and the fabric for my unborn baby's quilt was tumbling around inside the dryer.

A long day, a hard day, and a good day. For so many reasons.

I turned out the light, pulled up the covers, and laid my hand on my stomach. "Good night, Bean."

The next morning, while Sherry was at the office supply store buying ink cartridges for the printer, my phone rang.

When I picked it up, a deep, slightly familiar voice said, "Philippa? This is Bob Tucker. I just got off the phone with your dad. I hear you could use a mentor."

❧ 29 ❧

Margot

March

Paul squatted down to hold the dustpan while Philippa swept up a bright tangle of colored confetti and eggshells. "What a mess."

"But the kids loved it," Philippa said. "Margot, this was a great idea."

After a couple of weeks of sitting in and watching how she ran the youth group, Philippa suggested Paul and I get together and create our own lesson plans and activities. While we were sitting in Paul's kitchen talking about how difficult it was to engage some of the kids, James wandered in and offered a few relevant observations.

"It's too much like school," he said. "All day long, we sit in classrooms while adults lecture us about stuff we don't really care about. Like algebra. Who needs it? I'm going to play pro basketball when I grow up."

"James," Paul said, laying a hand on his son's shoulder, "I don't want to burst your bubble, but you're about a foot too short to play in the NBA."

"I'm still growing," James said defensively.

Paul nodded. "I wouldn't be surprised if you top me by an inch or two before you're done, but that'll still leave you too short for the pros, buddy. Don't give up on algebra just yet."

He smiled and ruffled his son's hair, but James pulled away.

"Whatever."

"James," I said, pulling out a chair, "do you have a second? I'd like to hear what kinds of things you would like to talk about at youth group."

"What *I* want to talk about?" James sat down. "Really?"

Our conversation was very illuminating. What it all boiled down to was relationships. James desperately wanted to feel understood, accepted, and heard even while he struggled to understand, accept, and hear others. It wasn't that surprising when I stopped to think about it. That's what everybody wants and what everybody finds so hard to do.

After a bit of brainstorming, Paul and I decided that our emphasis for the spring would be on relationships, focusing on how Jesus handled his human relationships while on earth and employing lots of discussion, games, and activities to keep the kids engaged and help drive home the point. Today's discussion centered around the story of Zacchaeus, a dishonest tax collector whose life had been transformed because Jesus took time to call him by name, seeing beyond the little man's sinful shell and into his heart, a heart that yearned for God's love and a new life.

Our quiet activity had been to pass out colored cards for each child and ask the others to, anonymously, write something positive about the person whose name was on the card. Our "active" activity had been the eggs. My quilt circle sisters, who only complained a little about not getting any quilting done that Friday night, and I blew out five dozen eggs and then stuffed the empty white shells full of red, yellow, blue, green, and orange confetti.

At the end of the night, the kids chased each other around the fellowship hall, shrieking as they cracked the eggshells on each other's heads, releasing explosions of colorful paper and peals of laughter. Both activities were supposed to encourage the kids to look beyond appearances or first impressions and search for the good that exists inside everyone.

"I don't know," I said as I walked around the tables picking up empty paper cups and napkins the kids left behind after their snack. "The card activity was good. I could see that a lot of them were really thinking about what to write, but the eggs? I think they were having so much fun that they might have lost sight of the point."

"Nothing wrong with fun," Philippa said as she swept eggshells out of a corner. "That's part of what keeps them coming back."

"Well, I hope the kids aren't counting on confetti eggs every week. It took six women three hours to make them, four minutes for the kids to destroy them, and half an hour for us to clean up the mess." I smiled and tossed a stack of cups into the trash can.

"James loved it," Paul said. "He didn't want to leave when Melanie came to pick him up."

Paul and his ex-wife have a shared custody arrangement. She is supposed to have James every other weekend, but sometimes she has to cancel at the last minute. That upsets James, but rather than take it out on his mother, he gets angry with his dad. Poor James. He's had a lot of changes in a short time. But Paul is a great father, so patient. Paul is a great guy in general. Why didn't I notice that right off? I guess I could use some practice in looking beyond the surface too. That beat-up car of his threw me off at first.

He's nice-looking too, more handsome than I realized at first glance. His eyes are deep brown with little flecks of gold, like pieces of polished amber held up to the light. He's taller than I am and has an oddly athletic build for a lawyer. But maybe that's not a fair assumption on my part. Geoff Bench is athletic. He's always so quick to point that out. But the way he wears a suit always makes me think of the Incredible Hulk, as if the seams might burst at any moment and reveal some kind of slobbering monster, barrel-chested and hideously green. I swear he buys them too tight on purpose, just to give that impression. But where Geoff Bench is preeningly masculine, Paul is just manly. Paul is sort of the anti-Geoff. Come to think of it, he's sort of the anti-Arnie, too, but in a different way.

He's creative and talented. Next week, we're going to talk about the church body and how everyone has something unique and special to offer to it. Paul came up with the idea of having a jam session to illustrate the point. Kids who play can bring their instruments, Paul will bring his sax, and Philippa will have a supply of percussion instruments—tambourines, bongos, and such—available for everyone else to use.

Paul said, "It'll either be fabulous or a huge train wreck, but it'll be fun either way." It won't be a train wreck. Paul is a very good musician. He and James played a duet for me one day when I was at their house—James plays alto sax—and it was great.

It's so wonderful that he's willing to put himself out like that for the kids. And that he spends so much time with James—playing music together, working on the car. If I were still in the marriage market, Paul Collier would be exactly the sort of man I'd fall head over heels for.

A few weeks ago, I would have done exactly that. But the accident changed everything. The things that used to worry me—my age, still being single, the way other people viewed me—are barely blips on my radar screen anymore. Now my focus is on Olivia and this custody battle. It has to be. I don't have energy for anything else.

Just as well. I'm sure Paul won't be single for long. In New Bern, the ratio of unattached females to available men is pretty high. And the arrival of any new bachelor sparks a lot of interest among the people who find that kind of thing interesting. Just last week, Wendy Perkins came into the shop in a flutter, saying how she'd heard that Paul and Philippa had been spotted having lunch in the back booth at the Bean. It's a ridiculous rumor. Not the part about Paul and Philippa having lunch, but the implication there's anything improper going on between them. Philippa is just as focused on her work at the church as I am on trying to win custody of Olivia; neither of us has time for anything else.

But I did see Jeannine Baskins flirting with Paul after the coffee hour at church. I don't really blame her. What woman wouldn't fall for a man like Paul Collier?

With the floor swept and the tables and chairs set up for Sunday, we put on our coats and headed upstairs. Philippa brought up the rear, turning off lights. It was dark when we stepped outside and chilly and the air felt heavy, as though it might rain. The last of the snow melted off this week. Breathing in, I could smell that wet, musty, grassy scent that means spring is on the way.

Paul walked to his car, which I now know is a 1973 Mustang hardtop, and a classic. Paul's father was a mechanic in Chicago and this was his car; he left it to Paul in his will. Paul and James are trying to restore it to its original condition. Progress is slow, but they just installed a new muffler so it runs quieter now. Well, a little quieter. I think it's sweet that Paul wants to fix up his dad's old car. And I'm impressed that he actually knows his way around an engine and is passing that knowledge on to his son, just like his father did to him. Arnie doesn't even know how to check the tire pressure on his car.

Paul got into the Mustang and started the engine, but instead of driving away, he rolled down the passenger side window and called out, "Hey, are you two hungry? Want to go to the Blue Bean for a hamburger or something?"

"Thanks," I shouted, "but I can't. I've got quilt circle tonight." When Philippa asked me to help with the youth group, the circle voted to move our meetings from five to seven on Friday nights. It turned out to be a more convenient time for everyone anyway.

Philippa put the keys in her pocket and walked to my side. "Sure you can't skip it? Just this once?"

"We're going on sort of a field trip, to the inn. Madelyn just finished remodeling the garage into a huge quilting classroom, and we're all going over for a tour. Everybody will be waiting for me."

Philippa gave Paul a quick glance and nodded her head. "Well, all right. I kind of wish I could tag along. I can't get the blocks on my baby quilt to come out the same size. Maybe I need some private tutoring from Virginia. But a burger is pretty tempting too. I'm starving."

Philippa had gained a little weight since coming to New Bern. Maybe the stress of running a big church was making her eat more, or maybe she was one of those people who always put on a few pounds in the winter. Abigail swears she gains six pounds every winter, but you can't tell by looking at her. She always looks skinny to me.

Paul, who couldn't quite hear us over the noise of the engine, shouted, "What about later? After your quilt circle? I don't mind eating late."

"No, no. You two go on without me. Maybe another time."

Philippa looked at Paul and shouted, "I've got to run home and take Clementine out. Can I meet you at the restaurant?"

"See you there," Paul said. "Margot? Can I give you a lift to the inn? It's not that far out of my way."

"That's all right. I brought my car."

We said our good-byes. Paul pulled away. As he did, I had a sudden impulse to run after him, tell him I'd changed my mind. I didn't, of course. I couldn't. Everybody was waiting for me.

I unlocked my car. Paul's blue Mustang paused at the intersection, made a right turn, and disappeared around the corner. Darn it.

❧ 30 ❧

Margot

It was starting to drizzle when I pulled up in front of the Beecher Cottage Inn. The hand-painted sign next to the brick walkway said No Vacancy and every light in the place was on, making the stately Victorian look warm and welcoming in spite of the rain.

I wiped my feet on the mat before stepping into the inn's bright, elegant foyer. It was hard to believe this was the same dreary space that I'd seen on my first visit to Beecher Cottage. Madelyn had transformed the run-down ruin, and she'd done it on a shoestring budget. For instance, she'd spent hours sanding the ornately carved staircase and replaced the dark mahogany stain with a rich cherry color. And, after stripping off rolls and rolls of truly awful paper, she painted the walls a warm ivory and hung a collection of elegant framed floral pictures from the floor to the ceiling. They looked like something you'd find in a very expensive interior design store, but the "pictures" were really just pieces of wallpaper samples. The frames, painted with an antique silver color on the outer edges and a thin strip of ebony on the beveled interior edges, had been salvaged from the attic of the house. In terms of sweat equity, those pictures were priceless, but in terms of dollars and cents, they were practically free.

I walked from the front door toward the back of the house,

peeping first into the living room with its eclectic mix of antique and modern pieces, including the dollhouse Madelyn had played with when she was a little girl, and the wall hanging she'd stitched and hung only recently, an abstract, paper-pieced creation with hundreds of brilliant, jewel-toned patches of fabric in various shapes and sizes outlined with thin black fabric leading that remind me of cathedral windows. In the dining room I spied the huge table Madelyn refinished herself, and more silver-framed florals, but no people.

"Is anybody home?"

"In here!"

Tessa was in the kitchen placing slices of cake on china plates. "You're just in time to give me a hand."

"Where is everybody? The place is lit up like a Christmas tree, but I don't see any guests."

"Madelyn didn't take any bookings this week. Made it easier for the construction crew to finish up. She's out in the addition, giving everybody the grand tour. Can you get a couple of tea trays out of the cupboard? I've got frosting on my hands. Over there," she said, pointing with the cake knife toward one of the lower cabinets.

Before she started making herbal bath amenities for boutique hotels, Tessa worked for Madelyn at the inn, so she knows where everything is.

I pulled out two trays and carried them to the counter. "Do we need anything else? Teacups? Wineglasses?"

"Nope. We're good," she said, continuing to slice the cake. "So, how're things? How is Olivia? Any good news on the custody front?"

"More of the same. My parents and I aren't speaking except through lawyers. But Olivia is getting better every day. Her ribs are healed and the head injuries don't seem to have done any damage to her brain. She's even starting to read a little bit. At least, that's what the nurses tell me. She's still not speaking to me."

Tessa made a sympathetic clucking sound with her tongue and wiped a glob of frosting off the knife with a paper towel before cutting the next slice. "What about your parents? Does she talk to them?"

"Nope. She's mad at the whole family. She's so stubborn! Mari was just the same. She and Dad could go ten rounds and still come back for more. But now that I'm working with all these junior high kids, I'm starting to think my sister wasn't much worse than most teenagers. It's the age. I'm sure I was the same way. . . ."

Tessa grinned. "Bet you weren't. I bet you never put a foot wrong when you were a kid. Admit it, Margot, you were the good girl in the family, a little angel."

"I was not!" Tessa rolled her eyes. "I wasn't! I did plenty of bad things."

Tessa wiped a final glob of frosting off the knife with her thumb and forefinger. "Like what?" she asked before sticking her fingers in her mouth.

"Well . . . when no one was looking, I used to slip my green beans under the table and feed them to the dog. And one time, I stole a pack of erasers from the drugstore."

"What did your parents say about that?"

"Nothing. As soon as I left the store I felt guilty, so I went back inside and told the clerk what I'd done."

"That was it?" Tessa deadpanned. "That was your big foray into a life of crime?"

"Stop it!" I laughed. "Okay, so I didn't do all kinds of terrible things when I was a kid. That doesn't make me an angel. I just didn't like upsetting my parents, that's all. It was easier just to do what they wanted than not."

Tessa carried the dirty knife to the sink and rinsed it off. "I was kind of a goody-two-shoes too. That's why Madelyn and I became such good friends. When we were kids, Madelyn did whatever she wanted, didn't give a hoot what anyone else thought.

"Come to think of it," Tessa said, "she still does that. And I still like her for it. Madelyn is much braver than I am. And stubborn? Oh, gosh, she can be stubborn! Kind of sounds like your niece. But the flip side of stubbornness is determination."

Tessa put the knife away in a drawer and then turned around. "Look at this," she said, spreading her hands to encompass the beautiful kitchen. "Do you remember what a wreck this place was when Madelyn moved in? A less determined woman . . . a less stubborn woman would have given up before she even started. Not Madelyn. There are worse things than being stubborn."

"I know. But my parents . . ." I sighed. "Everything is black and white with them. That's not all bad. I always knew where I stood with them, but what worked for me didn't work for Mari. We were so different. And Dad just couldn't acknowledge the other side of Mari's coin. If he could have just focused on her good qualities a bit more, he might have been able to help her bring them out. Because, you know, she really did care what he thought. No matter how much she pretended she didn't. She just wanted to be loved."

Tessa bobbed her head slowly, letting me talk. I guess she knew I needed to.

"I'm not saying it was all my parents' fault. If Mari hadn't gotten into drugs, I think everything would have turned out so differently.

"I finished cleaning the junk out of my spare room and turning it into a bedroom for Olivia a couple of weeks ago. I painted the walls a soft lilac color and added these decals that look like clouds because I thought it would look sweet with a white bedroom set. But I'm starting to wonder if she's ever going to sleep there. What if I go through all this, jump through all these hoops, alienate my parents and Olivia, and it all turns out to be for nothing? What if I end up all alone and with a family that hates me?"

I put the last three plates on the tray. "Don't listen to me. I'm just tired. It's been a long week—make that a long winter."

Tessa squeezed my arm. "You know, there's a couple of bottles of prosecco out in the studio. Madelyn says it's the perfect accompaniment to chocolate orange cake. And, I believe, a great cure for custody battle fatigue. What say we go find some?"

The transformation of Madelyn's carriage house into a state-of-the-art "stitching studio" was amazing.

A glassed-in walkway led from the back door of the kitchen to the studio. Two additional guest rooms with private baths were housed on the upper floor. The studio itself was on the main floor. It was a cheerful space with yellow painted walls, white woodwork, large windows that looked onto an herb garden, and lots and lots of bright lighting in the ceiling that made it easy to quilt even at night. There was a large stone fireplace on the back wall surrounded by a cozy collection of sofas and armchairs, a comfy spot to take a break from sewing. A wet bar stood on one side of the fireplace, a perfect place for Madelyn to serve tea or snacks to her guests. Walls on the opposite ends of the room were lined with low cabinets where supplies and extra sewing machines were stored, very convenient for guests who might be traveling long distances and couldn't bring their own. And all those cabinets were topped with thick padding and heavy-duty muslin and lined with wall plugs to create a roomy and convenient ironing station where as many as a half dozen people could work without bumping into each other. The sliding doors of a double closet in the corner were also padded but were covered with white flannel instead of muslin, creating a generously sized design wall where quilters could arrange and rearrange their blocks before settling on a final stitching plan.

"What are those?" Ivy asked, pointing to one of several black plastic rectangles in the wood floor.

"Covers for electrical outlets." Madelyn bent over and flipped up one of the covers, revealing two electrical plugs. "That way, however we arrange the tables, everyone can have their own outlet. I don't want to have a bunch of extension cords snaking around the floor and tripping people."

"You've thought of everything, haven't you? Right down to the chairs!" Virginia sat down in one of the ergonomically designed black sewing chairs that stood in front of every sewing station and shook her head with wonder. "I've been on a lot of quilting retreats over the years and, most of the time, the experience was a whole lot like camping, right down to the bunk beds and mosquitoes. Once, my guild rented a fishing cabin up in Door County for our retreat, and we blew out the electricity in less than an hour. Spent the whole rest of the weekend hand-stitching by candlelight and kerosene." She chuckled. "Of course, we still had a good time—a bad day of quilting is still better than a good day doing just about anything else—but this! This is a regular quilting palace!"

Madelyn smiled, pleased by the compliment, and topped off Virginia's glass with some sparkling cider—Virginia is a teetotaler.

Abigail, who was looking very tan and fit after spending the winter in Bermuda, said, "I couldn't understand why you wouldn't let *my* architect take on this project. That man is a genius. But I'll be the first to admit that it turned out well."

"I didn't use Guillaume because I couldn't afford to, Abbie. This whole thing was already enough of a gamble. But I think it was a gamble worth taking." Madelyn lifted her glass. "Ladies, a toast: to one hundred percent occupancy!"

When our glasses were empty, Madelyn said, "I think we should do a little beta testing. Let's plug in the machines and get to work. There are notepads on every table. If you think of anything in the way of improvements, jot it down. I want to make sure everything is perfect before my first group arrives so, tonight, you're all my guinea pigs."

"I'm game," Evelyn said and started unpacking her project bag.

"Wait a minute," Tessa said. "I want to propose something—a group project. Twelve-inch blocks, any pattern or technique you like, with white on white backgrounds and lilac as the principal color. If everyone makes at least two blocks and a couple sign up to sew three, we'll have enough for a quilt for Olivia's new bedroom. I'm willing to make three blocks. Anyone else?"

"I'm in," Ivy said.

"Yes, me as well," Abigail added.

"I can do three blocks and take care of the borders," Evelyn offered.

"I'll do the quilting," Virginia said.

Madelyn raised her hand. "I'll make brownies to keep up everybody's strength. That's what I do best. *And,*" she said with a dramatic pause, "I'll stitch the binding."

Tessa beamed. "Ha! See? I knew it! It was just a matter of time before you'd start stitching with the rest of us!"

"Well, I wouldn't get excited just yet," Madelyn countered. "It's possible I'll stink at this. But . . ." She shrugged. "I figured I'd give it a try. It's just the binding, right? If I mess it up, somebody else can fix it."

"You won't mess it up," Tessa said. "You'll do fine."

My eyes started to tear up. I hate being so emotional, but sometimes I just can't help it. "You shouldn't go to all that trouble. Not when I don't know . . . I mean, what if the judge sides with my parents? What if Olivia never—"

"Shh!" Tessa walked over and clapped her hand right over my mouth. "No more of that. Olivia is going to get out of the hospital and come home to her lilac cloud bedroom. Everything will work out. The quilt is just a pledge of good faith, a down payment on all the good things that are coming for both of you. Got it?" She raised her eyebrows into a questioning arc. I nodded and she removed her hand so I could speak.

"Got it."

Tessa was right—a piece of cake, a glass of bubbly—just one—and a couple of hours of quilting with my friends did a lot to lift my spirits. I felt better than I had in days and was looking forward to going home and getting a good night's sleep. But instead of taking the most direct route home, I ended up driving downtown, passing slowly in front of the Blue Bean Café. Paul's car was still parked in front.

It was dark and raining pretty hard by then, too hard to be able to see inside the restaurant. Not without parking my car, walking right up to the restaurant window, and peering inside.

What a ridiculous idea. Why would I even think of something like that?

✑ 31 ✑

Philippa

"Can I bring you anything else?" The waiter, who had introduced himself as Tony when we first sat down, glanced at the still-untouched bill.

I looked up and smiled. "Ummm. A little more coffee? Decaf."

Tony smiled, but only with his mouth. "Sure. You want me to clear away the dessert plates?"

"Yes. Thank you."

Watching him leave, Paul spoke out of the side of his mouth. "I think Tony wants to go home." We both reached for the check.

"I've got it," he said, pulling it away. "It's the least I can do after making you sit here all night listening to me gripe. Sorry."

I waved off his apology. "It was a fair exchange. You were very patient listening about my troubles with cranky Ted Carney." I gulped down the last sip of coffee, now lukewarm. "*And* the cranky boiler. I'm so glad winter is almost over."

Tony returned to top off our cups. Paul handed him the black plastic bill folder with his credit card tucked in the top.

"It's a wonder you and Sherry haven't come down with pneumonia," he continued. "But I'm glad things are going better now that Reverend Tucker is mentoring you."

"I like Bob. He's a good listener."

"So are you." Paul blew on his coffee before drinking it. "It's bad enough you have to listen to the tales of woe of a single father raising a juvenile delinquent. . . ."

"Will you lighten up? Getting caught smoking one cigarette does not make James a juvenile delinquent."

"It doesn't make him citizen of the month either. Didn't they realize that if eight of them were in the bathroom, all smoking at the same time, it would set off the alarm?" He shook his head in disgust. "Knuckleheads."

I laughed. "And you were worried about him making friends."

"Well, yeah . . . I was kind of hoping he'd make *smarter* friends."

"I'm sure two weeks of detention will add at least ten points to their IQs. Don't worry. It's just the age. They're testing their limits. And you made it very clear what the limits are."

"Well, I was proud of him for taking his punishment like a man. He's going to be washing a lot of windows next week, but he didn't gripe about it, just said he was sorry and that it wouldn't happen again." Paul smiled and stirred another packet of sugar into his cup. "I don't think it will either. Those cigarettes made him sick as a dog."

"James is a good kid. And it seems like he's finally settling in."

"You were right about me working with the youth group. I think it helped a lot. And I enjoy working with the kids. And Margot. Mostly. All but the part where she's driving me crazy and torturing me."

Letting his head droop, he heaved a melodramatic sigh and pretended to beat his head against the table. "This is pathetic. I'm forty-two. I'm too old to be suffering adolescent angst over a woman who won't give me a second glance." With his head still on the table, he mumbled, "I hate this."

"I'm sorry."

He jerked his head up. "You should be. This is all your fault. You're the one who introduced us. Now I can't get her off my mind." He peered glumly into the bottom of his cup. "But I guess I'll have to. She obviously has no interest in me."

The poor guy. I really felt for him.

"Margot has so much on her plate right now—her niece, her parents, this court battle, plus she works full-time. Maybe it's just an issue of timing."

"Or maybe she's just not that into me. Can't you do something? Talk to her or something?"

"You mean like pass her a note in study hall? You've been spending too much time with teenagers. Maybe she's gun-shy," I offered. "You know she was dating another lawyer in town, Arnie Kinsella, for more than a year. He had commitment issues so bad that when Abigail Spaulding said something about the two of them getting married, Arnie passed out cold. . . ."

"He what?" Paul's expression was incredulous. "You've got to be kidding."

"It's true. Ask anybody. There were plenty of witnesses. He fell face first into his dinner at the Grill on the Green restaurant. Margot broke up with him after that, but it was a pretty public humiliation. You can see why she might be a little nervous about getting into another relationship, especially with another lawyer, until she is really sure of her feelings and yours. I think you just need to give it time, Paul. For now just be her friend. Spend some time getting to know her."

"That's what I've been trying to do! Tonight, for instance, I invited *both* of you out to dinner. I thought that would be more casual, you know? Less pressure on everybody."

"I know," I replied, nodding my approval. "And I'm sure if she hadn't had her quilt circle tonight, she'd have come. Ask her another time. What about that gig you were looking into for Thursday nights? Playing at the pub in Warren? Did you get it?"

"Yeah," he said. "Starts next week."

"So why don't you ask Margot to come hear you play?"

Paul lowered his head, practically glaring at me. "What makes you think she'd come all the way to Warren to go on a date with me? She wouldn't even let me give her a lift to the inn."

I rolled my eyes. "Oh my gosh! Will you quit being so pathetic? She didn't need a lift. She had her car.

"Anyway, don't think of it as a date; think of it as a friendly get-together. Less pressure. If you want, I'll come too. That way it won't feel so awkward. You've got to be persistent. And patient. Margot was rejected in a very public and embarrassing manner. It takes a while to get over something like that."

"Well. Maybe you're right," he said. "It's worth a try anyway. You're sure you don't mind coming along? It would make things easier, less tense."

"Of course I don't mind. I like jazz."

"Okay. Thanks," he said, sounding somewhat more hopeful. "You know, I don't know who this Kinsella guy is, but he must be crazy to have let Margot slip through his fingers like that. How could he have let her go?"

Paul leaned toward me, resting his forearms on the table. "She's so bright and funny and she's got this . . . I don't know, this innocence about her, but at the same time, she's incredibly smart. James is crazy about her. She's just so beautiful, inside and out. After what her parents pulled, you'd think she'd be furious, but she never says a word against them. I've never heard her say an unkind word about anybody. At first, I thought she was too good to be real, but I think Margot might be the most genuine person I've ever met.

"And beautiful!" he exclaimed. "Have you noticed the way her skin glows? And her eyes. I've never seen eyes quite that shade of blue. And . . ."

I listened as Paul went on, or at least I made every appearance of listening. It wasn't that I wasn't interested, only that I'd heard it all before. Paul was head over heels and, while it is sweet to see, after a while people in that condition can be pretty boring. But I understood. He had to talk about Margot. He couldn't help himself.

When I fell in love with Tim, I bored my family and friends with an endless litany of his virtues, good looks, personal history, plans for the future, and the repetition of every adorable thing he'd ever said to me. Once we were married and a little time had passed, I stopped telling everyone everything I could about my fabulous husband. Not because the passage of time made him any less fabulous in my eyes, but just because I learned to restrain myself.

Let him talk. He's in love, and that's not something that comes along very often. Most of us are lucky to find it even once in a life-time. I was.

I yawned. I didn't mean to, but it had been a long day.

Paul looked at his watch. "Sorry. I should let you go home."

"That's all right," I said, trying unsuccessfully to stifle another yawn. "I'm just a little worn out. Clementine woke me up at five this morning."

We got up from the table, saying thanks to Tony and giving him a wave as we headed to the door. "Hang on a minute. I left my jacket hanging on the coat rack by the restroom."

"Wait right here. I'll go get it."

Paul walked to the back of the restaurant and disappeared around a corner. At the same moment, a voice said, "Reverend Clarkson?"

I turned around and saw a man wearing black-framed glasses and waving. He was sitting at a table near the window, eating alone.

"Hi, Arnie," I said, walking toward him. "Do you always eat this late?"

He had obviously just been served. His steak was only missing one bite and his baked potato hadn't been touched.

"I was working late—working up some notes for Margot's case. It's a mess. Her dad is serving as his own attorney. He keeps asking for all kinds of motions and information and generally doing whatever he can to make things as difficult as possible. I don't know if he's doing it on purpose or by accident, but it amounts to the same thing. Don't suppose you'd care to join me, would you? I hate eat-ing alone."

"Thanks, but I've already had my dinner. But why are you eating alone? Word around town is that you've been seeing Kiera Granger."

Arnie made a wry face as he chewed a piece of steak. "Well, the word around town is a little behind the curve at the moment. Kiera and I broke it off."

"Oh. Sorry to hear that."

Arnie shrugged. "It's better this way. We're still friends."

First Margot; now Kiera. For a man with so many friends, Arnie Kinsella seemed to spend a lot of time by himself. I spotted Paul, returning with my coat draped over his arm, and motioned him to come over. "Have you two met?"

Arnie rose halfway from his chair and stuck out his hand. "Arnie Kinsella."

Paul bent down to grasp Arnie's hand. "Paul Collier, nice to meet you. I've heard a lot about you."

"Paul Collier..." Arnie mused, his face brightening when he made the connection. "Oh, right! You're the new guy at Baxter, Ferris, and Long, right? You work with Geoff Bench. A pleasure," he said and pumped Paul's hand before resuming his seat. "I imagine you heard about me from Geoff. The court assigned him as guardian ad litem for a custody case I'm working on."

Paul nodded. "Margot Matthews is your client," he said. "I know. She's a friend of mine."

Arnie raised his eyebrows. "Oh?"

"We've been volunteering together at the church, working with the junior high kids. Margot's a terrific lady."

"Absolutely," Arnie said, looking down at his plate as he loaded his fork with potato. "A little intense sometimes, but..."

"Intense?" I asked, feeling a prick of irritation. An exact transcript of the exchange would lead you to believe that Arnie's regard for Margot mirrored Paul's, but his casual, almost dismissive tone told the real story. "In what way? You mean intense in her faith?"

Arnie jerked his head up, as if surprised by my line of questioning and the bite in my voice. I was a bit surprised myself, I must admit. Margot is a friend, so it's natural that I'd spring to her defense, but I'm a minister first, and Arnie is a member of my congregation. You can't tell by looking at him, but I'm sure he has scars of his own. Everybody does. Why else would a man who hates being alone on a Friday night find it so hard to stay in a relationship?

The barest blush of pink flushed the top of Arnie's ears. He swallowed quickly. "No...I mean...yes. Margot is intense about her faith, but there's nothing wrong with that. I...I was thinking more about her relationships. She's very...well, she's just intense. That's all."

He looked toward Paul, hoping to find an ally. "Sounds like

you've spent a lot of time with her. I'm sure you know what I mean."

Paul narrowed his eyes and tilted his head to one side. "No," he said slowly, "can't say I do. I do know she's a woman in a million and that the man who won her heart would be the luckiest man in the world. And the one who let her get away? Well . . . I can't imagine anybody crazy enough to let that happen, not without a fight. But if somebody did, I'd sure feel sorry for him."

A quick smile creased Paul's face, as if he was suddenly surprised to realize how long he'd been going on, but that wasn't the case. Every word he'd uttered was absolutely intentional.

"Hey," he said affably, nodding toward Arnie's plate, "we're keeping you from your dinner. Sorry about that. It was nice to meet you, Arnie."

"You too." Arnie shook Paul's extended hand and began to rise from his chair.

"Enjoy your food," Paul said before walking away.

I had to follow Paul, but Arnie looked so forlorn. I felt bad for him. I reached out and touched him lightly on the shoulder.

"Good night, Arnie. See you on Sunday?"

He glanced up and his lips bowed into a robotic smile. "Sure."

Paul helped me on with my coat before opening the door, letting in a sharp blast of cold air. I glanced toward the back of the restaurant and saw Arnie sitting at the table, knife in one hand, fork in the other, eyes fixed on a distant wall, lost in his private thoughts.

❧ 32 ❧

Margot

Every day, either before work or after, I drive to the hospital, ride the elevator to pediatrics, check in with nurses, and walk down the yellow corridor with the bright mural of rainbow colors that curl like spools of unwound ribbons to room 322.

Olivia has had a score of different roommates since they moved her to the pediatric ward. Caleb, age nine, suffered bruises and a broken arm after falling off a bicycle. Emily, also nine, had an asthma flare-up. Lauren, age eleven, had emergency surgery to remove her appendix. And Michael, only four, who was here for a whole week, had broken ribs, and black eyes, and surgery on his wrist after a car accident.

Children come and go quickly in room 322, except Olivia. And all of them are happy to talk to me, except Olivia. Every day I sit by her bed, chattering away about what happened at the quilt shop or the church the day before, or about a funny show I saw on television, or about how I'm remodeling the spare room in my house into a bedroom with lilac painted walls and white ruffled curtains at the windows, or the quilt my friends and I are making to go on the bed, or how I've been thinking about going to the humane society and picking out a kitten, or anything else I can think of.

I talk to her about everything in the world, everything but the custody battle. She has enough uncertainty in her life without hearing about that mess. But she never says anything in response.

Sometimes I feel like an idiot, talking to myself day after day. She doesn't talk to my parents either. I heard that from one of the nurses, not from my parents. The only time they speak to me is during our occasional, unproductive mediation sessions, and then mostly to tell me how unfit I am to raise a child and how it's all my fault that Olivia won't talk, that if I hadn't insisted on telling her that Mari had died everything would be fine.

Well, I'm sorry, I don't want to be disrespectful, but that is just ridiculous. We had to tell her. Not telling her would have been a lie, and if we started off by lying, Olivia would never trust us, not ever. And maybe she still won't, but I have to believe that, eventually, there's hope. Isn't there?

That's why I keep coming here day after day, because Olivia needs me, even though she doesn't know it.

There was no one at the nurses' station when I arrived. Olivia's room was empty too. Logically, I knew there was no reason to panic; she's out of the woods now. But my heart raced as I walked quickly back down the hall, peeking into doors until I found a nurse who was putting a blood pressure cuff on a teenage boy.

"She's fine," the nurse said with a smile. "Hang on just a minute and I'll take you to her."

I followed her down the elevator to the second floor and to a large room with mirrors on the walls, mats on the floors, and rows of dumbbells sitting on racks—the physical therapy room. In the far corner stood a set of very low wooden and metal parallel bars, like gymnasts might use. A white-coated physical therapist stood behind, offering support and encouragement while Olivia, looking pale and nervous, gripped the bars tightly and limped slowly forward, so focused on the task that she didn't notice me enter the room.

I stood in the doorway with my fists clenched and pressed my lips together to keep from crying out as my niece moved inch by painful inch toward the end of the bars. When she finished, the therapist whooped with delight and scooped Olivia up in her arms before depositing my exhausted but smiling niece into a waiting wheelchair. Applauding, I ran across the room and knelt down next to her.

"Olivia! Oh, honey! That was amazing! You did it! You really did it!"

I looked up at the therapist, who was grinning from ear to ear. "When did the casts come off?"

"Just this morning. She's a little wobbly and weak still, but we'll build those muscles back up. If she keeps going like she started, we'll be able to discharge her soon."

"Discharge her? To where?"

The therapist, who obviously didn't know about our personal situation, looked confused. "Well . . . home. Once she can walk, there'll be no reason to keep her here any longer."

She smiled down and ruffled Olivia's hair. "Hospitals are for sick people, and you're not sick anymore, are you? I'm sure you'll be much happier once you get out of this place and back home."

Still kneeling, I turned and looked into Olivia's wide, solemn eyes. She said nothing, but her thoughts were easy to read. Where was her home now?

I wish I knew.

❧ 33 ❧

Margot

Arnie's office was a mess. I counted no less than four abandoned cups of cold coffee sitting in different spots around the room, not including the one he held clutched between his knees as he used both hands to riffle through a drawer in the gray metal filing cabinet. His desk was covered with papers, file folders, manila envelopes, pens, unopened mail, a section of a newspaper, and several photographs of the accident scene.

While Arnie continued his search, I quietly slid one of the manila envelopes over the pictures. I didn't need to see them—the skid marks on the road, the mangled guardrail, my sister's car lying on its side shrouded in snow and half-hidden by the branches of the fallen tree that had stopped it from sliding even farther down the embankment—all those images were burned in my mind. I didn't need pictures to remind me.

Arnie jerked his head up. "Don't touch anything! I have a system. I know where everything is."

Considering that he'd spent the better part of ten minutes searching for one file, I sort of doubted that, but I didn't say anything. Arnie gets a little crazed before a court date—partly because he's not nearly as organized as he thinks he is, but mostly because he cares so much. Olivia's impending discharge from the hospital has moved our court date higher on the docket and kicked Arnie into high gear. Until he is as prepared as he can possibly be, eating, sleeping, and putting on clean clothes will take a backseat to work. That's why he's such a good lawyer, a much better lawyer than he was a boyfriend. But, our unpleasant personal history aside, I'm glad to have Arnie on the case.

A stale, half-eaten sandwich with wilted lettuce and cheese so old it was starting to sweat and curl sat on top of one of the stacks of paper. I picked it up with two fingers and held it aloft. "Are you done with this?"

Arnie looked up distractedly, taking a moment to focus his gaze. "Um. Yeah. Throw it in the trash," he said and immediately returned to his task.

After another minute of silent searching, he pulled a sheet of paper out of a blue file folder and waved it over his head like a flag. "Ha! I knew it was in there!"

He closed the drawer with a triumphant slam and pushed his feet against the cabinet, propelling his rolling chair back to his desk. I took a seat in one of the chairs opposite.

"Is that the same shirt you were wearing when I was here yesterday?"

"Could be," he said absently, pulling his nose as he read.

"Didn't you go home last night?"

Eyes still fixed to the document, he held up his hand to stop my question. "Okay, here's the part I was looking for. Margot," he said, glancing up, "do you take antidepressants?"

"No," I said. "Never. Why do you ask?"

"You're sure? Because your parents say you do. Or at least that you did."

I frowned, wondering what in the world this could be about. "Wait a minute. A long time ago, at least ten years, I told my doctor that I wanted to lose some weight and he wrote me a prescription for Prozac. He said there had been studies showing it might help with weight loss and that it might be worth a try."

Arnie reached to the far side of his desk, grabbed a pen and legal pad, and made a few notes. "And you filled the prescription?"

"Yes," I said. "I only took it for about two weeks. It didn't help me lose weight and it made me feel kind of funny, so I stopped."

"And you never refilled the prescription?" I shook my head. Arnie made another note. "We're going to need to get a copy of those medical records. Hopefully, the doc took good notes."

I sunk back in my chair. Suddenly I felt very tired. "This is crazy. My parents are trying to make the judge think I suffer from depression? How could they do something like that?"

Arnie raised his head and stared at me. "Because they want to win. Margot, things get crazy in custody cases. Family law is one of the toughest areas of the law because you're not just dealing with contracts, or money, or facts; you're dealing with feelings and resentments, dashed hopes. All the emotional baggage that people drag through life comes to the fore in a custody battle. For what it's worth, this probably isn't about you, not in the way you're thinking. It's more about your parents' relationship with your sister. I don't think they want to hurt you, but for whatever reason, they've convinced themselves that they, and only they, are fit to raise Olivia and they are willing to do whatever it takes to make that happen."

"Even if it means destroying our relationship?"

"Apparently," Arnie mused, scanning another section of the document. He sighed wearily. "Margot, I know this is a ridiculous question, but I have to ask it: Have you ever been arrested?"

"Yes."

Arnie looked at me as if he'd never seen me before. "You have? When? For what?"

"During my sophomore year of college. I think the charge was unlawful assembly and disturbing the peace. There were protests on campus because the college had money invested with corporations that were doing business with South Africa, back before apartheid had been abolished. About eight hundred students gathered in front of the administration building to demand that the college divest itself of those investments. We didn't have a permit, so the university called the police. When they arrived, a lot of the kids ran off, but I sat down on the steps and wouldn't budge so they picked me up, put me in a squad car, and hauled me off to jail."

Arnie smiled and scratched the side of his face, which was looking a bit stubbly. Had he remembered to shave that morning?

"Huh. Were you scared?"

I laughed. "Petrified. Which is pretty silly, since I was only in there about three hours. The judge fined everybody twenty dollars or something and let us go."

"What did your parents say about it?"

"Oh, Dad was furious," I said. "He drove down to school so he could chew me out in person. Said he hadn't spent his whole life unclogging toilets and replacing pipe to give me the education he'd never had just so I could go to college and spend my time protesting. He said he'd sent me to college so I could get a husband, an education, and a job, in that order, and that I should quit worrying about things that were none of my business. He also said if I wanted to worry about investments, I should worry about the investment he'd made in me, which, at the moment, was looking like a bad one."

Arnie frowned. "He actually said that?"

"Word for word. I remember the conversation vividly. It was the only time I ever really talked back to my father. I told him that justice was everybody's business, that I didn't see how he could call himself a man of God and not be concerned about the oppressed and unfortunate of the world, and that if he thought I was such a bad investment then he could just keep his money, that I'd get a part-time job and figure out how to pay for college myself."

"Really? *You* said all that? To your father?" Arnie rested his elbows on his desk and clasped his hands together, interlacing his fingers. "This does not sound like the Margot I know."

I blushed. "Well. Maybe it was a little out of character for me. I really shouldn't have spoken to my father that way. That was rude and disrespectful. But," I said, lifting my chin, "I'm not sorry I took part in that protest. I'd do it again if I had the chance. After the protests, the college did divest itself of those investments. And a couple of years later, the government of South Africa ended apartheid, partly as a result of pressure from the international community. I'm not saying that our protest was the straw that broke the camel's back, but I'm sure it helped. I'm sure it was the right thing to do."

"It was," Arnie said. "I'm proud of you."

He picked up the document and added it to a stack of others, part of his own mysterious filing system. "Listen, don't worry about this. It's not going to cause you any troubles. If anything, it'll help. Your dad was foolish to raise the issue. It makes you look moral and him look vindictive. But we are going to have to get your medical records. Can you take care of that?"

"Sure," I answered, rising from my chair. "I'll fax a request to the doctor's office. Is there anything else you need me to do?"

Absorbed in scribbling more notes, Arnie didn't say anything, just shook his head.

"Well, let me know if you change your mind." I moved toward the door, picking up a couple of abandoned coffee cups along the way. Cleaning up a little was the least I could do. "Don't work too hard, all right? I know you need to be prepared for the hearing, but I'm worried about you. I bet you haven't had a decent meal in days."

Arnie stopped scribbling. "Not really. In fact . . . I was wondering . . . do you want to have dinner?"

"With you?" The question was pretty straightforward, but the way he delivered it, clearing his throat before getting the words out and shifting his eyes nervously when he finally did, confused me. He sounded a lot like a man who was asking for a date.

"Yes . . ." More throat clearing. "With me. If you want to. I mean, if you're not seeing anyone else."

If I wasn't seeing anyone else? He *was* asking for a date. Now I was really confused.

"I'm not seeing anyone, Arnie, but I don't think that would be a very good idea, not right now." Actually, I didn't think it would be a good idea ever—we'd already been down that road—but I didn't want to hurt his feelings. "You know, since we're working together on the case and everything. But can I drop off some dinner for you later? I made a meat loaf and scalloped potatoes yesterday, the kind you like, with the smoked cheddar. Why don't I bring you a plate?"

Arnie waved his hand dismissively and lowered his head, once again appearing to be absorbed in paperwork. "No, that's all right. Charlie called this morning, wondering why I wasn't at poker night. I told him I was busy with your case and he offered to send dinner over from the Grill. I'll give him a call later."

"Are you sure?" I bit my lip, feeling guilty. But what did he expect after all this time?

"Yeah, sure. Not a problem. It was just a whim, thought you might be hungry. You probably already have plans anyway, with Paul or something. . . ."

"Paul? Paul Collier? I didn't know you two knew each other. Why would you think I'd have plans with Paul?"

Arnie shrugged innocently. "No reason. I just saw him at the Bean the other day. I know you're friends, so I thought you might be having dinner with him. Or Philippa. She was there too."

"We are friends," I said, hefting the handle of my purse onto my shoulder. "Not that it is anyone's business, but that's all there is to it. Anyway, I do have plans. I'm going to spend some time getting my house ready for Geoff's home visit—assuming it ever happens."

"I was starting to wonder about that myself," Arnie said, his tone more relaxed now that the conversation had returned to safer ground.

"Do you know how many times he's canceled on me?" I held up three fingers. "But he'll have to do it soon. He's got to have his report filed with the judge before the hearing. I'll be so happy to have this over with and Geoff Bench out of my life."

"Maybe that's why he's been putting it off," Arnie said in a playfully knowing tone, "because he knows that once the report is filed and the case is closed, he won't have a reason to see you anymore. Maybe he has a crush on you; did you ever think of that?"

I rolled my eyes. "Yes, that's it. Because men up and down the eastern seaboard are pining with love for me. Married men especially."

He grinned and held up one hand, pinching a spare inch of air between his thumb and forefinger. "A crush," he said. "A little one. It could happen."

"Don't be ridiculous, Arnie." I turned the knob and opened the door. "Anyway, I'm spending my evening checking items off the list of things Philippa said I should do prior to Geoff's home visit next weekend. My first stop is the drugstore, to buy the biggest first aid kit I can find, then the hardware store to get a fire extinguisher. Then I'll head home to install child locks on medicine cabinets and the cupboard where I store the cleaning supplies. Sound like fun?" I quipped.

"Weird that he's making his home visit on a weekend."

"It's the only time he had open. He's got three cases coming up."

Arnie frowned. "Mmm," he said, nodding slowly, "I guess that makes sense. Although you'd think sometime in the last three months he could have found time to make one home visit." He started digging through a stack of papers and mumbled, "Some people are just disorganized, I guess."

I ducked my head to keep from laughing. "Hey," I said before leaving, "are you sure you don't want me to bring you some dinner?"

"No. Thank you. I'm going to call the Grill. I'm in the mood for duck confit. But it's nice of you to ask, Margot. You've always been a good friend to me."

"Why wouldn't I be? That's how we started out. Right?"

He smiled. "Right."

✑ 34 ✑

Margot

When I was halfway out the door, Arnie remembered that he needed to drop some papers off with Judge Treadlaw's clerk. I said I'd do it for him and met Paul coming up the courthouse steps as I was going down.

"Hey!" Paul exclaimed when he saw me. "I didn't know you were in court today."

"I'm not. Just dropping off some papers. Have you got a trial?"

"In about ten minutes." He looked at his watch and frowned. "Actually, more like seven. In front of Judge Treadlaw."

He raised his eyebrows slightly, just enough so I knew he had no more affection for the judge than I did.

"Listen," he said. "I was meaning to call you. I'm going to start playing with a jazz combo over at the Rooster Tail Tavern in Warren on Thursdays. We start this week so I . . . I was wondering if maybe you might want to come."

Paul cleared his throat. His eyes shifted from my face to a point near my left shoulder and then back. He looked nervous. It almost sounded as if he was asking me out on a date. Was I really being asked out twice in one day? And by two different men?

My pulse started to speed up, but I told myself to calm down. It wasn't possible. Probably he was asking everybody he knew to come hear him play. That's the deal in these local spots. The owners expect the band to bring in their own audience. Any band that doesn't won't keep the gig for very long. But it might be fun. Other than Fridays with the quilt circle, I hadn't been out in weeks.

"What time?" I asked, thinking about Thursday night. I always went to see Olivia after work, and Warren was at least a half hour drive.

"Seven to ten. I know it's a little out of the way," Paul said, "but it's a pretty drive. And you've never ridden in my car. Just got her out of the body shop; the new paint job looks great. I need to get there early to set up. Can I pick you up at five-thirty?"

Pick me up? He was asking me on a date! But what about Olivia? She still wasn't talking to me, but I knew she counted on seeing me every night. I had the sense that she was on the verge of opening up to me. I didn't want to risk losing ground with her. But I didn't want to risk losing out on an evening with Paul either.

My mind flashed back to that night outside the church, watching his car turn the corner, feeling like I wanted to run after him and tell him to stop.

"It sounds like fun. I'd like to come, but..." Paul's mouth, which had curved up into a smile when I started to speak, flattened to a line when he heard the beginning of my caveat. "I've got to go to the hospital first to see Olivia. I can drive myself, but I might not be there right at seven. Is that all right?"

"Sure! Absolutely!" he said, smiling again. He opened his mouth to say something else, but stopped short and looked at his watch again. "Argh. I'm late. Treadlaw is going to lecture me again. Sorry, but I've got to run."

"Go. I know what Judge Treadlaw is like when he's 'displeased.' See you Thursday."

"See you Thursday."

Paul bounded up the stairs two at a time. Pausing at the top step, he turned around and called down to me. "I'll leave your name with the hostess, so don't worry about the cover. I'm really glad you're coming," he said, then hurried inside.

He had planned on picking me up? And now he was leaving my name with the hostess?

No one was around to hear, but I covered my mouth with my hand to keep from squealing. I was going on a date with Paul Collier!

❦ 35 ❦

Margot

I felt silly pulling on pantyhose while perched on a toilet in the bathroom stall, but changing at the hospital would save me time. When I was dressed, I looked myself over in the mirror. The little black dress with the deep V-neckline and figure-forgiving ruching clung to my curves, and I wondered if I wasn't a little overdressed. After all, I was meeting Paul at the Rooster Tail Tavern, not the Oak Room at the Plaza.

I turned to see how the dress looked from the back, trying to decide if the heels were a mistake. The extra three inches made my legs look slimmer, and even with them on I'd still be shorter than Paul, but still . . . Maybe I should run home and change into something a little less . . . everything. I grabbed a paper towel from the dispenser, blotted my lipstick, and practically ran out the door, heels echoing on the ceramic tile, almost running into Michael Barzini and his respiratory therapy cart.

"Whoa!" he yelled, holding up his hands as if to ward off a blow. And then, lowering his arms, he looked me up and down. He said it again, "Whoa!" but in a completely different tone and with a totally different meaning.

"Margot! You're completely hot! Look at you. You've got a shape! Who knew?"

I blushed, partly from embarrassment, partly from pleasure, and partly from irritation that Michael had not noticed I had a shape before now. But Michael is a nice guy, and married to a nice woman, so I ventured to ask, "Do I look all right? It isn't too much?"

"Where are you going? On a date?"

I bit my lower lip and gave a quick nod. "First date. Out to the Rooster Tail to listen to some jazz. Really, you don't think I'm over-dressed?"

Michael shook his head. "Naw. You look great. A man likes it when a woman goes to the trouble to dress up for a date, especially a first date. Gives him confidence. Just one thing . . ." He reached out and yanked a tag off the sleeve of my dress.

I blushed even more deeply. How could I have forgotten to take off the price tag?

I groaned. "Maybe this is a bad idea."

"It'll be fine," Michael assured me. "You look great, better than great. You look beautiful."

"You really think so?"

He nodded. "Any guy who didn't would have to be blind in both eyes." He started pushing his cart down the hall, turning to call over his shoulder, "Good thing I'm an old married man or I'd give your new boyfriend a run for his money."

By the time I walked from my car across the snow-covered parking lot and into the lobby, I decided that, slim legs or no, the heels had been a mistake. My feet were freezing, and melting snow was squishing around in the toe of my shoe.

I hung my coat on the rack and gave my name to the hostess. She glanced down at a list. "Oh, yes. Here you are. Right this way," she said.

In the mid to late 1800s, the Rooster Tail was a place where people traveling by coach would stop for a fresh horse, or a meal, or the night. It's charming, the kind of spot city people picture when they want to get away for a romantic weekend in Connecticut. The dining room serves good, classic New England fare. The Pub Room, serving drinks and bar snacks, is small and dark and cozy. The low ceiling is striped by hand-hewn beams. There is a long mahogany bar on the back wall, a big river rock fireplace on the center of the opposite wall, and a small platform for the band to the left of that. I glanced around the room, but didn't spot anyone I knew. Apparently, I was Paul's only guest. That made me smile.

There was a fire roaring in the fireplace and votive candles glowing on all the tables. The band was playing "Misty." They sounded great, but as the hostess led me into the room, Paul, who had his eyes closed as he played the solo, opened them. His expression was the same one Michael Barzini wore when he saw me come out of the bathroom. His shoulders jerked and his saxophone gave off an uncharacteristic squeak. The drummer shot him a look, but Paul didn't seem to notice or care. The hostess walked me to an empty table near the fireplace. Paul's eyes smiled and followed me as he continued to play, the notes falling sweet and slow from the bell of his sax like honey dripping from the comb.

My feet were so cold I couldn't feel my toes, but the shoes, I decided, had not been a mistake.

When the set was finished, Paul put his saxophone on the stand and walked over to my table. He smiled, bent down, took my hand. I thought he was going to kiss me on the cheek, but instead he squeezed my hand before letting go and waving to a passing waitress.

"That was great," I said.

His eyes twinkled. "All except that part where I dinged the note on the solo. Kinda threw me when you came in."

"Sorry."

"Don't be," he said. "I'm not. It was nice of you to come all this way."

"I can't believe this is the first time you've played with this group."

"We've had a few rehearsals in the last couple of weeks but, yeah, I thought we did all right, considering. Of course, it's not like playing with the guys back in Chicago. We knew each other so well we could practically finish each other's sentences. And we'd been together so long we hardly had to rehearse. At least, that's what we told ourselves." He laughed.

The waitress arrived with a bowl of nuts, another glass of chardonnay for me, and a beer for Paul. He took a drink.

"I bet you miss your old friends," I said.

He nodded, his face serious again. "I do," he said. "But New Bern is growing on me. I like my new friends too." He smiled and popped a few peanuts in his mouth.

Over the last weeks, while working together on lessons and activities for the youth group, and at odd moments when we weren't busy herding the kids, I'd learned a good bit about Paul's history and shared a good bit of mine with him. But I was eager to know more, so I asked him about growing up in Chicago, how he'd met his friends, and why they'd decided to start a band—"To impress girls, of course!" Between sips of beer and spurts of laughter, he told me the story, but I really didn't hear him.

That is, I heard him, heard the sound of his voice, a deep and resonant hum, baritone, like notes from his sax, but I didn't really follow what he was saying. I was too focused on his eyes, the way they crinkled at the corners when he laughed, the way they seemed to laugh on their own without making a sound, his hair, how thick it was with just a little curl to it and how that one piece kept falling into his eyes, the way he pushed it back using his ring finger, only that one finger every time. I wanted to memorize him, every gesture and glance, pressing them into my mind like leaf rubbings in a scrapbook, souvenirs of a day so perfect and fine that you want a keepsake to remind you of it, in case it turns out to have been too perfect too last.

He talked for a long time, but I didn't mind. He could have talked all night, as far as I was concerned. Finally, he rolled his eyes and said, "What a bunch of dopes, right? My dad grounded me for two weeks, but he never ratted out my friends, never called their folks. He didn't have to. The guys showed up the next day with a mops, paint, and brushes. They had the whole living room repainted before Mom got back from Aunt Amy's. She never knew what happened.

"But what about you?" he asked. "What was it like growing up in Buffalo?"

"Cold."

He laughed. "I'll bet. But, seriously, did you and Mari ever get into . . ."

The drummer, the one who'd given him the nasty look, walked by our table and jerked his head toward the platform.

"Sorry," Paul said. "I didn't realize I'd been talking so long. I've got to get back to work. After the next set you can tell me the rest of your life story, okay?"

"Okay."

I smiled as he walked to the platform and picked up his sax, playing a quick scale to warm up. The keyboard player sat down and leaned toward the microphone, thanking everybody for sticking around, and said they were going to start off with "I Got It Bad (And That Ain't Good)."

Paul adjusted his neck strap and wet his lips. As the leader counted off, Paul's eyes darted to the back of the room and his face lit up. He grinned, winked, and started to play. I turned around to see who he'd been looking at.

Philippa spotted me, waved, and walked toward the table. Forcing a smile, I waved back and scooted my chair to the left, making room for her.

Not wanting to make my disappointment obvious, I stayed through most of the next set. But I felt silly sitting there, listening to the music, chatting with Philippa between songs, knowing that I had totally misread Paul's signals. He considered me a friend, one of many in his life. Unlike other men who had used the "let's be friends" line as an excuse to get out of our relationship and then never speak to me again, I felt Paul really wanted to cultivate a friendship with me. He wasn't the sort to play games with someone else's feelings.

But I couldn't be Paul's friend. I just couldn't. The feelings I had for him already surpassed the platonic, and as time went on, I knew those feelings would grow even stronger. I couldn't afford that kind of distraction right now. I'd have to go around being pathetic and getting my heart broken another day—heaven knows I always seem to find opportunities to do just that—but not now. Olivia is what matters now. I shouldn't have allowed myself to be distracted from that, not even for an evening. It's not worth it.

Though . . . as many times as I've had my heart broken, I've never felt anything close to what I feel when I'm with Paul. Other men I've known made me feel anxious and uncertain, stirred, but in the way that a thrown stone stirs up muddy water, making everything cloudy, unclear, and unsettled. I don't feel like that when I'm with Paul. When he speaks to me, he's completely present and so am I. His eyes never dart around the room, looking for someone more interesting. When I'm with him, whatever I've been worrying about melts into the background and becomes less pressing, as if I know everything will come out all right in the end. Paul makes me feel peaceful, happy, and significant. These are feelings I could get used to very easily, feelings that I will not be willing to share with the larger audience of Paul's other friends, however much I might like them, feelings that will not be satisfied by friendship alone.

Unless I put a stop to this right now.

When the keyboard player announced that they were going to finish up the set with "My Funny Valentine" and then come back after a short break, I grabbed my purse and started to get to my feet. Philippa took hold of my sleeve.

"Where are you going?"

"I've got to run. Early day tomorrow. Tell Paul I said good-bye and thanks for inviting me."

"But he'll be so disappointed. Can't you stay just a little while longer?"

I stood up. "Can't."

Paul saw me rise and frowned, but he was playing and couldn't stop or say anything. I smiled and gave a quick wave.

"But you'll see him tomorrow, right?" Philippa asked.

Youth group. I'd almost forgotten. With all my heart, I wished I could quit. This would be so much easier if I just never had to see Paul again, but unless he decided to leave town, there was no real chance of that happening. Besides, I'd made a commitment to Philippa and the kids. And if I suddenly quit, Paul would probably figure out why. I didn't want him to feel sorry for me or to endure any awkward conversations.

"Yes. Of course. I'll see him tomorrow."

36

Philippa

"Paul," I said, resting my forehead in my hand as I talked, "for the tenth time, I don't think you said anything wrong. She just had to be at work early the next day."

"But I told her I'd talk to her after the set. She didn't say anything about having to leave early."

I sighed. Paul is my friend. So is Margot. But I'm their pastor first and friend second. I wish I'd remembered that before I allowed myself to get into the middle of this.

"I just don't understand what happened," Paul said. "She seemed really interested, you know? I mean, she drove all that way and wore that amazing dress. She looked beautiful. Did you see her?"

"I did." Margot is always pretty, but she truly had looked beautiful that night, elegant, sophisticated, and yes, even a little sexy. "That's why I don't think you should be worried. She went to a lot of trouble to look good for you, so obviously, she's interested."

"Then why was she so distant at youth group on Friday?"

"Paul, she's got so much on her mind right now. Her court date is coming up. You, of all people, should know what that's like. She's probably feeling overwhelmed. Too, I still think she's a little gun-shy. I'm certain she has feelings for you, but maybe she's worried about things moving too fast."

"Or maybe, once she actually spent some time with me, she decided she didn't like me after all."

I held the phone in one hand and used the other to go through my e-mail, deleting the unimportant ones. "I think you just need to be patient. And quit thinking about it so much."

"I can't help it. Can't you talk to her for me?"

"No, Paul. I can't. I'm your minister, not your matchmaker."

The intercom rang. It was Sherry, telling me Reverend Tucker was on the line.

"Paul, I've got to run. Look, just keep doing what you're doing. Keep it light, keep it friendly. Be persistent, but don't push too hard. She'll come around in time."

"Yeah. Maybe you're right," he said, but he didn't sound convinced. We said our good-byes and I pressed the blinking light to pick up the second line.

"Is this a convenient time?" Reverend Tucker asked. "Sherry said you were on another call. I can call back later if that would be better for you."

I wedged the telephone between my shoulder and ear so I could use my hands to log out of the computer. During my weekly phone appointments with Bob Tucker, I prefer there be no distractions.

"No, this is fine. I've asked Sherry not to disturb me unless it's urgent. So, before we start in on my list of woes, how are you? How is the book coming along?"

"Bah. I'm no writer. The *book*," Bob said with a facetious emphasis, "is really just a study guide on the book of Acts. Ted Carney made it sound like a bigger project because he likes the idea of having a preacher who is published, also because he thought it'd make my sabbatical a little more palatable to the congregation. He doesn't want them to think I'm just sitting around doing nothing. But the word 'sabbatical,' you know, is a derivation of 'Sabbath.' It implies a period of complete rest. When the church hired me, my contract called for a three-month sabbatical every seven years."

"And how long have you been at the church?"

"Thirty-two years in New Bern. But, all told, I've been in ministry for forty-four years."

"And in that time, how many sabbaticals have you taken?" I smiled to myself, anticipating the answer.

"This is the first."

I laughed. "Well, you were due. Honestly, there are days when I feel ready for one myself. How did you manage it for so many years? And all on your own?"

"I had a heart attack." He said this in such a casual tone that I had to laugh. Bob joined in with that big throaty laugh that has so endeared him to the congregation.

"But, seriously," he continued, "New Bern has been a wonderful place to serve. I'm going out of my mind up here. Too much scenery. And too many doctors, all lecturing me about diet and exercise. What I wouldn't give for an order of short ribs from the Grill on the Green right now." He sighed wistfully. "But let's get back to you. I looked at your sermon. . . ."

I could hear the sounds of papers shuffling as Bob flipped through the pages. He is one of the kindest people I know, but I felt tense, waiting for his verdict. I picked up a pencil and started drawing a series of intersecting squares on a pad of paper, then added lines that turned them into cubes. I always doodle when I'm nervous.

"It's good," he said in a voice that wasn't entirely convincing. "You have a clear and logical mind, and a gift for finding the practical in the spiritual. But . . . you've got it all written out word for word. Don't you think you'd be better off using an outline?"

Bob Tucker was not the first person to mention this. My seminary professors suggested the same thing.

"I'm afraid I might leave something out if I use an outline. When I read the whole text, I can be sure I'm getting in every point I wanted to make."

"But if you're so tied to delivering your text exactly as written, might you be limiting God to *your* script?"

I saw his point, but the idea of speaking from an outline was a little scary. What if I looked down at the bullet points and drew a blank? What if I couldn't remember how they tied together or what I'd been thinking when I'd written them?

"It seems to me," Bob said, "that a written text has become a kind of security blanket for you. And I get that. It's hard not to feel exposed when you're standing at the front of the church with two hundred pairs of eyes on you. I'm convinced that pulpits were invented not to give preachers a place to put their sermon notes, but to give them something to hide behind.

"But did you ever consider that maybe you *should* feel exposed when you're preaching? That's when you need to be at your most honest and vulnerable, exposed in all your weakness, because that's the only way you'll be forced to rely on God's strength. See what I mean? Also, I think you're making this harder than it needs to be. It's important to be prepared, but I think you need to give up the reins and let God steer the wagon."

While Bob was talking, I wrote *Let Go* in big block letters and underlined it three times. Easy to write—hard to do.

"I preached that exact sermon about two weeks ago," I said. "Maybe I need to go back and read it again."

"Well, that's one of those lessons we all have to learn and relearn. Next time I need a review, you give me a nudge. Okay?"

"Okay."

He paused for a moment, and then cleared his throat. "Philippa, there is something else I wanted to speak to you about. I hope you won't think I'm stepping into your personal business, but I'd be remiss as a colleague, and a friend, if I pretended not to have noticed. . . ."

I held my breath, waiting for him to speak, and my hand moved to my stomach, covering the swelling of flesh beneath my black blouse. It was still so small, how could anyone know? Especially Bob Tucker? He was in a whole different state. Had someone from the church noticed my baby bulge and called him?

Maybe I should tell him. I'd planned to, but not for a couple of weeks. Maybe I should just beat him to the punch and get it over with.

"Bob, I think I know what—"

"No. Hear me out. And know that I understand exactly what you're up against."

He did?

"I was a preacher's kid too, you know. I see a lot of your dad in you, which is good. But . . . some of what I see doesn't seem natural to you, especially when it comes to your sermons. A number of the phrases, even the illustrations, seem more like something your dad would say than something you would say. I'm not saying that you're borrowing from his material but, subconsciously, you might be trying to emulate his style. Sometimes it's almost as if you're speaking in his voice."

The spirals I was making snaked from one corner of the paper to the other like tiny tornados, curling into smaller and tighter coils as I drew, pressing down so hard that my pencil lead snapped off.

"Your father is a good man and you can learn a lot from him, but you don't have to be him. You are in this church at this moment not because of who your dad is but because of who you are. God has called *you*, not your imitation of Philip Clarkson. Do you understand?"

I think Bob knew he'd hit a sore spot with me, but I don't know if he realized just how sore. Part of the reason I resisted the ministry for so long was because I thought people would measure me by my father's yardstick. Sometimes they did. But I've been using the same yardstick, and every time I do, I find myself coming up short.

I coughed, unable to speak for a moment. There was a knock on the door. Sherry peeked her head inside.

"Excuse me for a moment, Bob."

I lowered the telephone and covered the mouthpiece with my hand. "What's up, Sherry?"

"Sorry to disturb you," she said in an apologetic stage whisper, "but Sylvia Smitherton called from the hospital. An ambulance brought Waldo in." She shook her head. "It doesn't sound good."

The gray-haired Smitherton girls, along with their spouses, children, grandchildren, and even one infant-in-arms, a great-grandchild, were gathered around Waldo's bedside when I arrived.

The tableau was almost identical to the one I had seen last time Waldo was admitted to the hospital, just a few weeks previously, with murmurs and whispered prayers and muffled sobs as Waldo's three older daughters wept into their handkerchiefs. But when I saw that Sylvia, the most stoic of the sisters, was also red-eyed and sniffling, I knew that this time it was different. Waldo truly was dying.

Sylvia walked toward me and clasped my hand in hers. "Thank you for coming," she said, blinking back tears. "He's been in and out of consciousness, but I think it would be a comfort if you prayed with him." She choked out the words and pressed her clenched fist against her lips, fighting to keep her emotions in check.

"Forgive me," she said, regaining her composure. "We talked about this moment so many times, Dad and I. I really thought I was prepared. I didn't know it would be so hard."

Sylvia pulled a chair up to Waldo's bedside, then turned to her husband.

"George, could you ask everyone to go down to the waiting room for a little while? It's too crowded. Let's have just the four of us for now," she said, glancing toward her sisters, "while Reverend Clarkson is praying with Dad."

George herded the mass of relatives out the door and down the hall, patting Sylvia on the arm as he left. I sat down. The noise, or rather the lack of it, seemed to stir Waldo to consciousness. He opened his eyes and blinked. His lips were still, but his eyes smiled when he turned toward me. He reached his hand upward, clutching the oxygen mask with feeble fingers.

Sylvia, who was standing on the opposite side of the bed with her sisters crowded behind, leaned down. "What is it, Dad? Do you want me to take the mask off?"

Waldo nodded, but very slowly, his movements as measured and laborious as an ancient and wrinkled sea turtle moving deliberately away from the shore to the beckoning surf, inching forward, drawn irresistibly to that hidden world and the quicksilver freedom that lay beneath the waves.

Sylvia removed the mask and was rewarded with a grateful smile. He lifted his hand again, resting it on hers. "Good girl."

"Dad, Reverend Clarkson is here. You asked me to call her."

"I know." Still smiling, he turned toward me. "How are you, Reverend?"

"I'm fine, Waldo."

"Good," he murmured. "Good. You know, Waldo is a good name. My father was named Waldo and his father before that. If it's a boy, think about naming it Waldo. It's a good name." Waldo closed his eyes.

I was speechless. I didn't know what to say or do, but Sylvia seemed unperturbed by her father's remarks. She lifted her head to look at me across the white expanse of the sheet. "Pain medication," she mouthed. "He's been hallucinating."

Waldo opened his eyes again and turned toward me, as if he'd just remembered something. "Reverend?" he rasped.

"Yes, Waldo?"

"You still got that file? For my eulogy?"

"I do, Waldo. It's in my office."

"That's good," he said. "Give me a good send-off. I know you will. And help my girls when I'm gone. They can be sad if they want, but not for too long." He twisted his head toward Sylvia as he said this last. Sylvia nodded dutifully and her sisters with her.

Satisfied, he turned to me again. "I'm not afraid to go, you know. But, if you wouldn't mind, could you stay for a while, Reverend? Pray me out?"

"I will, Waldo. I'm right here."

∾ 37 ∾

Margot

"Wait!" Madelyn said as I was about to step off the porch of the inn. "I almost forgot. I've got leftover apple muffins. Hang on a second, I want to send some home with you."

"But you already gave me the quilt," I protested, lifting up the white shopping bag that contained the beautiful lilac quilt for Olivia's bedroom. "You don't have to give me muffins too."

"I didn't make the quilt," Madelyn said. "I just stitched the binding. Anyway, the muffins will go to waste if you don't take them." She scurried off to the kitchen before I could say anything else.

I stood on the porch, looking at the mess in Madelyn's yard. There were leaves and limbs everywhere. The hard winter had given way to a hard and rainy spring. There had been a huge storm the night before with lightning, pounding rain, and howling wind. I'd lost power for a few hours and so had most of the town. Several houses in the area had lost limbs and even whole trees. This was especially true on Oak Leaf Lane, which, true to its name, is lined on both curbs with big beautiful oaks.

I heard the sound of a chain saw and looked up to see Paul, head down, cutting up the trunk of a tree that was blocking a driveway. Not his driveway—a neighbor's. Paul's place was on the other side of the street and three houses down.

Madelyn returned with a foil package of leftover muffins. "Here you go," she said. "If there are too many for you, take them to Olivia. Bet she's sick of hospital food."

"Madelyn, who does that house belong to? Why is Paul Collier sawing up their tree?"

Madelyn made a pitying face and clucked her tongue. "Didn't you hear? Waldo Smitherton died last night."

"Oh, no. Really?" I asked, genuinely regretful and a bit surprised. Waldo was old and always talking about dying, but he was such a fixture in the town that I never quite believed it would happen. Until recently, he'd never even been sick—not so much as a cold. "How sad. New Bern won't be the same without him."

Madelyn nodded her agreement. "Waldo was quite a character, wasn't he? He and Paul had struck up something of a friendship. In fact, Paul was the one who came over to check on him a couple of days ago, saw he wasn't doing well, and called Waldo's daughter, who ended up calling the ambulance. I think Paul just decided to take care of the tree so the family wouldn't have to worry about it. They've got so much to deal with right now. Paul is really a good neighbor. And a very nice man."

"Yes. Yes, he is."

The noise from the saw was so loud that Paul probably couldn't hear anything, so I just kept my head down and walked to my car quickly, hoping he wouldn't notice me.

I almost made it.

"Hey! Hey, Margot!"

My hand was on the car door. For a moment I thought about getting in and driving off, pretending I hadn't heard him, but that wouldn't be nice. I took a deep breath, let it out, and reminded myself that giving into the temptation to spend time with Paul was not an option. I couldn't just be friends with Paul. I couldn't. But I could be friendly without being friends. It was just a matter of being polite and keeping my distance.

I pasted a smile on my face and turned around.

"Hi, Paul."

He was puffing. He'd run up the street to catch me.

"Did you hear about Waldo?"

"Madelyn just told me. So sad. It's nice of you to clean up his yard after the storm."

Paul shrugged. "Oh, well. Sylvia is pretty torn up. It's the least I could do. Waldo was a good guy, sharp for his age. We played cribbage a couple of times and he practically wiped up the floor with me."

I smiled in spite of myself. How many men busy raising a teenage son, volunteering at church, and starting a new job would take the time to check on an elderly neighbor, even play cribbage with him?

"Waldo was one of a kind," I said.

Paul bobbed his head, glanced down at his feet and then up at me. Poor thing. It looked like he was really choked up over Waldo's death.

"Say, James has been making noise about checking out that laser tag place in Torrington. It'd be more fun with more people, so I was thinking, maybe you and Philippa could come along. We could play a couple of games, maybe get a pizza after? What do you say?"

"Sounds like fun, but I'm really busy getting ready for the trial. And I have this knee injury. . . ."

It was sort of true. I had injured my knee back in college, playing soccer. It hasn't been a problem for years, but Paul didn't have to know that. Still, I felt a little guilty about deceiving him.

"I just don't think it would be a good idea," I said.

That part was the absolute truth.

❧ 38 ❧

Philippa

"Clem. You're getting drool on the fabric."

I gave Clementine a firm but gentle shove—a nudge is completely ineffective when your dog wrestles in a higher weight class than you—and moved her big head and paws off my lap. She gave a throaty groan and looked up at me with a pitiful expression before laying her head on the sofa, wedging her big body as close to me as possible.

"I know," I said. "Life is hard. But you're just not a lap dog, Clemmie."

She groaned again, sputtered a sigh, and closed her eyes. I reached over and scratched her on the head before returning to my work.

This has become part of our nighttime routine. After finishing my deskwork, I sit down on the sofa in front of the fire and Clemmie climbs up next to me and sleeps while I work on the baby quilt. It's a relaxing ritual. I like having that precious few minutes, to unwind and think my own thoughts, mostly thoughts about the baby.

When I sit here in this room, silent except for Clementine's heavy breathing, and stitch the block of the week, I feel completely connected to the invisible life that is growing inside me. I make up lists of possible names, mentally conjure a little face with Tim's eyes and my nose, or vice versa, and imagine tiny hands and feet, dimpled arms and chubby legs, so filled with gratitude that sometimes it makes me cry.

But sometimes I worry as well, about what happens after the baby is born and what that will mean for my future in ministry. How many churches will be willing to hire an unmarried female minister with a newborn? Will motherhood mean postponing, or even re-scinding, my call to ministry? I hope not. These last months, work-ing in this community, have only sharpened my desire to minister. But it's all in God's hands and so, most of the time, I'm content to leave it there.

And when I'm not, I've noticed that working on this quilt helps to keep my worries at bay. It takes a long time to sew a quilt block by hand, to make tiny stitches that will stay tight and secure for years to come, a lifetime even. It's not something you can rush. And I've also noticed that even though you start with a pattern, you never really know how the block will turn out until it's finished. When you're faced with a pile of scraps it can be hard to see how it's all going to come together, how each patch will fit with the others and how the colors and patterns will play against one another. Of course, now and then you've got to go back, rip out a seam, and try again—what Virginia calls "unsewing." But, more often than not, everything turns out better than you could have imagined.

When I finish a block and hold it up, everything looks so right together, the connections so obvious, that I wonder why I wasn't able to see it from the beginning. But when I start on the next block I find that I'm just as confounded as I was the time before. It's a process, I guess. You can't rush it, so you might as well enjoy it.

And I am enjoying it, so much. I love making this little quilt and thinking about wrapping my baby up in it, safe and warm, bundling my little one inside this colorful cocoon. And I enjoy getting to know the women in my quilt class, listening to them talk about their stories, taking careful mental notes as they discuss pregnancy, child-birth, and child rearing. I've learned quite a bit about babies from the books I've been reading, but not nearly as much as I've learned from listening to these mothers and mothers-to-be talk amongst themselves. And I've enjoyed having two hours when I don't have to be Reverend Clarkson. Sometimes it's refreshing to take a break from being the woman who is supposed to have all the answers and just be one of the girls.

I won't be able to go to class tomorrow, though. I'll be conducting Waldo's funeral. There's going to be a big turnout. A dozen or more floral arrangements have already been delivered directly to the church, and there are three times that many at the funeral parlor. I was there earlier in the evening, for the viewing. The daughters are bearing up pretty well. I think the flowers were a comfort to them. It's nice to have a visible symbol of how much their father was loved. And he certainly was. I'm going to miss Waldo. Besides Margot, Waldo was the first friend I made in New Bern.

I've spent a lot of time on my talk for the funeral, working out every little phrase and nuance. I even practiced in front of the mirror, trying to force myself to look up more often. I figured it was worth a try. I owe it to Waldo.

It's probably just as well that I'm going to miss class tomorrow. This is the first chance I've had to work on my quilt since Waldo's death, so I'm behind. Hopefully, I'll catch up by next week. As I came to the end of a seam, doing a little backstitch to secure the seam instead of tying a knot, thus helping the block lie flatter, just like Virginia had taught me, the phone rang.

I sighed. It was after ten. I'm used to getting calls at all hours, but I'd really hoped that tonight would be quiet. Clementine grunted as I got up from the sofa, opening one eye, then immediately stretching out and claiming the unoccupied real estate as her own.

"Don't get too comfortable there. I'll be back. I hope."

I laid the partially stitched quilt block on the desk, out of drooling distance for Clem, and picked up the phone. "Parsonage. This is Reverend Clarkson."

"Bob Tucker here. Hope I'm not calling too late, but I figured you'd be at the funeral parlor. How was the viewing?"

"Nice. Big turnout and I'm sure the church will be packed tomorrow."

"Sharon and I are sending flowers. I sure wish I could be there."

"I wish you could too. You've known Waldo for more than thirty years; I've known him for three months. You're the one who should be speaking."

"Remember what we talked about—just keep it simple, be yourself, and let go of the reins. If you do that, everything will be fine. You'll see."

I murmured something noncommittal, thinking about the eighteen double-spaced typewritten pages, the text I'd been writing and rewriting during every spare moment of the last three days, that were sitting on my desk at that very moment.

"Listen," I continued, "I'm glad you called. Franklin Spaulding called me yesterday. He wrote Waldo's will. It seems Waldo left a bequest to the church, seventy-five thousand dollars."

"Really?" Bob sounded surprised.

Waldo was far from being a pauper, but I had no idea he had that kind of money put away. Apparently, neither did Bob Tucker.

"Do Sylvia and the girls know about this? I'd hate for the church to be the cause of any family squabbles."

"Sylvia told me that if that's what Waldo wanted, then the family had no problem with it. The other daughters were there when she said it, and they all agreed."

"Well. Isn't that something?" Bob paused a moment, as if he were still trying to take it in. "I'm not surprised he remembered the church in his will; Waldo was always a generous soul. But seventy-five thousand? We could do a lot with that. . . ."

"Which is what I wanted to talk to you about. Waldo didn't leave any instructions about how the money was to be used. What do you want to spend it on? Building? Programs? Benevolence? Community outreach?"

"It's not for me to decide. You'll want to bring it up at the next board meeting."

"I don't think it can wait that long. Somehow the word has gotten out. Members of the board have been calling to voice their opinions on the matter and—"

"Let me guess," Bob said. "You got ten calls and ten different opinions."

"Actually only nine calls, but you have it about right. What should I do?"

"Huh." I heard a sound of air being sucked in through teeth as Bob considered the question. "Well, I think we need to be careful here. A gift of that size can be a blessing, but if people start arguing about how we should use it, it could turn out to be a curse. We need to get everybody on the same page. This might be too big an issue to leave up to the board. What you should do is call up Ted Carney and suggest he call a church-wide meeting to discuss the options and take a vote."

The mere mention of Ted Carney's name made a knot form in my stomach. Thanks to Bob, our relations were somewhat improved, but Ted had yet to get behind a single idea I proposed, not unless the rest of the board outvoted him, which they had on more than one occasion. This did nothing to improve Ted's attitude toward me.

"I agree, but I don't think I should be the one to call Ted and suggest it."

"Philippa, we've talked about things like this before. I know your relations with Ted have been a little rocky, but . . ."

"Bob. This isn't a case of me avoiding a person I find difficult. If I propose the idea of the meeting, Ted is going to shoot it down. The call has to come from you. Please, you've got to trust me on this."

Another brief silence. "All right. If you feel that strongly about it, I'll give him a call tomorrow."

"Thanks."

When I returned to the living room, Clementine was no longer sacked out on the couch. She was at the far end of the room with both big paws on the top of my desk and her jaws working, drool dripping from her muzzle, as she chewed something.

"No!" I shouted. "Not my quilt! Down, Clemmie! Down! Bad girl!"

Clementine, startled by the noise, spun around and immediately dropped to the floor, looking very guilty even while she continued chewing. I sprinted to the back of the room, hoping to pry her big jaws loose and rescue the quilt block, but saw that the whole stack of blocks was sitting untouched on the corner of the desk, right where I'd left them.

What was left of Waldo's eulogy, the parts that Clementine hadn't consumed, was lying on the floor, ripped to shreds and covered with dog spit. I crouched down on my haunches and held my hand under Clementine's jowly jaws.

"Open," I commanded. She complied, letting a big wad of paper pulp and dog drool drop into my palm.

"Thank you. I'm not going to say you're a good girl because you really shouldn't be on my desk for any reason. Never again, okay? But just this once, you may have had a pretty good idea." Clementine's ears twitched and she lowered her head onto her paws.

I looked heavenward. "Or somebody did. Either way, I get the message."

❧ 39 ❧

Margot

The members of the Ladies in Waiting baby quilt class were right on time. That's not to say that the class started on time, only that everybody was actually in the shop by ten o'clock. These women, except Philippa, are expecting, and half of them have other children at home—this baby will be Jessica Gunn's fifth—so Virginia gives them a little extra time to get to class and get settled.

Colleen Murphy and Deb Funkhauser were the first to arrive, breaking into peals of laughter as they tried to come through the door together and ended up bumping bellies. Those two are so funny. They're expecting their first babies, one boy and one girl, in the same week in May. They'd never met before this class, but now they're practically joined at the hip, joking about how they're going to have their children betrothed from birth, a sure way to guarantee they like their future in-laws.

When Natalie Sorenson came in, with the handle of a car seat that held seven-month-old Celia looped over her arm, carrying two diaper bags and a project bag over her right shoulder and one of those designer purses that look like something a Pony Express rider would sling over the back of a horse on her left, I ran over to help.

"Thanks," she murmured gratefully as she took off a large pair of designer sunglasses and dumped her bags on a nearby table.

The purse, the glasses, and her cashmere sweater are remnants of Natalie's life P.C.—Pre-Celia, as she calls it—when she was a buyer for a big department store. She had intended to go back to work when Celia was six months old, but this new little "surprise" changed her plans. She doesn't seem bothered by the course correction, though I did hear her offer some advice to the other moms last week: "You know that old wives' tale about how you can't get pregnant when you're breast-feeding? Don't believe it."

Summer Sharp, a freelance writer, who was five months along and mother to Roger, who just started preschool, was next, followed by Jane Weissman, six months pregnant with her first child, and Antoinette DeClerc, who had a twelve-year-old son, Randall, had recently remarried and was expecting a little girl in June. Jessica Gunn, as usual, brought up the rear.

"Jessica, you're on time!" Virginia exclaimed.

"I know!" Jessica said, sounding as surprised by this development as Virginia was. "The twins are sick. I wasn't going to come, but my mother-in-law came to the rescue. Being punctual is easy when you don't have to wrestle two little tornados into their car seats."

Jessica's two oldest, Walt and Emerson, are in kindergarten and first grade, so they never come to class, but the twins, Brian and Michael, are just three. They're cute little boys, but definitely a handful. Jessica doesn't know the sex of this new baby, due in six weeks, but she's hoping for a girl.

I bent down to unbuckle the baby from her car seat. "I guess it's just you and me today, Celia." I picked her up and settled her on my hip. She gave me a gummy grin, cooed, and started grabbing at my charm bracelet. "Maybe we can just stay down here this morning. You can help me fold fat quarters. Doesn't that sound like fun?"

Normally, I take the children upstairs to the workroom to play while the mommies take their class. It's a nice break for the mothers and, I think, one of the reasons this class instantly fills whenever Virginia runs it.

"Do you mind, Natalie?"

Natalie, who was pulling fabric out of her project bag, shook her head. "Fine with me. The baby carrier is in the blue diaper bag if you want it. Then your hands will be free while you fold."

Natalie has more and fancier baby equipment than any mother who's ever taken this class. It seems like overkill sometimes, but the baby carrier did come in handy. Virginia helped buckle the safety belt around my waist while I slipped Celia into the carrier and put my arms through the straps. The baby faced me, her head crowned by a wispy halo of dark curls, riding close to my body, contented as a baby kangaroo in her mother's pouch. Celia reached for my silver heart necklace and began happily chewing on it. I looked a question at Natalie, wondering if she thought this was a good idea, but she waved me off.

"It's fine. It's Tiffany, I can tell," she said, as if all sanitary concerns were made moot by the reputation of the jeweler.

Celia continued gnawing on my necklace and I took a pile of fabric that Ivy had cut into fat quarters, those twenty-two-by-eighteen-inch rectangles that quilters collect by the boatload, and began folding them into tidy packets that would later be grouped into collections of complementary colors, tied with a ribbon, and displayed in baskets or stacked on shelves. Folding fat quarters is part of the job description of every Cobbled Court Quilts employee. They fly out the door so quickly we can barely keep up.

Telling the women to gather round and watch carefully, Virginia gave a brief demonstration on how to perfectly join the points on their blocks and then how to "spin" the center seam, carefully removing a couple of vertical stitches on the back of the block so it would press flat when finished. The ladies were absolutely silent as they watched Virginia work, grouped around her like chicks around a hen, their eyes bright with interest, craning their necks to get a better view.

Though Virginia is the first person to remind people that quilting is supposed to be fun, when she is teaching, she's all business. She expects her students to pay attention and stay on task, but she also cares deeply about them, and they know that. This is the third time we've run this class. In each of the previous sessions, at least one of the mothers decided to name her baby Virginia. I bet the same thing will happen this time.

Sometimes I like to think of myself being as old as Virginia is now, still working in the quilt shop and meeting all kinds of Virginias whose mothers named them after their old quilting teacher and who grew up to be quilters themselves. Wouldn't that be a fine legacy to leave?

When she was done, Virginia carried her work to the ironing board, her pupils trailing behind, gave the block a quick press, and held it aloft. "See? Flat as a Kansas prairie. Remember what I said about taking out those vertical stitches. Remove two. No more, no less." Virginia squinted through her thick glasses and stuck out her index finger, pointing at the circle of attentive faces. "The only bumps I want to see in this room today are baby bumps. Understand?"

The ladies nodded.

"Good. Well, go on," she said, shooing them back to the table. "I'll come around and check on you in a little while. Summer, come with me and I'll help you pick out a border fabric."

With the demonstration complete, the students returned to quilting—and talking. Quilters are fairly social animals, but our mothers' groups are more social than most. Jessica, who was still unpacking her project bag, lifted her head and looked around the room, suddenly realizing that there was one empty spot at the table. "Where's Philippa?"

"Preaching at a funeral," I answered. "Waldo Smitherton died."

"I heard about that," Natalie said, pausing for a moment while she threaded her needle. "He had pneumonia last month and recovered, but it damaged his heart. He was almost ninety-seven and still sharp as a tack. Isn't that amazing?" she asked, then continued without waiting for a response. "He left the church a hundred thousand dollars in his will."

"Seventy-five," I said without thinking, then pressed my lips together. I shouldn't be talking about the bequest with anyone not on the board. Ted asked us not to. Not that there seemed to be much point in trying to keep the secret. Natalie knew everything, and she doesn't even go to our church.

"Seventy-five," Natalie said, correcting herself. "I heard there's a big disagreement about how the money should be spent."

I knew I should stay out of this conversation, but I couldn't just sit there and do nothing while Natalie stirred up rumors. "Not really," I said, tying a length of blue ribbon around a stack of green fat quarters. "It just hasn't been decided yet. I only found out about Waldo's will yesterday, and I'm on the board. How did you hear about this so quickly, Natalie?"

She shrugged, stopping a moment to examine the seam she was stitching. "Oh, well, people talk. You know."

People do talk; Natalie certainly did.

"Well, I'm sorry to hear about Mr. Smitherton," Jessica said. "Sylvia was my fourth-grade teacher. She used to teach us geography by telling all about her parents' travels. Every year, Mr. and Mrs. Smitherton would fly off to some exotic location and send postcards to the fourth grade. We'd pin the postcards on a big world map and when they got back the Smithertons would visit the class and show slides from all the places they'd been. The year my brother was a fourth grader it was Japan. The Smithertons brought everybody a pair of chopsticks and a box of those sticky candies wrapped in clear rice paper that melts when you put them in your mouth. In my year it was India and Nepal. The Smithertons brought us bottles of Fanta orange—they said everybody in India drank it—and tiny animals carved out of sandalwood. Mine was an elephant. I think I still have it somewhere."

Jessica picked up a pair of scissors and trimmed a seam, frowning. "I wish I'd known about the funeral," she said. "I'll have to send a card to Sylvia. And maybe make a contribution or something. Is there a memorial fund?" she asked, looking in my direction.

"Yes, to benefit paralyzed veterans. I was planning on making a donation myself." Like Jessica, I would have liked to attend the funeral, but I'd already missed so much work since Olivia's illness that I wouldn't have felt right about asking for the morning off. "Philippa has the details. You can call the church later and ask."

Colleen, who was sticking her tongue out the side of her mouth

232 • *Marie Bostwick*

as she searched for the right place to join her points, pierced her needle through the fabric layers and said, "Philippa will be back next week, won't she? It's our last class."

"I think so. Barring any unforeseen emergencies."

"You know," she said thoughtfully, pulling her needle and thread through the other side of the block, "I've really gotten to like her. It was weird at first, having a minister in the class, especially since she wasn't pregnant."

"This was the only beginners' class that would work with her schedule," I said.

"Maybe," Colleen said. "But I don't think that's all there was to it. The way she's always asking questions about our pregnancies and our kids, it's obvious she wants some of her own. So sad that she never will."

Antoinette, who was still cutting out the pieces for her quilt block, put down her scissors and frowned. "Why do you say that? Because of her age? I'm forty-four, and I didn't need fertility treatments or anything. Ray and I just did what comes naturally and— voilà!" She put both hands on her swollen belly and smiled.

"True," Colleen said in a conciliatory voice, "but most women over forty do have a harder time getting pregnant. At least it takes longer. And you've got Ray. Philippa's not married."

Natalie, a knowing expression on her face, said, "Well, I think she has something else in mind. Word around town is that she and Paul Collier have been seeing a lot of each other and that their favorite rendezvous spot is the back booth at the Blue Bean."

Heads that had been bent over their sewing popped up to look at Natalie, who was looking very pleased with herself. A murmur of interest went through the room. The back booth? Everyone knew what *that* meant.

I turned my back, but couldn't stop from rolling my eyes. This was obviously the same rumor that Wendy Perkins had been spreading around, and now Natalie was going to spread it even farther.

"Really?" Colleen asked, in a shocked but clearly intrigued tone. "The minister and Paul Collier? You don't really think . . ."

"No," Natalie said. "Not that. Well . . . probably not. You never know. But more likely Philippa is hoping to get a proposal before her time is up in New Bern, followed quickly by a wedding and baby. Think about it," she said, spreading her hands in a gesture that dared anyone to defy the logic of her argument. "It all adds up. Why else would an unmarried, un-pregnant minister join a class for expectant mothers? Because she's hoping to join the club before long and wants to pick up a few pointers."

The women were quiet for a moment, considering Natalie's theory. Natalie sounded convinced and, I hated to admit, convincing. I don't like gossip, but as I thought things over, her explanation seemed . . . plausible.

I tossed the folded and beribboned fat quarter collections in a display basket and quietly began piling up the remaining fabric.

"Or," Jessica said slowly, raising her eyebrows and drawing out the word, "maybe she joined the class hoping that all this obvious fertility would kind of rub off on her. If so, she really ought to sit next to me. I can use Gary's toothbrush and end up pregnant."

The women chuckled. Jessica looked down at the mound of her stomach and shook her head. "If this is another boy, I swear I'm going to give up brushing my teeth permanently."

"That'd work," Antoinette said. "It'd sure keep Gary out of striking distance."

The chuckles gave way to laughter and noisy hooting, so noisy that I was nearly at the stairs before anyone noticed I'd picked up my pile of unfolded fabric and walked away.

Natalie called across the room. "Hey, where are you going? We didn't say anything to offend you, did we?"

"No, no," I said, glancing down at the curly head below mine, lolling to the left, eyes closed, with my necklace still clutched in her chubby fingers. "I don't want to wake Celia. I'll go finish in the workroom, where it's quieter. I've got a lot to do."

And I wanted to do it far from the chatter of female gossip.

∾ 40 ∾

Philippa

Cynthia Smitherton Reese, the oldest of the four sisters, and the largest, wrapped her arms around me and gave me a huge, breath-stopping hug.

"It was a beautiful service. I am . . . we're all so touched that so many people came to Dad's funeral," she said when she released me, smiling through a film of tears and looking around the fellowship hall, which was filled with people for the post-funeral luncheon. Every seat at every table was filled with people who were talking and smiling, sometimes laughing, telling and retelling Waldo stories.

"It's such a comfort to know that so many others cared about him like we did, but your sermon . . ." She made a single "tsk" noise, sighed and, still smiling, slowly shook her head, as if she simply couldn't find words.

"It was lovely," Sylvia said, filling in the gap for her sister. "Really lovely. Maybe I shouldn't say this, Reverend, but I was a little disappointed when I realized that you'd be conducting the service instead of Reverend Tucker."

"I don't blame you," I said. "Reverend Tucker knew your dad so well."

"True. But I don't think he could have done it any better than you did. It was obvious that you really spent time with Dad," Cynthia said. "You know, younger people often don't bother getting to know older people. It's as if, once you hit retirement age, they think you no longer have anything interesting to offer. Once I retired from the station, people I met would barely talk to me, and when they did it was only to ask how many grandchildren I had." She puffed indignantly.

"I love my grandchildren as much as the next person, but for heaven's sake, that's not all there is to me! But suddenly people started to look right through me, as if I couldn't possibly have any opinions. I produced the news at channel eight for twenty-three years! Opinions were my business! And I'll tell you something else . . ."

Rose, the next oldest of the sisters, a retired children's librarian who was the polar opposite of her elder sibling, as petite as Cynthia was full-figured and as soft-spoken as Cynthia was opinionated, grabbed her sister's hand. "I think what Cynthia was meaning to say is that we really appreciate the time you spent with Dad."

"It was my pleasure. He truly was one of the most interesting men I've ever met."

"You captured him to a tee," said Gloria, the third sister, a hand-some and stylish woman who owned a jewelry store and wore a stunning sapphire brooch that advertised the fact. "I know that he left you that big file with all his clippings and such for you to work with, but you really captured the essence of his personality and his faith." Gloria wiped away a tear.

Rose murmured comfortingly and put her arm around her sister's shoulders.

"No, no. These are good tears. Think how lucky we all were," Gloria said, scanning the circle of her sisters' faces, "to grow up with such a wonderful father."

"He was so proud of all of you," I said, and it was true. In looks, temperament, and interests, Waldo's daughters were about as differ-ent as any four women could be, and yet they were all accomplished, gracious, and caring. Waldo spoke of them often, delighting in their differences even as he worried about them and how they would react to his death.

He asked me once, "Do you think it's possible to love children too much? The girls and I have always been so close, and even closer after Rachel passed. They took her death very hard, you know, but Gloria was the worst. Took years for her to get over it. I don't want them to grieve like that when I'm gone. Tell them I've had a good life, no regrets, and that we'll be together again. Make them understand, Philippa. It's important."

Searching the faces of the four, seeing smiles through tears, I could tell that they did understand, but I knew it wasn't because of any superior effort or gifted turn of phrase on my part. All I did was stand up and say what I knew to be true.

One by one, the Smitherton sisters hugged me and thanked me. I didn't tell them they were welcome, knowing the gift had not been mine to give. Instead, I said how happy I was to have had the chance to know their father and now to know them. We all cried a little but, as Gloria said, they were good tears.

Cynthia looked as if she might be coming in for another hug, but Sylvia took her by the arm. "We should go greet everyone, Cyn. They'll all be ready to leave after they finish eating. Let's divide into teams. Cynthia and Rose, take the right side of the room. Gloria and I will take the left."

She spread her arms out behind Gloria's and Cynthia's shoulders, gently shepherding them across the room. I stood watching them for a moment. Gloria and Sylvia didn't even get to their side of the hall before an older couple, together with a younger man who might have been their son, got up to meet them, anxious to share some anecdote about Waldo. Gloria and Sylvia listened earnestly for a moment until the older gentleman, with a twinkle in his eyes, delivered what must have been the punch line, because Sylvia grinned and Gloria threw back her head and laughed.

Good. Very good.

Just then the baby, in the form of a ravenous hunger, made its presence known. I went to one of the long banquet tables and loaded my plate with sliced turkey and ham, potato salad, corn salad, cole slaw, baked beans, two rolls, and six pats of butter. The brownies and lemon bars looked good too, but there was no more room on my plate. I headed for one of the few vacant spots at one of the tables that the ladies of the hospitality committee had decorated with white cloths and vases of daffodils. But before I could reach my destination, I felt a finger poking my shoulder. It belonged to Ted Carney.

"I don't want to keep you from your lunch, Reverend, but..." He looked down at my overflowing plate and lost his train of thought. "You must really be hungry."

"Oh. Well, preaching burns up a lot of energy. As much as running six miles, some people say."

"Really? I never knew that. Anyway," he said, shifting his eyes left and right and lowering his voice to make sure no one could overhear him, "I wanted to talk to you about Waldo's will, the bequest he left the church, bless him. It's a pretty substantial sum and will certainly allow us to cross a few items off our wish list, but it won't take care of everything. We're going to have to make some choices, and I think we need to be very careful about how we go about doing that."

"I couldn't agree more," I said, working hard to shut out the enticing, salty-sweet aroma of ham and baked beans and focus on the conversation.

Ted nodded earnestly. "A thing like this can be a blessing or a curse, depending on how we handle it. It's so important that, as a church, we reach a consensus on what to do with the money."

"Absolutely."

Ted smiled. I pinched off a tiny piece of roll and nibbled it while he talked.

"Good. Now what I propose is that we call a meeting of the whole church to present some options, open the floor to discussion, and take a vote. We need to get everyone on the same page."

I swallowed, listening to him repeat Bob Tucker's words as if they were his own. "A very wise suggestion, Ted. How can I help?"

"Perhaps you could draft a letter to the congregation that we could both sign—show of solidarity, you know. And we should get a date on the calendar for the meeting right away. The quicker the better. You know how out of hand these things can get if people start talking."

"I can draft a letter first thing tomorrow. Or even this afternoon if you'd like."

"Tomorrow is fine," he assured me. "You've had a busy day, a busy week really. And you handled it all so well. I mean that. The service was wonderful, so was the eulogy. Very moving. Gave me a few things to think about myself."

"Waldo was a good man."

"He was, bless him. And he'd have been pleased with today. Well done, Reverend." He smiled and moved as if to shake my hand but, realizing they were both occupied holding the heaping plate, he laughed.

Looking up, he spotted Miranda talking to Cynthia and Rose on the opposite side of the room and walked quickly away. "I should say hello to the Smitherton girls. Enjoy your lunch!"

I did. Very much.

❦ 41 ❦

Margot

The walls of the workroom, like all the exterior walls in the quilt shop, are exposed red brick, but you notice it more up here, maybe because the light that streams in from the two tall, wood-framed windows makes it more noticeable. It's such a plain space—four walls, two windows, a few quilts hanging from wooden rods, a honey-colored wood floor, and a painted black door with a brass knob. That door is solid. When you shut it, you shut out the noise of the world as well. That's why this is my favorite room in the shop.

I don't like gossip, I never have, but as I sat in that quiet room with the sun streaming onto the table, casting a beam of light that intensified the colors of the fabrics, folded each length into tidy squares exactly the same size as all the others, unconsciously slowing my breathing to match the soft whispered whoosh of the little cherub who slept so peacefully against my breast, and let the tension drain slowly from my body, I realized that my agitation didn't stem from gossiping tongues but from my own heart.

I was jealous.

It took me a little while to realize it, but not because I'm unfamiliar with jealousy. I've spent plenty of time in my life feeling jealous of what someone else has, way too much time. It's embarrassing to admit, but it's true. Whenever I find out that someone is having a baby, I am jealous. Maybe that's why, when Evelyn came up with the idea of the mothers-to-be quilting class, I immediately volunteered to stay up here and watch the children; I didn't want to spend two hours a week in the shop with all those women who had what I had been denied. I don't think jealousy was the whole reason I volunteered to be the babysitter, but it was at least a piece of it. And even though I did all I could to support Mari when she was pregnant with Olivia, I was jealous of my sister too. I stuffed it down as quickly as I could, but it was still there.

And I've been jealous of others, so many, sometimes even strangers on the street, who looked to be in love, who had what I longed for, the protection and affection and attention of a man, the security and delight that must come when someone singles you out from all the world as *the* one, the pride that comes from knowing that you were chosen.

When you pull it apart and take a good hard look at that kind of jealousy, it looks pretty ugly, because it is. It took me a long time to acknowledge that ugliness and even longer to make any progress in expunging it.

The antidote to jealousy, I discovered, is to shift your focus from what other people have to what you have; in other words, to count your blessings. It sounds like a simple solution, but if you practice it diligently—and sometimes I've been more diligent than others—you can overcome the habit and remove the ugliness from your heart, cutting it out like a cancer and replacing it with contentment. It works, it really does. Over the years, I've gotten to be something of an expert on jealousy, so I know what I'm talking about.

Normally, I can spot jealousy coming from a distance of fifty paces, but this time it caught me by surprise. This time was different. Until now, I've always been jealous *of* someone, of someone else's relationship, or security, or status. This time, I was jealous *for* someone, for Paul.

The time that has passed since I first met Paul can be measured in weeks, yet I feel I know him, perhaps better than I've ever known any man. It all sounds so fast, and it was. But at the same time, it wasn't.

I liked Paul, almost from the first. He's funny and smart and interesting, I mean *really* interesting. He knows a lot about a lot of things and can talk about them—and not just work or sports. He reads news magazines and can discuss politics, really *discuss* it, not just rant or give his opinion, but engage in an actual exchange of ideas. He reads books, too, novels, not just thrillers or murder mysteries, though he likes some of that, but classics, things by Hemingway and Nabokov and even Jane Austen. When he told me he'd read *Pride and Prejudice* twice, my jaw fell open.

And he's likeable. Most men I know don't have friends, only competitors. Not Paul. He met Tom, Russell, Billy, and Steve when he was eight years old and stayed friends with them through school and life, playing jazz in a basement bar in Chicago every other Wednesday for seventeen years. I think that says something important about him. And, of course, he's a fabulous father—patient but firm, a wonderful example to James and all the kids in the youth group.

He such has a beautiful smile, white but not too white, no bleach for Paul, and his teeth are straight. Well, all but that one on the upper left that leans a little bit and has a chip off the bottom, but I like that. It gives him character. And that night at the Rooster Tail, I realized he's handsome, really handsome. Funny how I didn't notice that from the first.

Maybe it would have been better if I hadn't. I have dreams about Paul now. Sometimes there are other people in the dream—Philippa, Olivia, James, my parents, and once his friends from the band were in it, though since we've never met, I don't know how I knew it was them, I just did. Sometimes it is just the two of us. The dream always ends with Paul holding me in his arms, just holding me close, and it feels so incredibly good, so safe and right. Then I wake up and realize he's gone, that it was only a dream, and I feel so empty that I can't go back to sleep, sometimes for hours.

I know I sound like a schoolgirl with a crush, but there is more to it than that—just as there is more to Paul than a man who is funny, smart, interesting, likable, and handsome, much more.

One day, when we were sitting on a pile of snow, taking a break during a sledding party we'd organized for the kids, he told me more about his relationship with his ex-wife. Melanie was a court reporter. He met her on a Wednesday, had taken her out and taken her home on a Friday. Two and a half months later, she was pregnant. A justice of the peace married them the following month.

Melanie was ten years younger than Paul and they didn't have much in common. The marriage was rocky from the first, but when James was born and Paul held him, three weeks premature and mewing like a kitten, wrapped in a blue hospital blanket and wearing a tiny knitted stocking cap, Paul fell head over heels in love with his son and decided, for all their sakes, to do everything he could to make the marriage work. It wasn't enough.

Four years later, in spite of all the counseling and Paul's best efforts, Melanie left. Furious with his wife and with himself, Paul took a long walk along the shores of Lake Michigan in freezing weather. By the time he reached Navy Pier, he realized he had to make a change. He decided to go back to the beginning, to the things he had learned as a child, things he'd known to be right but had walked away from. And he decided to put away his anger and forgive Melanie, learn from his mistakes, and try to be a better man.

Paul is so many things that are fine. But that conversation was the moment I realized that Paul was ... a man. Not a perfect man but a *real* one, a man of character and integrity, the kind of man I had ceased to believe existed. Knowing all that, how could I not be jealous for him? How could I stop myself from falling in love with him?

I had to. That was all. I just had to. Paul wasn't mine.

I have spent so many years chasing after things and people that didn't belong to me, that God hadn't intended for me. Every time I did, I had humiliated myself and damaged relationships with people I truly cared about.

It had happened with my sister, but I was not going to let that happen again, not ever. Not with Philippa. Not with Paul. Not with Olivia.

That morning, sitting alone in the workroom, thinking, praying, remembering, folding, and folding, and folding, was my walk on the shores of Lake Michigan.

That was the moment I resolved to focus not on love that was never meant for me but on the love that had come to me at the proper time and according to a plan that I still could not begin to understand, the love I had longed and prayed for, the love of a child who needed me though she would not speak to me and who, by the whim of a judge or a wrinkle in the law, might yet be removed from my life but could never be erased from my heart, the child I loved so very much, the gift I never expected to receive: Olivia.

❧ 42 ❧

Margot

I stopped by the bakery after work, bought the two biggest chocolate cream cheese cupcakes in the case, and took them to the hospital with me, dessert for Olivia and dinner for me. Though she
won't talk to me, Olivia will accept my gifts, especially if they in-
volve chocolate and frosting.

Bit by bit I am wearing her down. A couple of days ago I was
reading to her from *The Giant Book of Knock-Knock Jokes* and I
heard a giggle. When I looked up from the page her lips were
pressed into a line and her eyes stared straight ahead, but I know
what I heard. It's a start. Maybe there'd be another today, or a smile,
or even a word! A sentence! Wouldn't that be wonderful?

When I got to Olivia's room it was empty. It was a little late in
the day for physical therapy, but they'd been working her harder recently, stretching out her sessions, so I wasn't too worried. I went to
the nurses' station, looked for a familiar face, and found Amy, who
has been on the job less than a week and seems a bit overwhelmed.

"Do you know when Olivia will be back from therapy?"

"Hmmm?" Amy, absorbed with filling out some paperwork,
looked at me, then looked at the clock and frowned. "They brought
her back a while ago. You checked her room?" I nodded. "How
about the bathroom?"

Together, we checked the bathroom, then the playroom, and all the other rooms in the pediatric ward. We even checked the cleaning closet. No Olivia.

"She couldn't have gotten too far," Amy mused as I followed her back to the desk, "but I'd better call security."

Four minutes later, two blue uniformed security officers arrived. Amy couldn't leave the nurses' station, but the officers and I searched every room, office, and closet on the third floor. The officers got out their radios and raised an alert, giving a description of Olivia and an order for all available personnel to search every room on every floor of the hospital and to station guards at every exit.

Seeing the look on my face, the officers told me not to worry, that they were only following procedure. "She's probably messing with us. Wouldn't be the first time a kid decided to play hospital hide-and-seek. The nurse said she was in bed and sleeping less than thirty minutes ago, so she couldn't have gotten far, not alone, not on crutches."

But what if she wasn't alone?

I hated even thinking what I was thinking. Even with the craziness of the last weeks, even amid the grief and arguments, I couldn't imagine that my parents would kidnap Olivia. But had you told me a few weeks ago that my parents would go behind my back and go before a judge in an attempt to snatch Olivia from my hands, or that they would try to distort my personal history in court, turning a failed attempt at dieting into an accusation of clinical depression and peaceful protest against an immoral act into a criminal record, I wouldn't have been able to imagine that either. And yet they had. And Olivia was missing.

Hesitantly, making it clear that I was only doing so out of an abundance of caution, I gave the security officers a quick overview of our family situation.

When I was finished, the older officer looked at the younger one and said, "Greg?"

"I'm on it." He pulled out a cell phone and pressed three numbers, 9-1-1.

"Oh! You don't...I mean, that won't be necessary," I sputtered. "I'm sure that it's just what you said. I'm sure she's hiding somewhere...."

"I hope so, miss, but in this kind of situation we have to call in the police as quickly as possible. The nurse should have done it first thing. That's the procedure."

"And your parents' address in Buffalo?"

"132 Bachman Circle," I replied, watching the policewoman scribble the information on a pad. "But she couldn't be there. Buffalo is nearly a seven-hour drive from New Bern. Olivia's only been missing for a few minutes. And I'm sure my parents have nothing to do with this...."

"I understand, Miss Matthews, but we have to send someone in Buffalo out to talk to your parents, just in case. That's the procedure in a situation like this."

"Yes. I know." I supposed the officer was right. If my parents were home and Dad opened the door and found a policeman standing on the porch, he would be absolutely furious. And if they weren't home...Well, I'd think about that later. The only thing I cared about right now was finding Olivia, and if enduring my father's fury was the price for doing that, so be it.

"Is there something I should be doing right now?" I asked.

"There are a couple of officers searching the grounds. You could go help them if you want."

The elevator had never been slower. When I finally reached the ground floor and the big mirrored doors slid slowly open, I took a right turn into the corridor. Another right at the end of it would have brought me to the main entrance but, for some reason, I took a left instead. When I came to a set of big double doors with a sign that said EMERGENCY DEPARTMENT: HOSPITAL PERSONNEL ONLY PAST THIS POINT. ALL OTHERS USE MAIN ENTRANCE, I pressed a button with a blue wheelchair logo and waited for the doors to swing open.

The hallway was wide enough to let two gurneys pass and was lined with a series of glass-fronted procedure rooms filled with monitors and specialized equipment. The hall led to a big rectangular "bullpen" with smaller, curtained exam areas that surrounded a U-shaped desk with room for three computer stations and had a white wipe-off board with notes and instructions about each patient. I remembered it all, much too vividly, from the hours I'd spent here on Christmas Day.

There was always a lot of noise in the ER, the sounds of beeps and tweets and bells coming from various monitors and alarms, the sound of moaning from people in pain and incoherent babbling from others out of their senses, the sound of doctors and nurses and aides and registrars exchanging information and instructions, but it seemed even noisier than usual. The sound of voices coming from the bullpen was nearly a babble. I had come in during the shift change.

There are always extra relatives and caregivers hanging about in the ER, and the cast of characters changes minute by minute as new patients arrive and others leave. I doubted anyone would question my presence there, but even so, I was quiet as I went from room to room peering through the glass walls of the procedure rooms, walking past if they were occupied, walking in if they were not.

The third room on the left was empty. I went in, looked around, saw nothing.

"Olivia? Olivia, are you in here?"

There was silence. I turned and started to leave but stopped when I saw a blue privacy curtain flutter and heard a soft voice say, "Aunt Margot?"

Two little feet wearing fuzzy pink slippers flanked by rubber-tipped crutches were visible under the curtain. With my heart pounding in my chest, I pulled back the curtain and found Olivia.

I dropped instantly to my knees, half a prayer, half a reflex, and pulled her close.

"Oh, Livie! Oh, Livie, there you are! I've been so worried, sweetheart. Everyone is looking for you. We've all been so worried! Promise me you won't disappear like that ever again." I loosened my hold on her and peered into her little face. "What were you doing all the way down here?"

Olivia's big brown eyes, shining like gemstones at the bottom of a pool, filled with tears. "I came to find her. Aunt Margot, you've got to help me."

And suddenly I knew what she was doing.

My eyes filled with tears as I grabbed her again and squeezed her tight, wishing I could hold her close enough to undo all the pain, close enough to turn back the clock to the day before Christmas and give my beloved child back to the one she was missing, the one I was missing too, the one Olivia, heaven alone knew how, had run away on crutches to search for, sneaking through the hallways and doors, past hospital workers, to the last place she had seen her mother alive.

"She is gone, Olivia. She is gone and she isn't coming back. She isn't here. Her body is in the ground and her soul is in heaven. That's what happens when people die."

The last time I had said those words to her, my little niece had flown into a hysterical rage. This time, she pulled her body away from mine and looked at me. Two huge tears, like dewdrops from a lily, fell down her cheeks. Looking in her eyes, I could see that she didn't want to believe me but finally did. In her eyes I saw the loss of innocence, the exit from Eden. It broke my heart.

"She never said good-bye, Aunt Margot. I never got to tell her good-bye."

No, she hadn't. Neither had I.

❧ 43 ❧

Philippa

If someone wanted to photograph the face of love, all they would have to do was click the shutter on a close-up of Margot as she sat snuggled next to Olivia in the hospital bed, one arm draped over the little girl's shoulder, hanging on to each and every word as though it were a precious pearl that had unexpectedly dropped into her hands.

"Ummm . . ." Olivia frowned and bit her lower lip, searching for an answer to my question. "How about this one?"

She pressed her hands flat against each other, tucked them under the point of her chin, and closed her eyelids. "I hear no voice, I feel no touch, I see no glory bright . . ."

Margot's eyes glistened and she joined in the piping prayer of her niece. "But yet I know that God is near, in darkness as in light. He watches ever by my side, and hears my whispered prayer. The Father for his little child, both day and night doth care."

Olivia turned to look at Margot, her eyes wide. "You know it too? Mommy used to say it with me every night before I went to bed."

"I do," she said, smiling through a sheen of tears. "Grandma used to say it with your mommy and me every night when we were little."

"Will that be a good prayer?" Olivia asked me.

"That will be a perfect prayer." I made a note on my clipboard. "Now what about music. Did your mommy have a favorite song?"

The thinking frown returned. "Does it have to be a church song?"

"You're the one doing the planning, Olivia. It can be anything you want."

"How about 'You Are My Sunshine'? Mommy sang that to me all the time."

I wrote it down quickly, swallowing hard. "That's a good idea."

The poignancy of Olivia's selection was not lost on me. The little one's sunshine *had* been taken away, and that was nothing but sad. But she had an aunt who adored her and would do everything in her power to help her heal, and in that she had been blessed.

Letting Olivia plan a memorial service for her mother, giving her a chance to say the farewell she had been denied, was just the beginning. Margot was going to have her work cut out for her. There would be hard days ahead for both of them, but in the end, Olivia would be all right—Margot too. I was sure of it.

"What about you, Aunt Margot? Do you want to pick a song?"

"How about 'Like a River Glorious'? Your mommy and I sang that when we were little. Mari played the piano and we both sang."

"Okay. Can we bring a piano to the garden?" Olivia asked.

"Well," I said. "That could be a little tricky, but," I said, addressing the rest of my answer to Margot, "Paul asked me to tell you that he and James can play if you want them to."

"That's a good idea," Olivia said before Margot could reply. "Better than just singing."

Margot didn't raise any objection, just stroked Olivia's hair, so I wrote *Paul and James* down next to the song titles and then glanced over my notes.

"I think that's about it. Unless you can think of anything else."

"Just one other thing," Margot said. "Olivia wants butterflies."

The little girl nodded vigorously. "Mommy's name was Mariposa. That means 'butterfly' in Spanish. Mommy told me once that when people die, it is like when a caterpillar turns into a butterfly. They go to sleep for a while, all wrapped in that blanket thing. . . ." Olivia looked up at her aunt.

"A cocoon."

"Right. A cocoon. And when it wakes up, the caterpillar climbs out of the cocoon and is a beautiful butterfly. So I think it would be good if we had a lot of really pretty butterflies."

"That's part of why we've decided to wait until summer to have the memorial," Margot explained, "so Olivia will be feeling better and it will be warm enough for butterflies."

"But we're planning it now," Olivia added, "so everything will be ready and we'll have time to invite people to come."

"Very wise," I said, slipping my pen and notepad into my purse. "Well, Miss Olivia, I'm going to get out of your way and let you consult with your florist and caterer." I rose from my chair and glanced back at Charlie Donnelly and Tessa Woodruff, who had been sitting near the window, waiting patiently for their turn.

Margot got up too. Olivia looked up, a bit alarmed. Now that she'd finally accepted Margot, she was afraid to let her out of her sight. Yes, there was still a lot of healing to be done. Well, bit by bit. That's the only way to do it.

"It's okay, Livie. I'm just going to walk Reverend Clarkson to the elevator and then I'll be right back. You and Charlie can start talking about the food. Be sure to ask him about the butterscotch cookies I was telling you about. They're heaven!"

Charlie rose from his chair, took a white bakery box tied with string from where he'd left it on the windowsill, and approached the side of the bed. "Here. I brought a few for you to sample. . . ."

Margot and I walked out into the hall. "Charlie will have her eating out of his hand in no time."

"She looks great, Margot. I can't believe the change. Letting her plan a memorial service is a wonderful idea. She needs this."

"She's not the only one," Margot replied. "It all happened so fast and then, with Olivia so sick and all this wrangling over custody, I hardly had a chance to think about Mari. Every time I did, I was so overwhelmed with guilt and bad memories that I just wanted to shut it out. Being Mari's sister wasn't always easy; I'm not trying to pretend it was. But it wasn't all bad. Now I want to remember that part of our relationship.

"Anything I needed to forgive her for, I have. I hope, before she left this earth, maybe while she was trapped in the car, she did the same for me and that she was finally able to let go of all the bad things that had happened and remember what was good about us. I hope that's the way it was. I hope she's finally found peace."

"So do I."

I pressed a button on the elevator. Margot gave me a quick squeeze and thanked me for coming. Our farewell was interrupted by the sound of hard-soled shoes pounding like an angry drumbeat against the linoleum flooring of the hallway and Werner Matthews's voice, just as insistent, just as angry.

"Margot! Hang on a minute!"

Margot turned around. "Hi, Dad. I didn't know you were coming today."

"No," he said sarcastically. "I'm sure you didn't. What the heck is going on in there?" He stabbed his finger in the direction of Olivia's room. "Who are all those people?"

Margot's flushed cheeks and she shifted her eyes to me, then back to her father. "There's just two, Dad. You met Charlie at Christmas, remember? And Tessa is another of my friends."

"Your friends." Werner's voice was flat, but his expression was smoldering. "I see. And what are *your* friends doing in Olivia's room?"

Margot straightened her shoulders and lifted her chin. "Helping Olivia make plans for a memorial service for Mari. Olivia never had a chance to say good-bye to her mother. She needs a chance to grieve her loss. She needs closure."

Margot's voice was calm and carefully modulated, but her posture was immovable. I couldn't help but recall that day I'd first seen her interact with her father, how she had bent like a willow branch to his will, ignoring every criticism, tiptoeing away from potential confrontation. How she had changed since then. She was still Margot, still soft-spoken and respectful and she still, I suspected, disliked confrontation. But if Olivia's welfare and healing demanded a confrontation with her father, then Margot would not back away from it. Sometime during the last few weeks a transformation had occurred; Margot had become a mother.

Werner rolled his eyes. "A six-year-old child needs closure. Hasn't the poor little thing gone through enough? She doesn't need to keep being reminded of sad things. She needs to forget about all of that and go on with her life. Closure. What kind of psychological mumbo jumbo is that?" He turned to me. "I suppose all this non-sense was your idea."

"No, Mr. Matthews, it was Margot's, and I think it was a good one. After Olivia ran away to look for her mother and Margot found her—"

"And tried to make the police believe that I'd kidnapped her!" He spun toward his daughter with furious eyes, poking her repeatedly in the arm with the stub of his finger, like he was poking at a pile of smoldering charcoal, trying to stir up a blaze.

"You sent the police to my house! You told them I'd come down here and kidnapped Olivia!"

"No, Dad. I never did. Olivia was missing and the police had to get involved; they had to go to your house. That's the—"

He didn't let her finish. "Do you have any idea how humiliating that was for your mother and me? To have a police cruiser parked in our driveway? In our driveway! For the whole neighborhood to see! And then to be questioned about the disappearance of my own granddaughter, like I was some kind of criminal? Some kind of per-vert! Do you have any idea?"

"Dad," Margot said evenly, "I'm sorry about that. I really am. But none of that was my doing. I told the police there was no need to go to your house, but that's the procedure when a child in a dis-puted custody case goes missing."

Werner closed his eyes and threw up his arms. He wasn't listening.

"I know what this is about. This is all about you trying to get your own way! You're trying to embarrass me, make the judge think that I'm some kind of nut job. And that!" he shouted, again point-ing to Olivia's hospital room. "That is all about trying to poison my granddaughter against me. Those are all your friends in there. They're all on your side!"

"Daddy," Margot said, taking a step toward her father and reaching for his arm, "I'm just trying to help Olivia. And it *is* helping. She's talking to me again, for the first time in weeks. That's what we all want, isn't it? There are no sides here."

Werner slapped her hand away. "Oh, yes. Yes, there are," he said coldly. "You created them, Margot, the minute you told the police to come to our house. I see how things are now. But if you think I'm going to stand idly by and do nothing while you weave your little schemes, you're wrong.

"I want those people out of that room right now. Either you tell them to leave or I will. I'm going to tell Mr. Bench to keep all *your* friends away from my granddaughter. And if he won't, then I'll go to the judge and get him to do it!"

He stormed down the hall. Margot stood and watched him go, her hands clenched into fists at her sides.

"What are you going to do?"

She shrugged. "The only thing I can do. I'm going to make some sort of excuse to get Tessa and Charlie out of Olivia's room without upsetting her. And then I'm going to call Arnie."

44

Margot

"I am not pleased."

He hardly needed to say so. The look on Judge Treadlaw's face made his sentiments crystal clear.

"Mr. Bench, I'm a busy man. Why are you bothering me with such a trivial matter? In less than two weeks, I will name a permanent guardian who, barring any special ruling from the court, can decide who will and will not be granted visitation rights. But for the moment, since there is a dispute, it seems best to limit the child's visitors only to immediate family members."

Geoff cleared his throat. "Normally I would agree. But there are special circumstances. For weeks, the child refused to speak to any members of the family, but after Miss Matthews found her last week, she's made excellent progress. . . ."

The judge pulled his brows together tightly. A valley of frown lines creased his forehead. "Found her? Found her where?"

"Hiding in the emergency room. The child snuck out of her hospital room and went off in search of her dead mother. The police had to be called."

My father stood up. "It was all a ruse, Judge! My daughter took advantage of the situation and led the police to believe that I was involved."

"Mr. Matthews," the judge growled in a low voice that was more intimidating than a shout. "Sit. Down. Now. I was speaking to Mr. Bench."

"Your Honor," Geoff continued, "if you'll look over the notes I sent, you'll see that—"

"Mr. Bench, I do not have any time to look over your notes or to waste on these sorts of trivial disputes." He moved his head from left to right, glowering. "Unless there is some sort of major development in this case, I do not want to see any of you in my courtroom before the hearing. Do I make myself clear?"

Out of the corner of my eye, I could see my father shift in his chair. My mother reached out and grabbed him by the arm, warning him to keep his seat. She nodded; so did I. Dad sniffed but kept silent. Only Geoff spoke.

"Yes, Your Honor. Perfectly clear."

"Any first-year litigator, let alone an attorney of your experience, should have been able to figure this out without my help. But since you seem to be suffering from a lack of good sense today, let me reiterate: Until the hearing, the only people visiting the child in the hospital are members of the immediate family. I will see you all back here in eleven days. And not one day before."

Geoff's ears turned red. Everyone rose as the judge left the room. My father tossed a triumphant glance in my direction. My mother nudged him with her elbow. I pretended not to see any of it.

I stood on the sidewalk in front of the courthouse, talking to Arnie. Dad and Mom had buttonholed Geoff and were still inside the courthouse talking to him.

"Isn't there anything we can do?" I pleaded. "It did Olivia so much good to see some fresh faces. When I came back in the room, Tessa was reading knock-knock jokes to her and Olivia was laughing so hard she nearly choked on Charlie's cookies. I wanted to bring Virginia and Evelyn over next. They were going to help Olivia make a baby quilt to donate to the hospital. Livie loves going down to the nursery to look at the newborns. And I was hoping Ivy could bring her kids for a visit. Bethany is sweet, and Olivia and Bobby are about the same age. They might end up in the same class at school. Think how much easier it would be for Olivia if . . ."

Arnie shook his head. "Let it go, Margot. You don't want to antagonize the judge any further, do you?" The expression on his face made it clear that this question required no answer. "I told you this was how he'd react, Margot. I'm surprised Bench was willing to bring it to the judge."

"He didn't want to," I admitted. "I pushed him."

"Well, you're lucky it didn't backfire on you. Next time listen to my advice, will you? I'm on your side, you know."

"I know, Arnie. I'm sorry."

My apology didn't make any difference. Arnie was still miffed at me. "I've got to get back to the office."

He walked away just as Geoff and my parents came down the courthouse stairs. My father kept his head down and walked past without even looking at me, but my mother, who was holding Dad's arm, turned to me as they passed.

"Hi, honey."

"Hi, Mom."

If someone had told me that a time would come when my father wouldn't speak to me and I wouldn't be able to think of anything to say to my mom, I'd have said that was crazy. And it is! This whole thing is nothing but crazy. If I didn't sincerely believe that Olivia would be better off with me than my folks and know for certain that I was doing what Mari wanted me to do, I would never go through with this.

I lifted my hand as they drove away, but I couldn't tell if Mom waved back. When I turned around, Geoff was standing there.

"That was fun," he said glumly. "I always enjoy getting chewed out by a judge before lunch."

"Sorry. That was my fault. But thanks for trying. I owe you one. Can I take you to lunch?" I asked. "It's the least I can do."

"Tempting, but I've got to meet another client in half an hour. But don't worry," he said, putting his arm around my shoulders and flashing that strobe-light smile of his. "We'll find a way for you to make it up to me."

45

Margot

"Close your eyes, Aunt Margot, and hold out your hands." I heard a sound of rustling blankets and a drawer opening, then a pause as Olivia turned toward the chair I was sitting in. "Don't peek!"

"I'm not. My eyes are shut tight."

More rustling, a drawer closing, the feel of Olivia's cold fingers brushing my hand, then something soft and warm. I already knew what it was and yet, when Olivia gave me permission to open my eyes, I gasped.

"Olivia! Oh my goodness! This is just beautiful, sweetie."

The baby quilt, made from five-inch squares of soft flannel in pastel colors, some solid, some dotted, some striped, some with squiggles and curlicues, all pre-cut from a charm pack I'd brought from the shop, had been only about three-quarters sewn when we worked on it last, but now it was all but done. Now all the blocks were stitched together, backed with pale blue flannel and tied in the center with lengths of yellow yarn. Once the extra blue flannel was double-folded, ironed to the front of the quilt, and blind-stitched to secure it, the quilt would be ready to donate to the next premature baby born at the hospital.

"How were you able to finish this so quickly? Did someone help you?"

Olivia had been surprisingly quick to pick up quilting. The accident had caused some lingering problems with her large motor skills—she still had issues with balance that the doctors hoped would improve in time—but her small motor skills were excellent. Even so, I couldn't imagine that she had been able to finish this quilt all by herself. Perhaps there was a secret quilter on the nursing staff.

Olivia nodded. "Grandma. She can sew a lot faster than me. But I did all the yarn thingies," she said, pointing to a green block with blue and yellow stripes, "after Grandma showed me how. She brought a really big needle." Olivia spread her hands out to a width that was much greater than any needle could be, but I knew what she meant.

"A tapestry needle."

Olivia nodded. "Uh-huh. Grandma is a really good quilter."

She is? My mother is an accomplished knitter, but as far as I knew, she'd never done much quilting.

"She's very nice too," Olivia said, playing absently with one of the yarn ties. "So is Grandpa."

"They are," I said. "Very nice."

"How come you never come to visit when they do?"

I scratched my nose, giving myself a moment to formulate an answer.

"Well," I said slowly, "it's a little bit complicated. Have you ever had an argument with a friend at school?" Olivia nodded. "So you know that sometimes when you have an argument, even with somebody you really like, you just need to take a break from each other for a little while. You know, until things cool down."

Olivia stuck her little finger in her mouth, gnawing on her nail, and thought about this for a moment. "Mommy had an argument like that with Grandma and Grandpa, but it wasn't for a little while. It was forever. I think they're nice. I think you should make up with them."

Olivia unfolded the baby blanket and smoothed it out so it covered her lap and knees, looking down at the pastel patches.

"I want to, Livie. I've tried to and . . . I'm sure everything will work eventually, but like I said, it's kind of complicated."

Olivia kept running her hands over the quilt, brushing her fingertips against its softness, but she said nothing.

"Listen, sweetie, I've got to go. I have to run by the quilt shop before my meeting at church, but I'll be back tomorrow. Would you like me to take your quilt home with me? I could iron the binding and then we can stitch it so it will be all finished."

"Okay." Olivia folded up the quilt, carefully matching the corners so the edges were all even. I smiled to myself, thinking she might have a future folding fat quarters in a quilt shop.

"Maybe when we take this to the nursery, we'll be able to get a picture of you and the baby who will be taking it home. Wouldn't that be cool?"

She handed me the quilt. "When do I get to go home?"

"Soon."

"With you?"

"Well . . . we're working all that out."

The big brown eyes stared up at me. "Is it complicated?"

"A little bit."

When I bent down to kiss her good-bye, Olivia kissed me back, then leaned back on her pillows and sighed. I couldn't tell if the depth of her sigh stemmed from sadness, resignation, or disappointment with adults in general, but whatever it was, it felt like an accusation.

Coming out of the elevator, my mind on other things, I bumped into Paul Collier, literally. In fact, I practically knocked him over. How embarrassing.

"Oh, gosh! I'm so sorry, Paul. I wasn't looking where I was going."

He grinned. "That's okay. You in a hurry?"

"A little. Why are you here? You're not sick, are you?"

I could have kicked myself. It was bad enough to blurt out such a personal question, but it was even worse to blurt it out in a tone of such obvious concern. The last thing I wanted was for Paul Collier to think I had some sort of schoolgirl crush on him.

"Dermatology appointment," he said with a dismissive shrug.

"When I was a kid, I worked as a lifeguard at the neighborhood pool. Never wore sunscreen. So now I have to go get all my moles checked out every year. It's no big deal."

"Oh. That's good. I mean, getting it checked out every year. Good idea."

"Yeah. Well. It's one of those things you've got to do. I'm going to see you at youth group on Saturday, right?"

"Saturday?" I hesitated, thinking about Saturday. There was something I was supposed to be doing then . . . wasn't there? Why couldn't I remember? Why was I getting so flustered? Maybe this was the kind of thing that started happening once you hit forty. I hoped so. Or at least I hoped Paul would chalk it up to that.

"We're taking the kids bowling, remember?"

"Oh, yes! Saturday!" I smacked myself on the forehead. How could I have forgotten? We'd scheduled it weeks before and on a different night than our usual, so it wouldn't conflict with quilt circle. "Philippa is going to fill in for me. I should have told you before. Geoff Bench is coming for my home visit. It's the only time he could do it. I'll be so glad to finally get it over with. I can't tell you how many times he's canceled on me."

"Really? Huh."

Paul frowned, and when he did a little series of lines, like folds in a paper fan, appeared at the corners of his eyes. How was it possible that frowning could make a man look even more attractive than he did smiling? None of the other men I knew looked more handsome when they frowned.

"Well, that's too bad. We'll miss you. I mean, the kids and all. You know. So, I guess I'll see you next Friday."

"Yes. Or later tonight, if you're going to the meeting at church."

"Right! The vote on what to do with the money. Thanks for reminding me. I promised Philippa I'd be there. You want to ride over together?"

He'd promised Philippa he'd be there? Well, that clinched it. The rumors were true. I wanted to be mad at him, but didn't have the heart. His face was an open book; he looked miserable and hopeful all at once. He couldn't help how he felt. Neither could

Philippa. And why should they? If Philippa wasn't a minister, I doubt anybody would have thought twice about it.

It was sweet in a way, how he was trying to disguise his interest in Philippa, but I wasn't in the mood to be anyone's decoy. Maybe at another time and with another man I'd have been able to pull it off, but not with Paul. If we walked into church together, there was no way I'd be able to hide my feelings. I'm an open book too, or at least I can be. But not anymore, not if I can help it.

"Thanks, but I can't. I've got to go to the quilt shop before. And I'm meeting someone after."

I've always been a terrible liar, but this lie came easily, slipping from my lips like silk from a spool. I knew I should take it back, but I didn't. I didn't want anyone, Paul especially, feeling sorry for me. I was tired of it. I was tired of feeling sorry for myself.

"Oh, that's too bad," he said, looking disappointed, as I was sure he was. But he and Philippa would have to work this out on their own. "Another time?"

"Sure," I said. "Another time."

46

Margot

The church was full. Not Christmas or Easter full, but more than half of the pews were occupied, which was fairly impressive for a weeknight. Clearly, the congregation had some strong opinions about where and how Waldo's bequest should be spent and they were eager to make them known.

Ted, I knew, wanted to buy a new boiler. I agreed with that wholeheartedly; I suspect everybody else felt the same way. We'd all endured so many frigid Sunday mornings that there could be no doubt of what our first priority should be. But what should be done with the remainder of the funds was a cause for debate.

Ted had an idea to use the money to buy cameras and recording equipment and broadcast our Sunday services on television and radio. And while I didn't think that was a terrible idea—well, not completely terrible—it didn't strike me as something that ought to be at the top of the list of possibilities.

There was a push among choir members to buy a new organ. The church librarians had proposed building a set of new book-shelves. The children's department wanted to create a church camp scholarship fund and buy new toys for the nursery. Somebody else proposed buying a new chest freezer for the kitchen to store meals for people who were ill or families with new babies. Another proposal called for using the money to pay down the mortgage. And that was really just the beginning.

Seventy-five thousand dollars sounds like a lot of money, and it is. But it wasn't enough to fund even a percentage of the good and worthy ideas that were floating around the congregation. I hoped we'd be able to come to an agreement.

There was a microphone and two chairs sitting at the front of the church, one for Philippa and one for Ted. I stood in the middle of the aisle looking for a place to sit. Evelyn, Charlie, and Virginia were sitting near the front in the middle of a full pew. They must have gotten there early. Evelyn saw me, fluttered her fingers and raised her eyebrows, silently asking if I wanted to join them, but I could see there was no room. I shook my head and mouthed, "See you after." Evelyn nodded.

Miranda Wyatt was sitting about halfway back and next to the aisle. She waved me over. "There's room here," she said. I sat down and shoved my purse under the pew.

"So what do you think we should do with the money, Margot?"

"Besides get a new boiler, I'm not sure."

"Well, I can tell you what we *don't* need to do," Miranda said, "and that is buy a bunch of electronic junk and start our own television show. What a silly idea. If you ask me, that whole proposal is just the result of testosterone poisoning. Ted just wants new toys to play with."

While I did believe that Ted's motivation for wanting to broadcast the church services was primarily spiritual, there was probably at least a crumb of truth in Miranda's observation. Men get pretty excited about new gadgets and gizmos. Evelyn is always teasing Charlie about how he has to have every new cooking utensil on the market. But then again, I once saw Evelyn go into raptures over a rotary cutting mat that could swivel. And I've been drooling over those machines that will create perfect fabric die-cuts in just about any shape you can imagine. So maybe the urge to collect new gadgetry isn't an exclusively male trait. One person's gadget may be another person's completely necessary tool.

I wondered if Miranda's interest in shooting down Ted's proposal was purely a matter of wanting what was best for the church. I'm not sure what happened between her and Ted, but something had. Whatever it was, I intended to stay out of it.

At the front, Philippa and Ted were having some sort of exchange, possibly to decide who should do the talking. Philippa shook her head and lifted her hand, appearing to yield the floor to Ted, who smiled and walked to the microphone.

He was just calling the meeting to order when Paul arrived. Paul saw me, pointed to his chest and then toward an empty pew, indicating that I could come back and sit with him if I wanted to. I made a "thanks anyway" face and tilted my head toward Miranda, so he'd know I already had someone to sit with. Paul shrugged and took a seat in an empty pew at the very back of the crowd.

Standing at the microphone, Ted waited for the conversations to cease, then gave an explanation of how this donation had come into our possession, followed by a moving tribute to the memory of Waldo Smitherton. When he was done everyone clapped.

"As you know," Ted continued, "Waldo left no instructions about how the money should be used, but I am sure he wouldn't have wanted us to quarrel amongst ourselves. I hope we'll keep that in mind during this evening's discussion.

"The ushers"—Ted nodded, and the ushers began moving down the aisle, passing out sheets of paper—"are passing out lists of various proposals and cost estimates. We've had a lot of ideas about how to use this generous gift, and I'm sure we'll hear a few more from the floor tonight. However, we're going to have to make some choices...."

Ted then went on to explain that, while tonight's meeting was about discussing ideas and trimming down our wish list, he didn't expect to take a final vote that evening. But he hoped we would be able to deal with one item of business—the boiler.

People were a little surprised to learn that the labor for installing the new unit and repairing the old pipes would cost nearly as much as the boiler itself, but after some grumbling and griping, they voted to go ahead with it. Looking to the front, I saw Philippa smiling and gave her a thumbs up. The discussion moved on. The library shelving was quickly eliminated as an option, as were the chest freezer, new carpeting for the vestibule, new landscaping for the grounds, and a proposal from the floor that we purchase an espresso machine for the coffee hour.

The conversation got a bit heated when the choir director, Alma Nadar, presented her proposal for the purchase of a new organ. As she rose to speak, the choir members, who were sitting in the two pews behind Alma's, also rose in perfect choreographed unison, a united front of support. They were silent but standing as a group and, thus, appeared larger in numbers than they actually were. Their eyes were glued to Alma; I almost expected them to start humming "The Battle Hymn of the Republic" as an underscore to her impassioned pleas. It was an impressive performance, and it was obvious that the choir members were enthusiastic about the prospect of a new organ. Nobody else seemed that excited about it.

Wendy Perkins stood up and said what the rest of us were thinking. "Why do we need a new organ? This one sounds fine to me."

"Technically," Alma said, "it is, for what it is: a two manual drawknob organ of middling quality. But this magnificent temple," she said, making a sweeping gesture—I wondered if she'd chosen to wear that purple blouse with the bell sleeves just for impact—"with its incomparable acoustics deserves an equally magnificent organ. For years, it has been my prayer to get a pipe organ in our church, something truly spectacular that would elevate the musical portion of our worship experience to a level that cannot be rivaled in this part of the state." Alma clutched her clasped hands to her breast and closed her eyes for a moment.

"I believe that this bequest from our dear, departed Waldo is an answer to that prayer, and could provide the seed money we need to purchase the kind of organ that our church deserves." Exhaling dramatically, Alma took her seat amid a spattering of applause from the choir, who, after the lead soprano quietly counted off one, two, three, also sat down exactly on cue, just as they did on Sunday mornings.

"Seed money?" Wendy asked. "What do you mean seed money?"

"Well," Alma said, "the money from Waldo's bequest, together with the money we would get selling our current organ, perhaps another ten thousand, would just be the down payment. A truly grand pipe organ, of the sort I have in mind and which I'm sure Waldo would want us to have, costs upward of one hundred thousand dollars, probably closer to two. But this initial investment would be a grand start to our capital campaign. . . ."

I didn't really hear much of what Alma said after that. That two-hundred-thousand-dollar figure she tossed out sort of rang in my ears, shutting out all other sound. Even some of the choir members looked stunned.

Needless to say, the purchase of a new pipe organ was quickly eliminated from the list. However, a motion was made and passed to give our current organ a tune-up and fix one of the sticky draws. Everyone seemed satisfied with this solution, even Alma. Ted returned to the microphone to discuss his plan for bringing the Sunday services of New Bern Community Church to the airwaves.

I looked at Philippa, wondering what she thought of Ted's proposal, but her expression gave nothing away. In fact, with her elbow resting on the arm of her chair and her chin resting on her hand, her eyes closed, unmoving except for an occasional shallow nod of her head, she appeared to be deep in prayerful thought.

"A thing like this could be a wonderful outreach to the community," he said, pumping his fist for emphasis. "And think what a help and comfort it would be for the elderly and shut-ins of our congregation if they could simply turn on their televisions to attend church. This is a forward-thinking—"

Ted wasn't finished speaking, but Miranda stood up and interrupted him.

"Excuse me, but I don't see who we'd be helping. We already have a CD and tape ministry for people who are too ill or infirm to attend services. We send recordings to more than a dozen people every week. It seems to be working perfectly well, and the program costs less than five hundred dollars per year, whereas what you're proposing would cost tens of thousands. To what end? There are already radio and public access broadcasts available from several churches in the area. What's the point in adding our congregation to an already crowded bench?"

Ted, who had been listening to Miranda's objections with barely disguised irritation, leaned forward and put his mouth right next to the microphone. "The *point!*" he said, inadvertently popping his "P" so loudly that everyone, including Philippa, whose eyes were still closed in prayer, jumped. Ted moved slightly back from the microphone, cleared his throat, and tried again.

"Ahem. The point is that people may find something here that they have not found in those other congregations. Wait just a minute, Miranda," he said, holding up one hand to stave off another interruption. "I'm not suggesting we suddenly start competing with other congregations, but this church has been a thriving part of the town of New Bern since before it was a town! I'd like to see it continue to grow and thrive. And it seems to me that a TV and radio show could help us do that. If people hear or see us on the airwaves, they'll be that much more likely to come visit in person—"

Miranda, whose right foot had been twitching during Ted's entire speech, couldn't hold back any longer.

"Or not!" she cried. She pushed past me into the center aisle and stood facing Ted with her feet planted apart and her hands on her hips. "I talked to one of my Lutheran friends, and she told me that the whole TV and radio thing has been a wash at best for them. Yes, they have attracted a few new people who came after they saw the broadcasts, but they also lost a few people. Some of the people who used to come to services in person, including a few formerly active members, stopped attending when they realized they could just watch the whole thing from the comfort of their living room while drinking coffee and eating waffles in their pajamas.

"If somebody actually can't get to church because they are physically unable to do so, then watching a broadcast is the next best thing. But, Ted! Church isn't a spectator sport! We're supposed to be *here,* serving, supporting, and learning from God and each other. Loving our neighbors as ourselves!"

While she spoke, Miranda had moved slowly down the aisle, nearer to Ted and the front. Now she turned to face the congregation, her eyes flaming and her hands spread wide. I leaned closer, anxious to hear what she had to say. So did everyone else.

"We have a chance to do that with this money. And isn't that what church is supposed to be?" she asked, her voice building in volume and intensity as she went on. "We're a community! A family! Let's start acting like one!"

When she finished, she pivoted one hundred and eighty degrees, facing Ted, who stood there with his hands dangling at his sides, clearly in shock.

What had come over Miranda? The mild-mannered, hand-raising elementary school teacher expressed herself with a passion and fire that would have done a tent revival preacher proud and a message that was difficult to dispute.

Ted shoved his hands in his pockets and stared down at his shoes. After a long moment, he looked up and addressed the crowd.

"You know, it's never fun admitting you're wrong, but I hope I'm man enough to recognize it when it's true. Miranda is right. There are bigger needs and better ways for us to use this money. I'm going to withdraw my proposal to buy broadcasting equipment. Assuming," he said, turning to the right so he could see Philippa, "that our minister agrees with my assessment."

The room was silent. All eyes turned to Philippa, who was sitting in the exact same position, with her chin resting on her hand and her eyes closed, as she had been for the last several minutes. We waited.

Her chest was rising and falling in a slow, constant rhythm, but she didn't move. Ted, looking a bit alarmed, walked over to her chair, laid his hand on her shoulder, and gave her a little shake. "Reverend Clarkson? Reverend?"

Her head fell forward and her chin thumped against her chest. The crowd gasped; I think they were afraid they'd driven yet another minister to death's door. Philippa's head jerked up and back as if attached to a spring. Her eyes flew wide open and she blinked a few times, as though she was having a hard time bringing the room into focus.

Ted dropped to his knees next to her chair and started slapping her hand, as if trying to bring her back to consciousness. "Philippa? Philippa? Are you all right?"

She looked at Ted, then the crowd, then at Ted again. "Yes, yes. I'm fine. I just..." She shifted in her seat, still sounding a bit groggy. "I guess I just fell asleep."

Ted drew back, affronted, got to his feet, and stared down at her. "You fell asleep. In the middle of an important meeting of the entire church, you fell asleep?"

Philippa, suddenly much more awake, exclaimed, "No, no!" and lifted her hands as if she were trying to wave off a swarm of flies. "It's not what you think! I'm not sick or anything. I'm just pregnant."

There was another collective gasp, and then a murmur as two hundred heads turned toward the back of the room and stared at Paul Collier.

He had a very guilty look on his face.

❧ 47 ❧

Philippa

"I'm just pregnant."

If you want to silence an entire room full of people, be an unmarried minister and say those three words out loud.

If I hadn't been so groggy and been woken so abruptly, I would never have blurted it out that way. The congregation was in shock, and I could understand why. What I didn't understand was why everyone was staring at poor Paul Collier. Neither did Paul.

When all those pairs of eyes turned toward him, Paul turned around to see who everyone was staring at. When he realized there was no one sitting behind him he blushed right to the tips of his ears, ducked his head, and pulled on the end of his nose.

I coughed. Two hundred heads snapped forward in one movement and two hundred pairs of eyes stared at me. That's when the lightbulb went on. Somehow, for reasons I could not begin to fathom, everyone in that room had gotten the notion that Paul was the father of my unborn child. Where in the world would they get such an idea?

I got up, pushed past Ted, and stood at the microphone, looking straight at the crowd, moving my gaze from left to right and back, pausing to peer into individual faces, some shocked, some confused, some accusing.

"I think I need to clarify a couple of things." I pulled the microphone out of the stand and held it in my hand so I could descend the steps in front of the altar, moving closer to the crowd.

"As most of you know, I am a widow. When he was diagnosed with colon cancer, my husband, Tim, decided to have his sperm frozen before undergoing chemotherapy. We had always intended to have children together, so this seemed like a wise idea to both of us. At the time, we believed that Tim would recover and, eventually, we would be able to go on and live the lives we'd always planned to live, having a family and growing old together."

I paused for a moment, lifting my eyes to the ceiling and blinking. I wanted to get through this without losing my composure.

"When it became apparent that my husband was not going to recover, he urged me carry on with our plans and undergo artificial insemination treatments after his death. For a long time, I couldn't bring myself to do so. However, a couple of years ago, I decided to begin the treatments, as my husband had wanted. By that time, this was what I wanted too—very, very much.

"As you can imagine, I was very excited about the prospect of having a child. Before he died, Tim had said that he considered the possibility of us having a baby together the 'chance of a lifetime' and I agreed one hundred percent."

I stopped again, just to give myself a moment, and saw Sara Pierce, a woman a few years younger than me, whom I didn't know very well but who I knew was childless. There were tears in her eyes and in the eyes of her husband, Tom, as well. He put his arm over Sara's shoulders. As she leaned close to him, resting her head in the crook of his arm, and looked up at him with a teary smile, I remembered something one of my seminary professors had said: "Most people are in way more pain than anybody knows." So true.

I closed my eyes for a moment and breathed a silent prayer of blessing on Sara and Tom Pierce before going on.

"Though I tried many times, the treatments didn't work. My doctors could find no reason for this and so I began to wonder if motherhood simply was not part of God's plan for my life. After much thought and prayer, I determined to undergo a certain number of treatments and then, if I was still unable to conceive, to accept that as God's will and go on with my life.

"In December, I underwent a final fertility treatment. I knew this would be my last chance at that chance of a lifetime Tim had spoken of, but after so many trials and disappointments, I was resigned, sure that this attempt would fail too.

"Soon after, as you know, I received a very important phone call." I smiled, remembering all the emotions that had washed over me when I'd heard the news that I was being called to my first pulpit—elation, excitement, anxiety, humility, and back to elation again. "The days between receiving the call and arriving in New Bern to serve this church, as well as the weeks following, were so busy I didn't have time to think about that final treatment.

"Coming here, getting to know all of you," I said, looking out to Margot Matthews, and Miranda Wyatt, and Paul Collier, and these many, many faces that had become so familiar and dear to me in such a short time, "was, and continues to be, an incredible blessing. I could not imagine asking for more. And so I was caught completely by surprise when I discovered that last treatment *had* worked and that after all those years, I was pregnant."

At this there was a smattering of applause and a few sniffles as people wiped their eyes with the backs of their hands or tissues they'd pulled from their pockets. Even through tears, every face was smiling.

I swiped at the tears in my own eyes and laughed. "I'm pregnant!" I said again, because it felt so good to hear the words aloud at last. The congregation laughed with me and there was more applause, louder this time, and from every corner of the room.

When the applause died down, I went on to explain my reasons for keeping my condition secret, how I had been bursting at the seams to share the news and how glad I was to be able to tell them at last. Everyone seemed to understand, and nothing more was said about my falling asleep in the meeting.

Miranda Wyatt raised her hand and Ted yielded the floor to her.

"This is such wonderful news, Reverend Clarkson. I'm sure I

speak for everyone when I say that we all want to do whatever we can to support you during your pregnancy." Miranda turned slightly, addressing her comments to the group.

"When I was pregnant with Mark, my oldest, I could barely summon the energy to sweep the floor or make dinner. I think it's just terrible that our own minister didn't want to tell us she was pregnant because she was afraid that we'd think of replacing her if we knew. . . ."

"Now, Miranda, I didn't say that."

"Maybe you didn't say it, but I'm sure you were thinking it. I just think we expect too much from our ministers. Look what happened to Reverend Tucker. And now here you are, working ten-, twelve-, even fourteen-hour days." She made a tsk-ing noise. "I just don't think that can be good for the baby."

Wendy Perkins, who was one of the first church members whose faces I was able to recognize and remember because she wore rhinestone-encrusted reading glasses with wingtips so shiny and pointy that they reminded me of the tail fins on an old Cadillac, bobbed her head so that light from the ceiling bounced off the rhine-stones and danced against the wall like reflections from a mirror ball.

"I couldn't agree more. Why, when I was expecting my Ruthie, I could barely lift my head off the pillow for the first six months!"

More heads bobbed as other women in the group nodded their understanding and a murmur arose as ladies turned to their seat-mates and began whispering fascinating tales of the trials of their own pregnancies.

The nausea! The weakness! The emotions! The fatigue! Oh, poor Reverend Clarkson. A widow alone in the world! And look how hard she has been working. Tsk-tsk! Who knows what kind of effect that might have on this poor unborn child!

The murmurs rose in number and volume until it sounded like a gaggle of geese had invaded the church. Ted, who seemed to have no clue as to how he had lost control of the meeting or how to re-gain it, dropped his arms to his side, looked at me, and shrugged.

I tapped on the microphone with my index finger, trying to get everyone's attention, but it didn't work; they went right on talking to each other. I briefly considered sticking my fingers in my mouth and letting out one of the ear-piercing whistles I used to call Clementine, but remembering where we were, decided against it. Instead, I began clapping my hands, loudly but methodically, until one by one, the group settled down and only Wendy Perkins was still talking to her nearest neighbor, Betty Pringle.

"And you should have seen my feet! Swollen like coconuts they were! But would my husband lift a finger to help? No. Even then, he was the most worthless, inconsiderate—"

Betty hissed and gave her a nudge in the ribs. Wendy looked up, startled. "Oh. Sorry about that. Go ahead, Pastor."

"I appreciate your concern, really I do, but I am fine. You don't need to worry about me. Or the baby."

Miranda, who had kept to her feet throughout the uproar and was still standing, shifted her gaze to Ted and said, very sweetly, "I'd like to hear what the president of our board thinks about this. Ted?"

And that was the end of our discussion about Waldo's legacy, at least for that evening. Ted told the story of his late wife's four pregnancies and how he'd helped with the housework when she was too tired to clean and taken over the meal preparation when she was too nauseous to cook, a story greeted with more smiles from Miranda and nodded approval from the women. The men, I noticed, were less enamored of Ted's story. A few even rolled their eyes, but Ted didn't notice. I don't think he noticed anybody besides Miranda.

And somehow, this led to a discussion of helping our neighbors as ourselves. The next thing I knew people were volunteering to help with hospital and shut-in visitations, edging and weeding the flower beds, and editing the church bulletins and newspapers. Barbara Stadler, a retired accountant, said she'd take the job of church treasurer, a position we'd been trying to fill for months. And Jim Demming volunteered to lead the discussions of the Early Bird Bible Study so I didn't have to get up at five o'clock on Wednesdays.

It felt odd, having all these people step up to do things I had been doing up until then, things I had been hired to do, and I worried that Miranda had manipulated the situation. But as I was sitting and watching all this play out, a conversation, not a voice, more an impression, came to my mind, one I had not put there myself.

This isn't Miranda's doing. Did you really think it was? Have you ever heard her speak so forcefully before? Rest now. You weren't brought here to do everything for them, but help them learn to do for each other. They need this. Be still.

When the meeting was done, I was encircled by well-wishers offering hugs and congratulations. Sara and Tom Pierce were among the first, which touched me so. I know how hard it is to be happy for someone who is expecting when your own expectations have been dashed again and again. I covered Sara's hand with both of mine when I thanked her. Tom's arm was over her shoulders as they walked away, and I could see him patting her.

Evelyn, Virginia, Margot, and Charlie came up to me in a clump, beaming.

"Aren't you the sneaky one?" Virginia said. "And to think I actually bought that story about you only being able to take class in the mornings."

"Wonderful news," Charlie said and gave me a peck on the cheek. "Tomorrow, I'm going to make a batch of chicken soup and bring it to the parsonage. Just the thing if you're feeling under the weather."

"I feel fine."

"Of course you do," Evelyn said. "You're glowing! We're so happy for you," she said, giving me a hug. "My only regret is that your time in New Bern will be up before the baby is born. Promise you'll come back for a visit and bring the baby. You can stay with us."

"It's a promise."

Margot was next, and she nearly squeezed the breath out of me. "Oh, just wait until I tell the Ladies in Waiting! They had all kinds of crazy theories about why you were taking a baby quilt class. Natalie said . . . Well, it doesn't matter. They were all wrong, weren't they?"

Paul worked his way through the crowd, wedging himself into a spot directly behind Margot. "Congratulations, Philippa. Let me know if you need help with anything."

"You're already helping with the youth group," I said, glancing from his face to Margot's. "That's huge. I really appreciate you both."

"Well," Paul said, smiling at Margot, "we make a pretty good team. Say . . . uh, Margot, would you like to go get a cup of coffee? We could work out the activity calendar for next month."

"Thanks, but I can't. I'm going over to the Grill with Charlie and Evelyn."

Charlie looked at Evelyn with an expression that said this was clearly news to him. Evelyn, her face giving away nothing, moved her elbow to apply a gentle pressure to her husband's rib cage, warning him to keep silent.

"Another time," Margot said.

"Oh, sure. Another time." Paul gave me a halfhearted smile before heading out the door. Poor guy. I wished Margot would give him a chance. Maybe I should talk to her about him? No. It was none of my business. I'd already gotten myself in too deep.

Saying they'd see me at the quilt shop, Evelyn, Virginia, and Margot left with Charlie, who was telling them about the restaurant's special offering for the day, black cod in a miso marinade. As the crowd began to thin out, I stood chatting with Wendy Perkins, who was quizzing me about my vitamin and calcium intake. Ted came by with Miranda.

"That was a wonderful sermon, Philippa. Just wonderful."

"Thank you, Ted. But it wasn't a sermon. It was just . . . telling my story."

"Well, whatever it was, it was very moving. I don't know what Bob Tucker told you to do, but whatever it is, keep doing it. You're turning out to be a fine preacher."

Miranda smiled and laid her hand gently on Ted's forearm. He moved his arm so it looped through hers, pulling her closer.

"We're just headed over to the Grill on the Green for a late supper, but I'll talk to you soon, Philippa. Congratulations again. This is wonderful news."

They walked down the aisle toward the door. Wendy watched them go.

"Well, isn't that nice? They're perfect for each other. Ted's the sort of man who needs a woman who'll get him to do the right thing, but always leave him thinking it was all his idea. I knew his late wife. She was just the same, and she and Ted were very happy. Now that they've worked things out, I'm sure Miranda and Ted will be too."

"You think so?"

"Oh, I'm sure of it," Wendy said with a wink. "So? How did your parents react to the news? Bet they were just over the moon when you told them they're going to have a grandchild."

"Oh. Well, of course they would be," I said cheerfully and then glanced at my watch. "Wendy, would you excuse me? I just remembered something."

By the time I got home and climbed into bed with Clementine sprawled out at the foot of the bed, it was a little past ten. I dialed my parents' number in Boston.

"Parsonage."

"Mom? It's Pippa. Is Dad there?"

"Yes, honey, but he's asleep. Why? Is something wrong?" I smiled. That was so Mom. I used to think it was silly, the way she worried about me as though I were still in grade school, but just then, I thought it was sweet. And I was sure that once my child was born, I would be just the same.

I snuggled down under the covers, drew my knees up so the little bump was a little bit bumpier, and laid my free hand on the mound. "Well, wake him up and ask him to get on the extension. There's something I want to tell you."

≈ 48 ≈

Margot

"This is good," Virginia said, sounding surprised.

Charlie was standing next to our table, looking pleased with himself. "What did I tell you? Would I steer my own mother-in-law wrong? Try the rice."

"This black stuff?" Virginia poked at it with her fork. "I thought it was burned."

"Try it," Evelyn urged. "It's forbidden rice. In China, only the emperor was allowed to eat it. It's Charlie's latest crush."

Charlie bent down and gave her a kiss. "You're the only crush I have, woman."

She squeezed his hand. "Honey, why don't you sit down and relax?"

"I've got to go fix the espresso machine. But I'll join you for dessert."

He kissed her again and headed back to the kitchen, stopping briefly at Ted and Miranda's table to check on them, though he needn't have bothered. From the way they were looking at each other, it was obvious that they were having a lovely time.

"Tastes like plain old rice to me," Virginia mumbled. "Maybe a little chewier. Are you sure it's not burned?"

"It's supposed to be that way," Evelyn said absently, glancing toward Ted and Miranda's table. "Looks like Miranda decided to give him another chance. What about you and Paul? Why didn't you go have coffee with him? He's obviously crazy about you."

"He is not," I said irritably as I cut a piece of roast chicken. "And, anyway, I wanted to spend the evening with you two."

"You see us every day," Evelyn observed.

I quickly popped a piece of chicken in my mouth so I wouldn't have to respond. There was no point in telling Evelyn that I didn't want to have coffee with Paul because I liked him too much. I was not going to allow myself to be distracted again. He might not be seeing Philippa, but on the other hand, he might. Just because she was carrying her deceased husband's child didn't mean she and Paul didn't have feelings for each other. I'd seen his face earlier, when we were talking about the meeting, and he said he'd promised Philippa he'd be there. It was the face of a man in love.

Evelyn gave me a sideways glance. "You know what your problem is? You're afraid to be happy."

I swallowed my chicken. "I've got an idea," I said in a deliberately cheerful tone. "Let's talk about something else. We should have a baby shower."

"I was thinking the same thing," Virginia said as she pushed her rice to the far side of her plate. "Why don't I call the Ladies in Waiting and tell them we're having a surprise shower for Philippa? I'll bake a cake."

"And I'll ask Charlie to provide a few appetizers," Evelyn said. "He'll be all over that."

❧ 49 ❧

Philippa

"This is darling!" I pushed the tissue paper aside and pulled out a quilted diaper bag with elasticized pockets and a long shoulder strap. The fabric had a yellow background with quarter-sized dots of sage blue surrounded by wreaths of tiny green leaves.

"You made it yourself? How did you have time?"

"It's easier than it looks. Open it up," Evelyn urged.

Inside the bag I found all kinds of presents for the baby—bottles, pacifiers, a changing pad, teething ring, baby wipes, baby powder, tiny T-shirts, and socks, as well as a present for me, an envelope containing a fifty-dollar gift card to the quilt shop. "Oh, Evelyn! How generous. Thank you so much."

She smiled, pleased that I was so pleased. "Now that you're a quilter, you've got to start building up your stash. This will give you a start. I just wish you could keep quilting here at Cobbled Court. Are you sure we can't talk you into staying?"

"Wish I could. But after Reverend Tucker comes back from his sabbatical, I'll have to head back to Boston to stay with my parents until the baby is born. And then I'm going to have to start looking for another job. Hopefully, another pulpit."

Abigail Spaulding frowned. Since she spends winters in Bermuda, we had met only recently, but she decided to come to my impromptu baby shower anyway, along with Wendy Perkins, Tessa Woodruff, Madelyn Beecher, and Ivy Peterman.

"Well, you don't *sound* very hopeful," she commented.

"I'm not sure how many churches will want to hire a minister with a newborn."

"Why should that make any difference?" She sniffed. "You're a fine minister. Even Ted Carney says so. And I thought your sermon at Waldo's funeral was lovely."

"Thank you, Abigail. And thank you again for the baby gifts. I'm . . . well, I'm just overwhelmed by your generosity."

I wasn't just saying that. Though she barely knew me, Abigail had given me a car seat, high chair, and an expensive stroller. It was very kind but yes, it was a little much, almost embarrassing. When we'd taken a break from gift opening to have some cake, I whispered as much to Margot.

"That's just Abigail's way. She gave me this necklace for my birthday," she said, pulling the silver chain out from her blouse so I could see the heart pendant dangling from it. "It's from Tiffany's. It makes Abigail happy to see people happy."

Apparently, there were a lot of people like that in New Bern. They weren't all as wealthy as Abigail Spaulding, but they had generous spirits. Natalie, Jessica, Antoinette, and the others from the class had given me all kinds of baby clothes. Virginia made a diaper stacker and bumper pads from some of the same fabrics that I had used on the baby quilt I'd made in class, so everything in the crib would match. Ivy gave me several children's books that her little ones had enjoyed when they were tiny. Wendy gave me a baby monitor. Tessa and Madelyn's gift was a whole box filled with baby toys, including a plush musical teddy bear. And Margot gave me a sort of backpack that you wore in front, so the baby could ride close to your heart while your hands were free to do other things. She assured me it would come in very handy.

I remember how nervous I felt when I came to New Bern, overwhelmed by the speed at which it all was happening, worried at how I would be received by the congregation, wondering what I really had to offer them—so many fears, all of them unfounded.

My unexpected sojourn to New Bern is already at the halfway point. Soon I will move on to...well, somewhere. I don't know what God has planned for me next, but coming to New Bern has taught me, once again, that I can rest easy, knowing the plan is a good one. Still, it is hard to imagine that anyplace could come to feel like home, and so quickly, in the way New Bern has.

The presents having been opened and the coconut cake with lemon filling now nothing more than shreds of coconut confetti and delicious crumbs, Virginia informed everyone that it was time for "Show and Tell."

Over the last eight weeks, we've seen each other's quilts at all stages of construction, but it's fun to see them finished at last. Though we all had the same teacher, and some even used the same pattern, every quilt turned out differently.

When it was getting near time to leave, Virginia passed out brochures with listings for the next term of classes. The reason I took the Ladies in Waiting class was so I could get to know other expectant mothers without giving my secret away—it wasn't about learning to quilt. But somewhere along the way, I fell in love with quilting. Even with a new crop of volunteers to help at the church, I still had so much to do, but I couldn't stop myself from scanning the class descriptions.

I felt a hand on my forearm and the presence of someone looking over my shoulder. "The machine-piecing class might be a good next step," Evelyn said.

"Oh. I shouldn't. And anyway, I don't have a sewing machine."

"I can loan you a machine. I've got a spare at home—nothing fancy, but it's got a nice, even straight stitch. That's all you really need. Or, if you want to continue stitching by hand, you could try this one," she said, pointing to a listing about halfway down the page.

"'Baltimore Basics,'" I read. "'An introduction to the history and techniques of the Baltimore Album style of quilting, utilizing a stress-free approach to needle-turn appliqué.' Hand appliqué?"

The photograph next to the class description showed a single block with a curved wreath sprouting dozens of evenly spaced green leaves and dotted with clusters of red berries. A bird, in a lighter shade of red, sat perched on a small branch that grew out from the wreath. It was far more intricate than anything in my baby quilt.

"This looks really hard."

Seeing Evelyn and me discussing the class, Virginia had come over to join us. "It's not so much that it's hard; it's just that it's not easy. That's why I allow four sessions just to finish the one block; this is something you need to take your time on. But I've been watching you, Philippa. You're a very precise quilter. You can do this."

Virginia had more confidence in my abilities than I did. Still, I loved the idea of sewing a block that had some history attached to it. This block, finished and framed, would make a wonderful present for my mom. She loves all things antique. Of course, the block would be new, but it looked old. And she'd love that I made it for her myself.

"How much is the class?"

"As it so happens," Evelyn said in a deliberately surprised voice, "this class runs exactly fifty dollars. And that includes the kit."

I grinned. "The voice of temptation."

"Don't be so coy. It's not like you're that hard to tempt," Virginia said. "We had your number from the minute you walked in here. First time I saw you, I turned to Evelyn and said, 'Evelyn, that woman is a born quilter.' "

Was that what I was?

I took the gift certificate out of my new diaper bag and handed it to Evelyn.

50

Margot

The doorbell rang at seven on the dot. Shoot! I was hoping he'd be a few minutes late. I quickly hung the last towel over the bar and gave the bathroom a final once-over. Everything looked good, but on second thought, maybe having an open flame in a home with a small child would be considered a bad thing? Philippa had advised me that child safety was absolutely key to making a good impression during my home study.

I blew out the candle, bared my teeth in the mirror, and rubbed off a lipstick smear. Would he mark me down for having only one bathroom? My parents had two and a half. Well, there was nothing I could do about it now. "Coming!" I shouted and ran down the stairs.

I took a deep breath and pasted a smile on my face before opening the door. I'd never seen Geoff dressed in anything but a suit and tie, so it was strange to see him standing on my doorstep wearing khakis, a blue sweater, and a loose-fitting suede jacket. He must have gone home from the office and changed. His right hand was behind his back, but he was carrying his trusty clipboard in his left.

"Hope I'm not early," he said and flashed a brilliant smile.

"No, no. Right on time. I was just in the bathroom. Come on in!" I opened the door wider and stood aside so he could pass.

He pulled his arm out from behind his back and handed me a bouquet of flowers, pink carnations nestled among deep green ferns and baby's breath. "For you."

"Oh." I hesitated just a moment before taking the bouquet. Did he usually bring flowers when conducting a home study? Maybe this was just his way of trying to help people relax. Probably he realized how nervous I was.

"Thank you. They're very pretty."

"Pink and green," he observed. "Your favorite colors."

"That's right." How had he remembered that? "I should put these in water. Do you want to see the kitchen first?"

Geoff made a little half bow. "Lead the way," he said and followed behind me.

"I'm so nervous," I said with a giggle and was instantly annoyed at myself for doing so. But that's what I do when I'm nervous; I can't help myself.

"Perfectly understandable. But don't worry. I've done this a hundred times. You're in very good hands."

I found a vase, filled it with water, and dumped the flowers in without bothering to arrange them, then stood back and watched, barely breathing, while Geoff inspected my kitchen, opening cupboards, trying out the flame on the stove top, looking under the kitchen sink where I keep the cleaning supplies. When the child lock on the door prevented him from opening the door fully, he smiled. "Good job," he said with a wink and made a note on his clipboard. I breathed a little easier.

Next, he looked in the refrigerator, which I had stocked with a variety of vegetables and fruits, orange juice, a block of cheese, a gallon of low-fat milk, yogurt, cottage cheese, a dozen eggs, a home-roasted chicken, a package of steaks, and a loaf of whole wheat bread, among other things. It was way more food than I normally keep on hand, but I wanted to let Geoff know that I was ready and willing to prepare wholesome, home-cooked meals for Olivia.

He gave the foodstuffs a cursory glance before looking at the shelves in the door. "Aha!" He pulled a bottle of white wine off the shelf.

I blanched and closed my eyes. No! With all the trouble I had gone to in the last days and weeks—buying things, repairing things, cleaning things, making sure absolutely every inch of my house was absolutely perfect—how could I have left an open bottle of wine in the refrigerator? Right in plain view!

Geoff held up the bottle and read the label. "Very nice. Where do you keep the glasses?" Without waiting for me to answer, he opened a cupboard and took out two glasses, filled both, and handed one to me. I didn't drink, just held the glass.

Geoff took a long swallow from his glass, working his mouth a bit, a look of concentration on his face. "That *is* good," he said after a moment's consideration. "Well, everything seems fine here. Can I see the rest of the house?"

"Sure. The living room is this way."

"Yeah, let's leave that for last. Why don't you show me upstairs?"

He followed me up the stairs, still carrying his wineglass. I had mine with me too. Since he'd just poured it, I couldn't think of a polite way to leave it behind. I didn't want to insult him. I showed him the bathroom first, apologizing that there was only one, but he assured me it didn't matter.

"I grew up in a house with two parents, four kids, and one bathroom, and I turned out fine. And this is a nice size," he said, flipping the fan, then the faucet to the tub. "Good water pressure too."

I smiled gratefully and showed him Olivia's room. It really did look nice. The clouds on the wall were so pretty, and the little white bed looked fresh and bright with the new quilt spread neatly on the top. I told Geoff about the quilt, about how my friends had all contributed blocks to it, hoping he'd pick up on the fact there were a whole cadre of wonderful women in this town who were more than eager to love my niece and make her feel at home. Maybe I didn't have a husband, but I had a "village," and I knew they would help me raise Olivia.

"Very nice," Geoff said before opening the closet door and peering inside. My house is old and the closets are small, but Jake Kaminski, who owned the hardware store, had helped me pick out a collection of baskets, shelves, shoe racks, and an extra rod, all in a matching white metal, to maximize the available space. He closed the door and smiled. "What little girl wouldn't love a room like this?"

Wineglass still in hand, Geoff extended his arm in a gallant gesture, indicating that we were done here and could move on. He followed me to the top of the stairs, but stopped me when I started to descend.

"Where is your room? Isn't it upstairs?"

"Oh. Well, yes. Right over there." I nodded toward the other end of the hall. "But I didn't think you'd care about that."

"But I do. I want to see everything," he said.

I walked him past the bathroom again, and the linen closet, then into my room. I switched on the light and set my still-untouched glass down on the top of my bureau. "This is it."

My bedroom isn't large, so I moved to the far side of the room, sandwiched in the three feet of space between the bureau and the foot of my bed, feeling awkward.

Geoff came into the room, partially but not completely closing the door behind him, and turned in a slow circle, stopping and facing the wide mirror that hangs over my bureau. "This is perfect. Very nice."

After taking a drink, he put his glass down next to mine, took three long steps toward me, which is all it took to get from that side of the room to mine, and kissed me. Not a peck, not a friendly or questioning kiss or even a romantic one, but a hard, demanding kiss with half-open lips and a probing tongue, with hands bent on doing the same thing.

His breath tasted like wine and old coffee. The feel of his tongue in my mouth, thick and wet and uninvited, made me nauseous. I was shocked, stunned actually, and for a moment I honestly couldn't move. It seemed so unreal. But when one of his hands slid down my hip and started moving up under the hem of my skirt, I came to myself. With one hand, I clamped my fingers around his wrist and with the other I pushed his body away from mine.

"Stop that! What do you think you're doing?"

He smiled languidly and took half a step back, still too close for comfort. "Well, I should think that would be obvious, even to you. I know you're innocent about these things, Margot, I heard that around town, and I think it's sweet. In fact, I find it incredibly arousing. But innocent or not, you can't pretend you don't have some understanding of what's going on." He grinned. "If only in the broadest general principles. Don't worry. I'll help you fill in the details. I'll be a very good teacher; promise."

He leaned forward as if to kiss me again, but I braced my hand against his shoulder, blocking his move. "What? You heard around town . . ."

"Don't act so offended. Word gets around. Even in a city, the supply of virgins over the age of consent is limited." He reached his hand up with two fingers, brushed the hair out of my face, letting his fingers run down my cheek, to my jaw. "Especially ones as pretty as you. In a town the size of New Bern, where the supply is even smaller, even nonexistent, word spreads quicker."

The last thing I wanted to do right then was cry, but I couldn't help it; I've always been emotional, even more so when I'm angry. And when I thought about Arnie, who I had trusted, who must have been talking about me, I was furious. Tears sprang to my eyes, but I blinked hard to keep them back.

Geoff, almost as if he could read my thoughts, said, "Don't get mad. It wasn't Arnie. He's too much of a gentleman to spread rumors. And so am I. I promise you, Margot, I won't say anything to anybody. It'll be our secret. I heard it from a guy who heard it from a guy who probably heard it from another guy who you used to date, or maybe whose wife you know. It doesn't matter. You know, I didn't actually believe it at first, but the more I've gotten to know you, the more I figured it must be true."

He paused and smiled, a strange mixture of excitement and fascination on his face. "It is, isn't it?"

Before I could say anything, he put his two hands on either side of my face and kissed me again, more softly than he had the first time but still insistently, then shifted his weight forward, pushing me down, easing me toward the bed. I pushed back, hard, so hard that his backside hit the bureau and he darned near smacked into the mirror.

"Hey! What are you doing?"

"I don't think you heard me before," I said. "I told you to stop it. I am not interested in sleeping with you. I'm not interested in you at all!"

I got up and moved toward the door, but Geoff stuck out his arm, blocking my exit. His expression was angry, but he fought to soften it and his tone of voice. "Come on, Margot. I'm not buying that. Okay, so you're nervous. I get that. Having remained . . . shall we say . . . intact for so long, I can see how you might have second thoughts. But there's no use in pretending you're shocked. You knew why I was coming here tonight. You wanted me to come. You've been leading me on for weeks."

"I did not! I never led you on!"

"No? What about all those lunch dates? You think most parties in a custody case meet the guardian ad litem once a week, sometimes twice, for cozy lunch dates? I didn't take your parents to lunch every week. And what about the way you flirted with me?"

"I never flirted with you."

He smirked. "Who are you kidding? All those questions you asked me about my work and my hobbies? You were hanging on to my every word. And the giggling? How you'd laugh at my jokes? Even the ones that weren't very funny."

"I do that," I protested. "When I'm nervous. I giggle."

"And the way you let me go on about my wife," he said, continuing as if he hadn't heard me. "And what about tonight? I told you that my wife was out of town this weekend. That's why I kept canceling, because she kept canceling her weekend visits to her sister. You can't tell me you didn't pick up on that. Conducting a home study on a weekend isn't exactly usual procedure. You knew what was going to happen. You had to. Nobody is that innocent."

No. Nobody is that innocent, not even me. I didn't remember him saying anything about his wife being gone for the weekend, but something had bothered me about the idea of him coming over after office hours. But wanting to believe the best about everyone, even Geoff Bench, and, yes, wanting him to like me, not because I liked him but because I was desperate for him to recommend me as guardian, I had ignored the red flags and my own feelings, the discomfort I had felt whenever I was in his presence.

"You misunderstood," I said. "You misinterpreted—"

"Uh-uh. I don't think so." He took a step to the right, putting his body between me and the door, and picked up one of the abandoned wineglasses. "I think that after all those years of waiting, you got curious and wanted to see what you'd missed. And now that the moment is here, I think you're just scared.

"It's okay, baby," he said in a low, even voice, the sort of voice you use when trying to slip a bit and bridle over the head of an unbroken horse. "It's all going to be okay. Shhh. Just relax and let me take the lead."

He draped his arm over my shoulder and down my back in a half hug, and with his spare hand, he lifted the wineglass to my mouth, tipping the glass up high so the liquid splashed against my lips. I twisted my head to the side, refusing to drink. In one swift move, Geoff put down the glass, slopping wine over the edge, and clamped his arm low around my back, pulling me close. He shifted slightly to the left so he could watch himself in the mirror. The look on his face was lewd and proud and his voice was hoarse. He rocked his hips hard into me.

"Feel that?" he asked.

I didn't think about what I did next; my response was pure instinct. I pumped my leg back as best I could and then forward, as hard as I could, driving my knee straight into his groin. With him standing so close, I wasn't able to get much leverage, but it was enough. He yelled, doubled over, and dropped to his knees, cursing.

"Feel that?" I asked as I stepped over him.

Downstairs, I wiped away my tears and tried to collect myself. My first thought was to call someone—the police, my parents, Arnie, someone—but when I picked up the phone and started to dial, I had a second thought—the hearing. And Olivia. That was still the most important thing.

I closed my cell phone and laid it on top of the television just as

Geoff, grim-faced and smoldering, descended the stairs. My heart was pounding and my hands were shaking. I was scared. Surely, after what I'd done to him, he wouldn't want to, perhaps wouldn't be able to, pounce on me again, but I kept a good distance between us, just in case.

"Don't come any closer. If you touch me again, I'll call the judge and your law partners and—"

"Oh, trust me, the moment has passed," he said in a flat voice. "But if anyone should be worried about someone saying something to the judge, it's you, at least if you want to have a prayer of getting custody. Judge Treadlaw is the laziest judge in the county. He's going to grant custody to whoever I recommend because that's what he does, relies on the guardian to do the work and tell him what to think. So if you don't want me to tell him that Olivia should go to your parents—with a side recommendation that you be denied visitation rights—you'd better keep your mouth shut."

I swallowed hard. Much as I dislike Geoff Bench, I would never have believed he'd do something so low. On the other hand, I would never have imagined that he'd walk into my house on the pretense of doing his job and then try to coerce me into bed. The flint edge set of his jaw told me he meant what he said. And I knew what he said about Judge Treadlaw was true; Arnie had said as much from the first.

Geoff stood at the bottom of the stairs, a safe distance away from me, studying my face as I considered my options. "And if you do say anything, even if they were to believe you—which I doubt—it'd end up being a case of he said, she said. The worst that would happen to me is I'd end up with a slap on the wrist and a scolding by the judge. For you, however, it would mean starting the custody clock all over again—new guardian, new round of interviews, new home study. It could take months.

"Olivia can't stay in the hospital much longer. But if I'm out of the picture and you have to begin the process again, Olivia will have to leave the hospital and go to a foster home—maybe for months. Maybe forever. Think about it, Margot. This whole thing could backfire on you. And Olivia. Are you willing to risk that?"

He was silent for a moment. "Didn't think so. Let's make a deal. You don't say anything and I'll not only promise not to write you a negative custody report, I'll never press my . . . unwanted attentions on you again," he said, unable to keep the smirk from his voice.

Even a knee to the groin hadn't convinced him that I had no designs on him sexually. Amazing. Geoff Bench was undoubtedly the most arrogant man I'd ever met.

"Of course, if you insist on talking about this. . . ." he said, shrugging as though it made very little difference to him what I did or didn't do.

"It's a deal," I said quickly.

His lips twitched in triumph, revealing a narrow crescent of too-white teeth. "Very wise. I'd shake your hand to seal the bargain, but I'd have to touch you to do it. And you wouldn't want *that*, would you?"

He strode toward the door, pausing briefly in front of the foyer mirror to smooth his hair. When he was done, he opened the door and turned toward me.

"Just for the record, Margot, I don't think you're an innocent. I think you're a frigid b****."

❧ 51 ❧

Margot

The doorbell rang. Heart racing, I peeked through the living room curtains, afraid that Geoff Bench was back. When I saw Paul, I ran to open the door.

"So? How'd it go?"

I couldn't answer. I burst into tears.

A minute later, I was sitting on the sofa—I really don't remember how I got there—and Paul was sitting next to me, looking into my eyes. How had he known to come when he did? It didn't matter. I was just grateful for his presence.

"Talk to me, Margot. You can trust me. Really you can."

Of course I could. I knew that. In other circumstances I wouldn't have hesitated to tell him everything, but Geoff was his boss. It wouldn't be fair to put Paul in the middle of this.

"I can't tell you, Paul. I can't talk to anyone about this."

"Sure you can. I won't tell anyone else, not unless you say I can. Promise. And just to make sure," he said, "have you got a dollar?"

52

Margot

Sitting in one of those uncomfortable office chairs with the curved backs, the kind shaped like a crosscut barrel, and listening to Arnie and Paul go at each other like attorneys from opposing sides instead of what they were supposed to be, my *team* of legal advisors, I wished I had never let Paul talk me into telling Arnie about what happened.

Arnie's ears turn red when he's mad. Just then, it looked like you could have lit a match just by holding it next to one of them.

"I told her to be *nice* to him, that's all! Why not? Tell me you wouldn't have done the same thing in my shoes."

Paul put both his hands flat on the desk and leaned toward Arnie, who was standing on the opposite side. "No. I'd have told her to be cooperative and pleasant and nothing more."

"It's the same thing."

Paul moved his head slowly from one side to the other. "It's not. And you know it's not. If Margot had been a *man,* you would not have told her to be *nice.* You realized that Bench would find her attractive and you implied that she should trade on her sexuality."

"I did not! I would never do that. I don't even think of Margot that way!"

Looking up at Arnie, I crossed my arms over my chest. "Well. Thank you."

Arnie glanced down as if he'd only just realized I was in the room, which might have been true. He and Paul had been arguing over the top of my head for a good five minutes, as if I weren't even there! It was like they were jousting or jealous or I don't know what, but it was crazy. What had come over them?

"Sorry, Margot. I didn't mean it the way it sounded. But I never figured Bench would go after you like that." He raised his head, looking Paul in the eye. "I didn't."

"Why not? You should have." Paul thrust his hand in my direction, an impatient gesture. "Look at her! She's beautiful! Who wouldn't be attracted to her?"

I froze for a moment, wondering if I'd heard Paul right. I've frequently been called cute and sometimes even pretty, but no man, except my father, has ever called me beautiful. Maybe in *wanting* to hear him say it, my mind had tricked me into thinking he had. Either that or he was using hyperbole to try and score some points in this weird game of legal one-upsmanship he and Arnie were playing.

Paul leaned even farther across the desk, a vivid picture of what the phrase "in your face" means. "Didn't you know Bench has a reputation as a womanizer? I've only been in town a couple of months and even I know that."

Arnie's neck started to turn a little red, not as red as his ears, but more pinkish.

"Well . . . I'd heard one or two things, but you know how people talk around here. I didn't think there was anything to it. And, anyway, he's married."

Paul's head hinged back and his eyes went wide. He threw up his hands and barked out a single skeptical cough, as if he couldn't believe what he'd just heard. He was very expressive. Was this the sort of technique he used when arguing a case? If so, I wouldn't want to be on the opposite side from Paul in a courtroom. It was beginning to look as if poor Arnie felt the same way. Paul really was picking on him too much. But it was kind of nice having somebody stand up for me, even if I was paying him to do so. That was the best dollar I ever spent.

"Married? What's that got to do with it? I mean, seriously! Are you a lawyer or a scout master? A wedding ring doesn't mean a thing to a scuzzball like Bench."

"I didn't know he was a scuzzball. I told you that!" Arnie walked around the end of the desk and stood toe to toe, actually more like chest to chest, with Paul. They looked like a couple of bucks, warring over the same turf. If Arnie had bent down and tried to ram his head into Paul's stomach, I wouldn't have been surprised.

"Unlike some people," Arnie growled, "I'm too busy attending to my clients to spend time keeping up on the latest gossip. Maybe that's a little easier when you've just gotten to town, but I happen to have a thriving practice!"

"If you tend to the rest of your clients like you did Margot, you won't have it for long. She told you she was uncomfortable around him. She came to you for help and you didn't listen, just patted her on the head and told her to be 'nice' to him and that if she wasn't, she might lose Olivia!" Paul wasn't quite yelling, but almost, and the veins on his neck stood out. "You left her vulnerable, completely unprotected!"

He thrust out his arm and shoved the heel of his hand hard against Arnie's shoulder. Then he did it again. Arnie, his ears now the same shade as a boiled lobster, shoved him back.

I pulled myself out of the chair and spread out my arms with my hands flat, like a cop stopping traffic in two directions. "Enough!" I shouted.

Both of them jerked, startled by the noise. Their heads swiveled and they stared as if, once again, they'd only just remembered that I was in the room with them.

"Enough," I repeated, but more quietly. "This isn't getting us anywhere. And anyway, if we're going to point fingers, I have to point at myself, at least a little."

"That's crazy. What are you talking about?"

"No, you don't. Bench was totally out of line—"

I held up my hand again, damming up their protests. "Believe me, I'm not making excuses for him. And even though I wasn't sending out the slightest hint of a signal that I had any romantic or,"

I stammered, turning a little pink myself, "physical interest in him—he completely misinterpreted that—I *was* trying to make him like me. I was. Not because I actually did like him but because I wanted him to write a recommendation that would favor me. I was trying to manipulate Geoff Bench and the legal system."

Paul started to speak, but I shook my head, warning him not to.

"I know. Maybe I wasn't completely aware of what I was doing, but I should have been. And probably Arnie shouldn't have urged me to be nice to Bench, but I'm a big girl. I should have realized that what I was doing was wrong. Maybe I did, at least a little."

Paul frowned. "No, I don't think so. And even if you did do anything wrong, you weren't doing it for yourself, you were doing it for Olivia. And for Mari."

"Paul's right," Arnie said, sounding slightly surprised to find himself agreeing with Paul on anything. "Don't be so hard on yourself. Your motives were pure."

"Two wrongs don't make a right, and pure motives or not, I was wrong."

"Okay," Arnie said with a conciliatory shrug of his shoulders, "let's say that you were—just for argument's sake. But Geoff Bench was more in the wrong. You've got to let me talk to the judge. If we tell him . . ."

"No, Arnie! No. I've absolutely made up my mind. There's no use trying to talk me out of it."

He did try to talk me out of it, so did Paul, but finally they realized that I was not going to budge and they let the matter drop. Arnie went back to work preparing for the hearing and I had to go to the quilt shop. It was my turn to open. Paul asked if he could walk me to work.

It was nine-fifteen, forty-five minutes before the downtown shops would open, so we strolled rather than walked to the shop, taking our time, enjoying the sunny morning.

I love New Bern like this, when the day is fine and the streets all but empty, when the flowerboxes in front of the merchants' windows are filled with blooming daffodils, when there is no sound in the air but the chirp of birds perched in the branches of trees on the Green and the steady, soft slap of shoe leather on sidewalk. There was so much bad going on in my life, but for some reason, just at that moment, walking down Commerce Street at Paul's side, I felt good. I wanted to loop my arm through his and let it hang there like a bangle on a bracelet but, of course, I didn't.

Claudia Simon was unlocking the door of the art gallery and glanced up. "Morning, Margot. Morning, Paul."

"Morning, Claudia."

As we passed, Claudia looked at me with raised brows and a curious expression that quickly became a smile, topped off by a knowing wink. Embarrassing. Thankfully, Paul didn't see her. He looked straight ahead as he walked and said nothing until just before we reached the alley that leads to Cobbled Court.

"Nice day."

"Uh-huh."

Paul stopped, touched me lightly on the shoulder, and peered into my eyes. "Hey, are you okay? You're not worried, are you? Everything is going to turn out fine."

I nodded. "I know. I'm not sure it's all going to turn out the way I'm wishing it would but, no matter what, I'm sure it will be for the best. Maybe that sounds a little naïve, but I believe it."

He smiled and we resumed walking, taking a right turn into the cobblestone alley. "You have an extraordinary faith, Margot. That's one of the things I admire about you."

I didn't quite know what to say to that, so I changed the subject. "I wish the judge had assigned you as the guardian instead of Geoff Bench."

"Me too," Paul replied. "But even if he had, I would have been forced to withdraw from the case."

"Why?"

"Because it would be a conflict of interest for me to serve as guardian in a custody case when I have a romantic interest in one of the involved parties."

I stopped. Paul went on for a couple more steps, then turned around, realizing I was behind him.

"I'm sorry," I said, certain that he could not have said what I just thought he said and that, once again, wishful thinking was getting the better of my good sense. "Could you repeat that?"

"I said I couldn't serve as Olivia's guardian because of my romantic interest in you." He cleared his throat, looking a little embarrassed. "I realize my feelings aren't reciprocated, but it's still a conflict."

"A romantic interest. In me? I thought..."

He tipped his head to one side and frowned. "Well... yes, you. Who else? You didn't..." He smiled and lifted one eyebrow, as if something comical had just occurred to him. He laughed. "Oh my gosh, you haven't been listening to those crazy rumors about me and Philippa, have you?"

"Well, um. No. I mean..." I could feel the color rising in my cheeks. "That is to say... I knew you *liked* her. I knew the two of you were close friends and all." I was beet red, blathering, and once again, on the verge of tears. I laid my hand on my chest.

"Me? You're sure you mean me?"

A slow smile, homey and unhurried and sweet, like syrup over pancakes on a Sunday morning, spread across his face. He opened his arms.

"Come here."

I walked toward him and he met me halfway, our lips meeting at the same time and in the same way as our bodies did, fully and sweetly. It felt like home to be in his embrace, familiar and safe, but at the same time it was exciting and new, the discovery of a strange and exotic land, a place I wanted to explore completely and know intimately.

His lips were so soft, so very soft on mine and his hands were in my hair, cradling my head. I tilted my chin up and opened my lips, just a little, a shy invitation. Taking his time, his tongue gently outlined the curve of my lips, tasting me, letting me taste him. Instinctively, my mouth opened wider, wanting more of him, thrilled to learn he wanted more of me as well.

For a moment, less than an instant, my mind flashed to the memory of Geoff Bench doing the same thing. No. Not the same thing.

There was no comparison. No kiss had ever been like this. No kiss ever would be.

There was no time when I was in Paul's arms, no thought of what came before or what would happen after, so I don't know how much of it had passed when he shuddered and pulled away gasping. "I have to stop."

"But I don't want you to stop. Why should you?"

His eyes smiling, he took in a deep breath and blew it out as if he were recovering from a race. "Well, aside from the probability of you not respecting me in the morning, there's the fact that you're supposed to open the shop in," he pulled up his sleeve so he could see his watch, "twelve minutes."

Twelve minutes?

"I don't care," I said and reached for him, wanting nothing in the world as much as I wanted to feel his lips on mine. I kissed him again for a minute or five, I don't know how long, only stopping when I pressed myself close against him and felt that stirring that had repelled me when coming from Geoff Bench but that coming from Paul flooded me with a tide of longing so powerful, so irresistible that it very nearly swept me away.

When he had stormed out of my house, Bench had called me a name I never have and never will say, preceded by an ugly adjective—"frigid." I knew he'd said it to wound me and soothe his vanity and that I should think nothing more of it. But that was easier to say than do. I had kissed men before, Arnie for one, and several others during college and my years living in New York. Occasionally, I had let things progress further than kisses. The kisses and caresses of those others, excluding Bench, had often been pleasant, sometimes sweet, never more than that. I'd had no difficulty in putting on the brakes with Arnie and men of his ilk, not ever. And so when Geoff Bench called me frigid, I couldn't help but wonder if it might be true.

Now I had my answer.

"You're right," I gasped, pulling myself away from Paul and

clamping my arms around my chest, hugging myself as tightly as possible to keep from grabbing him again. "We have to stop."

"We do. We should," Paul said in a voice that didn't sound entirely convinced. "But I have to tell you, Margot. Wow. I don't want to. I really don't."

"Neither do I! Isn't it great?" I laughed, not a nervous giggle or a self-conscious chuckle, but full-throated and joyous laughter. I couldn't help myself.

"What's so funny?"

"Nothing," I said and linked my arm with his, joined at last, as we left the narrow alley and walked into the wide and sunny cobblestone courtyard, past the brick planter stuffed with daffodils in bloom, and the bowfront display window stacked with pink, green, and yellow bolts of cotton, our salute to spring, stopping in front of the brightly painted red front door, and I kissed him again, lightly this time, on the lips.

"Nothing important. I was just remembering something silly someone said."

❦ 53 ❦

Margot

The next five days passed with a strange mixture of elation and anxiety. Paul picked me up from work almost every night that week and the three of us—Paul, James, and I—had dinner together. Paul cooked twice and I cooked twice.

It was a good thing that we had James along as unwitting chaperone for those dinners; every time I saw Paul it was all I could do to keep from grabbing him, but I enjoyed James for his own sake too. He's a very sweet kid (though I'm convinced he cheats at Rummikub; nothing else could explain my dismal score). I love seeing how he and Paul interact.

Evenings with Paul and James, followed by a too-brief moonlight stroll when Paul walked me from his doorstep to mine, too much of a gentleman to come inside though I often wished he would, and kisses good night that only became sweeter as the days passed, these were the hours of elation, the things that bore me up through the anxious hours until the hearing.

I spent at least an hour at the hospital every day, longer if my work schedule allowed. On Tuesday I picked up a pizza after work and took it to the hospital to share with Olivia. I wished Paul and James could have joined us, but so close to the hearing I couldn't risk it. If my parents found out and raised a fuss, I knew Geoff Bench wouldn't lift a finger to help me.

I didn't tell Olivia anything about the upcoming hearing, only that she would be getting out of the hospital soon. That seemed to satisfy her. She was more interested in our current project, layering die-cut fabric butterflies of different sizes together and gluing them to the front of blue note cards, invitations for Mari's memorial service, than in asking questions. I hoped I wasn't setting her up for another loss. The memorial was important to Olivia, but if my parents were granted custody, I knew they would put a stop to it.

Dad couldn't seem to grasp that few of Olivia's memories of Mari were sad. If he stopped to think it through, he might have come to the same conclusion. We'd had hard days as a family, maybe more than our share, but we'd had good ones too. Could he have forgotten?

On Thursday, after Paul walked me home, I got ready for bed, said my prayers, turned out the light, and . . . nothing. Sleep would not come.

I kept thinking about the hearing, the judge, my parents, Olivia's trusting eyes and Geoff Bench's deceitful ones. My thoughts were circular, tumbling one over the other like water rushing down a rapid; there wasn't any controlling or stopping them. I tried thinking about Paul, his face, his voice, his kisses, but even that didn't help.

Finally, I gave up and got up. After putting on my robe and making a pot of tea, I sat at the kitchen table while the dark world slept, a mug of steaming chamomile at the ready, holding my worn Bible unopened in my hands. I didn't have to open the pages to read; the verses I had always counted on in times of trouble flooded my mind and soothed my soul. And I prayed like I had never prayed before. The words were nothing, there was no eloquence or loftiness to them, but they poured from me in groans, like the moans of a mother laboring to bring a child into the world.

Thy will be done. Grant me wisdom to recognize it, courage to bear it, whatever it may be. Nothing less than Your will because I need nothing more.

❦ 54 ❦

Margot

Evelyn told me to take all of Friday off, but I went to the shop and worked until lunch. Better to have someplace to go and something to do than spend the morning pacing back and forth across my living room carpet.

At noon, Evelyn put a sign on the front door reading CLOSED FOR THE DAY. Everyone—Evelyn, Virginia, Ivy, and Dana—went to the courthouse with me. Abigail, Tessa, Madelyn, and Philippa were there when we arrived. Sitting in the gallery, my friends made quite a cheering section. Paul wanted to come, but I convinced him not to. Besides it being a workday, considering what he knew about Geoff Bench and that they worked at the same firm, it wouldn't have been a good idea.

Bench was sitting in the first row behind the railing. With his arm draped over the chair next to him and his legs crossed languidly, he tracked my progress as I entered the courtroom and took my seat next to Arnie. He had an appraising, slightly contemptuous look on his face, as though he were sitting at a café table in some beachfront town, watching the girls go by. My parents were already seated at the table opposite us.

The routine was familiar by now; Judge Treadlaw came in, we stood up, he sat down and glared at us as if we'd all barged into his house uninvited. After putting on his reading glasses and scratching his nose, the judge opened a file folder and started riffling through papers.

"Mr. Bench, where is your recommendation? I don't see it in the file."

I twisted in my chair so I could see him better. Bench got to his feet and smoothed the lapels of his jacket. "Yes, Your Honor. I'm aware of that."

His eyes shifted briefly in my direction and I felt the bottom drop out of my stomach. He was about to pull something underhanded; I just knew it.

"Your Honor, I could not submit a recommendation for custody because, ethically, I am forced to withdraw from the case. I'm afraid that I ... that a ... a personal relationship has developed between Miss Matthews and myself, the nature of which ..." He cleared his throat, feigning embarrassment, implying the worst without saying anything specific, "makes it impossible for me to continue as guardian ad litem for the minor child."

My mother gasped. My father shook his head. So did Judge Treadlaw.

"This is a very disturbing admission, Mr. Bench, especially at this stage of the proceedings. You and I will have a talk in my chambers later, sir."

Geoff's shoulders drooped with pretended shame, but as he resumed his seat I could see the flicker of triumph in his eyes. He knew Judge Treadwell, and he was confident nothing more would come of this besides a stern lecture given in private—the "slap on the wrist" he had mentioned.

"Miss Matthews," the judge continued, peering at me over the top of his glasses. "I cannot pretend that this reflects well on your petition for custody."

Arnie was instantly on his feet. "Your Honor, my client resents and denies Mr. Bench's implication. He has no proof to support this. And to allow yourself to be unfairly prejudiced against my client simply on the basis of—"

The judge held up his hand and glowered at Arnie. "Counselor,

I would never allow myself to be unfairly prejudiced against anyone who appears in my courtroom." He pointed his gavel straight at Arnie as if it were a scolding finger. "Do not presume to instruct me in my duties, Mr. Kinsella. Do not presume."

Arnie adjusted his tie and sank into his chair.

"Mr. Bench's assertions, while disturbing, are, at the moment, immaterial. However, without a recommendation for custody, I have no choice but to assign another guardian ad litem, one *not* personally involved with anyone in the case, and begin the process again. In the meantime, because the child's medical condition has improved, it's clear she can no longer stay in the hospital. Therefore, I am granting temporary custody of the minor child to the state. She will be placed in foster care until the new guardian can submit a recommendation."

I clutched at Arnie's arm. "No! She can't go to a foster home!" I hissed. "He can't—"

Arnie shook his head quickly, warning me to keep silent.

"I don't wish to delay, but given the circumstances," the judge said as he slid his glasses down his nose again, giving me another admonishing look, a look that said he had already made up his mind about me, "I want to give the new guardian ad litem time for a thorough investigation. And since I'm scheduled to be in Florida for three weeks in May, we'll reschedule the hearing for permanent custody to a date approximately four months hence."

"Four months!" I turned to grab Arnie's arm and caught a glimpse of Geoff Bench's smirking face.

He planned this whole thing, keeping to the letter of our agreement, not making a negative recommendation about me but knowing full well that withdrawing from the case because of a supposed "personal relationship" with me would have the same effect. He knew that seeing Olivia placed in foster care was one of my worst fears and that his unverifiable accusation would make Judge Treadlaw question my moral fitness to serve as Olivia's permanent guardian. What kind of man would do such a thing? And all to soothe his wounded pride? He was a horrible, evil person. I should have followed my instincts about him, but it was too late for that.

"Arnie! Olivia can't go to foster care, not after all she's been through. Do something!"

But before the words were even out of my mouth, I knew his hands were tied. The judge had ruled. There was nothing he could do to help Olivia. That was up to me.

I pushed my chair away from the table and rose to my feet. "Excuse me, Your Honor. I have something to say."

✥ 55 ✥

Margot

That night looked like any other meeting of our quilt circle. All my friends were in the workroom. And everyone except Ivy, who was perched on one of the windowsills, and Abigail, who was fingering a strand of pearls as she paced from one end of the room to the other, was sitting in her usual spot. The sewing machines were set up, the irons were plugged in, and there were piles of fabric, batting, and quilts in various stages of completion lying about. A big platter of Madelyn's Bourbon Street brownies sat on the table.

However, there was one telling difference between this Friday night and the scores of others I had spent in the room with these women—no one was quilting. I couldn't ever remember that happening before, no matter how bad things were. But then again, it was possible things had never been quite this bad before.

Everyone was shocked when I stood up in the courtroom and announced I was relinquishing my claim for custody, even the judge.

"Are you sure of this, Miss Matthews?"

It was the hardest question I've ever had to answer.

"Yes, Your Honor. I'm sure. I don't want Olivia to go into foster care." I turned toward my parents. My mother's eyes were filled with tears, and for the first time in weeks, my father's eyes met mine. "I would like to request visitation rights, if that would be all right."

The judge glanced at my dad, who gave a single nod.
"I'm sure something can be worked out."

Abigail, utterly unaccustomed to losing, stopped pacing and threw up her hands. "I can't believe you're going to lie down for this. Geoff Bench is a lying, double-crossing, lecherous leech. He's besmirched your reputation! You mustn't allow him to get away with it, Margot. It's not right! It's not fair!"

Madelyn let out a contemptuous little laugh. "Well, whoever said life was fair?"

Having spent a lot of her life among the highest of New York's high financial circles—swimming with the sharks, as she would say—Madelyn is more than a little cynical. But she has a point. I believe in fairness and justice, I just don't believe we always find them here on earth. Geoff Bench will get what's coming to him—eventually. In the meantime, I've got something more important to worry about than my "besmirched reputation."

"Abigail, it'd be a case of Bench's word against mine. Who do you think the judge is going to believe? You saw the way he looked at me."

Abigail started pacing again. She was pulling on her necklace so hard that I expected it to snap at any moment, sending a shower of pearls rolling across the floor.

"What's happened to you, Margot? You used to be a regular Pollyanna. Sometimes I've found it quite annoying, but not nearly as annoying as discovering that you've lost your optimism just when it might do you some actual good."

"Abigail, I'm not going to let them put Olivia in foster care."

"Yes, yes. So you've said. But . . . four months! What's four months? It's barely more than a season."

I was so tired of arguing with Abigail. It wasn't as if I hadn't already gone through all of this in my mind. I knew what was right in this situation, and I knew what I had to do.

"If you're six years old and dealing with grief, loss, and abandonment, four months is an eternity. If Olivia was placed with the wrong sort of family, it might turn out to be the four months that scar her beyond the possibility of healing. I can't do that to her, Abbie. I love her too much."

"Of course you do," Abigail protested. "But don't you see? That's exactly why Olivia *should* be with you."

"I'm not the only person who loves her, Abbie. Do I think that Olivia would be better off being raised by me than my parents? Yes. But they aren't monsters. After all, they raised me, and I turned out all right."

Abigail crossed her arms over her chest and set her jaw. "And your sister? How did they do raising her?"

She was treading on sensitive ground now. If someone I liked less than Abigail had asked me such a personal question, I'd have told them to mind their own business. But I know Abigail; once she asks a question, she won't give up until she gets an answer.

"Maybe not as well as they could have, but they loved Mari and they love Olivia too. That's the most important thing. That's what Olivia needs more than anything right now, love and stability. By giving up my claim for custody, I can give her that."

"But what about your feelings—"

"No!" I snapped. "This isn't about me. Please, don't make this any harder for me than it already is."

Abigail, looking slightly abashed, said, "Of course. I'm not trying to be difficult, I'm just worried about you, that's all."

"I know."

"What does Paul say about all this?" Evelyn asked.

By now, everyone knew about Paul and me. Funny how quickly the people who loved and knew me best assumed that Paul would naturally have a voice in any of my major decisions. They'd never thought about Arnie that way, but neither had I. And their assumptions were right on target. Paul was the first person I'd called after leaving the courtroom. He said he'd come right over, but I told him not to. He had to go to youth group. Philippa wouldn't be able to handle it on her own, and tonight of all nights, I needed to be with my quilting sisters.

"He understands I'm trying to do what's best for Olivia. But there was a lot of talk about inflicting bodily harm on Geoff Bench—pistols at fifty paces or something."

Abigail exclaimed, "Hear! Hear!" and the others clapped their hands. Ivy whistled through her teeth and said, "Forget fifty paces. Let's try rotary cutters at close range."

There was an idea. But as much as I appreciated the support of my girlfriends, it was nice to have a champion of my own at last.

"Paul seems like a very good man," Virginia said.

He is. None better.

When I came home after quilt circle, Paul was sitting on the stoop.

"How long have you been here?"

He put his arm around me as he walked me toward the front door. "Half hour or so." Anticipating my next question, he said, "James is fine. Philippa came over and brought Clementine. He's beating them at Rummikub."

"Hope she's not playing him for money."

He put his hands on my shoulders and turned my body toward his. "Are you all right?"

Isn't it funny how that question, asked by someone you love, someone who truly wants to know, can summon the tears you've managed to keep back all day?

"I'm sorry," I said, lifting my head from his chest.

"For what?"

"I got your shirt all wet."

He pushed open the front door and we went inside. "I've got other shirts."

~~ 56 ~~

Margot

I didn't set the alarm, but I got up before dawn just the same. I'd never really fallen asleep to begin with, knowing what the new day would bring. Today, I had to tell Olivia that she'd be leaving the hospital and going home with her grandparents. It was a conversation I dreaded.

I dawdled in the shower, drank three cups of coffee, and took an extra-long time at my prayers, hoping God would give me just the right words to say to Olivia and that I'd be able to say them without falling apart. No wise words came to mind, however, and just before nine, I decided to quit putting off the inevitable.

My purse was on my shoulder and my car keys in hand when I heard the sound of a car pulling into the driveway. When I pulled back the curtain, I saw Paul and my parents climbing out of Paul's car.

What was going on? Paul had never even met my parents. And why were the three of them standing on my front porch?

Between my parents, Dad was always the bigger talker, but today, Mom was the one with the answers. Dad sat silently at one end of the sofa looking small and weathered, like a balloon beginning to deflate and sink toward the floor. All his bluster was gone.

"We never wanted things to turn out like this," Mom said, glancing toward my father, speaking for him. Dad bobbed his head in agreement, but didn't look at me.

If I'd been an observer of the family drama that had played out in the last few weeks instead of a participant, I might have found Mom's statement hard to swallow, but I'd gotten caught up in the craziness too. Shock, grief, the festering of unresolved anger, and the need to gain and hold the upper hand had combined into a poisonous brew.

Arnie had told me that a court case is a competition, and he was right about that, but he was wrong too. There were no winners in this. We'd all been sucked into a game that left us sadder, lonelier, and poorer in spirit than we would have been if we'd never played in the first place.

"We were so tired when we got back to the hotel, but neither of us could sleep. We got up and started reading the Bible, the story of the two women who claimed to be the mother of the same child and came before King Solomon, asking him to settle the matter. When the king said he couldn't and that the only fair thing to do was to cut the baby in half, giving a piece of the dead child to each, one of the women relinquished her claim. She was the true mother. She proved that by being willing to sacrifice her rights and her happiness to protect her child from harm.

"When we finished reading the passage," my mother continued, looking at my father again, whose head was bowed so low that it was impossible to read his expression, "we realized that in this whole thing, you were the only one who had behaved like a true parent. Just about that time, the front desk rang our room and said there was someone in the lobby who wanted to see us. It was Paul. He called every hotel in town to track us down."

"There aren't that many hotels in the area," Paul replied with a shrug, indicating it was no big deal. "Werner and Lillian had already decided what they wanted to do."

"But you convinced us to come over here and talk to Margot," Mom said. "Margot, I know that saying I'm sorry can't even begin to make things right, but . . . I don't know how else to begin. I am sorry. We both are." Her gaze flickered toward my father and she paused just long enough to give him a chance to jump in and affirm her statement. When he didn't, she continued. "We feel awful, Margot. We didn't mean the things we said, you know, about the protest march and your medical records. It's just that—"

Head still hanging low, Dad lifted his hand, cutting off my mother's explanation.

"Stop, Lil. Don't. *You* were the one who pulled out the Bible and found that story. You were the one who read it to me and made me see sense. You were the one who stood up for Margot and Olivia. Don't give me credit I don't deserve. And don't apologize for me. I've made you do that too many times over the years."

I'd have argued with him if I could, but Dad was right. In our family, when it came to wounds, apologies, and forgiveness—it was Dad who inflicted the wounds, Mom who offered the apologies, and my sister and I who were expected to extend forgiveness. That was the way it worked. Every careless word or thoughtless gesture on Dad's part was always swept under the rug, out of sight but never completely out of mind, all of us complicit in the cover-up.

Dad opened his big hands, laid them flat against his thighs as if he were preparing to push off and get to his feet, but he sat still for a long moment before finally raising his head, revealing red-rimmed eyes.

"I can't think of any reason in the world you could or should forgive me, but even so, I want you to know I'm sorry. Everything that's gone wrong since Mari died, and for a long time before, was my fault."

"Dad. It wasn't just you. I should have called you, tried harder to work out some kind of solution. . . ."

He held up his hand. "Don't let me off the hook, Margot. I didn't listen, not to you and not to your sister. Everything always has to be my way. That's what drove Mari away. I think part of me knew it even before the accident, but it took Mari dying before I was willing to admit it. Since it was too late to make things right with Mari, I got it in my head to undo all my mistakes by raising Olivia. But I just made it worse, didn't I? I made it all about me. Again.

"I never gave you credit for all you've accomplished, never told you how proud I am of you, Margot. I was afraid to let you grow up, afraid you'd know more and do more than your old man, then wouldn't need me anymore. I treated you like a child, but you're a woman, a fine one. And you'll be a fine mother to Olivia. Mari knew what she was doing when she picked you. I'm going to go over to the courthouse and tell the judge that before we go back to Buffalo."

Avoiding my gaze, he got to his feet and walked toward the door. My mother followed him, but not before casting an imploring glance at me. She didn't need to. Everything I said and did after that was my own idea and came from the heart.

I reached out as Dad passed by, clasping hold of his heavy hand, freckled with age, calloused by work and the commitment to provide for his family, the hand that spanked me when I was bad, applauded me when I was good, embraced me when I was both, the hand of a man who had made mistakes but done the best he could, the hand of experience, the hand of a father.

"Daddy? Mom? Hang on a minute. Let's talk."

∽ 57 ∽

Philippa

April

It was raining hard, but that hadn't prevented people from coming to church. Word had gotten around that Reverend Tucker was home for a visit and would be preaching at Sunday services. They came in droves to hear him and wish him well.

I won't say the idea that people might compare Bob's preaching with mine and find me wanting never crossed my mind, but I was too interested in his sermon to think about it much.

He spoke about the early church as presented in the book of Acts. I couldn't help but notice and feel a bit proud of how our little church had moved closer to that model in the last couple of weeks. No, we weren't holding all our goods in common, or eating all our meals together, but we were behaving more like a community than we had when I arrived.

Attendance was up, and not just when Bob was preaching. We had more visitors every week, and greater numbers in children's and adult Sunday school classes. And we had more people serving, a lot more. Summer was months away and the roster of teachers and support staff for Vacation Bible School was filled. People were volunteering who'd never offered to help before. Adam Kingsbury, our former treasurer, who after serving four years in that job had certainly earned a break, had teamed up with Jake Kaminski, who owns the hardware store, to start a new ministry called "Helping Hands." Their idea was to devote one Saturday a month to home repair and maintenance for anyone in town who needed help.

Yesterday had been the first Saturday work session, and twenty-six volunteers had shown up to paint a kitchen, install smoke alarms, patch a leaky roof, haul away trash, and put in a new handrail on a staircase. They'd also installed a wheelchair ramp in the home of a family whose son had been injured in Afghanistan. Though the Grizzards weren't members of our church, they'd come to the service. Dennis and Jean were sitting at the left end of the front pew and Blake was right next to them, sitting in his wheelchair.

During the offertory hymn, I noticed Margot in the back, far from her usual spot. Her parents were there too, sitting to her left. Olivia, James, and Paul sat to her right. Margot was beaming, as were her parents. They looked right together, the six of them, all of a piece, like a family, a happy one. What an amazing change.

As the organist rolled into the final, triumphant chords of "How Great Thou Art" and I walked to the center aisle to receive the offering, I could not help but think, "How great. How great indeed."

I wanted to talk to Margot during the coffee hour, but I got caught up with the Grizzards. When I finished speaking to them, I spotted Margot at the fringes of Reverend Tucker's circle of admirers, but before I could join the group, Ted Carney, Miranda Wyatt, and Abigail Spaulding came looking for me. When they ushered me off into an empty Sunday school classroom, saying there was something they needed to discuss with me in private, my heart sank.

It occurred to me that maybe I should have been more worried about people comparing me with Reverend Tucker that morning. He looked healthy, energetic, and completely recovered. Maybe he had decided to cut his sabbatical short. Surely the church would be only too happy to have him back early. Who could blame them? If

I'd had to choose between Bob Tucker and me, I'd have gone with Bob too. But, oh . . . I was going to miss New Bern.

As Ted closed the door, shutting out the sound of chatter and laughter coming from the fellowship hall, I decided to beat them to the punch. It would be easier for them and less humiliating for me.

Perching my pregnant body on a chair designed to fit an eight-year-old wasn't easy, but I did my best. "Listen, Ted," I said, trying to keep my voice even and businesslike, "I think I know what you want to talk about."

"Excellent!" Abigail said briskly. "Then this shouldn't take long. Franklin and I have a two o'clock tee time. Assuming the weather clears up. April is such an unpredictable month." She sighed and I nodded. It certainly was.

"Well," I continued, determined to make this as painless as possible, "I want you all to know how much I've enjoyed serving here. It's been a wonderful experience."

"Good. I'm glad to hear you say so," Ted said. "You and I had a few rocky moments, but we sorted everything out in the end, didn't we?" He shifted his eyes from me to Miranda and back to me.

"Absolutely."

"We were worried that it might be too much for you, especially with the baby," Miranda said.

"No. Certainly not," I said, bristling a bit at the suggestion.

Never, at any point, had I let my condition prevent me from giving my very best to the congregation. Until the congregational meeting, no one had even guessed I was pregnant. It was one thing to rescind my contract because they wanted to bring Reverend Tucker back early, but saying they were doing so because I hadn't been able to handle the workload during my pregnancy was something else entirely. After all my long hours and hard work, that hurt.

"Since coming to New Bern, I've never worked less than a ten-hour day."

Miranda looked at Ted and Abigail. "That's why we've been worried. It's just too much. That's why we settled on a three-quarter position. It will be so much better for everyone."

"Three-quarter position?" I shifted in the pint-sized desk chair, trying to find a spot where the plastic backrest didn't hit me in the kidneys.

"I understand your hesitation," Abigail said. "We all know that there's no such thing as part-time ministry, but we're going to be vigilant about making sure that you have three full days off per week. I'm going to hold them to it, I can promise you that!"

Her posture, as always, was ramrod straight, but she pulled her shoulders back even farther, as if to underscore her immovability on this point—whatever the point might be. I had no idea what she was talking about.

"Excuse me. But aren't the three of you here to tell me you're going to terminate my contract early?"

Abigail's eyebrows shot up. "Terminate your contract? On the contrary, we'd like to extend it—"

"With some stipulations," Ted interrupted and then cleared his throat officiously. "Last week, I took it upon myself to make a few calls to board members, nothing official, mind you, to take something of a straw poll to discuss various options and opportunities that might be . . ."

Abigail set her jaw and crossed her arms over her chest while Ted droned on about staffing optimization, volunteer utilization, and some sort of statistical study he'd read about in the *Christian Science Monitor* that, at least to me, seemed entirely unrelated to either issue. Abigail glowered. The two biggest personalities on the board might be on better terms than previously, but it was clear the cessation of hostilities in the Carney / Spaulding battle was an armistice at best, possibly a short one. Abigail looked ready to explode, but Miranda came to the rescue and laid her hand on Ted's arm. Happily distracted by her touch, Ted stopped talking and turned toward her.

"I think what Ted is trying to say is that he, and the rest of the board," she said, nodding toward Abigail, who uncrossed her arms, "were concerned about our staffing situation even before Reverend Tucker's heart attack, but we were at a loss as to how to deal with it. Last week, Abigail and Ted got together for a bit of brainstorming and came up with a few ideas.

"Basically, it comes down to this: We'd like you to complete your original contract and then, after taking off a few months for maternity leave, come back on as a three-quarter-time associate minister. You'd preach once a month, which would give Bob a break, but your primary emphasis would be pastoral counseling and volunteer coordination. How does that sound to you?"

The proposal caught me by surprise, so much so that I hesitated a moment before answering. "It sounds ... perfect."

And it really was, a position that played to my strengths and a schedule that would make motherhood a bit easier. I only had a couple of concerns.

"But how are you going to pay for another staff position? The budget is pretty tight as it is. And ... will there be an allowance for housing?" I didn't wish to appear ungrateful, but at three-quarter salary, there was no way I could afford to pay for rent.

"The Wynne Foundation will fund the position for the first three years," Abigail explained. For all intents and purposes, Abigail *was* the Wynne Foundation, so I knew that the idea had probably originated with her.

"The foundation focuses our funding on projects that emphasize community involvement, matching grants and the like, getting people to participate in solving their problems instead of just expecting the foundation to throw money at them. The church's newfound emphasis on volunteerism makes it a perfect fit with our mission."

Ted took over from there. "Barbara Stadler did a bit of number crunching. Using volunteers from within the church should actually offset much of the cost of a new position. And the leftover money from Waldo's bequest will give us the money we need to remodel the third floor of the parsonage into an apartment for you and the baby." Ted grinned. "Assuming you don't plan on having any other children, it should be plenty big enough for the two of you."

I laughed. "I'm pretty sure that one baby will be as much as I can handle, but ... are you sure that the Tuckers will want to give up the space?"

"It was their idea," Miranda said. "With their children grown and gone, they don't need it. And Sharon is hoping you'll let her babysit now and then. So?" She clapped her hands together in a "let's wrap this up" gesture. "What do you think? After the baby is born, would you like to come back to New Bern?"

For a moment, I was so choked up that I couldn't speak. But I didn't have to. My smile said it all.

∾ 58 ∾

Margot

July

I opened the cardboard box, pulled out a ceramic cup with pink blossoms painted on the side and a green handle that looked like a twig. "Mom? Where do you want these?"

My mother was sitting cross-legged on the kitchen floor trying to figure out how to fit a small mountain of cookware into a cupboard about the size of a toaster oven. She looked up at me and groaned. "The Desert Rose dishes? Didn't those go in the garage sale?"

I peered into the box and shook my head. "Looks like they're all here, the whole set. What do you want me to do with them?"

"I don't know."

She climbed up off the floor and started opening cupboards, searching for an empty shelf. There weren't any. Every inch of available space in the tiny kitchen was already packed with dishes, glasses, serving pieces, pots, pans, and assorted bric-a-brac. In preparation for the move, my parents had sold or given away about half of their possessions, but they still had way more stuff than could be easily squeezed into the two-bedroom cottage they'd decided to rent for a year before buying a house in New Bern.

Mom turned around and stared vacantly at the box, then shrugged.

"Just tape it up and put it in the garage with the rest of the overflow. I think we're going to have to rent one of those storage units. Is that the last box for the kitchen? Please," she said and clutched at my arm in mock desperation. "Tell me it is."

I smiled. One of the several pleasures of having my parents move to New Bern was rediscovering my mother's sense of humor.

"Unless Dad and Paul are hiding more in the truck, that's it. Where are those two anyway? I haven't seen them for a while."

"I don't know," Mom said, quickly opening a drawer and riffling through a pile of silverware. "Margot, have you seen any other tea-spoons? I think some are missing."

"No."

"Huh. You sure? Well, I suppose they'll turn up eventually."

Mom shut the drawer as Olivia came running into the kitchen. Except for a slight limp that the doctor said she'd always have, you'd never have been able to tell that she'd spent so many weeks in the hospital and in physical therapy. Olivia would never be a track star, but she could walk and she could run. I was so grateful.

"Grandma," Olivia said in a voice that wasn't quite a whine, but close, "you promised to play with me. James is *so* boring. He's just reading his stupid book and I've been waiting for you for-ev-er!" Olivia moaned and draped herself over the back of a kitchen chair, feigning exhaustion. I pressed my lips together to keep from smiling. Olivia was Mari's child, all right.

"Livie," I chided. "Is that any way to speak to Grandma?"

She looked at me and squirmed a little, rolling her head side-ways. After a moment, she pulled herself to a standing position and sighed. "Grandma, could you please play with me?"

Mom smiled. "Of course I will play with you, sweetheart, right after I make lunch."

"I can do that, Mom."

Mom cast a doubtful glance at the pile of cookware that was still sitting on the floor. "You don't mind?"

"Not a bit," I assured her. "You two go on and enjoy yourselves. After all, isn't that why you've moved to New Bern? To spend more time with Olivia?"

Mom turned to me and smiled that sweet smile that, when I was little, first made me think I knew what angels looked like.

"Among other people."

The bond between Olivia and my parents has grown quickly; she's so open, so ready to give and receive love. For the rest of us, the process has been a little more complicated.

Spring and summer has been a period of getting reacquainted for my parents and me, a time for sloughing off old prejudices and shredding out-of-date biographies, making allowance for growth and change, casting off the assumption that what always was is what always must be.

It hasn't been easy. There have been arguments, not all of them instigated by Dad. I, too, have raised my voice in these last weeks, not often but more than once. I'm a peacemaker by nature, but I've come to learn that to attain real and lasting peace, you sometimes need to endure temporary disharmony, and that speaking your mind isn't disloyal or sinful. In fact, if you think about it, *not* speaking your mind can be the greater sin. After all, it's just another kind of deception, isn't it?

Paul taught me that. It's one of the things I love about him, his honesty. I never have to guess where I stand with him and I never have to pretend. It's so refreshing, different from any relationship I've ever had.

Bit by bit, my parents and I have gotten to know each other again, and to appreciate each other. And so, when Mom started dropping hints that she wasn't sure if she could endure another winter in Buffalo and Dad started talking about retiring and both of them finally came right out and said they'd like to move to New Bern so they could spend more time with Olivia and help take care of her when I was at work, I said I'd like that very much. And I meant it, for all kinds of reasons.

The transition from single woman to working mom has been every bit as challenging as I thought it would be. Without the help of my quilt circle friends, I'd never have managed. They cheered me on, offered me advice and shoulders to cry on, and helped me cobble together a schedule of play dates and babysitting that allowed me to work a full schedule in the quilt shop. Olivia is crazy about "the aunties," and it's easy to see why.

Take this weekend—Olivia stayed with Ivy while I drove up to Buffalo to help my folks with the move. When I picked her up last night, Olivia told me all about her adventures.

On Saturday morning, she and ten-year-old Bethany walked to the inn to visit Auntie Madelyn. Madelyn let them play with the dollhouse in the parlor and helped the girls bake a batch of lemon lavender shortbread cookies. Next, they walked to the quilt shop to help Auntie Evelyn sort fat quarters into colors and Auntie Virginia stitch bindings on two new baby quilts that were to be donated to the preemie unit at the hospital. At lunchtime, they walked to the Grill on the Green, where Uncle Charlie made them cheeseburgers and fries. Later, Auntie Abigail picked them up and drove them to her house for a swim in her enormous pool. Bobby, who had spent the morning fishing with Franklin, joined them. Finally, Auntie Ivy took the troops home and made them a picnic supper they ate inside a tent they made out of quilts and sofa cushions while they watched *The Black Stallion* on DVD. It had been a busy and wonderful day.

When she finished the story, Olivia let her head flop back onto the seat of the car and sighed. "I love having a big family."

So do I.

Families, I've decided, are a lot like quilts—they've got layers. The first layer is the family of choice, the people you pick out of the crowd and stitch together, as different in outlook and experience as patches in a quilt. Piecing it all together, figuring out exactly how the patches fit together, takes time and patience. You've got to find just the right balance of colors, shapes, and textures, but if you stick with it, before long you'll have created something unique but sturdy that keeps you covered and makes life lovelier. That's exactly how I think of Evelyn, Virginia, Abigail, Ivy, Tessa, Madelyn, and now, Philippa. Had I searched the world over for my pick of sisters, I couldn't have found any better.

Then there's that other layer—the family you're born with. You don't get to pick it; it comes all of a piece, a backing of whole cloth, intricately and deeply stitched by memory, a pattern that stays with us from birth and through life. The colors and design may not always be to your liking, but I've discovered that it serves its purpose. Without a good backing, your stuffing falls out.

Of course, just because you can't pick your family of birth doesn't mean you can't adjust it a little, maybe even take out a few stitches and take the design in a new direction. A three-strand thread of love, honesty, and forgiveness goes a long way in easing mismatched seams and quilting out the bumps.

That's what I've been busy doing these last weeks and months, stitching it all together, joining the layers one to another, making them fit, making it mine, creating something that will last.

I love having a big family. Oh yes, I do.

Even amid the chaos of moving, my mother made sure the refrigerator was well stocked. The selection of sliced meats and cheeses alone could have supplied a deli. Knowing that Dad preferred roast beef and Cheddar, Paul ham and Swiss, Mom turkey with Monterey Jack, Olivia ham with no cheese and no mayo, and that James could and would eat absolutely everything—a common condition among teenage boys—I decided to make a big platter of assorted sandwiches and let everybody figure it out on their own.

After gathering a collection of meats, cheeses, and condiments from the refrigerator, I laid slices of wheat and white bread out on the cutting board and, assembly-line style, started making sandwiches. I was putting on the lettuce when Paul came and gave me a peck on the cheek before stealing a piece of ham from the stack and popping it into his mouth.

"If you'll wait three more minutes I'll have a whole sandwich for you." I pretended to slap his hand away. Paul and Dad had worked side by side carrying furniture all day. He was probably starving.

"Thanks for helping with the move," I said as I spread mayonnaise on a slice of bread. "We couldn't have done it without you. I saw how you grabbed the heavy boxes without letting Dad know what you were doing. That was so sweet. You saved his dignity and his back."

Paul shrugged and pinched another slice of meat from the pile. This time, I didn't even pretend to scold. "Werner is still pretty strong. I hope I'm in half the shape he's in when I'm sixty-seven. And he's a good guy—interesting. I hear he volunteered to install the new furnace at church."

"Uh-huh." I nodded and started cutting the sandwiches into triangles. "Should save the church a couple thousand at least. And he's going to volunteer with Helping Hands too. Adam Kingsbury was thrilled. They've got a lot of helpers, but not many with skills. It's good for everyone. I know Dad says he's retired, but he's not much good at sitting around. He needs to keep busy."

I began piling sandwich halves onto a blue platter, arranging them into offset circles, like bricks in a wall. Paul leaned against the counter and watched, saying nothing.

I turned my attention back to the sandwiches, feeling a bit awkward and anxious. When Mom mentioned that Paul and Dad had gone for a walk and then so quickly changed the subject, as though she were trying to hide something from me, I'll admit that my mind wandered briefly—okay, more than briefly—to the subject of matrimony. Sure, at my age it was a little silly to think of a suitor asking my father for permission to propose, but Paul and I had been dating for several months now. And I thought it was odd that, after a whole day of moving furniture, Dad and Paul should feel the need to get even more exercise. And now here was Paul, who usually had so much to say, standing next to me and saying nothing while I arranged sandwiches on a platter. Maybe he was trying to work up his courage. Or maybe he was searching for the right words. Or maybe he was looking for an opening, or needed a bit of encouragement.

"So," I said, trying to sound as nonchalant as possible, "where did you and Dad get off to anyway? Mom said you went for a walk."

Paul nodded and shoved his hands in the pockets of his jeans, keeping his eyes on the platter of food. "Yeah. I wanted to talk to him."

"Oh?"

"I needed some advice. About my future."

His future? Our future? My heart started to beat faster, thumping so loud in my ears that had I looked down at my chest, I wouldn't have been surprised to see my blouse pulsing in a sympathetic rhythm.

"Really?" I said, still trying to sound nonchalant and, I'm sure, failing miserably. "That sounds serious." I grabbed a tea towel off the counter and wiped my hands. If Paul suddenly got down on one knee and tried to put a ring on my finger, I didn't want my hands to be slimy with mayonnaise.

"Well, it kind of is. I quit my job yesterday." He pulled a sandwich off the pile and took a bite. "This is good," he said with his mouth full.

The thumping in my chest stopped abruptly. In fact, for a moment I almost thought my heart stopped, but it only sank with disappointment. Why had I gotten my hopes up?

So much had changed in the last months. I didn't *need* a man, any man, to be a woman. I knew that now. And I didn't *need* Paul. But I wanted him. And I loved him, with all my heart.

When Evelyn and Abigail had lectured me about not settling for less than the real thing, hearts and flowers, roses and chocolates, swept off your feet L-O-V-E, they had been talking about the kind of love I felt for Paul, the genuine article, I knew that now. But just because I felt that way about Paul didn't mean he felt that way about me. Or maybe he wasn't ready. His first marriage had been such a bust—maybe he'd never be ready. It was a possibility I had to consider—but only for a moment.

I loved Paul enough to take him as he was, ready for marriage today, tomorrow, or never—there was no one else for me, and by now I knew there never would be. Even so, it was hard to mask my disappointment, but I did. Quitting his job was not something Paul would do lightly. Right now, he needed my listening ear.

"You quit? Why didn't you tell me?"

"You had so much going on," he said, spreading his hands to

take in the pile of cookware still sitting on the floor and the stack of empty boxes in the corner. "I figured I'd wait until today."

"But . . . why did you quit? What happened?"

"What happened was the stunt that Geoff Bench pulled with you. I couldn't do anything about it before because Mr. Baxter, the only one with seniority over Bench, was on an extended trip to Asia when it happened. When he returned, I asked for an appointment to see him, but he kept putting me off. I finally met with him yesterday and told him about Bench's unethical behavior, but he shrugged it off with a lot of managerial murmuring that didn't amount to more than 'boys will be boys.' So I told him I was going to file a complaint with the state bar."

"And he fired you?"

Paul shook his head. "Nope. He offered me a promotion and a raise. But only if I agreed not to file a complaint against Bench. So I quit."

"Oh, Paul. Not over me! You didn't quit your job because of me."

"I quit it because I can't work for people who tolerate unethical behavior. I'm going to hang out my own shingle, specializing in family law and guardianship. Seems to me New Bern could use a few good guardians ad litem. I'll make less money on my own, but I'll sleep better at night. That's why I wanted to talk to your father."

"About starting your own law firm? But Dad doesn't know anything about that."

"No, but he knows a lot about you. And he thinks that it's more important that your husband be honest than rich. And so," he said, reaching into his right pocket, "even though my lifestyle is about to be downsized considerably, he said I could ask you to marry me. And before I talked to Werner, I talked to James. All of us think it's the best idea I've ever had."

He pulled a blue velvet box from his pocket, opened the top, revealing a platinum ring with a single, perfect, princess cut diamond in the center, then sank down on one knee.

"It's not a fair bargain, of course. I'm sure I won't make you even half as happy as you'll make me if you agree to be my wife, but I'll spend the rest of my life trying. I love you, Margot. I love you and only you, and I always will. Please. Marry me."

Tears came to my eyes and I didn't try to keep them back, not this time. Suddenly I was on my knees too, not above him, not below him, but eye to eye and heart to heart, a perfectly matched pair. Worth the wait. So much more than worth the wait.

"Oh, Paul! Oh, yes!"

❧ 59 ❧

Margot

An unusually wet June with frequent thunderstorms had forced us to postpone Mari's memorial service until mid-July. But when the day finally came, I knew it had been worth the wait, both because time had given me deeper insight about my sister and because the day was beautiful and the flowers in full bloom.

Abigail had volunteered her garden for the occasion. It was newly landscaped with shrubs of purple hydrangeas and neatly trimmed boxwood hedges that ran like low walls on both sides of a long and lush lawn that led to a rock wall mounted with an espaliered apple tree whose branches stretched out from the trunk like leafy arms. It was a peaceful spot, and when we set up rows of white wooden folding chairs separated by a center aisle, the garden felt sacred and celebratory.

Abigail has been hinting that the garden would make a nice wedding chapel, and she's right, but Paul and I want to be married in the church, with Philippa officiating. After all, she's the one who brought us together. We're thinking about a winter wedding, near Christmas. Maybe even on my birthday. It makes me smile just to think about it. How different my forty-first birthday will be from my fortieth. What a difference a year can make.

Near the podium, we've set up an easel with a huge black-and-white photograph of Mari with Olivia on her lap, her eyes radiating love and her lips pursed as she bends forward to kiss her daughter's upturned face. Olivia had chosen it out of the box of photographs Mari had saved.

Olivia planned nearly every detail of the memorial service. I was just her staff, there to carry out her instructions. Olivia had the final say on the format, setting, songs, and even the menus.

When Olivia was very good, Mari would sometimes reward her by letting her have dessert before dinner. So when guests started arriving, waiters with silver serving trays offered miniature chocolate, strawberry, and caramel sundaes in tiny glass cups to be eaten with demitasse spoons while people milled around, waiting for the service to begin. Afterward, in another section of Abigail's garden, under a white tent, guests could drink sparkling limeade punch and help themselves to an array of appetizers made by Charlie. There were a few surprises on the menu, including peanut butter and jelly finger sandwiches and macaroni and cheese presented in canapé cubes. These were Charlie's version of Olivia's favorites.

When we'd tested the recipes, Olivia declared the macaroni and cheese "almost as good as Mommy's," at which point Charlie teared up and Evelyn pulled a packet of tissues out of her purse. "That is the best review I've ever received," he said, blowing his nose. "Nobody's food can compare to a mother's. Nobody's."

But today, Charlie was all business as he fussed over the food, barely grunting a response when I'd wished him good morning. Evelyn saved a seat for him in the third row on the left, which seemed to be the Cobbled Court Quilts section. Virginia was next to Evelyn, looking very spiffy in a pink suit and white hat with pink and white ribbons around the brim. Ivy was there too, with her children—Bobby was on his third mini sundae and had chocolate smeared around his mouth—and Tessa and Lee, Madelyn, Jake, Wendy, Dana, and a half dozen other friends I knew from the shop who, though they'd never met my sister, had come to lend me their support, which was sweet. But we didn't need stand-ins to fill the space.

It wasn't until I looked at Mari's address book that I realized how many friends she had. Olivia helped me figure out whom I should contact, and those people helped contact others of Mari's friends whose names didn't appear in her address book. So many people showed up that Jake Kaminski and Paul had to make another run to the hardware store to get more folding chairs.

What would I have done without him? I asked myself and then smiled. It was the first time I'd asked myself that question, but looking down and catching a glimpse of the diamond on my left hand, I knew it wouldn't be the last.

Philippa came, but only as a guest. After I found the name of Mari's minister in her address book, she said it would be more appropriate for him to conduct the service. Philippa sat in the fourth row, behind Evelyn and Charlie, wearing a bright blue maternity dress with capped sleeves, blooming as brightly as any flower in the garden. Since this was a celebration of Mari's life, not a funeral, we'd requested that no black be worn. Philippa couldn't even if she'd wanted to—just seven weeks from "launch date" and so big that none of her somber clerical clothes fit anymore.

When it was time to begin, our family took seats in the front row. Paul wasn't sure if he and James should sit with us, but Dad told him not to be silly. "You're part of the family now."

The minister from Mari's church, John, a small and smiling bearded man, wore a white polo shirt and pressed khakis instead of clerical garb. His ministry style was relaxed and informal, different from the tradition I had been raised in, but our faith was the same. I could see why Mari had been attracted to this caring and accepting congregation. John prayed and gave a short eulogy before inviting others to come forward and share their memories of my sister.

Mari had made a good life for herself in Albany. She was an administrative assistant at the nonprofit rehab center that had finally helped her kick her addictions. That I knew. What I hadn't known until recently was that she'd also volunteered as a peer counselor to other women trying to get clean. Several came to the memorial, and two got up to speak, saying how, if not for Mari, they would either still be slaves to their drug habit or dead. I teared up when I heard that. When I glanced to my right I saw tears streaming down my father's face too.

Next to speak was a petite woman, about fifty, with short auburn hair, who wore a white skirt, bright green cardigan, and pearls. Olivia squeezed my hand. "That's Mrs. Sylvestro! My old kindergarten teacher!" Livie said in an excited stage whisper, waving to her former teacher. Mrs. Sylvestro winked and wiggled her fingers at Olivia.

She talked about Mari as a mother, how she walked Olivia to school every morning and kissed her good-bye at the end of the sidewalk, helped her learn to tie her shoes, served as a chaperone on a class trip to a museum, and sent cupcakes for the class on Olivia's birthday.

"I remember that!" Olivia exclaimed. "We dyed the coconut pink and put jelly beans on top! Everyone liked them." Olivia beamed. Mom, who was sitting on Olivia's other side, sniffled as she reached out to take Olivia's little hand in hers.

Such simple things—a walk, a kiss, a cupcake—little acts of motherly love that mean the world to a child, things our mother had done for us that Mari had remembered and done for her little girl, things that Olivia would remember always and perhaps do for her children someday. When Mrs. Sylvestro finished speaking, I smiled wetly and mouthed my thanks to her, grateful for the memory.

There were others too, happy memories, funny ones, a story from Mari's next-door neighbor about how she had to jump-start my sister's car six times one winter because Mari was forever forgetting to turn off her headlights, another about the elaborate costumes my sister wore when handing out candy to the neighborhood kids on Halloween. One year she'd been a fairy, another time a pirate, another a giraffe, complete with a long neck and headpiece she'd spent weeks crafting from chicken wire and papier-mâché.

And there was another surprise. I knew that Mari had started going back to church after she finished rehab, but I didn't know she'd played guitar and sung as part of their praise and worship group. The group offered to provide music for the service. Before they sang a four-part arrangement of "Like a River Glorious,"

Stephen, a lanky man with a gold earring who sang tenor and played keyboard, spoke of Mari with such tender wistfulness that I wondered if his feelings toward my sister moved beyond brotherly affection. It was nice to think about, but I suppose I'll never know for sure.

I do know that as the music began, both my father and the tall tenor closed their eyes and struggled to keep singing as tracks of tears coursed down their faces. I prayed for them both, that the regret for whatever they had said or left unsaid, done and left undone, would, in God's good time, be washed away by the river that flows deeper and fuller day by day, the river of peace.

Afraid of losing control of my emotions, I hadn't wanted to speak. However, my parents felt someone from the family should say something, and Dad, over my protests, insisted that only I had the right to do so. I'd planned only to share a few anecdotes of Mari's childhood and then thank everyone for coming. But when I walked to the front, I felt compelled to speak of her incredible courage and fortitude, and lessons her life and death had taught me: that we're stronger than we think we are, and that it is never too late to begin again.

I didn't speak for long or with any special eloquence, but I hope whoever needed to hear Mari's message took it to heart. And I hope that when I face hard times in the future, as I surely shall, I'll remember that lesson, relearn it if I must, as many times as it takes. If you think about it, we're all starting over every day. Every time the sun comes up, we get another chance to do wrong, do right, do better. What we do with the chances we have is up to us.

When I finished saying what I had to say, I nodded to Paul. He and James took Olivia's hands and walked her forward, then stepped aside to pick up their saxophones. Paul's deep baritone notes blended with James's brighter alto tones in a poignant and reverent version of "You Are My Sunshine." I took a white box tied with teal bows out from behind the podium and held it as Olivia pulled at the ribbons, opening the lid of the box, and releasing the fifty butterflies inside.

The crowd breathed a collective "Ah" of delight and lifted their faces toward the sun as the butterflies, impatient with their captivity and eager to begin the journey, rose as one in a cloud of orange and black fluttering wings into the bright summer sky, higher and higher and higher still, to the treetops and above, to the home they'd never seen but instinctively knew they must return to, to the far horizon that is within reach but beyond sight.

Olivia tipped her head back, watching the butterflies for as long as she could. When there was only one left in view, she leaned her little body into mine, resting against me, and lifted her hand skyward.

"Good-bye! Have a good trip!"

A tear fell from my eye, the last I would shed for my sister. The time for tears had passed. Mari had no use for tears and no memory of them, not anymore. It was a new day, another chance. I put my arm around Olivia and pulled her closer as the last flutter of orange disappeared in the bright light of the summer sun.

"Good-bye," I whispered. "Good-bye."

❦ 60 ❦

Margot

When the service was over, people rose from their chairs and began milling about the garden, talking to one another, admiring the flowers, drifting toward the white tent where food and drink were waiting. Olivia skipped off to find her old teacher, Mrs. Sylvestro. My parents talked to John, the minister. Paul gave me a hug and a kiss and asked if I needed anything before getting involved in an impromptu jam session with Stephen and a couple of the other musicians. Evelyn came toward me with Virginia, Ivy, and Abigail on her heels and offered me a tissue.

"No, thanks. I'm fine. It was nice, wasn't it?"

"Nice!" Abigail scoffed. "What do you mean? It was a perfectly lovely service. Very moving."

Evelyn nodded in agreement. "Your sister was quite a woman. I'm sorry I didn't get to meet her."

"So am I. You'd have liked her."

Olivia, her Mary Janes tossed aside, came running barefoot across the grass and shouting, "Auntie Evelyn, Uncle Charlie says he needs help serving the punch!"

"Okay, Olivia. Tell him I'll be right there."

Grinning, Olivia turned around and headed back toward the tent to deliver the message. When she did, I noticed a grass stain on the back of her pink skirt. Already? She hadn't been out of my sight for three minutes. I wondered if I'd be able to get it out. Or find where she'd left her shoes.

Abigail put her hand on my shoulder. "It really was lovely, Margot. I think your sister would have been pleased."

"I hope so. Thank you again for letting us use the garden. It's so pretty."

"It is, isn't it?" Abigail replied, looking around. "Turned out very well, I think. Are you sure you don't want to have the wedding here? I'd be perfectly willing to help you plan the ceremony. I still have contact information for caterers and such from when I was planning Liza's wedding."

Ivy, who had been standing by silently, guffawed. She remembered, as we all did, what happened when Abigail took over, basically by force, the planning of her niece's wedding.

Abigail jerked her chin and turned sharply toward Ivy. "What are you laughing at? It wasn't my fault that Liza—"

Evelyn grabbed her arm. "Abigail, I need help serving the punch. Mom? Ivy? You come too. Margot has other people to talk to, and I'm sure Charlie has jobs for everyone."

Evelyn gave me a wink before herding the others across the lawn and into the tent. Abigail's head was bobbing and her fingers kept pointing at Ivy. They were out of earshot, but I was pretty sure I knew what she was saying.

I felt a hand on my shoulder and turned to see Bob and Sharon Tucker as well as Philippa. I tried to give her a hug, but her belly was protruding so prominently from her tiny frame that it ended up being more of a thump on the back.

"Well," I laughed, looking down at the bump, "I see things are coming along fine. Thanks for coming all this way, Philippa. It's so good to see you. We're all counting the days till you're back in New Bern."

"Me too. Wouldn't have missed it for anything. It was a beautiful service, Margot. Just beautiful. Be sure to tell Olivia I said so."

"She's over there somewhere," I said, motioning toward the tent.

"I think Charlie has made her his personal assistant. Or she's made him hers. I'm not sure. But you can tell her yourself."

"I wish I could," she said with an apologetic shrug, "but I have to get going."

"So soon? You can't! Everyone will want to see you. And Charlie will throw a fit if you go before trying his appetizers."

"I know, but I really do have to leave." She looked at the Tuckers. "Bob and Sharon are going to drive me to the hospital. My water broke."

ᴖ 61 ᴖ

Philippa

My parents must have made the drive from Boston to New Bern in record time. I wasn't even out of the recovery room and was still a bit groggy from the anesthesia when they showed up. Dad came in beaming and carrying the tiniest Red Sox baseball cap I have ever seen, and Mom was right behind him, weeping and laughing at the same time.

"How did you get in? There aren't supposed to be any visitors in here."

"I flashed the nurse my collar and a smile and she let us right in," Dad said with a wink. "What did I tell you? Works every time."

"Did you see the baby?"

"We did!" Mom exclaimed, trying to hug me without disturbing the intravenous tube that was taped to my arm. "The nurse let us peek in the nursery window. He's beautiful! Tiny but so beautiful! Did they let you see him?"

"They laid him on my chest for a minute, then they took him off to the NICU, the neonatal intensive care unit. He's only thirty-three weeks gestation, so they need to keep an eye on him. But he was crying pretty well when he was born and he had a good head of hair, curly, like mine."

"Well, he looks pretty good for homemade, honey. Good work. I think he has Tim's nose," Dad said, settling on the edge of my bed and laying the tiny baseball cap on top of the blanket. "Here. You're going to need this. Because I'm sure he'll have Tim's pitching arm too."

"And if he doesn't, I bet you'll take him out in the yard to play catch until he develops one." I picked up the cap. It was so small my fist would barely fit inside, but it was still too large for my newborn son.

"What did the doctor say?" Mom asked anxiously. "Did they tell you when you can bring him home?"

Just then, Dr. Mandel walked in carrying her clipboard and wearing a frown. "How did you two get in here?"

Dad got up, unfolding himself to his full height, and smiled his most charming smile. "I'm Reverend Philip Clarkson and this is my wife, Joyce. We're Philippa's parents."

Dr. Mandel narrowed her eyes, looking from short dark me to my tall blond parents for just a moment before figuring out the nature of our family connection. "Nice to meet you. I know you're anxious to check on your daughter, but you really can't stay. Philippa needs rest and the nurses need to do their jobs. She'll be transferred to a regular room in a couple of hours. In the meantime, perhaps you can go down to the waiting room with the rest of the crowd."

"Crowd?"

"Oh, yes," Mom said with a laugh. "There's a whole gang of people waiting to see you. Bob and Sharon Tucker are there, and all your friends from the quilt shop, and some people from church, and a man with an Irish accent who keeps passing around trays of food. It's like a party. Such nice people. One of your friends, Madelyn, insisted we stay at her inn free of charge. And she said to tell you she has a room for you too, for as long as you need it. Until the baby can leave the hospital."

Mom turned to the doctor. "When will that be?"

"The pediatrician will be the one to make that call, but I was just in the nursery and Dr. Markowski said he looked good for thirty-three weeks. His weight is good too, four pounds and six ounces.

Barring any complications, I'd guess you'll have him home in three or four weeks."

Three or four weeks? It sounded like an eternity. I felt myself tear up. Dr. Mandel clucked her tongue with motherly sympathy and patted my hand.

"Now, now. It's not so long. You'll be able to visit him every day for as long as you want. We encourage that. And as soon as he's breathing reliably, you'll be able to hold him. The important thing to remember is that he's here and he's healthy, just a little small."

"That's right," my mother echoed soothingly, patting my other hand. "Listen to the doctor. She knows what she's talking about."

"I do," the doctor replied and then looked at my parents with arched eyebrows, "so I'm tossing you two out of here. Go on, Grandma and Grandpa. Down to the waiting room with the rest of the fan club."

As if to underscore her meaning and her authority, Dr. Mandel stood by the door and opened it wider. My parents didn't give her any argument. I think they were so thrilled to hear themselves called grandparents that they'd have done anything she asked.

Mom gave me another teary hug. "See you soon, sweetheart."

Dad stood next to the bed. "Oh, I almost forgot! What did you name him? Your friend, Margot, wanted me to ask you."

I smiled and took a deep breath. "Timothy Philip Waldo Clarkson."

"Wow. That's a lot of name for one little baby. But I'm sure he'll live up to it."

"I hope so. I named him after the best men I've ever known."

Dad leaned down and kissed the top of my head. "I'm very proud of you, Pippa. And I love you. Very, very much."

"I love you too, Dad."

"Your parents seem nice," Dr. Mandel said after she finished listening to my heart.

"They are. I'm very lucky."

The doctor absently nodded as she made a note on my chart. "I know you're tired and sore, Philippa, but I need to give you a quick exam. After that you can sleep."

She walked to the sink and started to turn on the water but stopped when she looked down at the counter and saw a flat package wrapped in white paper that had been lying under her clipboard. "Oh, before I forget, I'm supposed to give you this."

"What is it?"

"Open it," she said with a smile. "It's a present. Something they give to all the preemies."

I knew what it was the moment she said that, but knowing did nothing to lessen my delight when I tore away the paper and saw the tiny flannel quilt, stitched from pastel patches and tied with yellow yarn, especially when I turned it over, revealing the soft blue backing and a white label that said, *A gift to you from New Bern Community Church and Olivia Matthews.*

"Pretty," the doctor commented, nodding at the quilt as she pulled the sheet down and my hospital gown up. "All right, Philippa, this won't take a moment. Just close your eyes and think lovely thoughts, dear. Think about holding your baby."

Following my instincts and my doctor's orders, I thought about leaving this place and bringing baby Timmy home, wrapped in flannel and love, and holding him in my arms.

With my eyes closed and my heart filled, I dreamed of that day, and the day after that, and the day after that, and the day after that. . . .

~ 62 ~

Margot

It was a bit after eight when we finally left the hospital. Olivia fell asleep in the car on the way home, so tired I could hardly rouse her.

"It's all right," Paul said, picking her up in his arms. "Let her sleep."

When we got inside, Mom went into the kitchen to make popcorn, and Dad and James started searching for a board game—Dad said he'd play any game James wanted, except Rummikub—while Paul and I climbed the stairs to put Olivia to bed.

While Paul closed the louvers on the shutters, I took off Olivia's grass-stained dress and tossed it into the laundry hamper. "Oh, shoot. Olivia's quilt is still in the washer. She gave her dolls a tea party yesterday—grape juice and chocolate mini doughnuts."

Paul smiled. "I thought boys were supposed to be the grimy ones. Olivia generates more loads of laundry than James ever did."

"Tell me about it," I said, slipping a clean cotton nightgown over Olivia's head. "Honey, can you get me another quilt out of the linen closet?"

While Paul went to the linen closet, I tucked Olivia between the sheets and knelt down next to the bed, holding my sleeping niece's tiny hand in mine.

"I hear no voice, I feel no touch, I see no glory bright. But yet I know that God is near, in darkness as in light. He watches ever by my side, and hears my whispered prayer. The Father for his little child, both day and night doth care. Amen."

Olivia squeezed my hand. "Amen," she said with a yawn and then rolled to her side, tucking her knees to her stomach and her hands under her chin.

Paul came back, carrying a very large quilt.

"Oh, honey, isn't there something smaller? A twin size?"

"There is, but I saw this one tucked up on the top shelf and pulled it down. It's gorgeous," he said, lifting the quilt by the corners and shaking it out to reveal its black cameo appliquéd with flowers and leaves and dewdrops and butterflies, surrounded by a band of yellow and border upon border in blue and teal and purple, butterscotch and honey and goldenrod. "Why haven't you shown this to me before? Did you make it?"

"It was a Christmas present for Mari. But I never got to give it to her."

I reached out to touch the most beautiful quilt I'd ever made, traced a butterfly with my finger. The fabric was soft, but not as soft as it would be with years of use and life and love, the way it was meant to be.

"It's too big," I said, looking down at Olivia's sleeping frame, curled up tight and safe in her narrow bed. "But maybe just for tonight..."

I took one side of the quilt and Paul took the other as we spread it over Olivia and tucked her in.

"And when we're married," Paul said, "we'll put it on our bed."

"Really?" I asked, pleased that he'd even suggest it. "Are you sure, honey? It's kind of ... girly, isn't it?"

He walked around the foot of the bed, brushed the hair from my face, and kissed me on the lips.

"It's beautiful. And filled with memories. And made," he said, pressing my hand to his lips, "by the person I love more than anyone else in the world. It's perfect."

"Oh, Paul." I wrapped my arms around his neck. "I love you. I love you so much."

In the dark room, illuminated only by the glow of Olivia's cloud-shaped night-light, silent except for the sound of her soft rhythmic breathing, we kissed and clung to each other. But not for long.

James's voice rang out from the bottom of the stairwell. "Margot! Dad! Are you coming down? The board is set up and the popcorn is getting cold!"

Paul sighed. "Are you sure you want to be a mother?"

"And your wife," I said with a smile. "Absolutely."

He draped his arm over my shoulders as we walked to the door. "Well, then . . . I guess we'd better go on down. Our family is waiting."

TIES THAT BIND

Marie Bostwick

ABOUT THIS GUIDE

The following questions are intended to
enhance your group's reading of
TIES THAT BIND.

DISCUSSION QUESTIONS

1. The story opens on Margot's fortieth birthday—an occasion she'd just as soon ignore. What about you? Do you like celebrating birthdays, or do you prefer to let them slip by unnoticed? What do you enjoy about getting older? What aspects of aging do you dislike or perhaps even fear?

2. We all know that there's no such thing as a perfect family, and Margot's is no exception. To the extent that you feel comfortable doing so, share some insights about your family. What did your parents do right? What do you wish they'd done differently? If you're a parent, how did your childhood experiences shape the way you raised or are raising your children?

3. Margot and her sister, Mari, were close as children, but when they got older, they became estranged. What changed their relationship? Was there anything they could or should have done to help heal it? If you have siblings, do you have a close relationship with them? Why or why not? If you're an only child, have you ever wished you had siblings? What do you imagine the benefits or strains of having brothers or sisters might be?

4. After Reverend Tucker becomes ill, the church board hires Reverend Clarkson to fill in for him while he recovers, not realizing that "he" is actually a "she" until Philippa arrives in New Bern. Some of the characters seem bothered that their new minister is a woman, while others feel her sex is immaterial to her ability to serve as their minister. What do you think accounts for the difference in their attitudes? If you attend a church, does your denomination allow women to serve as clergy? Do you think that this is a good idea or not? If you belong to a denomination that doesn't ordain female ministers, do you think they should?

5. Philippa had a number of careers before finally responding to the call to ministry. Why do you think it took her so long to do so? Have you ever changed career paths? Tell the group about your experiences. What was difficult about it? What was easier than you thought it would be? If you could do it over again, would you? And if you've never changed careers, do you wish you could?

6. People deal with grief and loss in very different ways. Margot, her parents, her niece, and Philippa have each undergone a terrible loss at some point in their lives. How did their responses to grief differ? How were they similar? What does the manner in which they respond to loss say about their personalities? If you have ever grieved the loss of someone close to you, how did you get through it? Or are you dealing with it still? What are some of the things that people did or said that were helpful or harmful as you were grieving?

7. Margot has had many male friends in her lifetime, yet those friendships never seem to blossom into romance. Why do you suppose that is? Do you think that all those men were truly uninterested in Margot romantically? Could she have been sending out unconscious signals that she wasn't interested in them?

8. Margot often says that she's given up looking for "Mr. Right" and would happily settle for "Mr. Good Enough," but do you think that's true? How might Margot's views about sex outside of marriage have affected her relationships with men? In our modern culture, is it realistic for a woman to wait until marriage before she experiences sexual intimacy?

9. Philippa and Margot both want children but, for different reasons, face obstacles to realizing that dream. Have you, or

has someone you know, been faced with issues of infertility? What about life as a single parent? Do you think it is important for children to be raised in a two-parent home? What are the particular challenges of raising a child alone? Can you think of strategies that would make the job of being a single parent easier?

10. In talking about the attitude of the church congregation in New Bern, the book makes mention of "the 10–90 rule," meaning that 10 percent of the people do 90 percent of the work. If you belong to a church or volunteer organization in your community, have you found this rule to be true? If you volunteer in your church or community, what are some of the benefits you've gained from that experience? What do you enjoy most about volunteer work? What do you like the least?

11. Geoff Bench's intentions toward Margot are less than honorable. Margot feels uncomfortable around him from the first, but dismisses her own feelings and ignores her instincts. Why is that? Do you think this is a common reaction among women? Have you ever been in a similar situation? How did you respond? Did you trust your instincts, or try to ignore them? What do you think is the best way to confront someone you believe may be trying to harass you or make unwanted advances, especially if the harassment isn't blatant?

12. When Margot first meets Paul, she could not find him less appealing. However, as the story progresses, her feelings toward him move from disinterest to friendship to true love. Do you think this is the usual way for romantic attachments to develop? Or do you believe in love at first sight? What about your story? If you're married or in a meaningful romantic relationship, how did you come to know that this was the one for you? Did love hit you like a thunderbolt? Or was it a slow burn? Do you think one is better than the other?

Dear Reading Friend,

It's hard to believe that this is our fifth trip to the fictional village of New Bern! When I was working on the first Cobbled Court Quilts novel, *A Single Thread,* I never imagined that such a thing could happen. And without your support, I know it never would have. Thank you so much.

The wonderful letters and e-mails I receive from readers are so encouraging. Your enthusiasm for this series keeps me going and fills me with the desire to make each book better than the last. I read every message personally, and everyone who writes receives a response. If you'd like to write to me, you can do so by going to my website, www.mariebostwick.com, and sending an e-mail via the contact form, or by mailing a letter to . . .

Marie Bostwick
P.O. Box 488
Thomaston, CT 06787

The friendship of my readers is such a gift. Sometimes I wish I could reach through the pages of the books and give you a gift right back. That's why, with the publication of nearly every Cobbled Court Quilts novel, I've offered a *free* downloadable quilt pattern to my registered Reading Friends.

My dear friend Deb Tucker, of Studio 180 Design, has come up with a fabulous project to celebrate the release of *Ties That Bind,* a darling baby quilt reminiscent of the quilt that Philippa makes in the story. As a new grandma myself, I can tell you this is a pattern I hope to make many times in the years ahead. (If you're reading this, kids, that was a hint.)

If you're already a registered Reading Friend, you can get this pattern (or any of the three others that are available) by logging in at www.mariebostwick.com. If you're not yet registered on my website, you can do so by clicking on the "Become a Reading Friend" box and submitting your registration information, which I will not share with anyone. Once you're registered, in addition to the free patterns, you'll be entered in the monthly readers' drawing, be able to post on my online forum, and have access to recipes and special content. **The pattern is available only as a computer download and only to registered Reading Friends for their personal use.**

In addition to the baby quilt, Deb Tucker has created a full-sized printed pattern of the quilt Margot made for her sister, and has made it available for purchase from her website, www.studio180design.net. I've loved all the companion patterns that Deb designed for my books—including Liza's "Star-Crossed Love" quilt and the "Providence" wall hanging that Tessa made and Madelyn embellished—but this quilt, "Garden Dance," is my favorite so far. When Deb sent me a photograph of the initial design, I smiled for the rest of the day. It's that beautiful. But don't take my word for it; go over to www.studio180design.net and see for yourself.

Thank you again, my friends, for joining me on another armchair journey to New Bern. I hope you enjoyed the trip as much as I did and that we'll meet again very soon.

Blessings,

Marie Bostwick